'As you know, the Sisters believe the Book foretells the future of the Three Kingdoms – or at least indicates *possible* futures, possible threats. One such was found by Alaria.

'Her interpretation has it that one day Ashar would send his minion to raise the Horde and bring the forest folk southwards, their own might fortified by the magicks of the one called the Messenger. As in all things, there was a balance to this – counterweighting the powers of the Messenger would be one born of the Kingdoms . . . You may be the one – the only one, if Alaria's text is correctly translated – able to defeat the Messenger.'

Kedryn's head was spinning with the import of Bedyr's words.

He was the saviour of the Kingdoms?

The coming of age he had longed for so desperately no longer seemed so attractive. He felt very young again. And very frightened.

THE FIRST BOOK OF THE KINGDOMS:
WRATH OF ASHAR

Angus Wells

SPHERE BOOKS LIMITED

SPHERE BOOKS LTD

Published by the Penguin Group
27 Wrights Lane, London w8 5tz, England
Viking Penguin Inc., 40 West 23rd Street, New York, New York 10010, USA
Penguin Books Australia Ltd, Ringwood, Victoria, Australia
Penguin Books Canada Ltd, 2801 John Street, Markham, Ontario, Canada l3r 1b4
Penguin Books (NZ) Ltd, 182–190 Wairau Road, Auckland 10, New Zealand

Penguin Books Ltd, Registered Offices: Harmondsworth, Middlesex, England

First published in Great Britain by Michael Joseph Ltd 1988
Published in paperback by Sphere Books Ltd 1988

Printed and bound in Great Britain by
Richard Clay Ltd, Bungay, Suffolk
Filmset in 10 on 11½pt Monophoto Ehrhardt

For Stephen Hall

Prologue

He was born in fire, not knowing who or what he was.

He existed, and that was enough for now. Knowledge of self and purpose would come with time; he knew that, though not how. For now, existence itself was enough. That and survival.

He sensed the fire: it surrounded him, its awful red light seeming to pierce his closed eyes, to lance deep into his mind, yet he was not afraid. Rather, he felt it as a newborn infant might feel the warmth and comfort of the swaddling cloth, nestling into its soft embrace, unafraid, knowing with insensate certainty that no danger – for him – lay in the conflagration.

He opened his eyes and found them unseared by the heat, though all around him great trees blackened and withered under the onslaught of the flames, the massive trunks no more than kindling to the fury of the blaze. Grass died, the very soil charring and crumbling to expose roots that burned and twisted in the holocaust, wrenched from the tortured earth to feed his birth pyre.

He mouthed inarticulate approval of the destruction and rose unsteadily to his feet, swaying as he peered about, not yet confident of the body in which he found himself.

He stood at the foot of a craggy outcrop of fire-blackened stone, a cave mouth gaping womb-like for an instant before superheated rock shattered and fell to obscure the opening. And he felt something close behind him and a beginning open before him. He watched as flame beat against the rock, showering sparks and pieces of burning timber in a hellish rain that died before it reached him, the ashes drifting around him, not touching him. He did not know how or why, but he knew that he was protected, that no harm could befall him in the flames. He opened his mouth and laughed, inhaling great lungfuls of incandescent air. It vivified him, filling him with an energy that set his nerves tingling, as if a myriad of nails danced over his skin. It was vital, demanding, and he laughed again, knowing that he was where he was meant to be and that he would do what he was meant to do. It was inside him, an imperative that he recognized would become clear with time.

He turned from the wreckage of the cave towards the surrounding trees, their fiery coronas filling the sky above with a red glare, the licking tongues of flame scorching and consuming all around save him; for him, the flames were a gentle caress as fond as any mother's. He could not see past the wall of flame so he studied his own form, seeking knowledge of himself before he obeyed the commands he could feel stirring deep inside him. He raised his hands before his face and saw charred flesh, the outer skin dark as the burning bark of the trees, cracked, oozing thick droplets of crimson. He brought them to his mouth, licking experimentally at the blood, enjoying the sweet, salty taste. He was naked, he saw, his body hairless, carapaced with the same burnt skin as covered his hands and arms. Still not knowing how, he knew that it was unimportant, that he would change; that he must find the means. He took a step and felt the strength inside him. Then another, and a third, until he strode calmly into the blaze, away from the rock, towards the south.

As he approached the timber the flames swirled and turned in on themselves, drawing back to expose a path that beckoned before him, showing him the way. The forest continued to burn all around him, but where he walked there was only the charred ground, comfortably hot beneath its heavy overlay of ash. He walked steadily, feeling nothing, and after a time – he could not tell how long for time had no meaning within the cauldron of flame – he left the blaze behind and found himself marching through forest only marginally seared, clear blue sky above ending abruptly where it met the great black column of smoke rising from the burning. He liked the clarity less than the conflagration, but his steps were guided by an instinct he accepted blindly, knowing that he must proceed.

In a while he came to a boulder-strewn slope that stretched down to a river, the water wide, the forest ending on the far bank in a grassy strand. He felt revulsion for the water, but knew that he must cross it, and began to make his way down the slope.

Close to the foot he halted, crouching in the shelter of a boulder as he studied the boat drawn up on the nearer bank. It was a sturdy coracle laden with the accoutrements of a trapper, a squat, solid-looking man transferring furs from a jumbled pile on the shore to the vessel, casting nervous glances at the ominous northern skyline as he worked, clearly afraid the blaze might spread to engulf him. He wore leathern breeks bound round with strips of fur, and a shirt of homespun, opened to expose a muscular chest matted with thick curls of dark hair that matched the tangled mane held back from a flat, wide-cheek-boned face by a circlet of hammered bronze. His only weapons, as far as the watcher could ascertain, were an unstrung longbow and the woodsman's axe resting in the coracle. The watcher rose and stepped from the concealment of the boulder, the unexpected movement alerting the trapper to his presence.

Horror showed in the man's eyes as he saw what approached him, and he passed three fingers before his face in a warding gesture, simultaneously reaching to the small of his back to draw a wide-bladed knife that he held expertly before him.

'Ashar save us!' he muttered. 'What are you?'

The words meant nothing and brought no response, the watcher continuing his steady approach as though oblivious of the knife's menace or the expression of disgust on the man's face.

'No closer!' warned the trapper. 'I'll gut you, demon though you be.'

His tone and the threatening motion of the blade made his meaning clear and the other halted, waiting, staring at the man.

'No demon, then,' the trapper muttered, 'but – man? Could a man survive such burns? Did you come out of the fire? Did it take your tongue? Speak if you can. Do you have a name?'

The watcher made a gesture with hands and shoulders that appeared to reassure the trapper: fleeting sympathy showed in the man's deep-set blue eyes.

'Burned, eh?' The knife blade lowered a fraction. 'Ashar knows how you survived – you look to have been roasted. Well, I am Hadrul of the Drott, wolf-taker, and I am renowned for my generosity. It would befit me ill to leave so sorry a thing as you to die in this hell-burned wilderness when you've survived thus far, so I'd best bring you to old Redek. He's a poor enough shaman, but he has the healing art and may find some magic to aid you.'

His eyes said that he doubted it, but the knife was slowly lowered as he spoke and the other felt confidence growing. He could not as yet understand the words, hearing them only as jumbled patterns of sound, but he was able to interpret the expression on Hadrul's swarthy face and the language of his stocky body. He stood silent, watching as Hadrul sheathed the blade and turned back towards his furs.

'I'll load these and we'll be gone. If you can aid me we'll be gone the quicker – and from the look of you, I'd say speed is vital. Do you understand me, or has the fire boiled your brain together with your flesh?'

3

The watcher was uncertain of the man's intent, but when Hadrul began to load the furs into the coracle he saw what was required and moved to assist the trapper. Hadrul grunted his approval, surprised that so hideously injured a creature possessed such strength. Indeed, he was surprised that life lingered at all in a frame so obviously damaged. Not since the Sisters had persuaded him to transport supplies to their hospice in the south had he seen creatures so malformed, and not even the forsaken ones, the pitiful victims of the falling flesh disease, had appeared so ghastly. They at least retained some vestiges of their humanity, but this . . . thing – Hadrul could think of no better word – lacked even that saving grace. It stood upright, and its contours were those of a man, but there was no sense of humanity about it, no kinship of spirit that he could feel. He doubted Redek would prove of much use, but could offer no other help. Perhaps the shaman would persuade Niloc Yarrum to send the creature south to the Sisters. Or perhaps – and far more probable – the ala-Ulan would have it killed on the spot. No matter, Hadrul told himself, it was the time of the Gathering, and that imposed an obligation of charity on the forest folk for as long as the great summer meeting lasted. He was committed now, and hopefully Ashar would look favourably upon him for this act of succour. He glanced surreptitiously at the ghastly figure and went on with his loading, anxious to ferry his furs over the river; anxious to deliver his unwelcome burden to Redek and be done with it.

It was close on sunset before the coracle was packed to Hadrul's satisfaction and he motioned the charred thing into the little vessel. The creature clambered gingerly over the rim of the bowl-shaped craft, casting nervous glances at the water and crouching against the piled furs. Hadrul shoved the vessel clear of the bank, swinging his own bulk on board in a flurry of spray that sent the thing huddling back as if terrified of the droplets. The trapper was too busy with the paddle to notice the contraction, steering the coracle out into the current and applying all the weight of his powerful shoulders to the task of guiding them over the swift-running Alagor. The fact that the creature faced him lent him strength, for it was not a pleasant thing to gaze upon. He found it disturbing that the creature showed no sign of awareness of its condition, nor seemed to experience any pain, and he wondered if it was some demon of the deepwood roused by the flames, using him merely as a means of crossing the river. Yet it had so far offered him no threat, and the warding sign had brought no response, so perhaps it was just a man, his reason destroyed by the ordeal of the fire. In any event, Hadrul was safe whilst they rode the river, and when they landed he would watch carefully despite his revulsion. And he wanted to reach the far bank! He wanted the thing ın front of him where he could see it as they trekked to the Gathering where he could dispense the duty imposed by Gather Law and pass the responsibility over to Redek. The sooner the better!

He guided the coracle skilfully towards the bank, driving it on to the grass where the river trail commenced and leaping ashore to haul the craft safely clear of the water. Only then did his passenger move, springing with obvious relief on to the firmness of the soil. Hadrul took the axe from the boat, its weight comforting in his hand, and propped the weapon against the vessel, where he could reach it quickly should such need arise. No threat was offered, however, and the creature assisted the trapper in the unloading, carrying the furs up to the treeline until the full catch was stacked beneath a mighty oak. Hadrul lifted the empty coracle and carried it a little way into the forest, hiding it in a tangled thicket of beech and bramble before, axe in hand, he joined his strange companion. The sun was closing on the western horizon now, bathing the woodlands in red-gold light that was eerily akin to the hell-glow of the forest fire, and the lengthening shadows brought a chill of apprehension to Hadrul's sweating frame.

'We've a night march ahead of us,' he remarked, avoiding direct observation of what remained of the creature's face, 'but the track will bring us to the Gathering in time. We'll eat first.'

His unwelcome companion gave no indication that he understood and Hadrul moved to the far side of his pack to rummage amongst his supplies for dried meat and journey cakes. He brought out a handful and held them towards the creature, retaining his grasp on the axe as a withered hand was extended, reminding him of the talons of a hawk. Then he shouted as the hand closed not on the meat and journey cake, but on his wrist. He felt himself drawn up and forwards and swung the axe in a clumsy blow that suddenly lost its direction as he saw the creature's eyes. He noticed for the first time that the pupils were as tiny red pinpricks set into orbs of pure black, not so much a colour as an absence. He felt his fingers loosen their hold, the axe falling unnoticed and useless to the ground as he saw the pupils expand until they filled the sockets with a baleful red that seemed to glow and pulse, robbing him of will, leeching him of strength. He moaned, dimly aware that the creature – a demon, surely! – held both his wrists now. Unable to do otherwise, he stood. And felt horror fill him as the thing drew him closer, its breath sour as the reek of a charnel pit, gusting hungrily from between cracked lips that parted in obscene parody of a kiss. Panic gripped him. He tried to speak, to scream, to plead, to rage; but only moaned as the awful thing released his wrists and placed its withered hands almost gently on his cheeks. The ghastly lips descended on Hadrul's and the man's eyes glazed, rolling up in their sockets, dulling as the life went out of them. The trapper's knees buckled and he sagged within the creature's embrace, falling as the hands released their grip to slump lifelessly to the loam of the forest floor.

The creature sighed contentedly. The sustenance of the living body was more nourishing than the flames and he could already feel the changes commence within him, his form shifting, firming, becoming as a man's. He stared across the river, smiling hideously at the conflagration that still raged beyond the Alagor, tainting the twilight sky with hell-fire.

He knew who he was now, and what.

'I am Taws,' he told the coming night. 'I bring desolation.'

The weathered stone of the Keep was cool beneath Sister Galina's palms as she rested her weight on the sill of the deep-cut window to stare out across the rooftops of Estrevan to the city walls where the light of day was already fading. The torches of evening were establishing a mosaic of glittering brilliance that defied the encroachment of night. Much as Estrevan itself defied the darkness she sensed was growing far away beyond the distant mountains. The room she had occupied from dawn until long after dusk each day, since the word came down out of the Beltrevan, was cut by four windows, aligned on the four cardinal points of the compass so that it was now lit by the red glare of the setting sun. Her aged skin was leant a healthy glow by the light, her silver hair transformed to a halo of salmon pink. To the east the sky was dark, save where the lowering disc washed the mountain wall of the Gadrizels, the high peaks reflecting the light back so that a band of fire seemed to illumine the horizon. On other days, in other times, Galina had taken considerable pleasure from the sight, but now it presaged the reality of the flames, as though the sky itself announced the coming of the Messenger. She narrowed eyes still keen despite their age and turned them slowly over the cityscape below her vantage point. The wide avenues and spacious plazas of Estrevan bustled, buzzing with conversation as the daytime occupants made way for those of more nocturnal bent, and Galina opened her mind to the multitude of emotions seething in the streets beneath her.

There was an overwhelming sensation of joy, of contentment and anticipation: the common emotions of the Sisters' sanctuary.

Would they still laugh if they knew? she wondered. Would I sense fear then? Do any of them remember?

She dulled her inner ear, cutting off the clamour of the many minds, and directed her thoughts to the matter in hand. She had spent long enough in research and contemplation without finding hope of alternative measures; she had debated the matter at length with the elder Sisters, coming always back to the single, unavoidable conclusion: act or watch the world devoured. There seemed no escaping it: she must act. A small enough act, to be sure, but perhaps one that, like a pebble dislodged from the rimrock of a mountain, would set in motion others, until an avalanche thundered down to dam the threatened flood.

Or perhaps it would fall unnoticed. She could not say, only hope and trust – as she had always done – in Kyrie's Book. It was all she could do, of that she was certain, just as she was certain that the future of the world she knew rested on the implementation of her decision.

Sighing, she allowed herself a moment of quiet, seeking the Lady's Peace, the solid stone beneath her hands reassuring. Estrevan at least would stand: Kyrie had chosen well when she selected this remote site for the sacred city that housed the Book. Geographic isolation ensured both physical and spiritual safety for those who chose to live within the walls, and determined that those who sought the privilege should face sufficient challenge their purpose would be firmed in the coming. Stone-circled, the city could withstand siege, the inhabitants living off the stored bounty of the surrounding farms and the springs that fed its fountains and bath-houses and gymnasia; peace-loving, the occupants were still able to defend themselves should the need arise, that need virtually negated by Estrevan's location. The Gadrizel plain spread out around, fading into the wilderness of the Unknown Lands to south and west, banded by the Gadrizels and the Lozin mountains to east and north, the sole pass guarded by the soldiers of Tamur stationed in high Morfah. Beyond the Gadrizels lay the Kormish Waste, that desolation a graveyard to more than one army, and below the Lozins, a barrier to any south-coming barbarians, lay brave Tamur, hardiest of the Three Kingdoms.

The Messenger will seek the riches of the Kingdoms first, Galina told herself. Before he thinks to turn the Horde westwards for Estrevan he must come south from the forests of the Beltrevan, down the Idre river road to the Lozin forts, and Andurel will be his aim. Any other course must leave his rear exposed to the might of the Kingdoms, so Andurel will inevitably be his first target. Perhaps his undoing. Might the Horde not break against the bloody stone of the Lozin forts, as Drul's Confederation had broken? Or against the walls of Andurel itself? Even should he succeed in taking the Lozin forts – Andurel too – the Morfah pass could be held by a handful.

She pressed her palms harder against the sill, remonstrating with herself for such prevarication. Lysse had seen the forest burning and heard the talk of the Beltrevan, and there was no room left for doubt – unless she doubted the Book itself, and that was to doubt her life and all it stood for, to rob it of point and purpose, leaving nothing behind. She rearranged her thoughts, denying the luxury of optimism.

How long do we have? How long for the pebble to fall? As best I read it, the Book promises us no more than two decades to make ready. Will two decades be sufficient to prepare for what faces us?

She permitted herself a final glance at the darkening city and turned to face the woman waiting patiently at the book-littered table that occupied the centre of the circular chamber.

The woman was young, a quarter or less Galina's age, and very lovely. The simple white shift of the acolyte flattered a figure that needed no flattery, the simple cotton emphasizing the raven darkness of her luxuriant hair, a plain silver fillet holding the waist-length tresses clear of an oval, unblemished face dominated by calm grey eyes and a generous mouth. Usually that mouth was smiling, but now it was devoid of humour, its seriousness matched by the solemnity of the gaze she turned towards the elder Sister. Had Galina not left such pettiness behind, she might have envied the young woman her beauty; as it was, she felt an emotion close to pity.

'There can be no doubt,' she said without preamble. 'It is as the Book foretold.'

'Can you be truly sure?'

Resignation rather than argument sounded in the modulated tones and Galina nodded. 'There can be no doubt, Yrla. Lysse was sure enough to quit our mission in the Beltrevan to bring word in person. Since then each report we have received confirms what she suspected – the Messenger has come.'

'Then we must warn Andurel,' Yrla suggested. 'King Gedrin will raise an army to destroy him before he has time to raise the Horde. Tamur, Kesh and Ust-Galich can mount a force no barbarian army

8

may withstand. He will not pass the Lozin forts, and from there Gedrin can march on the Beltrevan and stamp out the abomination.'

'Were it that simple.' Galina eased tired bones into a padded chair, reaching for the earthenware wine jug, but halting her movement to allow Yrla to pour for them both. 'But it is not. Gedrin regards us well enough as healers, but he has never held much faith in the Book and I suspect he would consider such forecasts mere doom-mongering – or an opportunity for sport. Lysse was only sure the Messenger *has* come, not who or where he is. Gedrin would be happy enough to march into the Beltrevan and slaughter every forest dweller he encounters, but that is not the way of the Lady and to instigate such a course would render us of no more moral value than the Messenger himself. Besides, there would not even then be any guarantee the Messenger himself would die – the forces that guide him are dark and devious, and they protect their own.'

'The Sisters could find him,' Yrla said confidently, then saw Galina's expression and added with less surety, 'could we not?'

'Perhaps,' Galina allowed. 'I am not sure. I am not sure of his strength, but I *am* sure that would be the wrong way. To instigate a war in order to eliminate one man? That is not the way of the Lady, child.'

Her use of the diminutive was fond rather than patronizing and Yrla took no offence, blushing instead as she murmured, 'No, Sister, of course not. Please forgive me.'

'There is nothing to forgive,' Galina said gently. 'The suggestion has been made by Sisters of considerably more experience and age than you; and dismissed. No, war will come soon enough without our speeding its arrival. What we must do is prepare for it – set in motion events that will counteract the Messenger's designs. To that end, I have studied the Book afresh for guidance, and now there is something I must ask of you.'

'What?' Yrla enquired, surprised. 'How may I help? What can an acolyte do?'

'Not *any* acolyte,' Galina told her, studying her clear-eyed grey gaze, 'but one related to the High Blood. Of the blood.'

'I am not alone in that.' Yrla was confused: it was the custom of all blooded families to send their daughters to study in Estrevan for a time, and she was but one of several currently resident in the sacred city. 'Nor is my connection especially close; I am but a distant cousin, Sister. I am not close to King Gedrin.'

'We speak of times to come,' Galina responded. 'It is doubtful I

9

shall live to see the Coming, and certain that Gedrin will not. He is already old, Yrla, and if I have read the Book aright, he will be dead long before the Horde presents itself. Darr will be king then.'

'And I *am* close to Darr.' Yrla nodded, perceiving the faint outline of a pattern. 'You wish me to find Darr's ear?'

Galina was silent for a moment, searching inside herself for the truth and the words that would show it to the acolyte. She sighed again and smiled poignantly. 'That is part of it, child. Darr's faith in the Book and the word of the Sisters is greater than Gedrin's ever was – he *will* listen. But that is only part of it; the rest is harder for me to say.'

Yrla's unblemished forehead creased in a frown of incomprehension, but she said nothing, waiting patiently for the elder Sister to marshal her thoughts. When Galina did speak again the words came softly as the twilight that was now filling the high chamber, her kindly wrinkled face almost lost in the gentle shadows.

'However tenuous your link, Yrla, you remain of the blood and that sets – as it always has – certain inhibitions on your life, binds you to the Blood Code. You must, for example, marry blood. Be it the blood of Tamur, Ust-Galich or Kesh, it is a limitation of your choice.' She paused as the acolyte nodded, acknowledging what she had known since she was old enough to understand what marriage meant. 'That, or retire into the Sisterhood. Should you choose to wed, what choices do you have?'

'The princes of Kesh: Jarl or Kemm,' murmured Yrla, 'though I scarcely know either one. Brann of Ust-Galich – though I beg the Lady to spare me that ordeal. They are the obvious . . .' she thought for an instant, seeking the correct word, deciding on, '. . . selections. I would assume, though, that Jarl or Kemm – one of them – is designated for Demetria of Ust-Galich. Kemm, I should imagine, for their preferences are similar. Perhaps some cousin as lowly as I.'

Galina smiled, affection for the girl clear even in the twilight. 'And of those lowly cousins?'

Yrla shrugged: 'Bedrac; Quorn; Lyac. Perhaps Caitin. Perhaps some other I have forgotten or never known.'

'Of those,' said Galina slowly and very carefully, 'whom do you most favour?'

Yrla's brow creased again as she thought. 'Wulf Bedrac is very handsome and wealthier than most, but he is said to prefer boys. Adoc Quorn drinks too much, and it shows. Vellan Lyac is older than my father and twice widowed. Bedyr Caitin? I have set eyes upon him no more than – what? – five times, and on each occasion he nas carried some fresh scar. I think he loves battle more than bed.'

'It was Bedyr Caitin saw Lysse safely through to Estrevan,' Galina murmured. 'He sent an escort of Tamurin under the Lady's colours. He need not have done that.'

'I believe he is an adherent,' Yrla nodded. 'What are you telling me, Sister?'

'Not telling,' Galina said quickly. 'Nor commanding. Understand me, Yrla – I will not impose any choice but your own, and that must be made of free will. I ask only that from the options open to you, you consider Bedyr Caitin a contender like the others.'

'Why?' Yrla wanted to know. 'Bedyr has expressed no interest. Nor, from what I have heard, will he allow such matters to be decided for him. Why should he choose me? Why should I consider him?'

Galina set a hand lightly on a small book, her touch caressing the stiffened leather bindings, obscuring the elegant lettering that decorated the covers. 'This is an extract from the Book,' she said, 'made after Sister Alaria's great study, at her direction. It crystallizes that part of Kyrie's teachings dealing with the Coming. It suggests the means by which the Usurper may be thwarted. *Suggests* only, I hasten to add: it is by no means certain, and it is prefaced with the reminder that no worthwhile choice may be forced – coercion invalidates choice, which must be made of free will alone. Forgive me – you already know that; you are, after all, one of the most adept students I have known.'

'You want me to marry Bedyr Caitin.' Yrla went directly to the point: there was little prevarication amongst the Sisters; little point when adepts could listen with the inner ear.

'I ask you to consider him,' Galina modified. 'No more than that. As for why he should choose you, you need look no farther than a mirror for one reason; inside yourself for others. As for Bedyr, well, it is thought in Andurel that Bedyr Caitin has delayed his choice too long, that he dissembles. He is close to Darr, and when Darr succeeds to the High Throne he will doubtless seek to cement that friendship with ties of blood. You represent a most suitable choice. But I emphasize again, that is *your* choice. The Code dictates that you may refuse any match not to your liking.'

'There is something else,' Yrla remarked, her perception bringing a smile anew to Galina's face. 'What does Alaria's text say of this?'

'I shall not be sorry if you opt for the Sisterhood,' said the old woman. 'It is minds like yours that enable us to follow the way of the

Lady. What the text says is that a saviour may rise out of Tamur, born of Andurel. I have read and read again – I believe I could recite the whole, word for word! – and my conclusion is that your destiny is to be a part of this. I believe that Bedyr Caitin is another part, but in that I may be wrong.'

'How, wrong?' asked Yrla. 'Of all the elder Sisters you are the most adept in the translation of Kyrie's words. Is there really any choice for me?'

'Life is choice,' intoned Galina, reaching to fill their cups herself, the sleeve of her pale blue robe rustling as it brushed the tabletop, 'That is why Kyrie's words are often obscure – to force choice upon those who would merely follow slavishly. The Lady does not look for blind obedience, but service freely given, born of desire not duty. I can be sure only that the saviour will be born of Andurel, out of Tamur. No more! I may well be wrong in suggesting Bedyr Caitin as a suitor, and so I ask only that you consider him. Your own heart will reveal the truth – if he finds no favour in your eyes, then he is not the one.'

'And if he does?' Yrla wondered, her voice not empty of interest. 'What then?'

'It will go as it goes,' Galina responded.

Yrla offered no comment and for a while the two women sat in silence, the chamber growing dark as the sun descended past the rim of the world to leave the sky vacant for moon and stars. A mild nightbreeze started up, too warm to necessitate the closing of the shutters, swirling the scents of jasmine, oleander and incense on its vagrant whims.

'When must I leave?' Yrla asked at last, reluctance in her voice now.

'When you are sure,' said Galina. 'When your studies are done.'

'Perhaps it would be best to act immediately?' suggested the young woman.

'No.' Galina shook her head, her coif pure silver now under the moonlight that streamed through the eastern oriel. 'That would be a sense of duty, not of choice. I would much rather you finished your studies before deciding. Until then you will not know all it means to forswear your birthright to embrace the way of the Lady, so no choice can be truly valid until then.'

She took the book she had touched from the table and held it towards Yrla. 'Take this and study it. When you feel you have some understanding you may, perhaps, feel better able to decide. But make no decision until your studies are finished. We shall speak of this again then. And Yrla – I do not wish you to feel coerced in any way. No one shall know of this conversation, nor have I shared my studies with any but the elders; whatever you decide, you will have my blessing.'

It was a great temptation to listen to the girl's thoughts, but she resisted it, respecting the privacy of Yrla's mind. Instead, she rose and stretched a body beginning to feel its age. Or the weight of her knowledge.

Is that it? she wondered. Is this small thing the pebble that will roll to dam the flood? I can do no more, save watch and wait. May the Lady guide us all.

Aloud she said pragmatically, 'I am hungry. Will you join me?'

Yrla nodded and rose to follow the elder Sister from the chamber, Alaria's text concealed within a fold of her acolyte's shift.

Chapter One

Borsus leant disgruntled on his spear and stared at the red glow filling the night sky above the woodland to the north. The damnable forest fire had been burning for more days now than he had fingers to count them on, but no matter what old Redek prophesied, he refused to believe the dotard's mumblings. It was all very well for the shaman to mouth portentous promises of messengers and messiahs, but Redek was not standing cold and lonely in the night watching the Alagor trail for a phantom designed, in Borsus's opinion, solely to enhance the standing of the thaumaturgist. No, Redek was comfortably ensconced in his lodge on the second circle of the great Gathering camp, close to the sacred fire and the ear of his master. Redek was wrapped in soft furs, probably enjoying – if he was still able – the attentions of a softer woman. But Niloc Yarrum had issued the orders himself, and to argue with the ala-Ulan was more than the life of a mere warrior was worth. Those who earned Niloc's displeasure were likely to find themselves locked in the embrace of the blood eagle, and that was a penance Borsus preferred to avoid. So, keeping his scepticism well hidden, he had taken his spear and buckler and gone out into the night to stand watch on a trail that would doubtless remain empty until dawn and his relief arrived.

He spat into the darkness and wiped a hand across his eyes, promising himself gargantuan excess on the morrow to compensate for the wasted night. There was nothing to see, not even a nocturnal creature to alleviate the stillness, for the proximity of the fire and so many forest folk had driven the animals of the deepwood into retreat. The prevailing wind continued, as it always did at midsummer, to blow from the south-east, so there was little danger of the blaze spreading across the river to threaten the Gathering, and the Caroc, like the Vistral, Grymard and Yath, attended their own Gatherings, rendering the likelihood of raids as improbable as Redek's toothless soothsaying. It was a time of peace, when the tribes of the Beltrevan met to renew old friendships and form new alliances, to settle disputes and trade, to barter and find brides, doing the things the forest folk had always done, year in and year out, since Ashar first gave them the Beltrevan for their domain. There was no danger of attack, and if – Borsus spat again at the ridiculous notion – Redek spoke true, surely Ashar's messenger was capable of walking into camp and announcing himself without honest warriors losing time better spent drinking and whoring. The thought reminded him of Sulya. Sulya of the wheaten plaits and enticing mouth; Sulya of the summer-blue eyes and buxom figure. She had almost, but not quite, promised him her favour, but now he felt sure she must have accepted Andrath's torque. Was probably lying even now with that braggart, whose prowess in any area came nowhere close to Borsus's. The guard hefted his long-bladed spear in calloused hands and slammed the shaft viciously against the bole of the oak beneath which he stood. The force of the impact echoed amongst the gloom-shrouded timber and Borsus cursed softly as shock tingled his wrists, listening instinctively for any responding sound. None came and he returned to his cynical introspection.

Out of the fire? Out of that hell-blaze? Nothing living could emerge from that, no matter what Redek claimed. No matter what he saw in spilled entrails and cast bones. No matter what Niloc Yarrum hoped for.

Borsus grunted as he thought of the tales of his childhood: that Ashar, who first lit the World Fire, would one day rekindle the flames to birth a messenger who would come out of the fire to show the folk of the Beltrevan the way south, past the Lozins to the rich, soft pickings of the Three Kingdoms. Not so soft now, Borsus thought, not with the Lozin forts standing across the Idre river road and the united armies of Tamur, Kesh and Ust-Galich standing watch on the passes. Ashar should have sent his messenger in the time of Drul, when the hef-Ulan held the tribes in the Confederation. That was when he might have been useful, when Drul stood at the gates of the Lozin forts with all the southland before him. Why was he not there then, to work his powers and bring the southern forces down in bloody defeat? Borsus's grandfather's grandfather had died in that battle; uselessly, for hef-Ulan Drul had gone down and the tribes fallen back in disarray. The southlanders had come swarming into the Beltrevan to harry the forest folk like driven wolves, sending them back into the fastnesses of the deep timber country to lick their wounds and slowly forget the dreams of conquest.

Borsus felt no great desire to go to war against the Kingdoms. That was Niloc Yarrum's dream; the warrior was happy enough to live out his life in the Beltrevan, enjoying the bounty of the forest. Wars were fine if there was a chance at least of winning, but there was no chance now: the Kingdoms were too strong. Niloc's dreams were no more than that – dreams. The Confederation would never form again; no Horde would rise to spill past the Lozin forts, down the Idre; the tribes would never taste the sweetness of the southlands. The forest fire was no more than that – a forest fire. It was, admittedly, larger than the conflagrations that often sprang up at this time of year, and had burned longer. The last of such size Borsus could recall had blazed for nine risings of the sun and taken three full hands of Drott, twice that many Caroc, but in the end it had burned out and now the ground was once more fertile, the blackened stumps hidden beneath flowering creepers and burgeoning undergrowth. This one was larger, nothing more. The fact that it appeared contained within a fixed area was no more than an accident of wind direction and location, holding it – fortunately for the Drott – north and west of the Alagor. For that Borsus accorded Ashar due gratitude, but for that and nothing more. No talk of messengers and messiahs would convince the warrior otherwise, and he knew that there were numerous others who shared his disbelief, though none would voice their doubts aloud for fear of Niloc's wrath.

The ala-Ulan wanted to believe, and wanting made it easy for him to listen to Redek's senile mumblings. He was closer than most to the old ways, dreaming of the Confederation, of raising the Horde with himself – of course – at its head. But Merak was Ulan of the Drott and unless Niloc challenged him – and won – the clan leader was no more than a bellicose voice in the tribal councils. Borsus chuckled softly: Niloc was no more ready to challenge Merak for the Ulan's torque than Borsus himself, and when the forest fire died away he would most likely punish Redek and return to his fruitless war-dreaming.

But meanwhile Borsus was standing lonely in the moonless night listening to shadows. He shook his head at the stupidity of it and adjusted his back to a more comfortable position against the oak. Perhaps Sulya would spurn Andrath's advances. Or would she wear his torque come morning? Borsus damned Redek and came close to damning Ashar, too.

'You doubt the word?'

The question brought Borsus to instant alertness. He pushed upright, his spear menacing the darkness as his feet braced and he dropped to a crouch, ready to parry or thrust. His eyes narrowed beneath the fringe of his unkempt hair, head shifting from side to side as he sought to pierce the shadows, thinking that the damned forest fire would be more use if it shed a little more light. With overcast obscuring moon and stars to shroud the woodland in featureless shadows it was impossible to identify the speaker's position.

'Redek?' He spoke the shaman's name softly, grateful for the protection of the oak at his back, thinking that the soothsayer was perhaps reinforcing his standing by spreading a little fear. 'Redek?' he repeated as it occurred to him that he could not be sure whether he had heard the words with ears or mind. 'Show yourself!'

'Not Redek,' said the voice, 'but the one Redek spoke of.'

'Ashar!' muttered Borsus. 'It cannot be!'

'Is it not written?' the voice enquired.

Reading was not amongst Borsus's accomplishments, but he understood the gist of the question and felt beads of sweat form beneath the bronze circle of his warrior's torque.

'Who are you?' he gasped, bracing his spear defensively across his chest. 'What are you?'

'The Messenger,' said the voice, and Borsus felt his scalp crawl with apprehension.

Doubt still lingered in the Drott's mind and he thought of Caroc outcasts seeking the easy pickings of the peaceful Gathering. Well, if that were the case the renegades would find hard Drott steel instead and their heads would decorate Borsus's trophy pole. He spun about the bole of the oak, thinking to confuse hidden archers. Then halted as he realized that bowmen would have quilled him by now were they outlaws.

'Show yourself,' he challenged, 'if you dare.'

Abruptly witchlight shone in the gloom and Borsus felt not a crawling of his scalp, but the stiffening of each individual hair. He stared wide-eyed as the point of light expanded, gaining strength as does a fresh-lit torch, spreading an eerie radiance that flickered and shifted, confusing to the eye, more so to the mind. Then he felt sweat bead his forehead and licked dry lips as the light coalesced and became a distinct shape. He loosed one white-knuckled hand from his spear shaft just long enough to pass the three warding fingers before his face as his mouth moved unbidden.

'Ashar! Am I dreaming?'

The light was fading now, but Borsus was able to see the man – if man the figure was – as clearly as though moonlight bathed the forest. He was tall, perhaps a full head higher than the warrior, and

17

seemed, despite the abundance of furs that swathed him, skeletally thin. Beneath the pelts of wolf and otter and fox his shoulders were strangely hunched, his hands long, too delicate for any forest dweller. Hair the colour of a winter moon fell straight and unadorned from the dome of his skull, and no badge of rank showed on his corpse-pale skin. His face was triangular, the brow wide and high, rising craggy to overhang eyes sunk so deep in the sockets they appeared as twin craters of blackness at the centres of which burned two pinpricks of red light. The nose was straight and long, a knife blade poised above the near-lipless gash of the mouth. The chin was the lowermost point of the triangle, drawn in towards the slender neck as the head bowed to study Borsus and the Drott warrior stood rigid, immobilized by the scrutiny. He was vaguely aware of the spear still clutched in his hands and for an instant, through his fear, he felt a loathing, as if some subconscious part of his mind sensed evil, urging him to plunge the blade into the creature. Then the thought was gone as the narrow mouth shifted slightly in what might have been a smile and Borsus experienced a chill such as he had not felt in the coldest depths of the worst winter, knowing that such action would cost him more than life itself. Soft laughter sounded as the spear point was lowered to the forest floor, and Borsus shuddered, for it was the sound of bones grating in an open wound, or the chittering of insects devouring a corpse.

'You need not fear me.'

That the words now came aloud did little to reassure Borsus; far less the hand the apparition raised to touch his cheek. There was a momentary impression of intense heat – or extreme cold – that was gone before the warrior's mind was able to define its nature. He felt a moment's giddiness, shaking his head to clear it, then saw the mantis-like skull nod almost imperceptibly as if something in the touch reassured the strange creature.

'I have come as Ashar promised I would come – to lead the Drott to glory. To raise the Horde.'

Borsus gasped, his throat still thick with fear. Was this truly the Messenger? Had Redek's prophesies been valid after all?

'Do you still doubt?' The enquiry was mild, but still succeeded in producing a fresh wash of sweat on Borsus's skin, a fresh prickling of his hairs. 'Do your legends not tell you that I should come? Come to raise the hef-Ulan who will lead the Horde south? Come to break the gates and bring the chosen ones to their rightful due?'

He broke off as though awaiting an answer and Borsus nodded

dumbly, a fresh thought forming. Whoever brought the messenger to Niloc Yarrum would surely enjoy great favour in the ala-Ulan's eyes, would be able to ask a boon of the clan chief. He need not lose Sulya! He would bring this . . . man? . . . to Niloc and ask for the woman. Niloc would surely grant so small a request in return for the answer to his dreaming.

'You shall have her,' said the fur-swathed figure, 'If she is what you want. More than that – the name of Borsus will be spoken for generations. You will know fame amongst your people.'

Despite his astonishment at this reading of his innermost thoughts Borsus felt a swelling of pride alleviate his fear, though that was rapidly diminishing as he accepted the apparition meant him no harm, replaced with awe. Not only at the strangeness of the creature, but also at the pleasant prospect of fame and, perhaps, fortune. His doubts faded and he saw the being as exactly that – Ashar's spokesman; the Promised One. He fell to one knee, bowing his head to expose his unprotected neck in the full obeisance to an acknowledged superior.

'Stand up, Borsus of the Drott.' The voice, emanating now in the usual way from the mouth, was firm but unthreatening, a voice accustomed to command and obedience. Borsus stood.

'I *am* the Messenger. Redek spoke true.'

All doubt quit the warrior with that statement and he smiled, extending his spear in gesture of fealty.

'I am your man, Messenger. Command me.'

'I am Taws,' said the fur-swathed creature. 'Use my name. Do you swear loyalty, Borsus? Will you follow me, accept my bidding over all others?'

Borsus nodded enthusiastically, and the slight, enigmatic smile showed fleetingly on Taws's lips as he set a hand upon the spear shaft in acknowledgement of allegiance. It was a brief enough ceremony but in the instant of its enactment Borsus felt he had taken the first step on a path he had never thought to tread and the enormity of the Messenger's promise filled him with a great wonder. Raising his spear in salute he opened his mouth preparatory to letting forth a bellow, but the hand that had touched the weapon touched his lips, quelling the cry stillborn.

'There is no need to announce my presence yet,' Taws said.

'But surely . . .' Borsus was confused. 'A fitting welcome . . . There must be a ceremony.'

'Not yet.' The words came mildly enough, but nonetheless the warrior's enthusiasm was instantly dampened. 'I would speak first with Niloc Yarrum, and if you announce my coming to the people it will be Merak's hospitality I enjoy.'

'Merak is Ulan,' Bosus protested, 'the leader of the Drott.'

'Has Merak – Ulan or not – spoken for war?'

Borsus failed to recognize the question as rhetorical and shook his head. It was common knowledge that Merak, like most of his people, accepted the boundaries established by topography and the strength of the Three Kingdoms. Ashar knew, the Beltreven was large enough to contain the woodsfolk, the vast tract of densely forested highlands sufficient for all their needs, the Lozins holding them from south-wards migration, the two great river forts a gateway locked against them, the key too costly for turning. Until Taws had appeared Borsus had accepted that, but now he found his head filled with visions of battle and glory, the price small enough. Merak, too, would see that now that the Messenger was come. He said as much to Taws, who made a small dismissive gesture.

'Merak is not the one I was sent to guide. The man I shall verse in the ways of power must want what I offer. It would appear that Niloc Yarrum is that man – does he not lust after battle? Does he not dream of conquest?'

Again Borsus nodded. 'The ala-Ulan dreams of taking Merak's torque for his own. But, whatever his opinion on war, Merak is a mighty Ulan. Nine have challenged him and died in single combat. Without the Ulan's torque, Niloc can command no more than his own clan.'

'And unless he become hef-Ulan he can command no more than the Drott,' Taws murmured thoughtfully. 'The Drott alone are not the Horde. For that we need the Caroc, the Grymard, the Vistral and the Yath. Only with the full force of the Beltreven joined to the single purpose can we hope to defeat the Kingdoms, and for that we must raise a hef-Ulan.'

'Niloc Yarrum?' Borsus's jaw gaped in blank astonishment. 'You would make Niloc hef-Ulan of the Beltrevan?'

'He appears suitable,' Taws said.

'But Niloc is *ala-Ulan*,' the warrior protested, emphasizing the diminutive. 'How may he aspire to *hef-Ulan*?'

'Did you think this would be easy?' Taws demanded, his tone patient as if he addressed a backward child. 'This path we tread is long, Borsus. Long and fraught with dangers. There will be many obstacles along our way, and the first is Merak.'

Borsus stared at the Messenger in amazement, scarcely daring to believe what he heard. 'You mean . . .?' he mumbled.

'I mean that I would first meet Niloc Yarrum. If he is, indeed, the one I seek, then it will be time to take the measures necessary for his advancement.' Taws paused, eyeing Borsus until the warrior's gaze faltered and he broke the contact.

'Forgive me, Master. There is much I must learn.'

'Learn only to accept,' Taws told him, 'to obey. You believe I can raise the Horde, so how much easier must it be for me to elevate the one I choose?'

Borsus lowered his head and heard that soft, dry laughter again, a sound such as the wings of bats might make in a cave filled with the desiccated remains of fallen men. 'Yes,' was all he could think of saying.

Taws set a hand gently on his shoulder. 'Believe in me, Borsus, for what I say to you is true. I have come to give the world to the forest folk, but first I must ready them for the taking. And for that I need men with blood and hatred in their veins. Men such as I judge this Niloc Yarrum to be.'

This time Borsus nodded in agreement. The ala-Ulan was, without doubt, such a man. Niloc had coveted the Ulan's torque from the day he slew Tharl Skulltaker to become clan leader, and though he had not resolved his natural and understandable wariness of Merak's combat skills he spoke loud and frequently for war against the Kingdoms. It was a bone of frequent contention between clan and tribe leaders; Merak protesting the fruitless impossibility of such an undertaking whilst Niloc cast doubts just short of insult on the Ulan's courage. Yes, Niloc Yarrum was filled with blood and hatred.

'I believe!' Borsus cried. 'Forgive my ignorance, Master, and tell me what you would have me do.'

'Bring me to Niloc Yarrum,' said the Messenger, 'but tell no one of my coming. There is time enough for that later.'

Borsus was disappointed. He had anticipated waking the Gathering to announce the Messenger's arrival; more, he had envisaged himself bathed in reflected glory, hailed as the one to whom Taws chose to first appear. He could not be certain whether the strange man read his mind or his face when Taws said gently, 'You will earn glory enough, Borsus. But it must be *earned*, not given. Prove yourself by holding your tongue and your reward will be great. First – tonight, perhaps – you shall have Sulya. Content yourself with that for now.'

The warrior was mollified by the thought of the woman, but then a doubt crept in. 'What shall I tell her?' he wondered. 'If she is taken from Andrath she will want to know the reason.'

'She will understand,' promised Taws. 'She will ask no questions and you will offer no answers. Remember that, or . . .'

His eyes fastened again on Borsus's and the warrior felt the crimson-cored orbs suck at the very essence of his being, negating any need for the finishing of the sentence. The threat of those rubescent pupils was sufficient to quell argument and he shrugged, docile; accepting.

'Now let us start,' said Taws, 'before dawn overtakes us. I would be in the ala-Ulan's lodge before sunrise.'

Borsus grunted an affirmative, shouldered his spear, and set out along the forest trail to the Gathering, Taws coming silent as a wraith behind him.

The trail gave way abruptly to the enormous clearing occupied by the lodges of the Drott. Generation after generation had felled the trees that originally held sway here, uprooting the stumps to prevent regrowth and steadily cutting back the forest as the tribe grew larger so that now the vast area was undisputably cleared to wait in permanent readiness for the Gatherings of summer and winter. What brush and undergrowth that did manage to gain a hold during the intervening months was rapidly crushed down beneath the multitude of the clans. Now, with the sky still dark above, the clearing appeared overtaken by a sprouting of gigantic piebald mushrooms where the lodges of hide and wood were erected.

They spread in fanned ranks from the mound that filled the centre of the clearing, the apex of each fan-shape the lodge – the largest – of the ala-Ulan, those behind ranked in series according to status. Closest were those of the shaman and the bar-Offas, the battle commanders answering directly to the clan chief, each one leading a group of warriors. Then came the shebangs of the warriors themselves, the fiercest and most cunning to the fore, the lesser set steadily closer to the forest wall. Borsus's own lodge was a comfortable distance from the surrounding timber, a rank or two behind his bar-Offa, Dewan, and one removed from Andrath's. Between each fan-shaped concentration of clan members lay an avenue wide enough for four men to walk abreast, converging – and thus focusing the eyes of anyone standing at the perimeter – on the central mound.

This was the tumulus of Drul. A massive earthwork standing higher than the largest lodge, it had been constructed after the hef-Ulan's demise, in honour of his dream and his attempt to realize the vision, an enshrinement granted to no other in the history of the Beltrevan. Drul's bones rested in the crypt beneath the grassy mound, accoutred in battle raiment and fully armed, reputedly accompanied by a wealth of gold and precious stones. It was a testament to the exaltation of the hef-Ulan that no grave robber had penetrated the tomb; or to the magics bestowed upon the mound by the shamans. Borsus wondered if Drul stirred there, beneath the soil and stone, sensing the Coming, knowing the Messenger walked amongst the Drott. He glanced automatically at the bonfire at the mound's apex; it burned low now, awaiting the dawn when the priests would rekindle the flames in honour of Ashar and Drul both, a reminder of the god's presence and the dreams of the dead hef-Ulan.

The Gathering was almost quiet this close to night's ending, the tribe mostly sleeping off the entertainments and excesses of the day, the lodge fires that stood before each hutment smouldering, the smoke-holes emitting thin plumes that rose in straight lines through the windless night to merge with the overcast. A few scattered voices could still be heard, arguing or carousing, the low mutter occasionally pierced by the shrieking of a woman, those sounds too muffled by furs and night to determine whether the results of pain or pleasure, or perhaps a combination of both. No guards were posted, for the Gathering was traditionally subject to inviolate treaty which only outlaw scum would think to break, and that only after much contemplation. Besides, the dogs were guard enough. The Drott had many dogs, all large and most ferocious to any they failed to recognize as belonging. They were beasts of burden in a land where horses were few, and highly prized, usually the possessions of the chieftains and the bar-Offas only; they warded the horses and the camp alike; they were loosed in battle; sometimes – when the game was scarce – they were eaten. Now Borsus readied his spear to use the butt on any canine that protested the Messenger's arrival, and to his surprise found no cause to strike.

He watched warily as a massive brindle hound with yellow eyes and fangs that reminded him of a bear's slunk up, hackles raised and lips drawn back from threatening teeth, only to halt and cringe as Taws stared in its direction. He gaped as the tail curled to descend between hindquarters previously braced to charge, the snarl falling from the muzzle, a low whine escaping from the throat. Then the hound turned tail and skulked away, disappearing amongst the lodges. Ashar! Had he needed any further convincing of Taws's identity, this would have provided verification beyond doubt. That had been Dewan's own war-hound! He had seen it bring down a full-armed Caroc and crush the man's swordarm with a single bite, take out his throat with a second and then turn to savage another warrior. Even Niloc Yarrum trod carefully around Dewan's hound, yet Taws paid the threatening beast no more attention than he might bestow upon a troublesome fly.

There was no further interruption of their progress as they marched between the serried ranks of lodges. The dogs that constantly patrolled the Gathering removed themselves as though Dewan's hound had sent out some mental warning, and no Drott showed as they passed amongst the odorous hide constructions. Borsus continued down the avenue towards the innermost circle of the great lodges. The largest of all was Merak's, positioned so that the rising sun lit the canopied entrance, the skulls decorating his trophy poles like clustered grapes, a mute testimony to his prowess as a fighter. The location of the ala-Ulans' dwellings was determined by the size of their clans and their own battle-fame, those belonging to the fiercest or most numerous closest to the Ulan's lodge. Niloc Yarrum, for all that he was the youngest of the clan chieftains, enjoyed pride of place to Merak's left, the Shield Post. Borsus paused there, not sure how he should announce Taws or – mundanely – how he might be received at so late an hour.

The slight delay seemed not to disturb the Messenger for he stood patiently enough, surveying the lodge. It was a sprawling construction of tanned hides sewn together and mounted on a framework of wood, a network of supporting cords and pegs holding the mainframe upright, the inner supports extending through the hide roof, each one carrying a gaily-coloured pennant that drooped lifeless in the still air. Poles bound round with ribbons of red, green and black supported a canopy that extended from the entrance of the structure to form a kind of loggia, its flanks boundaried by trophy poles. It was difficult to read any expression on Taws's pale features but Borsus thought he saw a flickering of interest as the man studied the skulls, each one boiled clean of flesh and bleached, then turned his white-maned head to scrutinize first those mounted before Merak's quarters, then those set before the lodges of the other chieftains. When he was done he returned his gaze to Borsus and motioned towards the entrance.

The Drott took a deep breath and stepped between the poles, approaching the entrance. The skins of two forest bulls formed a divided curtain at which he halted, grounding his spear and calling softly, 'Gavroch? Borsus of the Drott brings great news.'

24

Instantly, as if the call were awaited, the curtains parted and three men appeared at the entrance. These, together with the nine behind them, were the Gehrim, Niloc Yarrum's personal body-guard, each one sworn to defend the ala-Ulan to the death and answering solely to him. Each ala-Ulan had his own Gehrim and not even Merak could command them, for their loyalty was sworn in blood and secret oaths that bound them to their personal leaders, forsaking all other ties. The trio that faced Borsus was full-armoured despite the hour. Crested helmets covered pates shaven in the Gehrim fashion, nasal-bars and cheekpieces obscuring their features so that only fierce eyes and unsmiling mouths gave any hint of humanity. Link-mail tunics covered their torsos and padded leather breeches their legs, with greaves descending from knees to ankles, boots of stiffened leather, the toes pointed and reinforced with metal. Wide weapon belts hung from their waists, each man armed with shortaxe, dagger and longsword. The right hand of each Gehrim rested on the hilt of his sword as they glowered at the suddenly nervous Borsus.

'Great news?' Gavroch's voice was harsh, rasping past the scar tissue of an ancient throat wound, unwelcoming. 'What news cannot wait for dawn?'

Borsus found it difficult to meet the stare of the metallic face and fixed his own eyes on a point beyond Gavroch's shoulder. He could see three more Gehrim, unarmoured but holding swords, and deeper into the vestibule the remaining six stretched on couches, sheathed blades at their sides.

He was about to announce that the Messenger had come but suddenly remembered Taws's admonition that he speak only to Niloc Yarrum himself and glanced involuntarily at the silent figure behind him. Gavroch followed his glance and slid his blade a handspan from the beaded scabbard.

'You bring strangers to disturb the ala-Ulan's rest?'

'A stranger the ala-Ulan will wish to greet,' Borsus said quickly, anxious the blade should slip no further from its sheathing leather. 'My word on it, Gavroch.'

'Your word?'

The leader of the Gehrim made it sound insulting and Borsus felt his face flush, his hands brace instinctively on his spear. The small movement elicited an ugly smile from the bodyguard and Borsus bit back his anger: the Gehrim were an élite and to anger them was to die, their actions accepted as the will of the ala-Ulan. It was the

Gehrim who put the blood eagle on a man – unless Niloc chose that amusement for himself.

'My word,' Borsus repeated.

'Who is he?' snapped Gavroch, jutting his chin in Taws's direction. The question was deliberately insulting, addressed as it was to the warrior, as though his companion was beneath recognition. Before Borsus could answer, however, Taws spoke for himself.

'One who rapidly tires of your prevarication . . . watchman.'

Borsus felt his stomach lurch as Gavroch's jaw tightened, a furious gleam burning in his eyes. He stepped back, thinking to gain the advantage of his spear's length as he heard the soft hiss of metal against leather as the Gehrim's blade slid halfway from the scabbard. Before the sword came free Taws had moved past him, shifting to take his place before the incensed warrior.

'I bear no arms. Are you so cowardly as to draw steel against an unarmed man?'

Unarmed but not defenceless, Borsus thought. No, far from defenceless. He said nothing more, preferring to leave the Gehrim to Taws as he watched those small parts of Gavroch's face he could see through the helmet suffuse with rage. The man slammed his blade down into the scabbard and chuckled horribly.

'It would, indeed, become me ill to slay an unarmed man,' he snarled. 'So I shall leave it to my men to set the eagle on your back.'

Borsus watched in horrified fascination as Gavroch motioned for the two men flanking him to seize Taws. He opened his mouth, ready to bellow that this was the Messenger they insulted, that Niloc Yarrum would give them all to the eagle – Borsus, too, no doubt – if they slew Ashar's man.

The warning died stillborn. Borsus's mouth still hung open, but now in amazement, for although he had no doubt that Taws *was* the Messenger, and so equipped of supernatural powers beyond his understanding, he could scarcely believe what he saw happen.

The two Gehrim moved towards the moon-haired man who stood immobile, making no apparent effort to defend himself. They were grinning, reaching to clutch Taws's arms. Then they were flying back, their booted feet leaving the hard-packed earth, their hands closing on emptiness, their ugly grins replaced by gasps of astonishment. They struck the trophy poles colonnading the entrance and fell heavily to the ground, like men poleaxed. The skulls clattered. The two Gehrim lay still; the others gaped, weapons bared now; awaiting Gavroch's orders. Taws extended his right arm, forefinger pointing

26

past Gavroch to the entrance. Borsus saw a flickering of the same witchfire that had first announced the Messenger's arrival and then the opening was wreathed in cold flame, sending the Gehrim dancing back, beating at smouldering hair and scorched skin. One, either more courageous or more stupid than the rest, thrust a blade into the heatless fire. And yelped, dropping the sword as it glowed red and his hand blistered.

'So, you would give me to the eagle?'

Taws's voice was a viper's hiss; the susurration of sharp steel slicing soft flesh. It froze Gavroch in the act of drawing his sword, the eyes that now turned towards him stilling him as though cords bound him. Taws smiled, and Borsus saw that his deep-sunk eyes glowed more fiercely, rubescent now, more threatening than any blade.

'You overreach yourself, watchman. You deny that which must be and it is you who shall know the eagle.'

The witchfire burned more brightly about his pointing finger and Borsus saw sweat trickle from beneath the face-plates of Gavroch's helmet. He saw the Gehrim's mouth open wide, though only a hoarse, strangled moan of pain escaped his wide-spread lips. Taws made a gesture too small and too swift to note and white light lanced from his condemning finger to Gavroch's chest. Now Gavroch did scream. And Borsus came close to joining him, for as he watched he saw the Gehrim's link-mail tunic burst asunder, bulging out, the metal mesh parting, the leather tunic beneath splitting, riven by the horrendous eruption of flesh and organs that exploded from the man's body. A curtain of blood hung briefly on the night air, then fell thickly, spattering hides and ground and trophy poles with dark crimson. Gavroch stood for an instant, ghastly disbelief in his pain-wracked eyes, ribs showing white and crimson in the chasm of his chest, his lungs hanging, still inflated, to his belt, dripping gore on to his pointed boots. Then his eyes rolled up and his knees gave way and he crashed face-down on to the earth. His lungs made an awful, soggy sound as his weight burst them.

Taws gestured again and the fire sealing the entrance died. Not one of the Gehrim made a move to attack the fur-clad figure: they merely stared, awe-struck, at Gavroch's bloody corpse.

Long moments passed before Borsus realized that the Messenger spoke again, this time to him, and when the words sunk in past the dull echoing of the dead man's scream he could scarce believe them.

'It would appear the Gehrim have need of a leader. One less prone to insult strangers, I think. Borsus – I promised you advancement.'

'I?' Borsus licked his lips, not sure he welcomed so rapid a climb to so exalted a position; concerned by the resentment he saw in the nervous faces of the watchers, thinking that even the bar-Offa of the Gehrim could die should a knife find its way between his shoulder-blades. 'I am but a simple warrior.'

Taws made an impatient gesture, but before he could speak again the embroidered curtains concealing the inner reaches of the dwelling were flung aside and Niloc Yarrum himself appeared.

He clutched a shortsword in his right hand and the frontage of a heavy wolfskin robe in his left, the garment flapping to expose long, heavily muscled legs and a torso decorated with thick black hair and the white tracery of old scars. The arms that extended from the robe were equally muscled and marked, sinews standing out on the right as the sword's point traversed the tableau before his outraged eyes. They were bloodshot with the aftermath of the mushrooms he had eaten and the disturbance of his sleep, their anger matched by the curl of fleshy lip between moustache and luxuriant beard. He was a massive man, tall and broad, his physical presence commanding, his authority a palpable thing despite the lingering effects of the hallucinatory fungus. Instinctively, Borsus lowered his spear and ducked his head in acknowledgement of his clan chief. Niloc Yarrum, however, could see nothing but the riven corpse of Gavroch and the dumbfounded members of his bodyguard, and his gaze moved from the one to the other as though he found it difficult to drag his perceptions back from the mushroom-dreaming to the stark reality of what he saw.

'It is real,' said Taws into the silence. 'Your Gehrim require a more courteous leader.'

Niloc Yarrum wrenched his eyes from the body to the steady stare of the Messenger. 'Kill him!' he snarled.

The Gehrim turned warily towards him; more warily towards Taws. Their reluctance gave Yarrum reason to doubt: he must surely be dreaming still, for it was unknown that his own bodyguard should hesitate to obey a command. He wiped a hand across his eyes and took a step forwards, the point of his blade angled in the direction of Taws's belly. 'Kill him,' he repeated.

'They have seen my power,' said the pale man. 'They know they cannot harm me.'

A growl such as might rumble from the throat of an angered bear burst from the clan chief's lips and, despite the after-effects of the mushrooms, he sprang forwards with the ferocity that had made him ala-Ulan. Careless of modesty he let loose his robe to allow greater freedom of movement as his shortsword thrust viciously for Taws's abdomen. And cut empty air. He came close to overbalancing as his gutting stroke encountered no resistance and Borsus saw the battle skill that made him so redoubtable an opponent as he recovered, slashing sideways to hack at Taws's ribs. Only to find himself spun around by the unopposed force of the blow as – somehow, though Ashar knew, Borsus could not see how – Taws was again elsewhere. A third cut, directed this time at the white-maned head, again found no target. Nor the fourth, that would have cleft the chest of any mortal man. Yarrum paused then, eyes slitted and lips drawn back from gritted teeth, studying the fur-clad figure standing calmly before him, now easily within reach of the blade. He glanced at the Gehrim, who stood immobile, swords clutched in hands as slack as their features, and he shook his head, for all the world like some furious bull deflected from its charge and blindly outraged by its inability to drive horn to target.

'What are you?' He crouched in fighting stance as he spoke, the wolfskin robe hanging loose as his left arm curved protectively before the soft parts of his lower belly, the adrenalin now coursing his veins dispersing the last effects of the mushrooms.

'The one Redek spoke of,' answered Taws calmly. 'The Messenger.'

The angry, narrow eyes flickered with a mixture of disbelief and hope, and Yarrum circled, seeking to place the speaker between the anvil of the Gehrim and the hammer of his sword.

'Why should I believe you?'

Taws gestured casually at the body oozing blood on to the ground; at the silent Gehrim. He pointed to the north, where fireglow crimsoned the overcast.

'I came out of the flames. The one called Gavroch sought to harm me – You have seen my power.'

'I have seen mage's trickery before,' Yarrum snarled, lunging forwards.

Whether it was done in search of confirmation or in blood-fury Borsus could not tell. He had witnessed too much this night to be sure of anything he saw, and had he enjoyed the mushrooms that were the privilege of the Ulans he might well have assumed it all a dreaming for it had the quality of unreality, the movements seeming slowed, elaborate and visible as the mannered actions of dancers. He saw Niloc Yarrum's weight shift in a motion he *knew* was too fast for the eye to follow, left foot advancing as though the ala-Ulan intended to swing at the ribs, the action a feint that was abruptly replaced by the thrust of the right leg as the chieftain's body turned, swordarm extending forwards and up to drive the steel towards Taws's exposed throat. There was no doubt in his mind that the cut would have severed the windpipe of any human man: it should have left Taws choking on his own blood. Instead, he saw the deep-set eyes spark crimson as one long-fingered hand lifted with an insulting casualness to meet the blade and grasp it, oblivious of the whetted edges that should have parted the fingers to the bone.

He saw the expression of stark amazement on his chieftain's swarthy features as the thrust was halted a handspan from the mage's neck, and the bulging of muscle as Niloc Yarrum sought to overcome the supernatural strength of the Messenger. Niloc's left hand reached to punch at Taws's face, and was halted like his sword, held in an implacable grip that bunched the great muscles of his shoulders as though he pressed against something far more solid than mere yielding flesh and breakable bone. The ala-Ulan's features suffused with red and sweat formed in thick droplets on his forehead and chest, running down into the hair of beard and torso. Taws showed no sign of effort. No strain was evident on his face and his eyes remained calm, a slight, approving smile stretching his thin lips. Niloc brought a knee upwards, but somehow it failed to connect with the mage's groin and instead of crippling his opponent, he found himself going down.

Borsus gasped as he saw the ala-Ulan drop to his knees, unbound hair falling to his shoulders as he was forced to stare up at the figure now towering above him. Taws turned his left hand a fraction and the shortsword was wrenched from Niloc's grasp to be tossed carelessly aside as the Messenger transferred his hold to the Drott's wrist. Stark disbelief showed on Niloc's face – less, Borsus felt, at Taws's claim than at the fact that the mighty Niloc Yarrum was on his knees before an unarmed man.

'Would you continue this dispute?' Taws enquired mildly. 'Or will you acknowledge me?'

Yarrum's mouth closed in a tight line and for an instant Borsus thought he would see his ala-Ulan die, but then the compressed lips parted and the great head bowed briefly.

'You are no mortal man,' grunted the chieftain.

'No,' Taws agreed. 'I am the one you have awaited.'

There was still scepticism in Yarrum's eyes, but he said nothing to contradict the statement and Taws appeared satisfied with that. He raised his arms, drawing the kneeling man to his feet as the thin smile spread wider across his gaunt features.

'It ill befits the Ulan of the Drott to grovel like some common warrior,' he murmured, the insult tempered by the elevation in status.

'*Ulan?*' Niloc said thickly, massaging wrists that showed the bloodless imprints of Taws's fingers. 'Merak is Ulan.'

'How?' Taws asked, the question sounding accusing.

Confusion showed on Niloc's face as he replied, 'By right and might. How else? Merak has defeated all challenges for the torque.'

'Which you would welcome,' Taws said, more gently. 'Would you not?'

Niloc glanced in the direction of Merak's tent as though afraid the skulls hung there might carry word back to the High Chief, but there was no movement, no sign that any others were witness to these strange events. It was as though a shroud of silence enveloped his lodge, isolating it from the ears and eyes of the Gathering, Gavroch's screams unheard by any save those directly involved. He nodded, grunting his agreement.

'You can defeat him,' Taws said.

Niloc Yarrum stared at the skeletal figure for long moments, then shook his head.

'No,' he said with a candour that surprised Borsus, for it belied his chieftain's customary bellicose attitude, 'I cannot.'

'You want it, though,' murmured Taws, 'the torque of the Ulan.'

It was not a question but nonetheless it was answered by the blaze of desire that sparkled in the dark eyes of the ala-Ulan, and Taws smiled afresh at the confirmation. 'Let us discuss the matter,' he suggested, 'inside.'

Had Borsus not already received more than ample demonstration of the strange man's powers he would have been surprised at Taws's casual assumption of hospitality. Few amongst the Drott could have survived a struggle with Niloc and any who had would not have invited themselves so carelessly into the chieftain's sanctum; certainly not had they hoped to emerge alive. Even now he half expected to hear Niloc condemn the mage to the blood eagle. Instead, he saw Niloc duck his head in agreement, though he noticed that the motion permitted the ala-Ulan to locate the exact position of his fallen sword. So did Taws, for he took two long paces and picked up the blade, offering it hilt foremost to Niloc.

'A pretty thing, but of little use against such as I.' He glanced at the decorative scrolling of the blade and the silver inlay ornamenting the hilt, allowing the Drott chieftain to take the weapon as though it offered no more threat than a straw. 'Remember that, Niloc Yarrum. Remember that I am come to lead you to greatness and that you cannot harm me. It is best we have this understood, that we may talk honestly.'

Again Niloc surprised Borsus by nodding and grasping the shortsword loosely as he studied the slack faces of his Gehrim.

'What of these?' he asked. 'What magic have you worked on them?'

Taws's expression was enigmatic as he gestured with his left hand, the fingers spread wide, the palm turned towards the static forms of the bodyguard. Instantly they were freed of whatever spell had bound them, the muscles of their jaws and eyes regaining strength so that they no longer stood like blank-featured statuary, but regained the appearance of fighting men poised for struggle.

'Leave him!' Niloc's voice cracked their silence as they moved towards Taws. 'By Ashar's blood! Do you think you can harm him after what you have seen?'

'He killed Gavroch,' protested one called Vand.

'Gavroch was a fool to think he could harm this . . . man,' retorted the ala-Ulan. 'And I have no room for fools in my Gehrim. Strip the body and give it to my dogs. Unless,' he paused, turning to Taws, 'you wish the skull for a trophy.'

The mage shook his head. 'I have greater trophies than a fool's skull in mind. Let him feed your animals.'

'Do it,' Niloc ordered. 'And see that we are not disturbed.'

He raised his blade then, using it to part the curtain barring the way to the inner reaches of the lodge, holding the fabric back that Taws might enter before him. The mage paused, beckoning to Borsus, and the Drott warrior took a faltering step forwards, torn between his instinct to obey whatever summons the Messenger gave him and long-held wariness of his chieftain's black temper.

'He is my man,' Taws said as the ala-Ulan glowered suspiciously at the warrior. 'He goes where I go.'

Niloc Yarrum shrugged huge shoulders and motioned his assent, leaving Borsus no other choice than to lay down his spear, slip his buckler from his back and follow them into the interior of the lodge.

The curtain hissed across the entrance, obscuring the ugly sight of Gavroch's ruined torso as the surviving Gehrim dragged the corpse away, and Borsus cleared his throat, blinking as aromatic smoke assailed his eyes and nostrils. They stood in a kind of ante-chamber, the atmosphere thick with the pungent odours of the herbs sprinkled on the flame-pots that filled the place with shifting red light. Smoke curled against the hides that formed the roof, swirling as their entry disturbed the air, snaking leisurely towards the single hole in the panoply overhead. The floor was covered with a litter of rugs that, like the tapestries adorning the walls, showed the intricate workmanship of Grymard weavers, and at its centre stood a long table on which rested the remnants of a feast. High backed chairs of wood and leather, intricately constructed so that they might be broken down and stowed in bundles when the Drott migrated, flanked the table and Niloc Yarrum gestured towards them. It was an honour Borsus had not expected; less so what followed.

He waited as Taws – without disagreement from Niloc – assumed the place of honour at the head of the table and the ala-Ulan took the place to the mage's right, then, nervously because he had little experience of chairs, seated himself on Taws's left. His eyes were becoming accustomed to the smoke by now and he could not resist surveying the chamber at leisure, seeing that the tapestries depicted scenes of battle and hunting, the central character in each tableau unmistakably Niloc himself. The rugs were rich and thick, soft beneath his booted feet, coloured with wools both brighter and more subtle in their shadings than any he had seen before. He started when Niloc swept an arm across the table, scattering food and the utensils of its consumption carelessly across the floor. The ala-Ulan clapped his hands and a tapestry was thrust aside by a red-haired woman with sleepy, red-rimmed eyes and a thin robe of trader's silk, pale blue with a border of tiny cerulean flowers. Borsus swallowed, remembering Sulya and Taws's promise; almost forgetting it in the same instant as the woman – a Vistral slave, he guessed from her colouring – stepped into the chamber, the skirt of her robe shifted by the movement to expose thighs of a creamy paleness and exciting firmness. She smiled nervously as she hurried to stand before Niloc, running fingers through the copper-bright tangle of her hair, the elevation of her arms drawing the silken material taut across her breasts.

'Wine,' Niloc demanded. Then, aside to Taws, 'If that suits your taste?'

The Messenger nodded and the slave scurried from the chamber to return moments later with a tray of inlaid ivory on which rested a silver flagon and three goblets of Ust-Galichian origin. She set the tray down carefully and filled each goblet with the dark red wine. Niloc waved her away and she disappeared behind the tapestry, leaving Borsus with the memory of her hips. Their image still filled his mind when the ala-Ulan spoke.

'So you cannot be harmed and you have come to make me Ulan of the Drott. Who – or what – are you? And who is this?'

The obsidian gaze turned in Borsus's direction and the warrior was thankful for Taws's presence and the protection it offered, suspecting that had the mage not set claim to his loyalty Niloc might well have ordered him executed for the offence of seeing his chieftain bested by an unarmed man, mage or not.

'He is called Borsus,' said Taws, 'and he stands under my protection. As for me . . . you have listened long enough to Redek to know who I am and what I am.'

'How do you know of Redek?' Niloc demanded, some vestige of suspicion lingering still. 'Or did this one tell you? This Borsus?'

'I know what I must know,' said Taws obscurely. 'What matters is not how, but what. Did you not set watchers in the forest because Redek told you the Messenger would come out of the fire? Was Borsus not one of them?'

'This is true,' Niloc admitted, his natural assumption of authority returning within the familiar confines of his lodge. 'And what I have seen you do persuades me to believe you, though that may, perhaps, be because I want to believe you.'

Taws smiled approvingly at that and set down the goblet he held, standing with a strangely loose-limbed fluidity to cross the chamber to the nearest flame-pot. Niloc Yarrum and Borsus both turned in their chairs to watch as the mage extended a hand into the flickering tongues of yellow and crimson that rose from the brazier. The fire danced over his ashen skin but there was no stink of burning flesh, no indication of discomfort on his hatchet features. He held it there until the furs that cuffed his wrist began to smoulder, sending tiny sparks dancing on the redolent air, then lifted the pot from its holder and cupped it as he had earlier cupped the silver goblet. The tallow within the receptacle was liquid from its own heat, yet he raised the vessel to his bloodless lips and tilted it as casually as the two Drott tilted their wine cups, flame curling about his face as he drained the burning draught. He sighed as the pot was emptied, just as a man long-thirsty might sigh after quaffing a cool wine, and tossed the container on the floor. There was a hiss and the sharp, rank stench of scorching wool, a curl of smoke.

'That does not confirm you,' remarked Niloc as Taws reseated himself. 'A most powerful mage, without doubt; but the Messenger?'

Taws turned eyes that Borsus saw glowed red again towards

the ala-Ulan and when he spoke it was again in viperish tones.

'Some measure of doubt is a valuable thing,' he murmured, 'but further proof will cost you dear.'

A threat was implicit in his tone and Niloc's face paled, prompting the chieftain to conceal his sudden fear behind his goblet. To Borsus's eye it seemed he swallowed the wine with less ease than Taws had drained the flame-pot, and when he set it down he appeared to find it difficult to meet the mage's red-eyed observation.

'So let us be done with prevarication,' Taws continued, 'and speak of things to come. You say you cannot defeat Merak in battle. Why?'

Niloc Yarrum glanced at Borsus before he answered, and the warrior knew then that he *would* be dead were it not for the Messenger's protection, for no other man would have been allowed to live privy to the confession that followed.

'Merak is too strong,' said Niloc, his voice flat and filled with angry resentment. 'He is too cunning. Too fast. After Merak I am the greatest of all the Drott, but Merak could best me. Let a few years pass – sufficient that his strength wanes a little, that he grows soft unchallenged, and then I can – shall! – take his skull to decorate my trophy poles.'

'You do not have a few years,' said Taws.

'I can wait,' said Niloc, 'if wait I must.'

'You do not have any years,' said Taws. 'I came out of the fire to make you Ulan of the Drott, and that I will do this year. Not next, or in a few years' time, but now. Things move in the turning of the world and there are those – may they burn in Ashar's pit! – who already conspire to thwart my master's design. Trust me, Niloc Yarrum, for I am come to make you more than Ulan of the Drott.

'I am come to raise you higher than Drul himself. Obey me and you shall be hef-Ulan of all the Beltrevan. This *is* the Coming Redek spoke of; I *am* the Messenger. Obey me and the Horde shall rise in all its bloody glory to rend the Three Kingdoms asunder. And you shall be lord of all.'

'Hef-Ulan?' Niloc's voice was an awed whisper. 'Hef-Ulan of the Horde?'

'And lord of all,' Taws said again. 'Usurper of the Kingdoms. Only obey me and it shall be yours.'

The silver goblet fell unnoticed from Borsus's hand as he watched Niloc Yarrum go willingly to his knees before the white-maned mage, his hands raised in supplication, his dark eyes ablaze with longing.

'Master,' he said hoarsely, 'tell me what I must do.'

Chapter Two

The Lady Yrla Belvanne na Caitin felt a chill of apprehension despite the midsummer sunlight that bathed her as she stood watching from the ramparts of Caitin Hold. The massive stone blocks of the wall were warm beneath her feet and fingers and she sought to draw strength from their solidity, calm from the disciplines taught her in Estrevan, but despite the impassive countenance she presented to the women watching with her, she could not entirely quell the fluttering trepidation of her maternal instincts. It was, after all, her son she watched on the combat ground, and from her viewpoint he appeared horribly vulnerable, scarcely old enough to bear the weight of his destiny. And yet she knew he was of an age when the youths of Tamur gave up childhood to become men, and that he wanted this with all the fierce, fine pride of his Caitin bloodline; knew, too, that he must face the rites of passage that would ensure his inheritance. Perhaps ensure the future of the land he loved so well. Yet even so, even knowing that if she had correctly interpreted the meaning of Alaria's text the survival of the Three Kingdoms rested on his youthful shoulders, she could not help wishing it was not yet time for him to become a man and that she might hold Kedryn to her a while longer.

It could not be: there was not sufficient time left, so she sought to utilize those powers sacrificed to his birthing to project strength to the child she loved so well.

Her eyes narrowed against the glare of the sun, focusing on the sturdy figure, the physical heritage of his father showing in the broad set of his shoulders, the casually expert control he exercised over his mount as the warhorse wheeled and danced in the thick of the mêlée. He was armoured, not in full battle harness but in the toughened and padded leather suitable for such practice, and she wondered if that was sufficient to deflect the blows of full-grown men accustomed to war. Even the knowledge that the blades were the blunt, wooden implements of practice did little to reassure her: the Sisters of Caitin Hold tended a steady flow of young men damaged in these rituals.

Then, unaware, she sucked her breath sharply between clenched teeth as she saw him take a sweeping cut on his buckler even as a blade hacked at his leathern helmet, only partially deflected by his parry so that it landed hard against his shoulder. His sword arm was numbed – she saw it drop – exposing him to a counter stroke that swayed him in the high-cantled combat saddle, forcing him to heel his mount around to avoid the thrust that would have unseated him had it landed. Instead, the hard oak kabah slid past his midriff and he brought his animal half-circle, hauling on the reins to propel the big horse backwards against his immediate opponent. Simultaneously, he countered the secondary attack with his buckler and then, with some effort she thought, raised his blade to carry the fight forwards, lifting in his stirrups to hack down at a hair-plumed helmet.

His attack carried him into the thick of the mêlée and for long moments she lost sight of him amongst the surging riders, dreading that a blow might unseat him and tumble him to the trampled grass amongst the plunging hooves. Then he became visible again, marked by the green emblem of a clenched fist sewn by Yrla herself to his now-grubbied surcoat, the fist the badge of Tamur, the colour indicative of his rank as novice. She sighed as she saw him emerge from the group, only to gasp again as he turned his horse and plunged back into the heart of the fighting, kabah rising and falling, buckler both protecting and offensive. Dust roiled in obscuring clouds and she lost sight of him again, becoming suddenly conscious of pain in her lower lip as it was nipped between worrying teeth.

Telling herself she was – Lady of Tamur or not, Estrevan-trained or not – essentially no different from any other concerned mother witnessing her son's first full-scale mêlée, she called on the disciplines instilled by the Sisterhood to force at least a semblance of calm. But so much of that calm so prized by the Sisters depended, like their powers, on a state of celibacy, and Kedryn was living witness to her relinquishment of that condition. The Sisterhood by choice knew nothing of the maternal condition, and she wondered briefly how well they might retain their objectivity had they children themselves. The bugle call heralding the end of combat elicited a gusting sigh and heartfelt smile as she saw the riders move apart, Kedryn still seated in their midst.

She saw her husband, recognizable at first only by the dust-smeared gold of his badge, walk his great stallion towards their son. As she watched, Bedyr Caitin slid his kabah into its saddle scabbard and reached up to unlace the chin fastenings of his helmet, shaking his head as he lifted the casque to spill the thick mane of dark brown hair about his face. He was smiling, and as she watched Kedryn remove his own helm, she saw a matching expression, remarking as she so often did how alike they were. Kedryn might have been the young Bedyr, his features not yet marked by time and responsibility, the boyish plumpness that lingered about his cheeks promising the regal handsomeness of his father without the hint of austerity the passing years had set on Bedyr's dark-tanned face. That, she knew, would come soon enough; too soon if she had interpreted the text correctly.

Darkness intruded on the sunlit afternoon with that thought and she turned away, promising herself that she would not allow events she was unable to forestall to cloud her enjoyment of what was here now: the love of a man more worthy than any she had known and a son whose existence was testament to that love.

'Come,' she told her attendant women, 'they will want their baths and their talk, we shall see to their feeding. And whatever other needs they have.'

Giggling, her ladies followed her from the ramparts.

On the field below Bedyr extended his right hand, palm outwards, in greeting to his son, the approval shining on his face echoed in his voice.

'That was done well, Kedryn. I am proud of you.'

The boy's smile grew wider in the warmth of his father's praise, the accolade doing more than might any of the Hold's masseurs or Sisters to dispel his bruises.

'Thank you, father,' he returned, as solemnly as he was able. 'Should I have fared so well in real battle?'

He stared at his father, his chest swelled manfully, his gaze earnest, only the faint uncertainty in his eyes revealing his youthful need for confirmation. Bedyr nodded, still smiling

'I believe so. I saw Gavan and Lutah paired against you and you survived that onslaught, though you would do well to remember that cut Torim delivered.'

'I shall,' Kedryn promised, flexing an aching shoulder. 'The bruise will mark my memory.'

'You let your sword arm drop as you shielded against my blow,' advised Lutah, bringing his sweating horse close as the squadron moved towards the Hold. 'That gave Torim his chance.'

'Full armour would halt a sword there,' added Gavan, running fingers through sweat-lank blond hair, 'but not a war-axe.'

'I will remember,' promised Kedryn. 'It is as Tepshen says: two eyes are not enough for a warrior.'

'Indeed,' Bedyr agreed solemnly. 'And now I suggest we flee the field to find the bath-house before we meet your mother.'

Kedryn frowned at this, then shrugged his acceptance, knowing that in such matters his mother was, perhaps, more formidable than any barbarian. He took his father's cue and loped beside the great stallion as Bedyr heeled the horse and headed for the walls of the Hold.

They rose above the wide mountain meadow in dwarfed imitation of the Lozins that spread majestically across the northern horizon, marking the farthest boundaries of Tamur, dark with timber, but tipped even in midsummer with snow, a wall that held out the tribes of the Beltrevan from the Three Kingdoms, breached only by the mighty Idre, the river guarded by the Lozin Forts. Similarly, Caitin Hold stood in defence of Tamur, built in the time of Corwyn who was called Iron Fist, and who had driven back the great Confederation raised by Drul. In those times, before the unification of the Kingdoms, Tamur's peace was threatened on all sides. War brought raiders out of Kesh across the Idre to ransack the homesteads dotting the fertile river plain; the Beltrevan was a constant threat to the north; and from the south-east, the fierce Sandurkan would spill from the Kormish Wastes, while Tamur's own depradations of Ust-Galich would bring vengeful armies of mercenaries north of the ust-Idre in retribution. Corwyn himself had been a mercenary, a general, and a visionary. He had seen the dangers of internecine struggle and the benefits of unity, and had ruthlessly set about rectifying the situation. His morality being that of the mercenary, he had seen unity as a mighty step on his path of self-advancement, but nonetheless it had been a move of inestimable benefit to the Kingdoms.

First, he had seized the throne of Ust-Galich, the army at his back persuading King Valerian that abdication was by far the better part of valour, and then set about establishing blade-backed treaties with Tamur and Kesh. He had seen the Lozin Forts built, impregnable against attack from the north, and led his mercenary forces in defence of Tamur when the Sandurkan mounted an invasion. He had commenced the building of Andurel, the task completed by his son, Lewin, where the Idre divided into ust-Idre and Vortigern, the very division of the waterway symbolic of the new-won unification for the city stood at the meeting point of the Kingdoms, their boundaries touching there. His own sovereignty established, he had declared his desire for peace, and in earnest of his good faith announced that Andurel should not be known as the capital of the Ust-Galich, but the heart of the Three Kingdoms, and that the seat of government should rest there. The Tamurin had agreed readily, for Corwyn's might was as useful as the Lozins themselves against attack from both the Beltrevan and the Kormish Wastes. Kesh had disagreed and put an army in the field to be put down under the combined onslaught of Ust-Galich and Tamur, after which the proud horsemen had sworn fealty to Corwyn, thus completing the unification. To the surprise of the vanquished, Corwyn had proven as generous in victory as he was implacable in war, and Andurel had grown steadily. Tamur and Kesh alike had sent trusted men to participate in the councils the mercenary lord established, their words heard and acted upon until Andurel became the legitimate seat of tri-partite government, a vast walled city regarded as an entity in itself, belonging to no faction, but whole in itself, the very heart of the Three Kingdoms, solid symbol of their unity.

The unification completed, Corwyn had turned to the defence of the borders. South from Ust-Galich and east of Kesh, the Tenaj Plains formed a natural barrier, easily defended by the line of border forts he ordered established. The greatest threats lay to the north and west, on Tamur's boundaries, and here Corwyn set about blocking the invasion paths of Sandurkan and forest folk alike. Just as he had built Andurel at the heart of the Kingdoms and warded his boundaries with forts, so he suggested that defences be established along the edge of Tamurin lands with one great hold to the centre, from which the rulers of Tamur should govern, controlling the mountainous country as the mind controls the body.

So Caitin Hold came into being and the Tamurin said that if Andurel was the brain of the Three Kingdoms, then Caitin Hold was the heart of Tamur.

It lay not at the centre of the territory, but to the north, midway between the Lozin Forts and the Morfah Pass, close under the flanks of the great mountains. Cherek Caitin had been lord then, ruling from a wooden longhouse circled by a wooden pallisade. Cherek was long dead and the Hold no longer a timber construction, but a mighty creation of the stonemasons's art. The wall towards which Kedryn trotted stood tall as four men standing atop one another, their ramparts crenellated and spanned by internal walkways built wide enough that squads of defenders might pass unhindered, the upper faces marked by embrasures from which arrows might be fired, or poles thrust out to dislodge scaling ladders. Towers stood on the corners, each one equipped with ballistae and designed in such a way that it might be sealed off from the inside to form a last redoubt against the breaching of the walls. A single massive gate afforded wide entrance to the interior, great metal crossbars dropping into place as the need arose. Within lay barracks and stables, granaries and storehouses, armouries, a hospital where the resident Sisters might tend wounded folk, bath-houses fed by the springs that had first dictated the location of the Hold, and a school that, like the hospital, was administered by the Sisterhood. Inevitably, a settlement had grown with the fortress, spreading around three sides, the fourth ordered clear for battle training, and in times of war – though such times were distant enough few remembered them, and fewer still gave them any thought – the inhabitants could find security behind the stone of Caitin Hold. To Kedryn it was a place of wonder and delight, a repository of memories and the finest playground a boy could wish for, equipped with deserted passages and near-forgotten chambers, ancient weapons hung casually on the walls and the exploits of his ancestors depicted in the tapestries that hung beside them. There was even – though he used it somewhat less than other facilities – a library.

He slowed his prancing mount as Bedyr clattered into the courtyard beyond the open gate and swung easily from the saddle, dropping a hand to the boy's shoulder as he tossed his reins to the karl waiting to stable the great black warhorse. The karl's lined features grinned at Kedryn, and he winked a scar-slanted eye in approval of the youth's fortitude.

'Did you see me, Tevar?'

'I did,' said the stablehand, 'and I do not believe I have seen any warrior face the test with greater spirit.'

Kedryn's smile threatened to engulf his face: Tevar's praise was valued as the judgement of an experienced soldier, almost as respected as his father's, or the hard-won encomiums of Tepshen Lahl. He glanced at Bedyr. 'Shall I ride with you soon, father? When next you go against the forest folk?'

'You may be old enough by then,' Bedyr said. 'But there is no hurry, and plenty for you still to learn.'

'Tepshen Lahl said I was his most able pupil,' Kedryn protested, then frowned, afraid Bedyr might disapprove of such boasting and adding, 'I overheard him.'

Bedyr's handsome face assumed an expression of mock severity as he steered a path through the milling crowd of men and horses, none showing any great reverence for their overlord for that was not the Tamurin way. 'It ill befits a prince of Tamur to admit to eaves-dropping, boy.'

Kedryn's frown became exaggerated into a look of remorse. 'I did not intend to eavesdrop, father,' he protested. 'I was in the armoury sharpening my sword when I overhead Tepshen speaking with Tevar. I could not help but hear what they said.'

'Then you are not entirely responsible,' Bedyr allowed, 'but should you find yourself in a similar situation, you should make your presence known.'

'I will,' Kedryn promised dutifully, thinking that it was no easy thing to be a prince; that there was so much to learn and, it often seemed, insufficient time in which to absorb it all. The warrior training was the easiest because that was the most enjoyable, strength and a natural quickness of wit enabling him to excel in that area. Tamur had fought no more than a handful of border skirmishes during Bedyr's reign, but it was Tamurin custom that every able-bodied youth be taught battle-skill against the possibility of barbarian invasion. The most vulnerable of the Kingdoms, Tamur was also the poorest, a land of mountains in which homesteads were isolated and – in times past – dependent on neighbourly help to survive. The rolling plains of Kesh produced grain and horses in equal abundance, both protected against raiders by the natural boundaries of the Lozins, the Idre and the Tenaj Plains. Ust-Galich was guarded by the two northern kingdoms and the rivers, a land of vineyards and farms, abundant in natural wealth: Ust-Galich could afford to hire mercenaries, Tamur could not. Indeed, it was common practice in the olden times for Tamurin to seek service with the hireling armies of the southern kingdom, and it had been from that relationship that Corwyn Ironfist's respect of Tamur had grown.

But fighting skill, Kedryn had rapidly learnt, was but part of a prince's duty. There was also the more tiresome matter of formal education, and whilst it was interesting enough to learn of Tamur's past – which seemed at times to be largely a series of battles – there was, too, the less interesting business of language and politics and – least pleasant of all – courtly behaviour. He had not yet visited Andurel, but his formal presentation there loomed ever closer and to that end he was required to familiarize himself with the proper modes of address and conduct, learn to dance, even to acquire some degree of accomplishment in a suitable art such as the singing of ballads or the playing of an instrument. The quickness of foot that served Kedryn so well on the practice ground deserted him completely on the dance floor, and when he raised his voice in song Sister Lyassa claimed that the crows deserted the fields in terror. He was able, through dint of remorseless application, to pluck out exactly three simple tunes on the balur, the simplest instrument available, but no more. He had said nothing to Lyassa, but it was his personal conviction that the Lady had omitted to round out his character with artistic accomplishment and that the deficit was to be filled with military skills. That Lyassa understood this conviction but remained determined to impart at least some small degree of finesse to her pupil was merely another example of the dogged resolution of the Sisterhood, whose influence since Darr had assumed the High Seat in Andurel was spreading ever wider.

Another tiresome aspect of high birth was the irritating insistence on cleanliness, and had Kedryn not wanted to talk with his father – and known that the bath-house was probably the best place for it – he would have sought some excuse to escape the ritual. He had passed the better part of the day simply standing on the practice ground while the horsemen charged and wheeled about him. He understood the need – both his father and Tepshen Lahl had explained the value of cavalry against men on foot, and the need for personal experience of the terrifying effect of watching a line of screaming riders charging directly at him – but such training did not produce the muscle-numbing weariness of a day spent wielding a sword or riding at full gallop that afterwards made the bath so welcome. He was, in his own estimation, barely sweaty, and could see no great need for bathing. But he wanted to talk, so he lengthened his stride to match Bedyr's long-limbed gait and accompanied his father into the low-roofed structure that housed Caitin Hold's baths.

The doors stood open on a tiled portico from which there were two exits, the facilities divided by sex. Bedyr took the door to the right and Kedryn followed him into an ante-chamber where they divested themselves of clothing and accepted voluminous towels from the waiting attendants. Kedryn had heard that in Ust-Galich such establishments were often communal, but in Tamur ablutions were regarded as a private affair and only close friends or those related by blood would think of bathing together, so father and son were ushered into a smaller room with a sunken pool just large enough to contain four bodies at its centre. Only after they were clean, and Bedyr had relaxed, would they continue to the steam room, where groups congregated to talk or gamble as the vapours rising from the pipes that lay beneath the floor completed the cleansing process and eased the final aches from weary bodies. Beyond that room lay the great pool, fed by a spring, its water chill and invigorating to dispel any lassitude produced by the steam. That was an enjoyable experience, for the pool was large enough for swimming, and even in winter slightly warmer than the rivers.

Kedryn dropped his towel on a stone bench and gingerly followed Bedyr into the water. It was already warm, but on Bedyr's shout an attendant adjusted the valves controlling the flow and it grew steadily warmer. Kedryn watched, not yet quite ready to speak, as his father pushed shoulder-length hair streaked with grey back from his face and, sighing luxuriantly, slid down chin-deep into the tub.

As the heat pinked Bedyr's skin Kedryn studied the tracery of scars that became visible, the damaged tissue white against the darker Tamurin colouration. That puckering on the left shoulder came from a Sandurkan arrow; the wrinkled mound above the right hip from a lance thrust; the thin line across the leftside ribs the legacy of a Caroc broadsword. There were more, and Kedryn could identify the origin of each one; could name the time and place and enemy as surely as he had leant to recite the dates and names and places drilled into him by Sister Lyassa. His father's body was a living history text to the boy, and he gloried in the story it told, not yet quite old enough to accept Bedyr's dismissal of the wounds as avoidable mistakes rather than objects of pride.

He was reciting the origins of a cut that ran from Bedyr's right shoulder to the point of the elbow to himself when his father spoke.

'You took the charge well, Kedryn, but remember that you knew each man there; and knew we were unarmed. I do not seek to belittle what you did, but that was not the same as facing an enemy intent on killing you.'

'I know that,' the boy responded, too confident of his father's affection to consider the comment any kind of disparagement. 'Tepshen Lahl has told me no man can be truly sure of himself in battle until he has fought one. He says no man knows how he will conduct himself until he faces an enemy intent on killing him; nor what kind of warrior he will be until his sword is bloodied.'

'Tepshen Lahl is wise,' murmured Bedyr, 'and a true warrior.'

'The finest,' said Kedryn. 'After you.'

Bedyr grinned and began to scrub his shoulders with a block of coarse soap as he spoke. 'And Tepshen *does* consider you a most able pupil, though I had sooner you had not overheard that particular comment.'

'But,' Kedryn blurted, no longer able to contain his impatience, 'if Tepshen says that – and you agree – it means I can ride with you.'

44

'To where?' Bedyr enquired mildly, obscuring his expression with soap.

'Against the barbarians!' Excitement routed the boy's earlier determination to approach the matter tactfully. 'When you go north.'

'Is this something else you have overheard?' asked Bedyr. 'Accidentally, of course.'

Kedryn grinned, far too eager to feel any guilt: 'King Darr's messenger was sent to estimate our strength, and secure your promise of support. I heard that in the stables when I was grooming Valand.'

'That is nothing unusual,' Bedyr said calmly, lifting a foot to scrub his toes. 'It is the duty of the king to know the strength of his kingdom, and kingly commonsense to know where support may be found. You have met royal messengers before, so why has this one produced such excitement?'

'His visit followed that of Rycol.' Kedryn referred to the commander of the Tamurin detachment manning the western Lozin fort. 'Why else would Rycol send a special envoy? Unless the Beltrevan threatens?'

'I see your studies have not been wasted,' Bedyr acknowledged. 'Do you smell smoke then?'

Kedryn nodded. 'Sister Lyassa has shown me the Book,' he said, 'and I believe that I have read enough to know woodsmoke from cookfire.'

Bedyr laughed affectionately and slid beneath the surface of the steaming water. When he emerged again his expression was serious. 'A full moon has come and gone since Rycol's envoy visited us; almost as much since Darr's emissary – your patience is commendable.'

'But may I come with you?' the boy demanded.

'How do you know I am going anywhere?' countered his father.

'The fire burns, consuming all. Let warriors quench it, lest they fall,' Kedryn recited. 'The smoke comes from the Beltrevan – Rycol has smelled it. He sent his man overland to bring you word while the River Guild took the news to Andurel. The King's messenger travelled by boat to Gennyf and took horse from there. It *must* mean the fire burns in the Beltrevan. And that King Darr considers it a danger.'

Bedyr's features remained serious despite the smile that stretched his lips.

'That old rhyme has been a part of Tamurin folklore since long before my father's time, you know.'

'So it must be true,' Kedryn announced, unwilling to be deflected, 'or no one would remember it. If it were false, it would be forgotten. Besides, I heard that the King sent riders to Kesh as well. Why send a personal messenger, rather than trust to the River Guild?'

'You have become the recipient of much knowledge,' Bedyr said slowly, his tone thoughtful, 'and I commend you on your interpretation – it shows a firm grasp of politics. But even if I were planning to ride north, do you really consider yourself old enough to accompany me?'

'You were no older when you fought Li-Chiall of the Sandurkan,' Kedryn pointed out. 'And I must fight sooner or later.'

'Later is oftimes better than sooner,' murmured Bedyr. 'Childhood is a gift men are sometimes too eager to relinquish.'

'But if you *are* planning a sortie,' Kedryn said cautiously, curbing impatience to choose his words with care, 'may I ride with you?'

'*If* I am,' Bedyr responded, 'then I shall consider the possibility. After discussing it with Tepshen Lahl. And your mother.'

Kedryn's grin was not entirely triumphant: Tepshen, he felt sure, would approve the blooding; he was less certain of his mother's reaction.

'I will abide by their decision,' he allowed gravely. 'But I hope they agree.'

'Their decision will doubtless be made wisely,' Bedyr said, 'and in your best interests. Will you accept it?'

Kedryn studied his father's face, trying to fathom the expression he saw there. It was impossible to gauge which way Bedyr would vote on the matter and Kedryn found himself torn between the desire to plead with his father to argue his cause and the youthful determination to behave in as adult a way as he could manage. He was, after all, claiming his right to manhood and he did not wish to appear whiningly childish in Bedyr's eyes. Mature acceptance was, he estimated, the best way to convince the Lord of Tamur that he was ready to take the warrior's sword and so he nodded solemnly.

'Of course, Father.' Then could not resist adding, 'I hope they agree.'

Bedyr succeeded in resisting the impulse to smile at his son's eagerness: he could remember a similar conversation with his own father and was not sure he had behaved in quite so dignified a manner. 'Tonight,' he promised, 'I shall raise the subject with your mother.'

'It might be best to seek Tepshen's opinion first,' suggested Kedryn, thinking that the weapon master was the more likely of the two to approve his going and thus sway his father's vote so that two voices would oppose the objections he feared his mother might raise.

'Indeed it might,' Bedyr agreed, deliberately noncommittal.

Kedryn opened his mouth to add further argument but Bedyr surged to his feet then, sending a wave rippling across the surface of the water and the words were lost as the boy gasped and spat. He knew his father well enough to recognize an implicit closing of the conversation, and followed Bedyr out of the bath, wrapping a towel about himself as they proceeded to the steam room. The place was rapidly filling with the members of the squadron and Kedryn settled cheerfully on a bench, content for now to listen to their conversation and bask – with, he hoped, due modesty – in the praise they voiced of his conduct on the training ground.

He remained in the aromatic chamber as long as he was able, then moved to the larger room that contained the pool. The water there was icy after the heat of bath and steam and he grunted as he plunged in, the shock numbing at first, but then invigorating. He swam the length of the pool several times and then dried himself, accepting the clean shirt and breeches offered by an attendant. His father emerged shortly after, but when Kedryn moved to join him, Bedyr waved him away.

'I shall speak with Tepshen now,' Kedryn was told. 'Find your mother and tell her where I am.'

The boy accepted the dismissal and hurried off in search of the Lady Yrla as Bedyr made his way to the armoury to find the weapon master.

As he expected, Tepshen Lahl was occupied with his unceasing search for perfection, and Bedyr waited silently at the entrance to the high-ceilinged practice room, unwilling to disturb the concentration of the man. He did not object to the wait, for it afforded him an opportunity to assess his mood and order his thoughts; besides, it was always a pleasure to observe the actions of the kyo.

Tepshen Lahl had arrived in Tamur when Bedyr was half Kedryn's current age, offering his services as warrior to Bedyr's father. He came, he said, from the east, from a land that began where the sun rose and that was ruled by an emperor notorious for his cruelty and his avarice. Lahl was the youngest son of a noble family that, with others, had risen in rebellion against the depredations of the Quijo, as the ruler was called. Naked fear had proven the Quijo's most potent weapon against the rebels, persuading too many potential supporters that discretion was the better part of valour and thus denying the dissidents vital support. The emperor's armies had routed the opposition and Lahl's father and two brothers had fallen in the epic struggle. A third brother, together with two sisters and Lahl's mother, were executed, Lahl himself escaping only because he had taken a wound and lain unconscious in a barn whilst the Quijo took his revenge. Recovered, he had seen the impossibility of raising a second army in a land robbed of its spirit by the emperor's depredations and fled, knowing that his life was forfeit should he ever return home. A demonstration of his skills had persuaded Bedyr's father that the strange, slit-eyed man with his carefully-tended plait of oiled black hair would be a most useful ally, and Tepshen Lahl had found a second home. Bedyr was uncertain of his age: when Lahl had been set in charge of his own warrior training, the easterner had seemed ancient as the Lozins, and equally solid. By the time Bedyr assumed the lordship of Tamur Lahl seemed no older; now he seemed ageless. His face remained unlined, if a little thinner; his hair, still oiled and plaited in the manner of the sunrise lands, barely streaked with grey, but his body was lean and hard as any youth's, his jet black eyes keen as ever. And Bedyr recognized him as the finest swordsman in the Three Kingdoms.

He was standing now before a straw and leather practice dummy, man-shaped effigy attached to a thick wooden post seated in the flagstones of the armoury's floor, dressed in the Tamurin fashion of loose shirt, breeches and high boots. The long, slightly curved sword he had brought with him from the east was sheathed at his waist, a traditional Tamurin dirk worn on the opposite side. He was short, his head tilted back a little so that he could stare at the grotesque face painted on the front of the dummy, which was constructed to Tamurin proportions. He appeared casual, lounging with arms loose and feet close together, a stance apparently more appropriate to conversation than swordplay. Then he moved and Bedyr smiled at the fluid grace that brought the longsword from the scabbard in a high arc that curved almost too fast for the eye to follow above his head and down, the motion ending with the blade resheathed and Tepshen Lahl again facing the dummy in relaxed manner. Now, however, the dummy was divided in two. Part remained fixed to the pole, but the rest, cut on a line from the base of the neck to the division of the legs, struck the floor as the easterner slid his blade back in the scabbard.

Bedyr thought he might be smiling, but it was still hard, even after so many years, to discern any change of expression on the usually inscrutable face. He clapped once and Lahl ducked his head in acknowledgement, jet eyes searching the floor where the riven half of the dummy had fallen. As Bedyr came towards him he stooped, picking something from amongst the wreckage of leather and straw, and grunted in satisfaction. Bedyr saw that he held the severed remains of a fly, bisected as cleanly as though cut with a surgeon's blade, and shook his head in admiration.

'You are still the best, Tepshen.'

'Perhaps.' Lahl blew the two pieces of the insect from his palm and wiped his hand on his breeches. 'For a while. No one remains the best forever, and there is one who may soon surpass me.'

'Who?' Bedyr asked.

Lahl looked up into the face of the tall, broad-shouldered man and said, 'Kedryn. Your son.'

'That good?' Bedyr's tone was thoughtful, and not entirely happy.

'Kedryn is the most able pupil since I taught you,' Lahl said. 'And you are good as any easterner. You would be kyo in my country.'

'Tamur is your country,' Bedyr said, pleased with the compliment, 'and you are the finest sword in the Three Kingdoms.'

Tepshen Lahl bowed his head briefly in acceptance of the truth and probed the fallen half of the dummy with one booted toe. 'It is not the same, cutting straw men. A warrior needs blood on his sword.'

'The Sisterhood would disagree,' Bedyr suggested.

Lahl shrugged. 'I respect the Sisters, but I do not agree with their peaceful ways. Love does not blunt a sword, nor the words of the Lady deflect its path.'

'They take a longer view,' Bedyr said. 'Their teachings build a better future.'

'I live now,' Lahl said. 'I have lived until now behind my blade. I shall keep it sharp.'

'And I shall remain grateful for its keenness,' averred Bedyr.

'You did not come here to discuss my prowess,' Lahl announced with his customary bluntness. 'Has Kedryn asked to ride with you yet?'

Bedyr nodded, unsurprised that the weapon master should already know the purpose of this meeting. 'You saw him take the charge?'

Lahl nodded in turn. 'He took it well. He can learn no more without battle. Take him with you.'

'You appear as certain as Kedryn himself that I shall ride north,' said Bedyr. 'Am I the only one not yet sure?'

The kyo shrugged again. 'Perhaps I do not agree with all the teachings of the Sisterhood, but I have learnt that their judgements are usually sound. I believe you will.'

'You believe the fire burns in the Beltrevan?' Bedyr asked.

'I believe that sometimes the Sisters see things invisible to others,' Lahl said. 'I believe that King Darr listens to their words. I know he sent his messenger to ascertain the strength of Tamur and your willingness to follow his direction. This business of fires and messenger I do not pretend to understand, but I do know that the wise man takes pains to discover the strength of those who profess themselves his enemy. And gauges his actions accordingly. I believe you will go north because I do not think you have any other choice: like your son, you were never a man to await the arrival of an enemy.'

Bedyr stared at the scattered straw for a while, then swung his gaze back to Lahl's face, his brown eyes intense now.

'And you think I should take Kedryn?'

'He will be safest with you.'

'With me?' Bedyr's voice was doubtful. 'Beyond the Lozins?'

'He will acquit himself honourably,' said Lahl. 'I have no more doubt of that than I do of your ability to protect him. Besides, I shall be with you. Let the boy become a man, Bedyr. There is little more I can teach him here, but much he can learn in action. Leave him behind and you may well sow the seeds of resentment – he thirsts for warrior status, and if he cannot find it soon, here, he may seek it in mercenary service.'

'He would not desert Tamur!' Bedyr protested. 'He is prince of Tamur: my heir.'

'He cannot be your heir unless he become warrior first,' said Lahl. 'Who would follow him? How could he claim Tamur if he stands behind the blades of others? This is not Ust-Galich – Tamurin fight their own battles, and will not accept a lord who does not.'

Bedyr grunted his acceptance of this truth and said, 'You are certain he is ready?'

It was not really a question and Tepshen Lahl did not answer it with anything more than a look. Bedyr stared into the calm, black eyes and nodded his acceptance of the truth.

'You will stand at his back?'

'You need to ask me that?'

'No,' Bedyr said, smiling now, 'but I think I shall need to tell the Lady Yrla that I have.'

'Tell her Kedryn will be safe,' said Lahl. 'I am his shield. My life is his. Kedryn is the only son I shall know. Tell her that.'

'I believe she knows that, old friend,' said Bedyr, 'but I shall tell her anyway. Whether she will listen, however . . .'

Tepshen Lahl frowned, though it would have been difficult for anyone who knew him less intimately than Bedyr to discern the change of expression. He had lived a good half of his life in Tamur but even now he sometimes found it hard to accept certain customs of the hill folk – this strange insistence on listening to the counsel of women, for example. The Sisters of Kyrie were different, and while he could not fail to recognize the feminine delineaments of their bodies, he did not regard them as *women*, and consequently was prepared to grant them the status of priests, or soothsayers. Which, in many ways, they were. The Lady Yrla – for whom he felt the greatest admiration and, indeed, a grudging affection – had spent some time in Estrevan as an acolyte, which experience, in the eyes of Tepshen Lahl, rendered her more sensible than the average. But she had forfeited the powers the Sisters attained through their celibacy when she married Bedyr, and so her judgements must inevitably lack the weight he was prepared to accord those of the Sisters. By marrying she had become first and foremost a wife; in birthing Kedryn, she had become first and foremost a mother. Neither condition equipped her well for the decision Bedyr would ask of her: a youth's blooding was a thing for men to discuss and decide upon, not women.

'You are Lord of Tamur,' he said, expressing his opinion with customary economy.

'And she Lady,' Bedyr pointed out loyally.

Tepshen Lahl grunted and gestured at an arched doorway, through which Bedyr could see some twenty young men practising the lethal form of hand-to-hand combat the easterner had taught the Tamurin warriors of Caitin Hold.

'No doubt you will take some of these, so I had best make sure they are ready.'

It was an admonishment, and Bedyr accepted it, grinning as the small man strode towards the group. They would be worked hard and by nightfall the resident Sisters would be called on for poultices and ointments to ease strained muscles and sooth burgeoning bruises, but most of them would in time prove as deadly unarmed as a warrior with a sword. And, the Lady knew, Tamur might soon have need of men like that.

His mood darkened somewhat as he left the armoury and paced

across the grass surrounding the pale stone building. It was late afternoon and the sun was still, at this time of the year, high in the western sky. It painted the dark granite of the Hold with summery colours, lightening the great slabs of the walls and gleaming off the lighter stone of the buildings. From the stableyard he could hear the shouts of the grooms as they put a yearling through its paces, commencing the training that would one day equip the animal for war, teaching it to react to the lightest pressure on reins or ribs, to stand calm amidst the sound and fury of battle, to use its teeth and hooves as weapons. Much as Tepshen Lahl trained the young men. Perhaps, thought the Lord of Tamur, we are not so very different from those horses. Perhaps we concentrate too much on the act of survival, rather than on the point. But what else can we do? If the Sisters are right, then we shall need every warrior and every war horse, and all we can do is ready ourselves. That, and hope.

His face more sombre, he traversed the grass to the entrance of the great hall that housed his council chambers and his family. As Tamurin custom dictated, the doors stood open in mute statement of the Lord's availability to his people, but to Bedyr's relief no suppliants awaited his judgement and he was able to make his way swiftly to the private chambers where, as he had known she would, Yrla awaited him.

She stood before a window, the sun glistening on hair still sleek and dark as a raven's wing, emphasizing the soft curves of her body, and Bedyr paused as he always did, staring at her with a smile forming. Logically, he knew she must look older than that first time he had seen her at the Morfah Pass, but his heart denied that logic so that his eyes saw the girl he had loved from that initial heart-lurching moment when he had known with a greater certainty than he had ever experienced that he wanted her. Not only from lust – though that had unquestionably stirred as he handed her from the simple wagon that had carried her away from Estrevan – but also from something he saw in her clear grey eyes; heard in her soft voice; felt in her touch. He had scarcely dared believe he might win her. She was of Andurel, High Blood, and he a blunt, plain soldier, knowing that some day he must wed and beget an heir, but expecting a sensible political alliance if he did not fall to Sandurkan arrow or Beltrevan spear. And yet, when he had pressed his suit, she had accepted him, chosen him rather than the princes of Kesh or Ust-Galich, or any of the many others who danced attendance on her. There were those, he knew, who had said he was too old, too bloodied in war for such as she;

more who could not understand how so lovely a creature *could* choose a homely warrior with no more to his name than a poor, hilly kingdom whose people, it was said, though seldom in their hearing, were too busy fighting to farm, and too busy farming to know how to enjoy themselves. Yrla had laughed at the gossip and told him she would rather the clean, hard body of a soldier in her bed than the soft flesh of a courtier; and he had believed her because somehow he knew she spoke the truth. Even when the rumours drifted north up the river and he heard it whispered that the marriage was a matter of convenience, devised by the Sisters who had sent Yrla from Estrevan to further their own devious ends, and that there was no love in it, save his infatuation – which might well be some magicking of Estrevan – he had not believed them. His faith in his young wife was strong enough that he could ask her and trust her answer. Which was that indeed the Paramount Sister, Galina, had suggested Bedyr Caitin as a possible husband, but only one of several, the choice being entirely Yrla's decision.

'What,' he had asked her then, staring from the same window that now framed her in light because he could not bear for her to see the fear in his eyes, 'would you have done had Galina not asked you to return?'

'I do not know,' she had replied, and he could feel her eyes studying his back, knowing that she read the language of his body as only those trained in Estrevan might. 'Perhaps I should have remained in the Sacred City and become a Sister. But then I should have remained celibate, so that my powers might develop.'

She had paused and Bedyr had felt a coldness distil within his soul until he heard her laugh and felt her hands on his shoulders, turning him to face her, to look down into her smile.

'And you, my foolish, frightened warrior, have taught me that there are joys enough to compensate for any loss of what might have been. I need not have quit Estrevan – I did that through free choice. I need not have chosen you – that, too, I did of my own volition. And I have never regretted any of those free choices; nor ever shall. I continue to serve the Lady as best I may, but She blessed our union and it would ill become me to question Her judgement. There are always rumours, Bedyr – they are usually the products of envy. Laugh at them as I do, and know that I love you.'

Then she had drawn his head down and kissed him and it seemed that magic did surround them, for his recollection of what followed was both hazy and clear as a dream, and all that he could be certain of

53

was that he had come to his senses on a rumpled bed with a heart so full of love there was no room in it for doubt.

'You are pensive, my Lord.'

Her voice woke Bedyr from his reverie and he smiled at her, moving across the simple chamber to place his hands on her shoulders as he said formally, 'My Lady, I must talk with you.'

She dispensed with formality by the simple expedient of stepping inside the circle of his arms to grasp his long hair and tilt back her head so that he could do nothing other than kiss her.

'It is about Kedryn,' she said when the kiss had ended and her cheek rested against his chest.

'Yes,' Bedyr replied into the sweet-smelling luxuriance of her hair, 'he asks to accompany me.'

'Into the Beltrevan.' It was a statement, not a question, and he felt her body stiffen slightly as she said it.

'If I go,' he responded.

'*If?*'

'When,' he amended.

She eased gently from his arms and leant against the wide ledge of the embrasure. Bedyr settled himself on the sill, one leg dangling, the other drawn up, hands cupping the knee. Yrla placed a hand on his thigh, the touch reassuring and still exciting.

'Is he old enough?'

They both knew the mother in her spoke, just as it was the father in Bedyr that would almost have welcomed argument; dissuasion. But he was also Lord of Tamur, Guardian of Morfah, Marshal of the Lozin Forts – amongst several other antique titles – and in those capacities his answer was shaped for him. He said, 'Yes, he is old enough. Tepshen Lahl sings his praises – as much as he praises anyone – and you saw him on the field today.'

'I saw my son behave with dignity and courage,' Yrla murmured, 'and as a mother I was proud of him. And frightened for him. As a mother, I would argue, but . . .'

'You are also the Lady Yrla Belvanne na Caitin,' he finished for her, 'Mistress of Caitin Hold and Lady of Tamur, and your duties extend beyond those of a simple mother.'

She heard the anguish in his voice and looked up into his face, her long fingers gripping his thigh more tightly. He was so strong, this great, wide-shouldered man she had chosen, strong enough to let his fear show, knowing that with her he had no need to hide it; she knowing in turn that such display of doubt was as much a statement

54

of his love as any spoken words. He was a warrior, revered by his men, his prowess and courage in battle proven, but now his eagle-proud features were forlorn, his brown eyes clouded with paternal concern. She touched his cheek, the forming bristles abrasive as he turned his face into the cup of her hand.

'We knew it would come,' she said gently.

'But not when,' he retorted. 'Not so soon.'

'Soon?' She chuckled softly. 'We have known for years, my Bedyr. Do not all the young men of Tamur seek out their manhood battle sooner or later?'

'Tamurin have had little other choice,' he murmured. 'But the young men go against the southern tribes – Yath or Grymard – or Sandurkan raiding out of the Wastes, not what your Sisters say awaits us beyond the Lozins.'

'*May* await,' Yrla said without any real conviction. 'Galina was not absolutely sure, and I have read the extracts until I can recite each word, but I am still not sure.'

'Darr is,' said Bedyr. 'You heard his message. Even Kedryn pointed out that only events of the utmost gravity would prompt the king to despatch a personal messenger. Something stirs there. It may not be the fire, but it is something.'

'And you will seek it out,' Yrla said.

'As I must,' replied her husband, taking the hand that touched his cheek in both of his and holding it as though physical contact with her aided his decisions. 'Darr's request was clear enough in that area.'

'He asked for your assessment of the situation,' Yrla murmured, absently stroking the hands that held hers, 'that does not necessarily mean you must venture into the forest yourself.'

'Does it not?' Bedyr recognized the wife and mother speaking. 'You are better equipped than I to judge the abilities of the Sisters Darr has established in Andurel, but I would judge from the tenor of his message that they have achieved as much as they can using the Sight, and that what are needed now are human eyes and a mind accustomed to assessing military situations. More directly – Darr wants my personal opinion.'

'Rycol is in a position to judge the situation in the Beltrevan,' Yrla said.

'Yes,' agreed Bedyr, 'but Rycol's duty is to guard the west bank of the Idre; to maintain the fort there, just as Fengrif holds the Keshi fort on the east bank. They do that well, but they are attuned to that task: their thinking is influenced by that, and the Lozin Forts have held back the tribes so long they seem impregnable.'

'Perhaps they are,' Yrla hoped.

'Mayhap.' Bedyr's grip on her hands tightened slightly. 'But neither Rycol nor Fengrif has the good fortune to enjoy marriage to a woman schooled in Estrevan. Rycol comes close to scoffing at the prophecy, and he is not alone. Ust-Galich is far enough removed from the northern border that Hattim finds it easy to forget the danger – or choose to ignore it – whilst Jarl maintains that he can raise all his Keshi soon enough should the forest folk attack. They have known peace for so long they forget their comfort was won with blades and blood, and neither pays heed to Estrevan as does Darr, or I. In this matter, I am Darr's eyes. He can trust no other: nor can I.'

'No,' said Yrla, Lady of Tamur now, 'but I wish there were another way to it.'

'There is not.' Bedyr shook his head slowly, his gaze fond as he studied her face. 'I must go north and see what I may see.'

'And Kedryn must go with you.' Yrla answered his gaze with clear eyes. 'To leave him behind would be too great a slur; too dangerous. There would be resentment – the suggestion that the Lord of Tamur protects his own son while other young men face their test like Tamurin. We must not allow our concern for him to weaken his position. The Text indicates that Kedryn is the hope of the Kingdoms, and as such he must have valid claim to Tamur, or he is nothing. There can be no questioning of his courage.'

Bedyr nodded, her words helping the clarification of his own thoughts. He did not properly understand the Book – not even the Sisters claimed full comprehension – but he had faith in its veracity, and its usefulness, and so was willing to listen. He knew, too, that Darr was a believer; indeed, amongst the initial acts performed by the King on his assumption of the throne had been the establishment of the college in Andurel, granting the Sisterhood its own place in the great city and a voice in the tri-partite council. But Darr's position was not that of Corwyn: his rule was democratic, at times close to a balancing act as he sought to satisfy the demands of Tamur, Kesh and Ust-Galich alike, maintaining equality amongst the Three Kingdoms of which he was nominal ruler. In this affair, his emissary had made clear, Darr's trust was placed firmly in Bedyr, for of all the Kingdoms, Tamur was the most alert to barbarian threat. Kesh was content enough with trilateral government, but by nature of isolationist bent, a land of nomadic herdsmen little given to concerted action. Ust-Galich was too far south and far too rich to consider the Beltrevan a potential danger, and Hattim too concerned with pleasure to wish his palace games disrupted by prophecies in which he placed so little faith. Tamur, alone it oftimes seemed, remained alert to the danger lurking beyond the Lozin wall, and if that danger was now becoming so great as the Sisters' interpretation of Kyrie's words averred, then procrastination was an invitation to horrors undreamt of.

'No,' he said. 'Not of that, or his right to take my place.'

'So really we have no choice,' Yrla said firmly. 'You must go north and Kedryn must go with you. It will be hard for you, my love – to be both commander and father.'

'The boy knows where his duty lies,' Bedyr said with paternal pride. 'He expects no familial concessions. Nor can I afford to grant them, for his own sake. But Tepshen Lahl will ride with us, and he is as fine a bodyguard as any prince could wish.'

Yrla nodded, smiling. The kyo was stiff in her presence and she knew that he felt Bedyr placed undue emphasis on her counsel, but she knew also that he loved her son as fiercely and as proudly as though Kedryn were his own; that should harm befall the youth, Lahl would be dead, for while he lived he would put his life between his charge and danger. Apart from Bedyr himself, Tepshen Lahl was the staunchest ally she could wish for Kedryn.

'It is settled then,' she said. 'When do you ride?'

'On the waning of the moon,' Bedyr answered. 'Overland to the Lozin Forts, then into the Beltrevan on the waxing. The forest folk stir with the moon, and if the fire does burn, I shall see it more clearly by moonlight.'

'Will you go deep?' she wondered, wife now as much as Lady of the Hold.

Bedyr shrugged, slipping from the embrasure to place an arm about her shoulders, drawing her close for the comfort and the sheer pleasure of feeling her body down the length of his as she nestled into the embrace, one arm encircling his waist as her head came to rest upon his shoulder.

'The southern Beltrevan belongs to the Vyath and the Grymard, and they enjoy the benefits of trade. Consequently, they tend to peace, having more to lose than their neighbours. Rycol's spies tell of movement deeper in the woodland, though most of it was merely rumour. I think we may have to penetrate the territory of the Caroc or even the Drott to satisfy Darr's request.'

Yrla shuddered, prompting Bedyr to hold her tighter, remembering tales of Drott savagery, Caroc viciousness.

'We go to look, not fight,' he said into her hair. 'I shall not seek to attract attention, nor invite attack. It may be that I can learn all I need from the southern folk.'

'I pray the Lady guard you,' Yrla said, 'and return you safely.'

'Amen to that,' Bedyr intoned reverently, steering her gently across the chamber towards the doors of their dressing rooms. 'Shall we now prepare ourselves for dinner? And the announcement I shall make.'

'Kedryn will be delighted.' Despite her reservations, Yrla could not help smiling at the pleasure she knew her son would take from such confirmation of his adulthood.

They robed themselves in the casual manner of the Tamurin, who set greater store on what they ate than on the apparel they wore for the consumption. In Andurel the evening meal was a formal occasion; in Ust-Galich, a fashion parade. In Caitin Hold it was considered proper that some small degree of formality should accompany the presence of Lord and Lady in the dining hall, but there was no great pomp to it and their attire was chosen as much for comfort as for show. Bedyr simply combed back his shoulder-length hair and fixed it in place at the nape of his neck with a clasp of hammered silver before tugging on a light surcoat of wool died rusty red that hung to his feet. He draped the necklace of his office about his shoulders and was ready, filling a heavy crystal goblet with the pale, light wine Tamur produced as he waited for his wife to complete her toilet. Yrla emerged not long after her husband, her glossy hair wound in two thick plaits to either side of her lovely face, bound with the blue ribbon that pronounced her a devotee of the Lady. Her gown was of darker blue, embroidered with chasings of silver thread and drawn in at the waist with a girdle of blue and silver filigree work. Bedyr offered his arm and together they descended to the dining hall.

The room was flagged, the square blocks of stone worn smooth by generations of Tamurin, the high windows cut into the thick walls allowing in the last of the day's light. Long tables backed with simple benches ran down two sides, the shorter trestle that faced the outer door reserved for Lord and Lady, and what family or guests they might entertain. Two huge hearths gave heat when heat was needed, but now stood empty, and over the door there hung a minstrels' gallery that on festive occasions could fill the chamber with music. Appetizing smells already drifted from the kitchens and the hall was beginning to fill as Bedyr and Yrla took their places. Tepshen Lahl appeared, still dressed as Bedyr had seen him in the armoury, pausing before the upper table to execute a formal bow, as was always his custom, before assuming the seat to Bedyr's right. Kedryn emerged from the kitchen door, nibbling a scavenged biscuit with an expression pitched midway between anticipation and apprehension. Bedyr motioned for him to sit, holding his own face deliberately impassive as he saw from the corner of his eyes the anxious glances his son sent towards father, mother and kyo. Then he clapped his hands and rose to his feet, stilling the numerous conversations that murmured about the hall.

He waited for full silence, ignoring the irritated tutting of a manciple poised to carve a side of roasted meat, his face solemn as he studied the curious eyes now turned towards him.

'King Darr has asked that I be his eyes in the Beltrevan,' he announced without preamble. 'It seems the Sisterhood fears the fire burns again, and if another Horde is rising, Darr would know of its coming; would prepare for the struggle. Perhaps douse the flames before they take hold.

'Kesh and Ust-Galich doubt the wisdom of such a venture, and Darr relies on Tamur. I ride on the waning of the moon, with a single squadron. I have yet to decide who shall accompany me and I ask those I leave behind to understand – this is not an army, but a scouting party. And if our fears are true there will be fighting enough for all in time.

'I do, however, know of one who shall be at my side: Kedryn rides with me.'

As the hall filled with the babble of discussion that followed the announcement Bedyr turned to his son. Kedryn's face was alight with pride, his eyes ablaze with excitement. Bedyr felt proud as the youth showed princely discipline, rising to bow as he said simply, 'Thank you, Father.'

Unconsciously, Bedyr reached for Yrla's hand, and found it waiting, reassuring.

Chapter Three

The ligaments that had once held Merak's jaw bone in place were not yet entirely rotted away, giving the bleached skull a lopsided grin, as though it found the events it witnessed from its vantage point on Niloc Yarrum's trophy pole cynically amusing. Borsus could seldom resist making the warding gesture when he found his eyes drawn, as often they were, to the white sphere set at the apex of the tallest pole. He made it now, his fingers passing almost furtively before his face, though not escaping Sulya's attention, eliciting a laugh from the buxom, wheat-haired woman sprawled on the furs beside him.

'Do you still fear the old boar?' she murmured, stretching on one elbow to nuzzle his bearded cheek. 'Surely he has been dead long enough, with no sign that he will return.'

Despite himself, despite the warmth of the day and the body heat of the woman pressed so close against him, Borsus shivered a little as he shook his head. Ashar knew, the Beltrevan held quadi enough now without Merak's shade joining the host that must already inhabit the forest, and Taws himself had assured the warrior that the great Merak, once Ulan of the Drott, was now no more than a servitor in the other-kingdom of the god. Yet sometimes in the darkest hours of the night Borsus would awake convinced he heard the skull whispering, the words never quite clear enough to discern, but nonetheless chilling in their inarticulate susurrations. He had mentioned this to Sulya, who denied it fiercely and told him it was no more than the night breeze whistling through the empty sockets and that a warrior – especially one so favoured by the Messenger – should pay less attention to the dead and more to those living. At such times Borsus found comfort in her arms, and for a while the night voices would go away, but then, in time, they would return to whisper fear into the darkness and he would again feel the prickling chill along his spine and the cold sweat bead his chest.

He had told himself it was foolishness, that he needed only time to adjust to the great turning of the world to which he was fortunate witness, that his fears were no more than the vapours of a man caught up in the maelstrom of history, nothing more. But still he felt uneasy around the skull that had once graced the great bull body of the dead Ulan, and no matter what Taws or Sulya told him, the unease persisted, even so long after Merak's death.

He grunted, extending his drinking horn that the woman might fill it with the sweet, red wine taken from the last Yath holding the growing Horde had looted. Cromart had led that clan of the soft Yath, and he had dissembled when Niloc Yarrum's invitation to place himself and his people under the command of the Drott had been presented. In response, Niloc had surrounded the palisaded settlement and put it to the torch, then slaughtered Cromart and all his followers as they fled the blaze. It had been a good killing and Borsus had taken his share of skulls, wondering idly why he felt no fear of opponents slain in honest battle, wondering if perhaps it was that particular distinction that made the difference: the skulls Sulya so proudly strung on his poles were taken honestly, while he could not feel the same for Merak's death.

He drank deep of the wine and gestured for more, feeling the soporific effects of the beverage and the sun's warmth kindle memories still vivid in his mind.

He was no longer sure how long it had been since Niloc took the Ulan's torque. Times were it seemed but yesterday, at others a lifetime since, but always the memory of the fight and the events that preceded it were clear as the summer sky, undimmed by time or any of the momentous events that had come to pass since Niloc presented his challenge.

Exactly what Taws had said to the ala-Ulan as he knelt before the mage Borsus could no longer recall. The shock of seeing so proud a warrior as Niloc Yarrum abase himself had blurred recollection, though he could remember Taws's words as he motioned Niloc to stand again.

'There is a favour I promised Borsus – a woman called Sulya.'

'Let him have her,' Niloc had answered, far more concerned with his own future than with that of a lowly clansman.

'She may have accepted another's torque,' the pale man had said. 'One called Andrath.'

Niloc had shrugged and bellowed for Andrath and Sulya to be brought to him.

When they stood, dishevelled and frightened, in the lodge of the ala-Ulan Sulya was, indeed, wearing Andrath's torque about her slender neck, presenting Niloc with a problem, for Sulya expressed no great desire to forfeit her new relationship and it went against all custom that she should be forced to relinquish the bronze circle that marked her as Andrath's woman. Taws had resolved the problem in horribly direct fashion. While Borsus gaped and Sulya shuddered, he had fixed his rubescent gaze on Andrath and taken two long, gliding strides across the floor of the lodge to place his hands upon the warrior's shoulders. Andrath had looked up into that red stare as not long before he must have looked into Sulya's eyes. Borsus had known what it was to experience that examination and shared some of the chill he knew must now surround Andrath's soul. Then Taws had ducked his head forwards, like some predatory beast seeking to fasten fangs in the exposed throat. Though not the throat, Borsus had seen, but the lips, which Taws kissed, the caress obscene and deadly. Andrath had stiffened, his body jerking rigid, his eyes rolling up in their sockets as he experienced the awful embrace of the Messenger. Then Taws had loosed his grip on the warrior's shoulders and Andrath had collapsed to the floor of the lodge, loose-limbed and somehow deflated, as though more than life was sucked from between his lips. The mage had turned then, sighing contentedly, to fix Sulya with his stare.

'Take off that dead man's torque.'

The lodge had been very quiet as she wrapped strong fingers about the bronze and bent it from her neck, tossing it carelessly beside the corpse, her cornflower eyes never leaving the mage's.

'You belong to Borsus as Borsus belongs to me. Go to him and take his torque. It is what you want.'

She had obeyed, and when Borsus saw her eyes he could scarcely believe the devotion he found there. He had removed his own neck-ring and handed it to her; watched as she closed it about her throat, her eyes never leaving his face. Then she had taken his hand and Taws had said, 'She is yours. Take her.'

What else had transpired in Niloc's lodge that night Borsus did not know, nor never thought to ask, but the next day Redek the shaman was gone to join Andrath and Gavroch, and the ala-Ulan announced the assumption of a new priest. By sunset the entire Gathering knew of Taws and Niloc Yarrum was summoned to the lodge of Merak, who demanded to know what manner of man the ala-Ulan chose to elect as his spiritual advisor. Borsus had been present at that meeting, the Ulan assuming him to be a member of

Niloc's Gehrim, which was now commanded – at Borsus's suggestion – by Dewan, whose continuing friendship he sought to maintain by the elevation. He had sat with his heart in his mouth and his hand on his sword hilt as he waited for Merak to explode in wrath at Niloc's arrogance. Indeed, several times the blades were loosened in their scabbards as the Gehrim of Ulan and ala-Ulan alike prepared to defend their masters, but Merak's confidence had forestalled open conflict between the factions and led him easily into the trap prepared by Taws.

'You dream high,' he had informed Niloc contemptuously. 'Do you dream of wearing this?'

Niloc's dark eyes had followed the Ulan's hand to the ornate torque that encircled the thick neck, his ambition rendering words unnecessary to confirm Merak's supposition.

'It can be yours,' Merak had continued, 'if you are man enough to take it.'

As Taws had instructed him, though such reticence sat ill, Niloc had resisted the temptation to respond with a challenge. Instead he had said only, 'I have no desire to destroy the unity of the Drott.'

'Or to die,' Merak had sneered, interrupting. 'And die you will if you face me in honest battle.'

'I have no wish to die,' Niloc had agreed, 'though whether you could kill me . . .' He had allowed the words to tail away, leaving doubt hanging in the tension-laid air as the attention of all those present focused on the Ulan.

Merak's features suffused with rage. There was a susurration of inhaled breath as his right hand descended to the sword resting across his knees, his left clamping about the scabbard in a fist balled so tight his knuckles shone white. Borsus felt his mouth fill with saliva, but was loath to tear his gaze from the two men long enough to spit and too afraid of drawing down the palpable danger that burned beneath the awning of Merak's lodge. At the periphery of his vision he could see Taws standing still and silent, the narrow mouth a knife slash across the snowy skin, the deep-set eyes expressionless, waiting. Abruptly, Borsus thought of a kite watching from its vantage point on a thermal updraught for a forest creature to die.

'You think I could not?' Merak snarled.

Niloc Yarrum shrugged, the gesture more eloquent for its wordlessness.

Merak chewed the trailing edges of his thick moustache, tugging red-black hairs unnoticed from his upper lip. His face was purpled, a nerve throbbing furiously beside his left eye. For long moments he glowered at the ala-Ulan.

Then, in a voice harsh and husky with barely-contained anger, he said, 'We shall see. We shall see which of us is the better man, Yarrum.'

'Do you challenge me?' Niloc enquired, unable to hold all the triumph from his voice.

'Yes!' Merak thundered, the bull-bellow sending the dogs that waited about the lodge scrambling for safety. 'By all the gods of the Beltrevan, I do! I challenge you, Niloc Yarrum, and by the morrow's sunset your head will decorate my trophy pole and your carcase shall feed my dogs.'

'So be it,' Niloc had responded with uncharacteristic aplomb. 'I accept your challenge, Merak. And by the morrow's sunset the Drott will hail a new Ulan.'

Borsus had thought the combat might commence on the spot. His legs were tense beneath him, readied for a spring that would carry him to his feet and across the floor of the lodge headlong into Merak's Gehrim. He could smell the battle-readiness of the men about him, and in the set of Dewan's broad shoulders see that the leader of Niloc's bodyguard shared his apprehension. But then the moment passed as Taws spoke, his voice soft and deadly cold as deep winter snow.

'Come, let word be issued so all the Gathering may know that the Ulan Merak has challenged the ala-Ulan Yarrum to mortal combat.'

With that and no further word or glance, he turned and strode from Merak's lodge, Niloc and his followers drawn in his wake as flotsam sucked along by the currents of the Idre.

They had returned to the tent of the ala-Ulan, where Niloc had shouted for wine and, on Taws's murmured suggestion, all but Borsus were dismissed from the inner sanctum. Outside, they could hear the camp criers already passing word of the combat, the news shouted from tent to tent, spreading amongst the lodges of the Gathering as a forest fire spreads, jumping from tree to tree. There was excitement and anticipation in the babble, though within the confines of Niloc's lodge the mood was more sombre. Niloc himself appeared far less confident than when he had confronted Merak, slumping in his chair and draining three goblets of wine in rapid succession, his swarthy features clouded.

Borsus had remained silent. Taws had stood, his inhuman face thoughtful, one long-fingered hand absently stroking the flames that rose from a fire-pot as a mortal man might caress the petals of a flower. Finally, when Borsus thought the silence would go on forever, he spoke.

'Do you doubt the outcome?'

Niloc ran his hands through his oiled hair, wiped them on his tunic, and shook his head as if weighing the question in his mind.

'In open combat I may well kill Merak, but I think he will wound me unto death. He is a mighty warrior.'

'So are you,' Taws had said, deep-sunk eyes studying the ala-Ulan's face, 'and you have me behind you.'

'On the combat ground?' Niloc asked, smiling cynically.

'In spirit,' Taws countered.

'That will be great consolation when I feel the bite of Merak's axe,' grunted the chieftain, spilling fresh wine as he filled his goblet again. 'I am not sure this is the best way.'

'How else would you have it?' Taws demanded. 'Would you have me slay Merak for you? Would that persuade the Drott to follow you?'

Niloc shrugged, doubt showing clear in his dark eyes. 'Knowing you stand behind me they would not dare to question my right to the torque.'

'Not openly perhaps,' Taws had said, 'but behind your back . . .?'

He left the question hanging in the stuffy air, and Borsus saw the sense of it. The Drott were a straightforward folk, prizing courage and battle skill above all else. Should the Messenger choose to work his magic to ensure Niloc's victory it would be said the man could not fight his own battles, that thaumaturgy had won the day. In time that could well lead to dissent, perhaps even rebellion. He glanced at Niloc, wondering how the ala-Ulan would respond.

'I care to win,' said Niloc. 'Not how.'

'How remains important, nonetheless,' retorted the mage. 'It would be easy for me to destroy Merak and all who questioned that destruction, but that would not ensure loyalty. Ashar sent me to find his Chosen, and that is you, Niloc Yarrum, but some effort on your part is necessary still if you are to be hef-Ulan and lead the Horde south.'

'I shall lead nothing dead,' grunted Niloc, the wine fortifying his black temper. 'What use am I to Ashar or you dead?'

'None whatsoever,' Taws responded carelessly. 'I have no more wish to endanger your life than you, but it is vital to our purpose – to Ashar's design – that you be seen to defeat the Ulan in honest fight. There can be no questioning your right to wear the torque. Thus the *how* of it is important.'

Niloc drained his cup and filled the bowl again, dark eyes locked on the opaline features of the fur-clad creature watching him.

'I am committed in any event. I must fight or flee, and I will not flee.'

'Good,' said Taws, his tone that of a parent gratified by a child's appropriate response. 'A wolfshead is no use to Ashar.'

'I hold a wolf by the ears,' Niloc snapped. 'I feel trapped.'

'You are,' Taws told him calmly. 'You have no recourse but to fight.'

'We come full circle.'

Niloc's tone was irritable, his expression dour. Borsus felt a chill dance along his spine, anticipating the sudden explosion of the ala-Ulan's temper; Taws's reaction. To his surprise, the mage smiled, bloodless lips stretching back from pointed teeth, his voice mild.

'Do you have so little faith?'

Niloc glowered, seeming torn between fear of death at Merak's hand and Taws's. 'In myself,' he muttered reluctantly, 'not in your power.'

'It is my power that will ensure your victory,' Taws said. 'Though not in any way that men shall know.'

Niloc frowned, scratching at his beard. 'I shall face Merak in the circle, alone. How can your aid not show?'

Instead of answering directly, Taws asked, 'What will be your weapons?'

'Sword,' said Niloc, 'and shield. Merak favours the axe.'

'Have them brought,' the mage commanded, 'by the slave who loves the Drott the least.'

Niloc Yarrum appeared confused by this, but shouted for the Vistral girl to bring the blade and the buckler. She came from the interior of the lodge, the sheathed sword resting on the underside of the shield, and set them down on the table before the ala-Ulan, her eyes averted. As she turned to go, Taws said, 'Wait. How are you called?'

'Neera,' she replied, her tone sullen and wary.

Taws rose from his chair and stood before her, reaching out to cup her chin, his fingers pallid against her tanned flesh, the russet luxuriance of her hair a dramatic contrast to his own ashen mane. She tried to avoid his stare, but the mesmeric power of his red eyes drew her gaze towards him and she stood in angry silence before him, her chin jutting defiantly. Taws nodded and let go his grip, turning from the girl to the shield.

Borsus had seen both blade and buckler before, but even so he marvelled at the artistry that had gone into their making. Amongst the chieftains of the Drott only Merak possessed finer weaponry. The shield was a disc of cured bull hide stretched over a frame of fire-hardened wood, tough enough to deflect a sword. The central boss was a cone of iron, and iron was riveted about the rim, the hide between reinforced with artful designs of beaten silver melded with more iron. It was a shield worthy of a chief, and the sword matched it. That was a good arm's length from hilt to point, the cutting edges honed to a razor sharpness, curving at the tip to a needle point, a shallow groove running along the spine to allow free flow of blood. The downslanted quillons were decorated with silver chasings that continued amongst the leather of the hilt, winding into the great knob of solid silver that formed the pommel.

Taws ran his fingers over the shield, his triangular features thoughtful, then drew the sword clear of the scabbard and held it before his face, oblivious of the deadly edges. He seemed satisfied with his examination for he set the blade down and turned again to Neera.

'What is your tribe, child?' he asked.

'The Vistral,' she answered proudly.

'How did you come here?'

'I was taken.' Her green eyes swung briefly towards Niloc Yarrum, flashing raw hatred. 'My village was burned. My man was killed, my parents, too.'

'If it were in your power,' Taws said, 'if you were not a slave, but free, would you seek vengeance?'

Shock danced in her startled gaze and she nodded dumbly.

'Tell me what you would do,' Taws murmured, the gentle tone prompting Borsus to think of a cat purring with pleasure as it studies the discomfort of a mouse. 'Tell me what vengeance you would extract.'

Neera glanced again at Niloc, then locked her eyes with Taws's. 'I would drive the filthy Drott from the face of the Beltrevan. I would kill them all. I would give their corpses to the crows and the carrion beasts they sprang from.'

Her breasts heaved as she said it, her skin paling, her eyes burning. Niloc's jaw snapped tight and he came partway from his seat, as though he would strike her down. A motion from Taws halted him, however, and he sank back with black fury writ in ugly lines upon his scarred face. Borsus wondered how many times the ala-Ulan had

67

taken her, and what pleasure it gave him to spend himself into so much hate. It appeared, though, that it was that very hate Taws sought – approved of – for the mage nodded and said, 'Excellent. You are the one I need.'

Confusion showed again on Neera's face, matched by that on Borsus's and Niloc's. It was compounded by the Messenger's subsequent action, for he turned his back on the Vistral girl and lifted the sword, the blade resting loose on his palms as he stared at the shining metal. His fingers locked tight around the length of it and he muttered something in a guttural tone, the words indistinct and alien, what little was audible sounding impossible for human tongue to utter. Borsus felt suddenly cold, shivering as if a creeping winter wind had entered the lodge. Taws raised the blade to his lips, kissing it as fondly as mother ever kissed a beloved child.

Then he spun and plunged the blade deep into Neera's belly, continuing the strange, singsong chant as the steel sank through robe and flesh and internal organs. The girl's eyes opened wide in pain and surprise, but some cantrip held them locked with the mage's and she made no sound other than a small, soft sigh as the sword emerged from her back, the shining metal now glistening red. More crimson filled the central groove, then was lost as Taws drove the blade quillon-deep into the yielding flesh. Still chanting, he let go of the sword and turned to the shield, taking it by the rim. Borsus expected the girl to collapse then: he had seen men gut-thrust like this in battle, the first shock stilling them, killing pain so that they stood numbed, but then they would scream and fall, kicking and clutching at the metal that leeched their life. Neera, however, remained upright, her arms hanging loose by her sides, the skirt of her robe staining dark as the fuller allowed her blood to flow out, the longsword jutting redly from her back. Her eyes were still open and all the pain that should have sent her screaming to the floor showed there in a silent, visual wail of agony. Taws stooped before her, placing the shield at her feet, then took the hilt of the sword in one hand and placed the other flat against the girl's breasts as he drew the blade from her body. A wash of blood gouted out as the awful wound was unblocked, spouting over the shield and running on to the floor of the lodge. The mage made a pass with his left hand before Neera's face and the Vistral girl abruptly crumpled, toppling on to the buckler, covering it with her riven body. Taws looked down at her, his eyes glowing red, his mouth moving to issue words Borsus could not hear for the pounding of blood inside his skull and the thunderous beating of his heart.

The spectral face was satisfied as it turned again towards Niloc Yarrum and Borsus. Both Drott watched in silence as the sword was raised and passed through the flames of a fire-pot, the blood spitting and giving off a sweet, sharp odour. Then it was gone as Taws ran a hand down the length of it, shining clean metal giving no sign of the gory ceremony as the mage returned the weapon to its scabbard. He kicked the lifeless girl from the shield and passed that, too, through the flames, restoring the buckler to pristine state with a single pass of his right hand. He set the metalled leather beside the sword and smiled at Niloc.

'Doubt no more, Ulan. Merak's axe will blunt on that; your blade will take his life.'

Niloc stared for long moments at the instruments of combat, his features clouded. Borsus wondered if Taws read the doubt there, the fear of handling ensorcelled weapons, then knew that the mage did, for he said, 'They offer you no harm – that is reserved for Merak, or any other who stands against you. The girl was rich in hate and that is now in the blade. When you face Merak that hate will defeat him. Your victory is ensured, but only we three shall know what I have done. And none of us will speak of it.'

A threat lay implicit in the words and Borsus shook his head as the crimson eyes caught his. Niloc found them reassuring, his right hand moving across the table, tentatively, to dart fingertips against the shield, the hilt of the sword. He gave a start, as though the touch shocked him, then smiled grimly and nodded to himself, locking his hand about the decorated hilt. He took the scabbard in his left hand and drew the blade, studying the metal.

'I feel it,' he murmured. 'I feel the power. I can defeat Merak with this.'

Abruptly he sprang to his feet, the chair toppling unnoticed behind him as he swung the sword experimentally, prompting Borsus to duck as the edge passed dangerously close to his head. The lodge filled with the ala-Ulan's triumphant laughter.

Borsus's exact position in the hierarchy of the tribe was not clearly defined. He was not bar-Offa, certainly not ala-Ulan, and could not be a shaman, but he *was* recognized as the confidant of Taws, and since the mage was favoured of Niloc Yarrum – and, as the rumours of his powers spread, feared – Borsus was regarded with a new respect. Thus it was that he stood amongst the foremost rank of onlookers as the combat began, shoulder to shoulder with Dewan, Taws on his other side, amidst the ala-Ulans and the shamans, in front of the bar-Offas. Thus he saw the combat.

As tradition dictated, it was held atop the great tumulus that marked Drul's resting place, with flambeaux set to augment the dying rays of the setting sun. Prayers were offered up to Ashar, and a goat sacrificed to the god with the plea that he look with favour upon both men, accepting the loser into the ranks of his followers in the other-kingdom. The blood of the animal was smeared on the foreheads of both men and battle was commenced.

As Niloc had predicted, Merak chose to fight with the axe, a weapon well-suited to his great size and strength. That his left hand be free to add power to his blows, he wore a small buckler of solid metal strapped to his left forearm. Neither combatant wore a shirt, their torsos bared and soon oiled with sweat. Merak's exhibited the scars obtained in the getting of the Ulan's torque in addition to those won in battle, while Niloc's was less disfigured, but no less muscular. Their hair was drawn back from their faces, Merak's hanging in a long plait that swung and slapped against his back as he fought, Niloc's contained within a silver fillet that glittered as he ducked and parried and swung the enchanted sword.

Had Borsus not known of the ensorcellment he would, like all the other watchers, have assumed the fight to be fair, a contest between two warriors of great prowess, for it appeared at first to be a matching of evenly skilled duellists. Indeed, it seemed at first that Merak's greater strength would eventually wear down Niloc's defence, stamina winning the day for the Ulan.

Merak carried the struggle to his opponent, charging like a berserker, the heavy axe whistling in his right hand as if it were no more than a willow switch used to disperse troublesome flies. Niloc backed away, circling the tumulus, staying out of reach of blows that would decapitate had they landed, utilizing speed and agility rather than the shield. Merak followed him, the bearded axe slicing air and reversing as if weightless, a stream of insults bursting from his lips. Niloc fought in silence, measuring his enemy as though not totally confident of Taws's spells, or perhaps merely endeavouring to make the combat appear more honest, for after they had circled the mound five times he sprang suddenly forward, the sword flashing in his hand.

The Ulan's bull-charge had imposed a kind of rhythm on the fight, the arcing of his axe assuming a horizontal pendulum motion.

As he raised the weapon at the commencement of each swing he brought his left arm across his chest. As the blade cut air with Niloc dancing before it, his body turned at the waist, right shoulder briefly exposed before the swing was reversed, the buckler still protecting his chest and belly, but his right side open to attack. The returning axe came back so fast there was scarcely time for Niloc to strike, but as the two men began their sixth circling of the tumulus, Niloc demonstrated the prowess that had won him his place amongst the leaders of the Drott. Foregoing the protection of the shield, he brought his blade up above his left shoulder and cut savagely across Merak's returning swipe. The sword caught the Ulan high on the right arm, carving a red-lipped gash over his bicep. Droplets of crimson spattered the trampled grass as Merak grunted, driving Niloc away with the return stroke, and crimson flowed down the corded arm. A tight smile showed beneath the ala-Ulan's moustache and as the axe swung again, he put the shield in its way.

Merak's axe struck the disc with a force that jarred Niloc's body. Borsus saw him gasp at the force of it, and thought he saw doubt flicker in the ebony eyes. But the shield took the blow without splitting or dropping, and Niloc cut again, this time aiming for Merak's ribs. The larger man deflected the blow with his buckler, the clamour of metal striking metal loud in the hushed silence, sparks dancing to join those given off by the torches. The blow should have numbed Niloc's wrist and arm, but the sword seemed to dance over the surface of the buckler to strike against Merak's ribs and carve out a gash to match the cut on his bicep. This time he gasped with the pain, and Niloc began to press the advantage.

Merak began to slow, realizing that sheer strength and ferocity were insufficient to win him the victory. He backed away, axe clutched in both hands now, and Niloc moved forwards, crouching behind his shield, using it to fend off the blows Merak rained down against the hide, stabbing with the sword so that the Ulan was driven steadily farther back as the point pricked wounds on belly and thighs. Soon he was forced to concentrate on defending himself, using the small buckler to hold off the snaking blade that threatened to disembowel him. Niloc screamed his battle shout – 'Yarrum!' – and drove the attack home. Merak fell silent, the beginnings of fear showing in the set of his jaw, in his narrowed eyes. He used his axe to ward the blows, clutching the haft close to the head, his breathing rapid as the initial flush of battle madness drained from him and he began to see defeat looming.

71

Warily, he back-pedalled, his direction around the circle reversed. A lupine smile stretched Niloc's lips and he hacked at the shaft as though cutting timber. Merak saw the danger of losing his weapon and let loose his left hand. It was a cunning move, for it allowed no resistance to Niloc's downswing and the sword cut earth as the Ulan stepped back. Instantly, the axe was lifting, the flat side of the head a hammer that would have shattered Niloc's jaw and most of his face had it landed. It did not, for the shield was interposed and the axe crashed against the reinforced leather with a force that came close to tearing the weapon from Merak's grasp. Then the sword lifted from the earth in a great arcing swing that scored a livid track from Merak's waist to left shoulder. Disbelief showed on the bearded features, soon lost beneath a frown of concentration as the blade danced and flickered in the firelit air as though possessed of a life of its own, driving Merak hurriedly back from the torrent of blows.

Niloc was remorseless now, confident of Taws's magic and so confident of taking Merak's life. There was no blood on his naked torso, no wound to slow and weaken him, only a few bruises that went unnoticed in the fury of the combat. The shield a barrier before him, he thrust and cut, inflicting draining hurts on the Ulan, slickening the grass with blood. Desperate, Merak threw himself into a fresh bout of frenzied action, bellowing '*Merak! Merak!*' as he rammed the axe directly at Niloc's face, turning the head as the ala-Ulan lifted his shield to hook the curved extension of the blade over the rim. The move gave the stronger man the advantage, for Merak was able to yank Niloc towards him as he slammed the buckler at the darkly smiling visage.

Again, a lesser warrior would have found himself stunned or crippled by the blow, his defence lost, his body exposed to the Ulan's axe. Again, Niloc's swordarm appeared to move faster than the eye could follow and instead of seeing him stagger back with blood coming from his mouth, the watchers saw Merak's left arm speared through by Niloc's blade. The sword had pierced the Ulan's wrist, forcing his arm up and a scream of agony from his mouth as Niloc twisted the metal and tugged it raggedly loose. Blood came in great spurts from the opened veins and the hand hooked, claw-like, where bones and tendons were cut. Niloc smashed his shield hard against Merak's chest, sending the man back with the axe swinging in ineffectual defence, the weakening effect of his many wounds now showing clearly, his breath coming in harsh, panting gasps as ragged as the hole in his wrist.

The sun was descending below the treetops now, combining with the light of the torches to bathe the scene in fiery radiance. Niloc stalked Merak, deflecting the axe blows with an almost casual air, his eyes bright, the wolfish smile fixed rigid on his mouth. Then he turned, taking the axe on his shield as he brought his blade down in a great swing that severed Merak's arm. Fresh blood gouted over the shield and a great sigh went up from the onlookers as Merak's axe, the hand still locked about the haft, fell to the ground. Merak took three tottering steps backwards, staring at the stump of his right arm, his massive head turning from side to side as though he could not believe the evidence of his failing sight. Niloc shouted and swung his sword in a tremendous blow that landed against Merak's neck, just above the gold and silver circle of the Ulan's torque.

The head fell. Blood jetted vertically from the opened throat. Then Merak's great bull body fell to its knees and pitched forwards at Niloc's feet. The ala-Ulan stood with the sword still moving in his hand, as though the blade sought more flesh to sunder. He seemed to still it with an effort, driving it into the earth beside the twitching corpse. There was a great silence throughout the clearing. Niloc loosened the shield and set it gently down beside the sword, then knelt to draw the Ulan's torque from the dead man's neck. He raised it bloody, setting sun and firelight glinting on the reddened twining of gold and silver, holding it aloft for all the Gathering to see as he paraded the tumulus.

Borsus heard Dewan whisper, 'Ashar!' Then Taws's crow-dry voice say, 'Niloc Yarrum! Ulan Yarrum!'

And the words were taken up by all, reverberating around the clearing, ringing off the encircling trees, Borsus's own shout adding to the tumult.

'Niloc Yarrum! Ulan Yarrum! Niloc! Niloc! Ulan!'

Even the members of Merak's Gehrim took it up, swords raised in salute, spears rattling against shields. It had, after all, been a fair combat, and Niloc had proven his right to wear the Ulan's torque; proven it in honest fight. None doubted that.

Borsus watched as the Ulan Niloc Yarrum stripped the silver torque from his throat and fastened the gold and silver in its place. He stared out over the massed ranks of the Drott, raising his arms for silence. A sea of upturned faces stared back, awaiting the words of their new chief.

Niloc's voice rang loud. 'I am Ulan! I wear the torque! Does any gainsay me?'

There was not a voice lifted in protest and he smiled, wiping Merak's blood from his hands.

'Let the Ulan Merak be given to Ashar. Let his women find new men. Let his possessions be distributed amongst you.

'Let us feast!'

There was a great roar of approval at the announcement, and warriors climbed the flanks of the mound to lift their new Ulan on their shields and carry him amongst the people so that all might see him. Borsus, stirred by the moment, moved to join them, but Taws set a hand on his arm and held him back, murmuring, 'You serve me, warrior; no other.'

The words, and the winterchill tone, dampened Borsus's spirits, but then Taws smiled momentarily and added, 'You serve the power, not its outward manifestation, and I have need of you.'

What need Ashar's Messenger might have of a humble warrior, Borsus was not sure, but he had no wish to argue and returned with Taws to Yarrum's lodge as Dewan and the Gehrim stripped Merak's tent of those items they deemed more suitable to their master than the common folk. The rest, as custom dictated, was distributed amongst the tribe, and for the remainder of that night and all the following day the Drott feasted.

Niloc Yarrum assumed the position of Ulan with ruthless enthusiasm. Old scores were settled, and when the great Summer Gathering ended the tribe left Drul's mound ringed with scaffolds, the carrion eaters of the forest gorging on those given to the blood eagle. The hierarchy altered as Niloc deposed all those who spoke against his dreams of war, elevating new ala-Ulans, appointing fresh bar-Offas, surrounding himself with men who, like him, saw the Confederation rising, the Horde massing to march on the Three Kingdoms.

Taws stood behind him, hailed now as High Priest of the Drott, and beside Taws stood Borsus, still – somewhat to Sulya's disappointment – only a warrior, but now one against whom no one dared speak, favoured of the Messenger and consequently protected as surely as though ringed by Gehrim. His lodge moved forwards in the circle, standing directly behind Niloc's and adjoining that of Taws himself. It was a great advancement, but the warrior was not certain but that he preferred the old days, the old ways, before the coming of the Messenger.

He drained the horn Sulya filled for him and reached for the venison set on the platter at his side. Across the grass lounged Dewan, resplendent in the looted armour with which Niloc now equipped his bodyguard. That, Borsus recalled, had once been worn by a Yath chieftain whose name he had forgotten, if not the battle in which it had been taken. It had been long and bloody, for the Yath had shown little enthusiasm for the suggestion that they join forces with the Drott, and had fought like cornered wolves when Niloc's ultimatum that they ally or die had been presented.

Indeed, the men of Borsus's tribe had at first looked askance at Niloc's announcement that they join forces with the other forest folk, for their conception of the Horde's rising was simplistic in the extreme: Ashar's Messenger had come to the Drott, not the Caroc, Grymard, Vistral or Yath, and therefore the Drott were paramount, the rest mere battle fodder, their destiny to obey or be destroyed. It had taken some argument on Taws's part – and some blood letting by Niloc – to convince them that conquest of the Beltrevan tribes would prove a slow and depleting process, ultimately weakening the Drott, and decimating the rest, to the extent that the Horde would be insufficient to defeat the allied might of the Three Kingdoms.

Niloc himself had, at first, been doubtful, and Borsus had wondered for a while if the whole great design might not founder on the rock of the Ulan's pride. He had listened to Taws spell out the game on Ashar's Eve, the shortest night of the year and customarily the final night of the Gathering.

They had been alone again, the three of them, in the lodge now set aside for Taws. The mage had no slaves, refusing Niloc's offers of the pick of the camp. So far as Borsus could tell, he neither ate nor drank, though he sometimes sipped at wine without lowering the level of his cup, as might a man seeking to appear normal, and his lodge was – for men – unnaturally warm. The hides that formed the roof and walls had been further augmented with furs; the floor itself was spread with pelts; and despite the summer heat, a fire burned constantly at the centre of the main chamber.

Niloc had requested the audience, and Taws had called Borsus to attend, refusing entry to all others. Dewan and his Gehrim ringed the lodge, while inside Borsus and Niloc sweated.

'You will make an announcement at dawn,' Taws had commanded. 'You will tell the people they stay together.'

'Together?' Surprise had shown on the Ulan's face. 'How can we stay together? The clans will seek their own lands – there are holdings to tend, crops to harvest, animals to herd. When the Gathering ends, all return to their own.'

'The Drott form the nucleus of the Horde,' Taws had replied, 'How else shall the tribes form the Confederation?'

'The warriors will fight,' Niloc answered, shrugging as though this was a foregone conclusion that required no debate. 'The women and the old ones will tend the holdings. That is the way. That is how it has always been.'

'No longer,' Taws responded. 'There is a new way now.'

'Drul made no such announcement,' argued Niloc. 'If we are to raise the Horde, it must be an army. An army consists of fighting men, not women and children.'

'You won your torque on Drul's mound,' Taws said in a voice that pricked icy fingers down Borsus's spine. 'Drul lies beneath the ground there, when his tomb might have been the marble of Andurel. Drul failed. Do you understand that? Drul failed!'

The statement – near blasphemy to Drott ears – shocked Borsus, but he deemed it the wiser move to keep his mouth closed. Not so Niloc Yarrum.

'Drul raised the Horde,' he countered sullenly, envisaging, Borsus thought, open rebellion amongst his followers should he suggest such departure from custom. 'No other has done that.'

'And the Horde broke on the Lozin Forts and Drul died there,' said Taws stonily. 'When the Kingdoms were weaker. They are stronger now, and the forest folk are scattered through the Beltrevan.'

'The warriors of the Drott will follow me,' Niloc grunted, eyes narrowing as he stared at the mage, then swinging abruptly to study Borsus. 'Will they not, warrior?'

Borsus had swallowed then, once more torn between twin fears. 'Unto death, Ulan,' he dissembled, 'if that be Ashar's wish.'

Taws had smiled slightly at that, pouncing on the prevarication. 'I am Ashar's Messenger and I give you his word. You hold the torque through my design – now you will follow that design as I paint it for you.' Threat rang in his tone. 'Do you heed me, Ulan?'

Reluctantly, Niloc ducked his head in acceptance.

'Then listen,' Taws had continued impatiently, 'for there is no more time to waste and I have lingered here long enough. The men of the Drott will follow you, of that I have no doubt. But what of the rest? What of the Caroc? The Grymard? The others?'

'We offer them alliance or death,' Niloc answered. 'Who will not join us, dies. It is simple.'

'It is *not* simple!' Taws rasped, his voice the hiss of a striking serpent, 'It is not at all simple. Listen to me, man, and bend your

76

mind to understanding – what I came here to achieve is not some tribal war. It is not a matter of the Drott conquering all, for that can only weaken all. I need men *willing* to give me their lives, ready to die for Ashar. The strength of the Horde will rest in its belly. I told you I came to raise the Beltrevan against the Kingdoms and I spoke of *all* the Beltrevan. The warriors, the women, the children. All! The mightiest Confederation this world has known, or ever will know. Do you grasp that, man? Can you think in larger terms than petty tribal warfare?'

Niloc noticed the absence of title, the contempt in the cold voice, and scowled.

'How shall such a Horde eat? What does it live on?'

'Hunger,' said Taws. 'Belly-hunger, and more than that – the hunger for what they do not have. Hunger for what lies beyond the Lozins. The Drott will set the example, the rest follow.'

Niloc Yarrum's mouth gaped open. Borsus wiped droplets of sweat from his eyes, unable to take them from the ashen face of the Messenger as the enormity of what Taws suggested sank in.

'You begin to see it.' Taws's tone was milder now, the threatening red light that had sparked in his deep-set eyes dimming. 'On the morrow the Drott will leave this camp in a single mass. You will abandon your holdings, your farms, your traplines. All of it. What you cannot bring with you, you will forsake. Those too old or sick to travel you will leave. Let the forest have it all – your destiny is southwards.'

'And when we encounter the Caroc? Or the Yath?' Niloc demanded. 'What then? Warriors can fight and run. Burdened by the entire people we move but slowly – like some lumbering bear that Yath or Caroc arrows may wound at will.'

'The Yath are the first you will encounter,' replied the mage. 'With me beside you, you will offer them a place in the Confederation. They will fight a little, but the weight of Ashar's design will tell and they will join us. Then we continue across the Beltrevan, through the lands of the Grymard and the Vistral and the Caroc. To the Lozins, with *all* the Beltrevan behind us.

'The warriors will march to the fore, but behind them will be their families, their possessions – everything they hold dear, everything they will fight for. They will know that defeat is not a matter of running back to the old ways, for the old ways will be dead. They died with my coming! There will be nothing to run back to. There will be no direction save forwards. Southwards!'

'Ashar!' Niloc Yarrum had muttered, his face suddenly pale, his throat moving above the Ulan's torque. 'You ask much of us, Taws. You ask that we forsake the ways of our grandfathers' grandfathers. The ways we have always known.'

'I offer you much in reward,' the mage had replied. 'I offer you the world.'

Niloc had thrust a hand to his chest then and scrubbed at the perspiration that darkened his shirt. Then he had nodded and said, 'Do I have choice in this?'

'No,' Taws had told him flatly.

And Niloc had made the announcement, and executed the nine ala-Ulans who rejected it, and led the Drott away from Drul's mound towards the territory of the Yath.

The Ulan of the Yath had at that time been a warrior called Yanador. His scouts warned him of the unprecedented movement of the northern folk and he had halted his tribe's return to their hunting grounds from their own Gathering, massing a force of some seven thousand fighting men across the path of the Drott advance, sending his eldest son, Vran, out under a truce banner to demand that the Drott turn back.

Taws had spoken alone with Vran, persuading him – if that was the correct term to apply to the mage's hypnotic power – that Yanador was a man of too small a vision to perceive the greatness of the quest, which would be better implemented by a warrior such as Vran himself, and that the Yath would fare better under a new Ulan.

Vran had 'seen' the wisdom of alliance and the chance to further his own ambitions with little personal danger. He had knelt before Niloc Yarrum and kissed the Drott Ulan's sword in token of fealty. Then he had returned to his father, accompanied by the Messenger and a mightily reluctant Borsus, to present the Drott terms. Borsus had thought he might well die then as he saw Yanador's features suffuse with a rage prompted both by the notion that he accept a subservient position to a man he described as nothing more than the outcome of an unnatural coupling between a Drott wanton and a forest hog and his own son's desertion, but Taws had once more demonstrated his powers. The mage had brought his hands together, producing a thunderclap that rattled the skulls on Yanador's trophy poles, a ball of white fire appearing as he opened his palms to engulf the Yath Ulan, dancing over his armour so that he stood dumbstruck, his hair standing on end and his teeth chattering in concert with the clattering bones as stark fear showed in eyes that watered. His Gehrim had reached then for their weapons, intent on defending – or revenging – their chief, but Vran had shouted for them to be still and Taws had gestured, sending fresh bolts from his clawed fingers to still them as he had once stilled Niloc Yarrum's bodyguard.

It had been agreed that mage and warrior be allowed safe return to the Drott battle lines, taking with them Yanador's counter proposal: the tribes would merge under *his* command, not that of some northern whorespawn who had doubtless won his torque through treachery.

Taws had been impatient – Borsus had thought he might kill the Yath chief on the spot – but rather than weaken the Horde through battle, he had played out the political game, informing Niloc of the suggestion, and the insults, and gone again to the Yath lines with a further suggestion of his own devising: Yanador and Niloc Yarrum should meet in single combat, the outcome deciding the leadership.

The proposal was supported by Vran and those Yath ala-Ulans who backed the chief's son, or sensibly sought to avoid open warfare with a folk renowned for their savagery in battle, and the two Ulans had faced one another on the ground between the two forces.

Niloc had won, and Yanador's skull had joined Merak's on his trophy pole.

Borsus felt little liking for Vran, for although he was privy to the thaumaturgy that had convinced the man, he could not help feeling that filial loyalty should have proved stronger. Besides, he had noticed the way the Yath regarded Sulya, and while he could take his pick of the many women thronging the enormous camp the Horde established each night – and sometimes did – he retained a proprietary interest in the buxom blonde. Vran, he felt, was not to be trusted. The man's eyes were set too close together, and the pale russet of his hair suggested Vistral blood, which spoke of softness and a willingness to live in harmony with the Southerners.

He studied Vran now, lounging easily on Niloc's left, his horn filled by a Grymard slave girl, a second feeding him titbits of venison that she held between her teeth, dropping them into the Yath's mouth with little cooing noises of pleasure as he stroked her breasts through the blue robe that had come from a batch of cloth saved from Cromart's hold.

Cromart had been one of the few to reject the alliance, taking his people from the scene of the duel immediately the outcome was declared, fleeing in the confusion that had followed as the Yath mourned the death of their Ulan and Vran rode his horse up and down the lines shouting for his people to sheath their swords in obedience of their new Ulan.

There had not been many like Cromart. A handful of minor clans had quit the Yath Gathering before the encounter and a few chieftains had rejected the alliance out of hand. They had sought the safety of the forest and their own holdings, but on Taws's insistence the Horde had turned aside from its southward migration to confront each dissenter. In some cases the sheer mass of numbers surrounding the holds had persuaded the ala-Ulans that resistance was futile and they had surrendered, only to find themselves sacrificed to the Messenger's design. Laying down their weapons, they had been promptly given to Taws in the privacy of his lodge. Having already witnessed the vampiric leeching of Andrath, Borsus was not surprised when dry-husked corpses were dragged from the tent and fed to the dogs that now roamed in great packs amongst the shebangs, while those who had not previously known of the mage's habits found their fear of the white-maned creature growing daily. Eyes were averted when Taws wandered the camps, and fingers passed before faces in the warding gesture against dark magic. Others, offering open resistance, were slaughtered out of hand – a move Borsus preferred, for it at least gave the chance of honest fight and decent death, which was as much as any warrior could ask for.

He thrust his horn at Sulya again, finding himself gripped with a sudden desire to cloud the memories. Like Niloc, he had envisaged the Confederation as a thing raised in the old way. He had thought Taws came amongst the Drott to imbue them with battle-vigour, perhaps aid them in the fighting with his cantrips, but this manner of absorption was little to his taste, and he was careful to take only those skulls he won fairly. Only those, he felt, remained silent as trophies should; the others whispered too much, too discomfortingly.

He quaffed the sweet, red wine and shook his head, slapping at a fly that found his face of interest. There were too many flies about the Horde, as though the great mass of forest folk carried with it the odour of decay, and these days, whenever he looked up at the sky, he saw crows and ravens flapping and circling as if they sensed something dying.

He was less than comfortable in the midst of so many folk, even though his lodge was now more luxurious than he would previously have dared dream. Even though he had Sulya to warm his furs at night. Even though men stepped aside when he approached them, fearing to offend the favoured of the Messenger. Even though he sat witness to the councils of the Ulans.

Borsus was a simple warrior, and in many ways he longed for the simpler days when men fought without the aid of magic, before Taws appeared to make reality of Niloc Yarrum's war dreams. But he was also pragmatical, and he knew that those days were gone forever, his simple life with them. Whether he liked it or not, whatever he felt about it, he *had* been the one to first greet the Messenger, and that marked him out as a special man, forced upon him a special destiny.

Ashar's will, he thought. I must accept it. I have no choice.

He caught Dewan's eye and saw something in it that made him wonder if the leader of Niloc's Gehrim shared his doubts. If so, Dewan had given no sign, said nothing to suggest anything other than grateful acceptance of his elevation. He had presented Borsus with a fine sword in expression of his gratitude, for he knew that it had been on Borsus's word that he found himself raised so unexpectedly, and they had had little opportunity to speak privately since then. Dewan's duties kept him close to Niloc, or busy quelling the arguments that so frequently erupted amongst the mass of folk, and his position by now had become virtually that of peacekeeper. Borsus wondered – and decided that silence remained the wisest course. If Dewan, too, had doubts, let Dewan voice them first; so close to Taws, Borsus could not risk the danger: he had no wish to feel the lethal kiss of those milky lips.

He thought of what they had achieved and had still to do, and found himself marvelling at the enormity of it all. Drott and Yath bound together; ala-Ulans of the Grymard and Vistral presenting themselves in open disobedience of their Ulans to swear loyalty to the cause; the Horde moving, remorseless as the north fire that had spawned Taws and now lay far behind them, across the Beltrevan, leaving nothing save the dead in its wake. Already there were more folk than he could number, more than he could believe *could* be, moving, always moving, pausing only to destroy opposition, consuming all before them, stripping the Beltrevan of food just as Taws had said. Moving steadily south towards the Three Kingdoms.

The Grymard and the Vistral were insufficient threat to waste time thinking of. If they chose to oppose the joint strength of Drott and Yath they would go down in bloody defeat – those who had not already allied themselves with the Horde. If they chose alliance, their numbers would further swell the ranks of the Confederation. Only the Caroc might prove a problem, for they were fierce as the Drott, and their territory lay in the path of the migration: open warfare could prove disastrous.

But there were Caroc emissaries here now. They sprawled on furs across the grass from Borsus, the ala-Ulans Denn, Jevart, Kagir and Grax, sent by Balandir himself, Ulan of the Caroc.

Sent to parley. To talk peace or war. Borsus wondered which it would be.

If war, then the Beltrevan would know a spilling of blood such as must surely slake even Ashar's thirst. If peace – alliance – then how could the Three Kingdoms stand against the Horde?

Chapter Four

Weary though he was from the long ride, and for once in agreement with his father that a bath was in order, Kedryn found it hard to resist the impulse to linger as the squadron of Tamurin cavalry approached the Lozin Forts. He had seen the great strongholds before, but this was the first time he had approached them as a warrior – albeit a fledgling – and he found he viewed them through changed eyes. Always they had impressed him – it seemed impossible that anyone should not be impressed by such great structures – but on previous visits he had seen them as vast playgrounds, whilst now his new status prompted him to take what he considered a more adult attitude, and regard them with the eyes of a soldier concerned with his country's defence.

And surely they were a mighty defence. They sat facing one another across the Idre where the river widened after its passage through the mountains, tumbling in a foam-wracked spill of white water from the mouth of a gorge flanked on either side by sheer stone walls that seemed to touch the sky. It was impossible to gauge the height of those walls for the stone merged, grey, with the heavens, and the chasm through which the river ran was filled with mist from the water, the very air thrumming with its tumultuous passage. The forts in turn seemed to merge with the stone, appearing less like man-made edifices than some natural protrusion of bastions and barricades thrusting from the living rock. Both, he knew from his lessons, housed a garrison of some five hundred fighting men and as many more supporting cadres of cooks and farriers and blacksmiths and Sisters hospitaller: sufficient that the forts were, in effect, self-contained settlements akin to Caitin Hold.

Below them, where the Idre became wider and slower, towns stood on either bank, foregoing palisades in their confidence of the forts' strength and consequent ability to protect the inhabitants from any danger. Boats plied the river there, ferrying Tamurin to the eastern side and Keshi across to Tamur in a constant exchange that, as much as Andurel itself, evidenced the unity of the Three Kingdoms. But Kedryn had little time for the towns, being wholly consumed with his assessment of the forts, and he slowed his horse, allowing the column to pass cheerfully by as he stared in awe at the spectacle rising before him.

The citadel on his side of the river stood a fraction higher than its Keshi counterpart, and was thus known as the High Fort, its neighbour being called the Low Fort, but that was the only real difference. Both rose above the towns, turning lofty, crenellated walls to the south, approached along a glacis which the Tamurin party now rode towards monumental gates that stood opened in greeting, soldiery lining the entrance as Bedyr's party commenced the ascent. To either side of the gates the walls joined with the Lozins themselves, melding on the one side with the precipitous stone and continuing on the other along the line of the Idre to overlook the waterway, their surfaces pockmarked with embrasures and battlements from which jutted the stark outlines of arbalests and catapults.

Whatever force had carved out the chasm of the river had left it wedge-shaped, wider at the southern extremity than to the north, where the great walls continued in a semi-circle to meet again with the mountains and block the narrow path that snaked up from the forests of the Beltrevan. Although he could not see that side, Kedryn knew that the defences were stronger there. The walls were deliberately angled and tricked to slow any approach and bring any penetrating warband under attack from a whole series of redoubts that commanded the approaches, effectively sealing off landward invasion.

At the base of the walls, where they descended into the river, there were fortified extensions against which the water splashed and broke, foaming over gigantic hinged booms that could be loosed from their moorings to swing out, impelled by the force of the Idre herself across the river to meet at the centre, where they were designed to lock and block the waterway. Thus any riverborn invasion would be halted, barbarian vessels meeting the barriers and stranding under fire from both High and Low Forts.

There seemed no way through the Lozins, the twin citadels plugging the passage through the mountains as effectively as a cork hammered tight into the neck of a bottle, and Kedryn could not help wondering why King Darr felt concern as he studied the gargantuan strongholds. They were, surely, impregnable.

He started as his horse frisked, drawing his attention back from the forts to the more immediate approach. Tepshen Lahl swung his own animal away, a minimal smile showing briefly on his impassive features as he motioned the lingering youngster forwards to join Bedyr at the head of the column.

'You have princely duties, boy. Attend your father.'

Kedryn nodded, grinning, and heeled his mount up the glacis to join Bedyr, the kyo close on his heels.

Bedyr was halted before the gates, awaiting formal invitation to enter, remaining in the saddle until a shout from beyond the porticoes called for the riders to come in, the men lining the gates raising pikes in greeting as the Lord of Tamur urged his horse forwards on to the wide, flagstoned plaza immediately beyond the entrance.

A guard of honour awaited there, mail glittering in the afternoon sunlight, surcoats emblazoned with the emblem of the Kingdoms, the chatelain standing a pace before in rust red surcoat, the chest marked with the fist badge that announced his Tamurin antecedents.

He was a tall, thin man, clean-shaven and sparsely haired, the greying strands tugged severely back from an austere visage that was lit by a surprisingly warm smile as he raised a hand in formal greeting, shouting loud enough that the words rang from the surrounding stone, 'Welcome to Bedyr Caitin, Lord of Tamur!'

Bedyr responded, 'Greetings to our loyal commander, Rycol, holder of the Lozin Pass!'

The formalities dispensed, Bedyr climbed from his saddle and took the hand Rycol extended, his own smile warm as he studied the man, the warmth echoed in his voice.

'How fare you, Rycol, old friend?'

'Well enough,' Rycol answered, 'though my joints begin to heed this watery place, and your visit persuades me the rumours I have heard may be more than mere border talk.'

'Perhaps.' Bedyr's tone was mild, but Kedryn knew his father well enough to recognize the underlying seriousness. 'But let us discuss the purpose of this visit more privately. I'd lief bathe the memories of the ride from my limbs before we settle to serious business.'

Rycol shrugged angular shoulders, hooking thumbs into his swordbelt. 'Indeed, my Lord, and I'll send a boat to fetch Fengrif from the Keshi side. It'll save you hearing the same story twice.'

Bedyr nodded his assent. 'You recall the stripling?' He gestured at Kedryn as he spoke, and Rycol swung his hawkish gaze towards the youth.

'Kedryn? By the Lady, I'd not recognize you – the last time you were no more than a child. Now . . .' He paused, turning full around to duck his head in acknowledgement. 'I bid you welcome, Prince.'

Kedryn grinned, drawing himself to full height, somewhat embarrassed and not sure how to reply correctly. Settling – for once grateful to Lyassa for the tedious lessons in protocol – on, 'I thank you, Commander. And join with my lord and father in felicitation.'

Rycol laughed aloud. 'We leave the formalities to Andurel, Prince. I am called Rycol by my friends.'

'And I am Kedryn . . . Rycol.'

Embarrassment departed as Rycol smiled afresh, clapping an iron-like hand to Kedryn's shoulder as he chuckled and said, 'Good, you have your father's way, and I have no complaint with that. And I see you brought that slant-eyed bloodletter with you. Silent as ever, eh, Tepshen?'

The words surprised Kedryn more than a little, for the kyo had made no previous mention of knowing the chatelain of High Fort, but Tepshen Lahl clearly took no offence for a smile creased his face as he nodded and answered, 'I thought to see for myself how fat you grow on peace.'

At which Rycol laughed hugely, ushering them on to the bath-house as he bellowed orders for their horses to be stabled and food prepared for the travellers, leaving Kedryn to wonder how long they had known one another and how much more he needed to learn of the kingdom he would one day inherit and the men he would lead.

Neither Tepshen Lahl nor Bedyr had mentioned any particular feeling for the chatelain, but it was clear that both knew him well, and respected him in equal measure. There was an ease to their conversation as they entered the steaming room and stripped out of their riding gear, sinking gratefully into the hot water. The talk continued along casual lines, the purpose of the visit left, by mutual consent, for later, as the stiffness and the aches imparted by the long ride from their last waystop were driven out by the warmth and the attentions of Rycol's masseurs.

Later, dressed in clothes provided by Rycol, they attended the dining hall, where Fengrif, commander of the Keshi fort, awaited them.

Kedryn had encountered few of the plainsfolk, but those he had met, and his studies, had suggested the Keshi were short and bow-legged from their traditional acquaintance with horses. The majority of the Tamur riding animals were bred from Keshi stock, the union producing beasts that enjoyed the speed and intelligence of the eastern bloodlines in combination with the hardiness of the smaller Tamurin hill ponies. There was a scurrilous legend extant in Tamur that the Keshi themselves were the product of an unnatural union between man and mare, which explained their undoubted skill in all things to do with horses, and no doubt the Keshi held similar exaggerations concerning the folk of Tamur. He was, consequently, surprised to see that Fengrif was only slightly bowed in the legs and as tall as Bedyr himself, if considerably larger of girth. In addition, the man was friendly as Rycol, greeting the Tamurin with obvious pleasure as he took his place at the head table of the dining hall, clutching his belly in pantomime of discomfort.

'Only for you, Bedyr Caitin,' he announced, gratefully accepting the wine a servant poured him, 'would I cross that damnable river. By all the gods, I hate water! We Keshi were born to the earth – liquids are for drinking and washing! Were it later in the year I'd suffer more, though even now my stomach heaves. How does the River Guild find men? Give me the plains or my fort, and may the Lady protect me from boats and water.' He drank deep, beckoning for the jug as he shook his head and laughed at his own aversion.

'Should we need to meet again, I'll cross to your side,' Bedyr promised, 'but today speed appears of the essence.'

Fengrif's dark face became more serious as he nodded. 'I presume you come on Darr's bidding?'

'Yes,' Bedyr confirmed, 'the King is concerned with these rumours out of the Beltrevan. What news have you, Fengrif?'

The Keshi shrugged. 'Little enough. Something stirs, but what I do not know. Rycol and I both have our spies amongst the forest folk, but they have told me little.'

'Nor mine,' Rycol added. 'There is talk of war between the Drott and the Yath, but whether fought or impending I am not certain. The very absence of information worries me.'

Fengrif nodded at this and said, 'Indeed. It is as though the forest folk hide their intent, and that in itself is worrying. Usually we can count on our spies advising us of the comings and goings of the tribes, but this past year or more there has been a silence. I have no great liking for such a quiet – it bodes ill.'

'Aye,' said Rycol, 'I concur. As you know, there is some degree of trade, but for some time now that has fallen off. It seems almost as though the tribes cut contact, whilst before they were anxious for our goods.'

'Do they raid?' Bedyr asked. 'Have you seen scouting parties?'

The commanders shook their heads as one. Rycol said, 'No. In the course of a year we might expect – *do* expect – a few attempts to slip past us, but there has been nothing. The traders from the town complain their profits are dropped.'

'I care little for their profits,' Bedyr said dismissively, 'but I do need information.'

'They are a source of that,' Fengrif said. 'That is why we allow them to continue. The Grymard and the Vistral hold their Gatherings not far from the forts and usually drift south after to trade. That has customarily given us news of the woodsfolk, but this summer no more than a handful showed their faces and the traders came back with empty pockets and scant information.'

Bedyr frowned. 'Perhaps that is the answer: Darr seeks word, the traders seek profit. Perhaps a trade party should make an excursion into the forest.'

'Risky,' said Rycol in a dubious tone, 'the people of the Beltrevan have little enough love for the Kingdoms and barely tolerate even those traders they know.'

'But they allow trade.'

Kedryn guessed the direction his father took and recognized the logic of it. An armed expedition was unlikely to achieve much more than a fight, and if the tribes were as ferocious as legend claimed, the squadron from Caitin Hold would gain little more than arrows from the woodland: there was no profit in that; but a seemingly innocent party of merchants – appearing to seek only commercial dividends – might well learn something of value.

He listened attentively as Rycol began to speak again.

'Some, my Lord, but not really very much. And those who do venture through the pass seldom go far into the woodland – the tribes are generally agreed upon certain locations as acceptable for trading purposes, and hold truce at those places, but elsewhere . . .'

He glanced at Fengrif, as though seeking support, which came in the form of a nod as the Keshi shoved one ornate braid back over the shoulder of his green robe and turned serious eyes on Bedyr.

'A plainsman went north early this summer, Lord Bedyr. A man I knew well – Gathir, he was called. He travelled with a band of some forty good men – fighters as much as they were merchants – and none returned. I sent a party into the Beltrevan, but all my scouts found were the remains of Gathir and his men. Some were killed in honest fight, but the majority were given to the blood eagle.'

Bedyr's face showed his distaste, and Kedryn winced at the notion of any man suffering so horrible a death. Fengrif spread his hands, rings sparkling on the fingers, in apology and explanation. Rycol added, 'Gathir strayed from the accepted trade sites, but even so . . .'

'I can speak only for the Keshi,' said Fengrif, 'but I would advise most strongly against the Lord of Tamur risking such a journey.'

'Darr requires information,' Bedyr responded doggedly. 'How else to obtain it?'

'The Sisterhood, perhaps?' Rycol suggested. 'I agree with Fengrif that you should not risk yourself or your son in the Beltrevan, Lord Bedyr. Even disguised as a trader you might be recognized – even as a trader, you might well be killed. The Sisters here are hospitallers, but could King Darr not request far-seers from Estrevan? Has he none in Andurel?'

Bedyr toyed with his cup, swirling the wine as if seeking inspiration from the movement, his face unusually solemn.

'My own suggestion,' he said at last, his voice low, 'and yes, Darr has far-seers in Andurel, but what they see is fire. No more than that. It is a matter of concern to the King – the very obscuring of the vision suggests a danger hitherto unknown.'

'What does Estrevan say of this?' Fengrif asked.

'The same.' Bedyr shrugged, leaning forwards to rest elbows on the polished oak of the table. 'The Sisters can warn, but no more. As best I understand it, they have applied all their efforts to penetrating the Beltrevan, but to little end. They are certain danger lurks beyond the Lozins, but can be sure of no more. It seems that if the fire does burn in the forests, the smoke clouds the source.'

'The Lady Yrla,' Rycol began, halting abuptly when Bedyr shook his head.

'The Lady Yrla forfeited her power when she married me. Celibacy is the source of that power, as you know.' He glanced at Kedryn, smiling as though to reassure his son no blame was attached. 'She is able to advise me; from her studies of the Book she surmises there is great danger. But the precise nature of that threat remains obscure to all.'

He drained his cup then and set it down, his hands flat on the table to either side, his face more serious than Kedryn had ever witnessed. 'She believes the Horde may be raised again.'

'By the Lady!' whispered Rycol, his gaunt features drawn suddenly tighter, as though some internal spring tensed in horror. 'Are you sure?'

Kedryn stared at the chatelain, shocked by the abrupt ageing of his face; at Fengrif, whose jovial visage was now equally emptied of humour; at his father, on whose familiar features he could discern nothing save an expression he would have thought fearful had he not known Bedyr incapable of fear. Only Tepshen Lahl remained unmoved by the statement, but the kyo's face seldom showed any emotion.

Fengrif let out his breath in a long, slow hiss, one hand moving to stroke the drooping moustache that hung to either side of his lips, his own pale eyes swinging from one face to the other. 'I think the Lord of Tamur is sure,' he murmured softly, 'though by the Lady, I wish it were not so.'

'You see the importance of this expedition?' Bedyr asked them.

'If this is so,' Rycol said, choosing his words with care, 'then surely it is not a matter for the Lord of Tamur alone, but for the Three Kingdoms in unity. Let us not send a scouting party but an army. Fengrif and I can muster close on a thousand men. Let Darr send the war banners through the Kingdoms and we'll put an army in the field that will scour the Beltrevan clean.'

'Or meet the Horde here,' said Fengrif. 'And let them break on the Lozins as they did in Drul's time.'

Bedyr glanced about him, ascertaining that the servants were still safely out of earshot, and even then lowered his voice as he said, 'My Lady believes there may be more, and Darr's far-seers are of the same opinion.'

He paused then, as if what he was about to say sat uneasily on his tongue, his tanned features creased with distaste. Kedryn experienced a strange discomfiture, for he recognized that his father was being unusually circumspect, the frankness with which he would customarily address these trusted captains somehow blighted by the nature of his announcement. Rycol and Fengrif, too, saw the hesitation and frowned their curiosity. Then, in a flat tone that added to the ominous mood, Bedyr continued, 'The Horde – if Horde there be – may be raised by Ashar's Messenger.'

Kedryn had thought the fort commanders startled by mention of the Horde, but this new announcement produced a reaction close to horror. He saw Fengrif's plump features contort in an expression of disgust, the tails of the Keshi's luxuriant moustache disappearing into his mouth, a tic starting on his temple. Saw Rycol's tanned face become snow-pale, the hand that held his goblet clenching with an involuntary abruptness that sent wine spilling across the table. A servant moved to mop the spillage, then halted as Rycol barked an inarticulate dismissal that stopped the man in his tracks. He glanced at Tepshen Lahl and saw that the kyo's right hand gripped the hilt of his dagger. In his belly he felt a thing stir and realized it was fear.

'It cannot be,' Rycol said slowly, enunciating each word as does a man seeking to convince himself even though he knows he cannot.

Bedyr looked at the man soberly and Rycol's eyes faltered, falling away from the Lord of Tamur's gaze as though afraid to acknowledge what he found there. Fengrif let loose the strands of his moustache and drew a hand across his eyes.

'How certain is your wife? How certain the far-seers?'

'Uncertain,' Bedyr replied softly. 'That is why Darr would have me penetrate the Beltrevan.'

'Madness!' said the Keshi. 'If the Messenger *has* come, then it is utter madness.'

'If not,' Rycol added hoarsely, 'then it is still foolishness to risk your life. If true, then – as Fengrif says – madness!'

'How else to know?' Bedyr demanded. 'Wait here? Wait for the Horde? We could defeat the Horde . . . but if the Horde is led by the Messenger?'

'Can even Ashar's creature bring down the Lozin Forts?' Rycol asked, his tone suggesting a lack of conviction. 'Surely not even he . . .'

'Do you believe in the power of the Lady?' Bedyr demanded abruptly, interrupting the hawk-faced soldier.

Rycol nodded, 'Of course.'

'Then why not in Ashar, too? Are they not, perhaps, the two scales of a balance? If the one exists, why not the other? And with equal power?'

Rycol licked his lips and motioned for the waiting servant to pour fresh wine, emptying his cup in a single draft and gesturing for more while Fengrif said, 'Would it not be the wiser course to wait? If this is true, then surely we shall know soon enough?'

'And perhaps too late,' said Bedyr. 'Perhaps the fall of the Kingdoms would be the confirmation.'

The silence that fell upon the group seated around the head table at this utterance communicated to the others and within moments the whole great hall was voiceless. Laughter, conversation, the shouts of the soldiery for wine and food, even the growling of the dogs died away. It was as though Bedyr's words were of such moment that their importance, the awful threat contained in them, impressed itself upon the gathering by telepathic means. Kedryn saw the faces that turned towards them, eyes questioning, hands frozen in the act of lifting cups, jaws poised motionless between bites of meat and bread. A chill wind seemed to blow through the hall and he felt hair rise on his neck.

Then Bedyr laughed. A loud, ringing guffaw, such as a man makes when the true meaning of a complicated joke has sunk in, and turned sideways in his chair to clap Rycol boisterously on the shoulder. The chatelain was startled by the reaction and Bedyr muttered, his lips still contorted in facsimile of humour, 'For the Lady's sake, man, laugh!'

Rycol took the cue and forced his mouth to curve, echoing his lord's cachinnation. Fengrif, too, leant sound to the pantomime, while Tepshen Lahl set to pounding the table as though applauding some subtle piece of wit.

Under cover of this display, Bedyr said, 'This information is for your ears alone. Do you understand? No other must hear it.'

Still smiling, Rycol murmured, 'Surely we must prepare, my Lord Bedyr?'

Kedryn had followed suit with the others and realized that he was giggling insanely. He forced himself to stop, though retained a false smile as he watched the diners relax, returning to their ease as they sensed the moment pass, the throbbing of a multitude of conversations again filling the hall.

'We do prepare,' Bedyr assured the man, 'but in a fashion that will not – hopefully – give any warning to our enemy.'

'No warning will come from High Fort,' Rycol grunted, somewhat affronted.

'Nor Low,' added Fengrif.

'My friends, please do not mistake my meaning,' Bedyr responded quickly. 'There are none I trust so well as you; you and your men, both. But if what we fear is true, then we cannot afford *any* risk. If the fire does burn in the Beltrevan, then mayhap it has been lit by Ashar's Messenger. And if that be so, then we face an enemy such as we have never known – one possessed of powers to equal those of the Sisterhood. Perhaps surpass them. We cannot know, and until we do, we cannot afford to risk any word slipping out. By any means!' He paused, letting his eyes fall upon each face in turn before he said, 'If the Messenger has come to the Beltrevan, it may be that he can see our thoughts. Therefore, the fewer who share them, the better. Do you see the sense of it?'

Reluctantly, the two men nodded.

'We must give no indication of what we suspect,' Bedyr continued, affecting a normal tone. 'To announce our suspicions would merely raise the likelihood of panic, and that would be to play into Ashar's hands – if, indeed, his bloody hand does lie behind this. If not, then we merely raise groundless fears that can do nothing but aid the barbarians, whatever their intent. Perhaps it is all no more than some vagary of the gods, and nothing at all will come of it. But until we *do* know more it seems the wisest course to hold our counsel to ourselves.

'Do you agree?'

'I do,' Rycol said after a moment's thought. 'Both forts stand firm against invasion and there is little more either Fengrif or I can do to harden our defences. If we do face the coming of a second Horde, then we fight as men have always fought and we shall break the tribes as Corwyn broke Drul.'

'But if the one you speak of is come . . .' Fengrif glanced around as if afraid some spectre might stand at his shoulder to bear word back to the Beltrevan, 'then do I doubly question the wisdom of your entering the forests in guise of a merchant. If word might flee these walls, surely the danger magnifies when you leave them.'

'Aye,' Bedyr agreed, 'but my lady has provided me with some protection against that eventuality. And I can see no other way to gain the information we need than to penetrate the Beltrevan.'

'What protection is there?' demanded Rycol. 'What protection can there be?'

Kedryn waited agog for his father's answer. He had anticipated danger on this mission – had welcomed it with all the enthusiasm of a young man eager for his blooding – but what had previously seemed an exciting excursion into barbarian territory was now taking on the dimensions of an epic quest. It appeared that there was far more than just his life at risk; it appeared the very future of his world might depend on the mission, and he wondered what safeguards his parents had in mind.

'Your nursing Sisters,' Bedyr said, 'they have a means of stilling pain, do they not?'

Rycol and Fengrif nodded, their faces evincing confusion. The Keshi commander said, 'As do all the hospitallers. It is their talent.'

'The Lady Yrla explained it to me, though I do not pretend to understand the intricacies of it,' said Bedyr. 'She told me to seek the aid of your Paramount Hospitaller, whose skills, it would seem, may set a veil about our minds that will block intrusion. Thus – should we fall captive – the messenger will learn nothing from us.'

'Which brings us back to the simple question of physical danger,' Rycol said. 'The threat of arrow, axe and blade.'

'Those I have faced before,' Bedyr smiled. 'And I can see no other suitable guise than that of trader.'

'Perhaps there is one other.' Fengrif smoothed his chewed moustache against his plump cheeks, his expression enigmatic as Bedyr met his gaze with an unspoken question. 'Though it may not appeal to the Lord of Tamur.'

'I have no room for niceties,' Bedyr said, waiting.

'There is a man called Brannoc,' Fengrif murmured, pausing as Rycol grunted irritably, 'some call him renegade.'

'Some call him outlaw scum,' Rycol snapped.

'But few deny his courage,' Fengrif continued unabashed, seeming, even, to find some degree of enjoyment in his comrade's obvious irritation, 'or his knowledge of the forests. He has been known to hire out to those merchants finding favour in his eyes.'

'And willing to pay him,' Rycol interjected. 'He is not to be trusted, Lord Bedyr. Please – in this matter pay my friend no heed: he has a soft spot for the wolfshead, whilst I would hang the man, had I legal justification.'

'He is, indeed, cunning,' said Fengrif, turning the point. 'He bends, rather than breaks, the law. His woodcraft is unsurpassed and he is respected by the forest folk. He is expert with bow and blade, and his knowledge of the hidden trails is equalled by none. On occasion I have found a use for his services myself. I believe he might well be the only man capable of taking you safely through the Beltrevan.'

'Are you in touch with him?' Bedyr asked.

'He can be found,' Fengrif answered.

'Why should I not trust him?'

Rycol met his lord's gaze with a steely, disapproving expression. 'He is neither Tamurin or Keshi, but a mixture of both – with barbarian blood, in addition. He is as likely to sell you to the tribesmen as guide you safely. Or slit your throat while you sleep.'

Tepshen Lahl spoke for the first time then, his voice calm, as if stating a fact so well known as to be scarcely worth the mentioning. 'Not while I live.'

Rycol swung to face the easterner. 'Even you must sleep, old friend. And while honest men sleep, Brannoc goes about his business.'

Bedyr set a hand on the chatelain's wrist as though to reassure him, saying, 'I have two good blades to guard my back, Rycol.'

His eyes caught Kedryn's as he spoke and the youth swelled with pride. 'No man will harm my lord while I live!' He was immediately embarrassed to speak in such a fashion to a senior warrior, but the approving glance of Tepshen Lahl and the grin that creased Bedyr's lips at the outburst made up for that and he added courteously, 'Forgive me, Rycol, but I would die before I should allow an outlaw to harm my father.'

'You have raised a wolfcub.' The hawk-faced soldier smiled approvingly at Kedryn as he spoke. 'But still I do not trust Brannoc.'

'I may not trust him,' said Bedyr, 'but perhaps I have no other choice than to secure his services.'

'I believe he may well be the only one you can trust to guide you,' said Fengrif, 'and my own notion of his honour differs from that of my friend.'

'Perhaps there is a way to guarantee his loyalty,' Tepshen Lahl murmured, surprising the group with the sheer length of the sentence. 'Can the Sisters not look into a man's mind and read what intent lies there?'

'By the Lady!' chuckled Bedyr. 'When you do speak, the words make sense. Of course!'

'That talent depends on the willingness of the subject,' Rycol said doubtfully. 'Surely it is only the adepts of Estrevan who may poke unbidden through a man's innermost intentions. And there are no such adepts here, so Brannoc could disguise his true thoughts. Or refuse the test.'

'If he refuses, he is not to be trusted,' said Tepshen logically. 'If he hides his intent, the obfuscation will be seen.'

'Perhaps,' Rycol admitted, still dubious. 'But the man is mightily devious.'

'Devious men are not swordproof,' said the kyo as if that ended the matter.

'Let us put it to him,' suggested Bedyr. 'Providing he is willing to hear out the proposal – and Fengrif is able to contact him.'

'What if he hears you out and then refuses to co-operate?' Rycol demanded.

'Then you hold him here in chains until we return,' said Bedyr. 'Or until such time as you feel we shall not come back.'

'I do not like it,' Rycol maintained. 'There is too much at stake.'

'Too much, indeed,' said Bedyr, 'to overlook any advantage. And it would appear that this Brannoc may well offer great advantage.'

'Do I seek him out then?' asked Fengrif.

'Immediately,' Bedyr replied. 'But tell him no more than is needful to arrange a meeting. Certainly nothing of our suspicions.'

The Keshi nodded, some small semblance of his good humour returning.

'And Rycol,' said Bedyr, 'I would speak with your Paramount Hospitaller. How is she called?'

'Wynett,' Rycol answered, head turning instinctively to the lower table, where by custom the ladies of the fort sat, the colourful gowns of the soldier's women contrasting with the simple blue of the hospitallers. 'Shall I summon her?'

'Later,' Bedyr murmured. 'What I would ask of her is best kept secret.'

His smile requested the chatelain's understanding for his excessive caution and was answered with a compliant nod, though Kedryn could see that Rycol was unhappy with the situation. Indeed, it was most uncharacteristic, for it was not the Tamurin way to hold secrets; rather, events of importance were discussed openly that all might have a say and let their views be known. Consequently, it was further impression of the momentous nature of Bedyr's suspicions that he should insist they be kept from the men manning the two forts. The youth longed to press his own questions on his father, but recognized that this was not the moment and determined to hold his tongue, quelling his curiosity until such time as Bedyr should see fit to enlighten him. That, he decided, was how a grown warrior would act – and he was adamant that he would prove to his father that he *was* now a warrior.

Bedyr, in turn, seemed determined to lighten the mood, engaging Rycol and Fengrif in conversation that was interlaced with jokes and anecdotes, none of them producing quite the response they might in other times. The commanders did their best to behave naturally, but all at the head table were relieved when the meal finally ended and the opportunity presented itself for Bedyr to stretch, yawning, and announce himself ready for sleep.

Fengrif took his hand, promising to contact Brannoc as swiftly as possible and return word to the Lord of Tamur, even though it meant a night crossing of the Idre, and Rycol escorted his guests to their chambers. Kedryn had expected to be dismissed then, but Bedyr beckoned him and Tepshen Lahl into the room, asking the chatelain to send Sister Wynett to them. As the door closed on the grey-haired soldier, Bedyr turned to his son, addressing him as he would any full-grown man.

'I ask your forgiveness, Kedryn. I do not enjoy secrets, but for your own safety your mother and I agreed you should hear all this no sooner than Rycol and Fengrif.'

Kedryn studied his father's face in the roseate glow of the lanterns mounted about the plain stone walls, and squared his shoulders.

'You are Lord of Tamur, Father. You act in the best interests of the Kingdoms – how can I argue with that?'

'Well said!' Bedyr clapped his son on the back, bringing a flush of pride to Kedryn's cheeks. 'I shall leave Tamur in good hands.'

'I have no wish to rule,' Kedryn responded, feeling suddenly less manful as he realized Bedyr spoke of a future that was not necessarily very far away. 'Not for a long time.'

Bedyr turned away, loosening the clasp of his dagger belt and tossing it on to the bed. Kedryn moved towards him, but Tepshen Lahl raised a hand and he stopped the movement, watching instead as Bedyr crossed to the window and pushed the shutters back, peering out into the night. There was nothing to see, for the vast bulk of the Lozins filled the canyon of the Idre with stygian blackness and the moon was not yet filled to the point where it illuminated the darkness. Instead, the murmuring of the great river entered the room, as though a myriad voices babbled in confusion. Bedyr braced his hands against the parapet and cocked his head as if he sought to discern some message in the sound of the water. Tepshen Lahl fetched a jug from the table at the centre of the chamber and filled three cups, carefully adjusting the skirts of his surcoat as he lowered himself into a chair and motioned for Kedryn to join him.

'I wonder. Are we right? Is this the right way?' Bedyr spoke into the darkness, his voice low so that it almost merged with the tumult of the Idre. Kedryn frowned, unused to hearing doubt in his father's voice.

'It will be as it will be,' said Tepshen Lahl. 'We shall do what we must. The rest is for the gods.'

Kedryn saw his father's shoulders sag momentarily, then straighten, and recognized a communication between the two men he was not yet old enough to appreciate. He thought of asking what – beyond the obvious – weighed so heavily upon Bedyr, but a knocking on the door prevented the question.

Bedyr called, 'Enter.' Tepshen Lahl's right hand dropped to his dagger, then eased away as Rycol ushered a woman into the room, excusing himself on the grounds of midnight rounds. The woman said, 'I am Wynett, Lord Bedyr. You sent for me?'

She was, to Kedryn's surprise, little more than a girl, the soft blue gown that marked her as one of Estrevan revealing a pleasantly curved figure that was complemented by the abundance of honey-golden hair escaping from beneath her snood. He saw the blue opal ring on her left hand and the plain silver and agate necklace that encircled her slender throat, thinking that it was a pity she chose celibacy.

'I thank you for coming at so late an hour, Sister,' Bedyr said.

'No doubt it is needful,' replied the hospitaller. 'I sense disturbance.'

Bedyr grinned ruefully, nodding. 'My wife, the Lady Yrla, suggested you might bend your talents to our aid.'

'In what way?' asked the Sister.

Bedyr invited her to a chair, settling himself upon the bed as he outlined the gist of his conversation with Rycol and Fengrif. When he was finished Wynett studied his face with troubled eyes.

'It is possible, though I would not have thought of such a usage myself. The Lady Yrla would have made a fine adept had she not chosen marriage.' She smiled to indicate no criticism was intended. 'I do not see why it should not work. I am less certain of Brannoc.'

'You know him?' Bedyr asked.

Wynett nodded. 'I have tended him on occasion. He collects more hurts than most men. And inflicts more. He is a godless man, but not necessarily as bad as my Lord Rycol would have him. I believe he has his own honour, though it is not always easy for others to see that.'

'If he plans treachery he will surely hide it,' said Bedyr. 'And you will see the hiding of it, will you not?'

'Perhaps.' Wynett frowned. 'It is not straightforward. Brannoc's loyalties are confused; primarily to himself. I do not think I can guarantee it.'

'Your best belief must do,' said Bedyr. 'If the messenger is come we have no choice but to gamble.'

'No,' Wynett agreed, sipping the wine Kedryn had politely poured for her, enjoying the smile of gratitude she gave him, 'we do not. When will you leave?'

'As soon as possible.' Bedyr met her level gaze. 'And as secretly as possible.'

'Brannoc is very good at that,' said Wynett. 'But I shall need several days to set the hiding on you and your men. I presume all are to be treated?'

'All willing,' said Bedyr. 'I believe that will mean all of them.'

Wynett nodded. 'I shall be ready. You can find me easily.'

'Thank you.' Bedyr rose to escort her to the door. 'Pray for us, Sister.'

Wynett nodded again and went out into the torchlit corridor. Bedyr turned, rubbing thoughtfully at the stubble sprouting on his jaw. 'I have done all I can. The rest, as you say, Tepshen, is with the gods.'

Tepshen Lahl grunted, rising cat-like to his feet. 'Sleep on it.'

'Aye.' Bedyr grinned ruefully. 'And may our sleep be dreamless.'

Kedryn's was not. He was far too excited for that. He left his father and paced the empty corridor to his own chamber, pausing at the door to raise a hand in farewell to Tepshen, then latched the door even though he knew he must be safe in this great stronghold. He leant against the thick oaken panels, studying the room. It had a soldierly austerity that was both gratifyingly complementary to his new-found status as a warrior of Tamur and more than a little forbidding. It was built into the great eastern wall of the fort, with a single window looking out over the Idre, slatted shutters drawn across the embrasure. The floor and walls and ceiling were of sleek grey stone, sparsely decorated with rough tapestries of antique design, the hearth fireless at this time of the year and only the lantern bracketed above the bed was lit, transforming that corner to a welcoming haven. Like Bedyr's room, it had a table at the centre with three chairs surrounding the dark, carved wood, and a wine jug and three cups on the table. Against one wall stood an armoire in which he found his riding gear set out, the leathers fresh-oiled, the protective undergarments washed. His weapons – sword and bow – racked on a stand of polished black wood, beside it a washstand and beside that a gutter into which he urinated.

He cleansed his hands and face, then scrubbed his teeth, smiling as he recognized his mother's hand in the packing of his personal gear. Then lost the smile as it occurred to him – for the first time – that he might not see his mother again. So far it had all seemed a tremendous adventure, an expedition of great excitement, surpassing his wildest expectations. Now, alone, the wind got up so that it whistled eerily down the chasm of the Idre, and he realized that he might well be riding to face far more than hostile barbarians.

It was as if the fright-tales told around the fires of a winter's evening were come suddenly true, the demons those yarns contained given flesh and fangs and talons. His lessons had contained mention of the barbarians' gods, but they had seemed to him the childish nonsense of ignorant savages, too intent on their bloody ways to heed the sensible teachings of the Lady. Now, however, it appeared that those tales he had thought mere folklore were fleshed out. Indeed, fleshed out to such extent that brave warriors gave them wary credence.

He stripped hurriedly out of his robe, shivering with a chill due not entirely to the cool air, and jumped beneath the covers, gasping as something struck his feet, snatching them back with an unbidden cry before he realized it was merely a warming pan placed there by a thoughtful servant. Even then, the heat made him think of fires, of Ashar, of formless, threatening things. He was reluctant to dim the lantern and give the room over to the night, and when he did, and sleep took him, he fought battles in his dreams and fled from faceless enemies.

He was grateful for the dawn and the familiar rattle of hooves and armour, the sound of men talking and birds singing. He climbed sleepily from the bed, ashamed of what he considered childish night-fears, to pull on his familiar riding gear and throw open the shutters on a bright morning, the early sun reflecting off the rimrock of the chasm to sparkle on the mist far below so it seemed he looked down on cloud, as might one of the birds that swooped and circled beyond the window. Dressed, he made his way down to the dining hall, his stomach rumbling in anticipation of food.

Naturally, he said nothing to either Bedyr or Tepshen of his troubled sleep, and both men appeared preoccupied with the task ahead. After consulting with Rycol they decided to advise the squadron from Caitin Hold of their plan and send the men singly to Sister Wynett, rather than wait for word from Fengrif.

In the event, this came whilst Kedryn himself was with the hospitaller. Bedyr was the first to undergo her treatment, then Tepshen Lahl, their enthusiasm rendering her task easier, but nonetheless requiring a full day, so that it was not until the third day after their arrival at High Fort that Kedryn found himself with the blue-gowned woman. Neither Tepshen nor his father had been able to describe exactly what course her treatment took, and Kedryn was aflame with curiosity – and oddly disappointed when it all proved remarkably painless.

An acolyte summoned him to the chambers set aside for the sick and hurt and he was invited into a sunny room, lit by high windows and filled with flowers and plants that trailed and climbed from pots hung about the walls, filling the room with soothing scents and bright colours. Sister Wynett invited him to seat himself on a low couch and took a chair beside it, clutching both his hands in hers as she gazed deep into his eyes in a manner that would have aroused him had he not known – and respected – her celibate state. He was given a small cup of some sweetish liquid that induced a condition of pleasant torpor, lulling him to drowsiness as Wynett's gentle voice murmured in his ear and he gazed drowsily into her calm blue eyes. The next he knew, she was shaking him awake, telling him it was done, and he rose from the couch wondering why he felt no different as the Sister smiled and ushered him from the room.

He went to find his father, learning from one of Rycol's men that Bedyr was at the signalling station on the river wall. He obtained directions and hurried through the multi-layered complexity of passages and courtyards and parade grounds to the keep. It was a solitary tower, noticeably separate from its neighbours, as if the function it served demanded space, jutting in isolation from the great wall and facing a similar column on the far side of the river. A guard bade him enter and he began to climb a stairway that wound upwards until his head began to swim with the spiralling climb and he thought he must emerge into the sky itself, wondering if his breathlessness was the result of haste or thinning air. He paused when he reached the final door to still his pounding heart so that he might appear calm and manly rather than show his excitement.

He stepped into a chamber that did, indeed, seem suspended in the sky. There was more window than stonework in the walls so that as he looked around he caught his breath afresh, for it seemed that he looked down on cloud and mountain and fort as might an eagle from its eyrie. His head spun with the emptiness and he thrust out an involuntary hand to contact the reassuring stone, narrowing his eyes against the glare that filled the chamber as he peered curiously about him. Machinery such as he had never envisaged stood at the centre, a great bulk of cogs and winding wheels and levers mounted on tracks that it might be moved around the circumference of the room to face any window, any direction. Great discs draped in cloth, like covered shields belonging to the giants of fable, protruded from the device, and at the orifice looking towards Low Fort men stood about an uncovered surface. Kedryn squinted as he stared at it, the magnified reflection of sunlight nearly blinding him so that he barely saw the two signallers busily working the levers that shifted numerous horizontal slats covering the disc, and sending flashes of pure white brilliance across the chasm. From the opposite side came answering flashes and after a few moments Bedyr's figure emerged from the dazzle, Tepshen Lahl close behind and Rycol bringing up the rear.

'Fengrif has located Brannoc,' Bedyr said. 'He has agreed to talk to us.'

Kedryn was surprised that an outlaw should *agree* to an audience with the Lord of Tamur; more so that Bedyr should accept the terms. He had assumed that the man would simply be summoned and instructed. Bedyr saw the confusion on his son's face and as they descended the stairs he spoke casually, as a man speaking to an equal, reminding rather than instructing. 'It is sometimes better to request than to order, Kedryn. Some men will agree readily enough to a thing asked of them, whilst refusing the same thing in the form of a demand.'

Kedryn thought about it and nodded his agreement, wondering what manner of man this outlaw would prove to be.

He found out, to some extent at least, after dusk fell, for it was not until then that a boat put out from the landing stage below the eastern fort to ferry Brannoc across.

Darkness came early to the lower levels of the canyon and Kedryn watched excitedly as the glow from the lantern mounted on the boat's prow grew steadily brighter and the slap of oars became discernible above the murmuring of the river. He made out the shapes of two men standing at the bow, behind them the squat bulk of hefty rowers and the helmsman on his high seat by the tiller. This latter rose slightly as the western jetty hove into view and shouted a command that instantly reversed the oars, bringing the craft to a smooth halt directly below the steps leading up to the landing platform. A rope was secured to a mooring ring and Rycol's men went down to assist the passengers ashore.

Kedryn saw that Fengrif accompanied the outlaw, partly, he guessed, that the chatelain might be privy to the exchange and partly as guarantee of Brannoc's safety. It was clear from the expression on Rycol's angular features that had he his way, Brannoc's greeting would have been a squad of armed men with waiting chains.

Kedryn went with his father to meet the arrivals, watching as the Tamurin soldiers helped the plump Keshi commander on to dry land, the torches they held revealing a face that was mute testimony to Fengrif's dislike of water. Brannoc sprang to the jetty as if accustomed to the crossing of the river, halting with his back to the Idre and his eyes warily on Rycol.

'My Lord Bedyr,' Fengrif bowed briefly, one hand pressed firmly to his stomach as if to hold down its contents, 'I present Brannoc. He comes under my promise of safety.'

This latter statement was clearly directed at Rycol, who stood glowering at the outlaw, left hand fidgeting with the fastenings of his sword belt.

'Bedyr?' Brannoc spoke presumptuously, ignoring protocol, before the Lord of Tamur could respond. 'Bedyr Caitin?'

'Aye,' said Bedyr, ignoring the breach, 'and I offer the same guarantee. You have safe conduct, Brannoc.'

The outlaw was dark of eye and skin and hair, so that it was difficult to ascertain the expression on his face, though his voice was cold and more than a little suspicious as he cast a swift glance at Fengrif and said harshly, 'You spoke of merchants, Commander, not the Lord of Tamur.'

Kedryn noticed that his right hand lay close to his dagger, and that the blade was not the customary dirk, but a weapon more suited for throwing. He touched the hilt of his own blade and saw that Tepshen Lahl had moved slightly to the side, thumbs hooked, seemingly casual, in his belt, so that the kyo's dirk was set on his open palm. Kedryn knew that Tepshen could draw and throw whilst most men closed their fist, yet something about Brannoc prompted him to wonder if even Tepshen could beat the outlaw.

Brannoc had about him an animalistic wariness. He was not particularly tall, nor did he appear very muscular, but his stance, the set of his shoulders and the placement of his feet, suggested both speed and strength. He seemed untroubled by Rycol's obvious dislike or the superior number of men facing him, and Kedryn thought that if events should turn against him he might well chance his throw and risk a dive into the Idre: a calculated recklessness emanated from him.

'Would you have agreed, had you known?' Bedyr's voice was friendly and Kedryn saw white teeth flash in the torchlight.

'Perhaps not.' Brannoc shrugged, showing no deference to Bedyr's status. 'But now that I am here, what is it you would ask of me?'

He gave no due to Bedyr's title and Kedryn felt himself affronted on his father's behalf, though Bedyr continued to smile, courteously motioning Brannoc forwards.

'Shall we talk over food and wine? Or do you prefer the river bank?'

'I'll eat with you.' Brannoc allowed. 'I am intrigued to hear what the Lord of Tamur can want with a simple guide.'

Rycol snorted at this and Brannoc threw a mocking smile in his direction, following Bedyr across the jetty to the private room earlier set aside for the meeting.

Within the torch-lit chamber Kedryn seized the opportunity to study the man at length, simultaneously intrigued and offended by his air of self-reliance. He watched as Brannoc took the chair offered him, eyes the colour of the Idre at midnight swiftly checking the room, noticing that Tepshen Lahl seated himself to one end of the laden table whilst Bedyr faced him, Rycol and Fengrif to either side, Kedryn himself at the other end, sensing – to his annoyance – that the outlaw dismissed him as a threat. Brannoc appeared, as described by Rycol, to be a mixture of Tamurin, Keshi and barbarian. He was straight as any Tamurin, though smaller, like a Keshi, his skin the dark brown of a sun-ripened nut, almost black, so that his eyes were permanently veiled, hooded by unusually long lashes of a raven hue that matched his shoulder-length hair. This, too, spoke of mixed blood, for it was cut in the simple Tamurin style, but then teased into several braids in which hung coloured feathers and pieces of shell. A silver circle hung from his left ear lobe and a necklace of leather and beadwork sat at his throat, two rings of Keshi design on left thumb and the third finger of his right hand. He wore a jerkin of leather worked supple and dyed in motley shades that seemed to merge with the brown of his breeks. Kedryn realized that such an outfit would afford excellent camouflage in the forests. The slightly curved blade of a Keshi sabre hung at his back, the throwing knife on his right hip. When he reached for the wine Bedyr offered him, Kedryn saw the hilt of a second knife strapped to his left forearm and realized that Brannoc had made no attempt to keep the weapon concealed, wondering if that was a gesture of trust or contempt. He watched as the outlaw lounged in his chair, tilting it back and turning it somewhat, apparently seeking a more comfortable position, but in fact positioning himself so that he could watch both Bedyr and Tepshen Lahl, and still see the door.

'You are a cautious man,' Bedyr remarked, noting all these things himself, 'but there is no danger here.'

Brannoc shrugged, smiling, without replying.

'Are you for hire?' the Lord of Tamur continued.

'Perhaps,' said Brannoc, helping himself casually to roast meat, eating it daintily, wiping his clean-shaven chin. 'For what purpose?'

'I would travel into the Beltrevan,' Bedyr said.

'The tribes will kill you,' Brannoc said equably, as though commenting on a foregone conclusion.

'Perhaps not if I had a suitable guide,' smiled Bedyr. 'A man who knows the secret ways. One familiar with the forests and the folk.'

'Why?'

'Do you need a reason?' Bedyr shrugged, staring at the outlaw as he filled his cup. 'You will be well rewarded.'

'I have no wish to view life from a trophy pole,' said Brannoc. 'Or to meet the embrace of the blood eagle. You cannot pay me enough for that.'

'I could offer you amnesty,' Bedyr suggested, motioning the spluttering Rycol to silence. 'A pardon for any crimes in addition to a purse of your own naming.'

Brannoc's dark eyes glittered with interest. 'I still require a reason, Lord Bedyr. You offer much – your need must be great. Consequently I anticipate great danger.'

Bedyr laughed. 'You are astute, Brannoc.'

'For an outlaw?' Kedryn saw that the man was handsome when he smiled. 'I have lived this long because I think things through. I have every intention of gaining respectable old age.'

'I might aid you in that aim,' said Bedyr.

'Perhaps,' Brannoc nodded. 'But the Beltrevan is no place for the Lord of Tamur at this moment in the world's turning.'

'Why not?' Bedyr asked innocently.

'Why do you seek to go there?' countered Brannoc. 'Does the chicken precede the egg?'

Bedyr laughed at this, openly. 'Shall we continue riddling, or speak without dissembling?'

Brannoc smiled back, then leant forwards, hands spread flat upon the table, his eyes firm on Bedyr's, challenging.

'The tribes migrate, Bedyr Caitin. Drott and Yath stand in alliance. There is talk of war with the Caroc; or a joining such as the Beltrevan has not known since Drul raised the Horde. Some say Ashar drives them. Whatever, their direction will be south. Have you heard as much? Or are your spies less well-informed that I?'

Kedryn saw his father's features stiffen at this news; heard Rycol's sudden intake of breath. Only Tepshen Lahl and Fengrif remained impassive, the one from custom, the other – presumably – because he had heard this during the river passage.

'You are right,' Bedyr nodded. 'I need knowledge. I must know whether the Caroc join the Confederation or fight. I need a man such as you. Will you help me?'

Brannoc toyed with his cup, his face expressionless. Then, 'Rycol does not trust me. Why should you?'

'I will obtain proof,' Bedyr said slowly, weighing his words. 'I will ask you to submit to a reading by the paramount Sister of High Fort. Let her see your innermost thoughts, and she will tell me whether or not I should trust you. Will you agree to that?'

Brannoc snorted. 'Were I to disagree?'

'Then I travel without a guide,' Bedyr said evenly. 'And you remain in custody until I return.'

'What if you do not return?' Brannoc wondered.

'After sufficient time has passed you go free.' Bedyr glanced at Rycol. 'You have Tamur's word on that.'

'Tamur's word has some reputation,' Brannoc acknowledged. 'A pardon, you say?'

'And a purse,' said Bedyr.

Brannoc reached for the wine jug. Filled his cup and drank, his smile enigmatic in the silence.

'Do you trust me, Bedyr Caitin?'

Bedyr stared at the man as the torch-lit chamber filled again with silence, his face calm as he reached a judgement, as if this were nothing more than some petition presented for his decision, then he nodded once.

'I do, Brannoc.'

The outlaw's smile became more open and Kedryn realized with surprise that his father had, in turn, been judged.

'Send for your Sister,' Brannoc said. 'I'll take you into the Beltrevan.'

Chapter Five

'And I say that you'd as well send a jongleur to announce our presence. Perhaps carrying an invitation to sit and feast with us. Or on us!'

Kedryn stared in wide-eyed amazement at Brannoc, scarcely able to believe that even so unusually outspoken a man as the outlaw would dare address his father in such a manner. He saw Tepshen Lahl stiffen, the inscrutable features hardening at this fresh outrage, though the kyo, instead of reprimanding the man as he would usually have done, merely glanced towards Bedyr, awaiting his lord's reaction.

That was mild, accompanied by a smile that suggested if Bedyr did find the outlaw's tone insulting he also found some justification in the complaint.

'You have convinced me we have little chance of passing ourselves off as merchants, Brannoc, so how else do you suggest we travel?' He gestured lightly at the squadron of Tamurin cavalry busy with the last minute checking of saddle gear and weapons. 'Rycol would send five times this many to ward me, and I believe that if I agreed with you, he might well mutiny.'

Brannoc snorted at the notion of so dutiful a commander as Rycol even contemplating mutiny, but took the point of Bedyr's argument, albeit with ill grace.

'These are soldiers,' he protested, 'not foresters. They carrry themselves as soldiers – look at those horses! Do you think they ride mounts like that in the Beltrevan? Do you think merchants set their fat backsides astride animals like that?'

'I thought we had forsaken the notion of disguise,' Bedyr replied cheerfully, cinching a girth tight. 'On your suggestion.'

Brannoc snagged a bit between the teeth of a tall, mottle-coated beast and shook his head in frustration. 'I said you would not pass as merchants, Bedyr Caitin. I suggested a handful of men might – guided by me – succeed in passing unnoticed. This is not a handful of men.'

'Nor is it an army.' Bedyr checked the firmness of the girth to his satisfaction and looked to his saddlebags. 'And nor am I some thief in the night – I am Lord of Tamur, man! And that forces certain trappings on me. What I say about Rycol is not far removed from the truth.'

'Enter the Beltrevan with all these men and your head may well be removed from your body,' Brannoc snapped. 'And that is not at all removed from the truth!'

Bedyr shrugged, his clear gaze roving over the assembly yard, taking in the readiness of his men. 'I cannot leave them,' he said, 'but what I can do is compromise. Listen – we ride forth in squadron, but once into the woodland you will take me and one or two others deep into the forest. The rest may travel separately, drawing attention to themselves so that we may move unnoticed. The barbarian leaders cannot believe the Kingdoms know nothing of their movements, so a scouting party will not seem out of the ordinary. What do you think?'

The outlaw fiddled with a shell-bedecked plait, winding it about a finger as he contemplated the suggestion. He appeared mollified, for he nodded at last and said, 'That may work.' Then, with a reluctant grin, 'It is not a bad plan.'

'Thank you.' Bedyr ducked his head in a parody of courteous acknowledgement. 'I am gratified you accept.'

'I have undertaken to show you the Beltrevan,' Brannoc grunted, lifting his horse's hooves one by one to check the padding lashed there, 'and bring you safely out. Should I fail, my life is doubly forfeit – the tribes will kill me if I am captured, and Rycol will kill me if I escape. I know the Beltrevan, Bedyr Caitin, and I know its dangers.'

'The very reasons you lead us,' Bedyr responded.

Brannoc sniffed. 'Four men at the most may go unseen – providing they do exactly as I tell them. You, me, and who else?'

'Tepshen Lahl and Kedryn,' Bedyr replied without hesitation.

'The boy?'

It was the first time Brannoc had openly recognized Kedryn's presence and the contempt in his voice was a goad to the youth's pride. He drew himself up to his full height, glaring at the outlaw across the torch-lit space that separated them, so thoroughly taken aback at the dismissal in Brannoc's tone that he was unable to frame a suitable reply before Bedyr made it for him.

'The young man. And you need harbour no concern for his competence as a warrior: he stands with the best of us.'

Brannoc's dark eyes swept over Kedryn as if in judgement and the warmth imparted by Bedyr's words was momentarily chilled as the outlaw studied him as dispassionately as he might regard a horse or a blade he was thinking of purchasing. It had not occurred to the youth that he might be considered a liability and it struck him forcibly, filling him with dread, that perhaps Brannoc might refuse to travel with him. He gritted his teeth, determined to allow none of his confusion or fear to show on his face as he concentrated on a thorough checking of his equipment. He found a hoof-pad not fastened to his liking and readjusted the strings binding the material to his animal's fetlock, fixing the muffling pad more securely in place. As he straightened he heard Brannoc say, 'He'll do – so long as he does what he's told.'

Relief mingled with irritation as Kedryn met the outlaw's gaze. 'I am Tamurin,' he declared, 'I obey my Lord Bedyr.'

'In the Beltrevan you obey me.' Brannoc's midnight eyes locked with Kedryn's brown ones, presenting the young man with a quandary he found difficult to resolve until Bedyr nodded almost imperceptibly from behind the outlaw.

'As long as my Lord Bedyr so instructs me, I will obey you.'

Brannoc nodded as though satisfied with this, then turned towards Bedyr. 'It had best be understood from the outset that I command in the forest.'

Again, Kedryn saw Tepshen Lahl stiffen and the thought sped through his mind that these two men might well fight before the venture was over. The men of Tamur were by no means docile, and their regard for the niceties of discipline and formality was notoriously scanty, but their loyalty to Bedyr was unswerving, their toleration of insult equally strict. They might well omit formal titles when addressing their lord, but not a man there would use the tone Brannoc affected, and the outlaw's tone and attitude was clearly abrasive to the kyo's sensibilities.

Leader that he was, Bedyr recognized the potential for disruption and sought to quell it before it grew to proportions dangerous to his purpose.

'You are our guide and therefore you will be listened to,' he assured the man, 'but remember that you deal with soldiers accustomed to *my* command, not some outlaw rabble. Perhaps your commands are best channelled through me.'

Brannoc showed no sign of resentment or retraction at this diplomatic admonishment, merely shrugged, tilting his head back slightly so that he could meet Bedyr's stare, his voice flat as he spoke. 'It is hard to know the Beltrevan and easy to die there, Bedyr Caitin. You had best channel my commands swiftly – and see that they are obeyed instantly.'

Kedryn watched as his father nodded, his expression impassive, and it came to him that Brannoc was enjoying himself hugely. It had been obvious from the initial meeting that the outlaw was mightily independent, relishing his protected position in Rycol's stronghold and enjoying to the full the status afforded him by Bedyr's need of his services. In other circumstances Bedyr would have set the man firmly in his place, and it occurred to Kedryn that the very fact his father accepted such effrontery was dramatic indication of his reliance on Brannoc. He found a buckle to refix as Bedyr turned away, moving amongst the men, exchanging words of encouragement as he un-obtrusively checked their preparations. He saw Tepshen Lahl tug loose the gaily-coloured cords that held his scabbard in place on his belt and hike the eastern sword to his shoulder, fastening it there for ease of riding before moving, seemingly casual, to Brannoc's side. The kyo's words were almost too low for Kedryn's ears.

'My Lord Bedyr is a mighty warrior and a great lord, woodsman. He deserves respect.'

From Tepshen Lahl that was a warning and a command: Brannoc appeared to recognize that. He nodded, a small smile decorating his lips, and said, 'I respect him well enough, stranger. I also respect life. Have you ridden the Beltrevan?'

Tepshen, in turn, appeared to find the response satisfactory, for he shook his head and said, 'No, but I have killed men before.'

Brannoc studied the kyo with the same appraising insolence he had earlier directed at Kedryn, then smiled openly and said, 'I believe that.'

Tepshen Lahl smiled back and said, 'You had better.'

Kedryn was not sure he fully understood the exchange, but it seemed to settle the matter for both men turned back to their horses and stood waiting for Bedyr.

The Lord of Tamur strode back across the assembly yard to halt before the outlaw.

'We are ready.'

'Good,' said Brannoc, and swung into his saddle without further preamble.

Bedyr followed suit without comment and gently eased his mount past the outlaw's to lead the way from the enclosed yard into the high-roofed corridor beyond. At the end of the torch-lit passage the column emerged on to a wide, open space surrounded by the north wall of High Fort. Rycol stood waiting there, left hand clamped fast to the hilt of his sword and a disapproving expression on his gaunt features. Bedyr halted, leaning down to take the commander's offered hand and murmur a few words too indistinct for Kedryn – who had managed to place his horse close behind his father's – to hear. Rycol turned as Bedyr straightened in the saddle and called a low-voiced order to the soldiers waiting alertly by the postern gate. Instantly all torches were dimmed and three men ran back the heavy lock-bar securing the gate. Two more eased the portal open, and Bedyr led the way out of the fort on to the Beltrevan road.

Instantly, no longer muffled by the walls of the fortress, the roar of the Idre filled the night. It came like the growling of some un-imaginable beast from the canyon of the river, pounding against the flanking rise of vertical stone to swell and grumble at the sky. Above, indifferent, hung the slender crescent of the waxing moon, sur-rounded by courtier stars, and veiled by narrow threads of drifting cloud. Looking up, Kedryn felt his head spin, his senses assailed by the sheer size of the chasm, the sky no more than a gash cut into the looming darkness of the walls. Looking back he saw only the vast, dark bulk of High Fort, the deceptive light furthering the impression that the citadel was some natural outcropping of the western Lozins, as solidly impregnable as the mountains themselves. Ahead, he could make out little save the dim outlines of Bedyr and Brannoc, the Lord of Tamur dressed now – as were all in the party – in the same camouflaging motley as the outlaw. Bedyr had remarked that he was not a thief in the night, but to Kedryn it seemed they took all the precautions of a thief. On Brannoc's insistent suggestion they had accoutred themselves in clothes designed to blend with the woodlands; their horses' hooves were muffled that no sound of metal on stone might betray them; their gear was fastened in ways that allowed no chinking of buckles or clatter of loose-held weaponry. They might well be, Kedryn thought, some outlaw band slipping wraith-like from the protective walls. He raised a hand to wipe wind-driven spray from his face and grinned at Tepshen Lahl, riding close beside him. The kyo favoured him with a brief responding smile, then jerked his chin in indication that the youth pay attention to the path.

Kedryn returned his gaze to the front, his eyes adjusting gradually to the stygian darkness of the canyon. They had descended the glacis fronting the north wall of High Fort and were now on the Beltrevan road proper, the way narrowing as it ran farther from the citadel, becoming little more than an enlarged ledge between mountains and river. Five mounted men abreast would fill the path, hemmed on one side by the Lozins, on the other by the drop to the river. Kedryn was not sure how deep that drop was, but from the sound of the water funnelled between the rocky banks he held little hope for anyone luckless enough to tumble in. He could not imagine any army, barbarian or otherwise, succeeding in an attack on the Lozin Forts: that roadway must surely prove a deathtrap for any force foolhardy enough to attempt it, the great walls that sealed it off from the Three Kingdoms too strong to storm, the defenders needing merely to sit and wait, secure in their impregnable stronghold. Yet even now he was leaving that stronghold behind to penetrate the Beltrevan. He shivered suddenly, fingers of ice tattooing his spine; it seemed, for an instant, that something nameless stirred in the night, listening, waiting. He grunted deep in his throat, flexing his shoulders as he told himself these were foolish – childish! – fears, and concentrated on maintaining the steady pace set by his father and the outlaw.

They held the pace until the first hint of dawn pearled the sky, and were still on the narrow roadway winding beside the river. It had begun to slope down sometime during the night and as the darkness gave way to the flush of morning, Kedryn saw that the surrounding stone was no longer sheer and blank but had become broken into great jumbles from which stunted undergrowth thrust scoured limbs, accusing as pointed fingers. Brannoc said something to Bedyr and the Tamurin lord raised a hand to slow his men, allowing the outlaw to assume the lead as Brannoc turned his horse off the path and began to pick a way through the maze of broken rock.

By the time daylight reached the foot of the chasm the party was settled in a natural amphitheatre formed by a spur of the mountains and numerous gigantic boulders. The horses were hobbled and left to crop on the sparse vegetation that had found a rooting in the dirt trapped amongst the stones. The men settled to eating a cold meal and then wrapped themselves in cloaks, preparatory to waiting out the light hours. Guards were posted and Kedryn was proud that his father gave him first watch, clambering to a vantage point with his bow and a quiver of barbed war arrows.

He hunkered down with his back to a boulder and chewed on cold meat as he watched the sun illumine the land around. It was a bleak and forbidding landscape that came into view, all hard stone and scrubby, wind-scoured trees. The trail they had followed through the night was no longer visible and it seemed that he sat alone in a wasteland of desolate stone, the Lozins rising massive about him, the fabled forests of the Beltrevan hidden by the ridges ahead. It seemed improbable that their presence should be noticed, but Brannoc had been most insistent that until they were inside the woodlands they should travel only by night, and Bedyr had accepted that as sound strategy, which left Kedryn with nothing to do but sit and watch. He did so dutifully, resisting the temptation to drowse as the sun rose higher and filled the stone maze with warmth. He saw kites wheel high against the blue and the fleeting shape of a small cat dart by at the periphery of his vision, but nothing else until Tepshen Lahl came to relieve him. He acceded his place gratefully, returning to the amphitheatre where he rolled into his cloak and fell almost instantly asleep.

Bedyr woke him as shadows crept between the rocks. The sky above was still bright blue, but the lower mountain slopes were a hinterland where night came early. He rose shivering in the twilight chill, wishing they could risk a fire, and found more meat and a chunk of hard journeybread in his saddlebags. He was still chewing on the jaw-breaking bread as the squadron saddled its horses and started out again into the darkness.

The river canyon was widening now and the expanse of sky visible above was noticeably larger, whilst the murmuring of the Idre diminished as the waterway expanded again. The trail continued to slope down, moving away from the river, and by the time the moon stood directly overhead Kedryn could make out the shapes of taller, closer spaced trees along the slopes ahead and to his left. When they camped again it was on a sward of luxuriant grass surrounded by tall pines, and Brannoc passed word that the hoof pads might be removed. There was still no fire and although the temperature had risen steadily as they descended from the high country, cloaks remained securely about shoulders as the party settled to eat and sleep. Kedryn was given a later watch, but instead of seizing the opportunity to rest he lay awake, listening to Bedyr and Brannoc as they lounged talking on the grass.

'This is no-man's-land,' he heard the outlaw say. 'The forests begin tomorrow and we must be careful. We enter Grymard territory, and while they are the softest of the tribes, they will kill us as readily as most.'

'I must go deeper,' his father replied. 'The Drott and Caroc are the greatest danger, and it is their movements I need to scout.'

Kedryn heard Brannoc snort laughter then and say, 'If the Horde is raised I can tell you the direction now.'

Sunlight bathed Bedyr's features and Kedryn thought that he looked carved from solid oak as he stared northwards, as if seeking to utilize talents given only to the Sisters, to drive his vision beyond the limits of the physical. Then he became human again as he sighed, smiling at the dark-featured outlaw.

'I must know for sure. Perhaps they fought.'

To Kedryn's ear he sounded unusually wistful.

Brannoc did not: he remained pragmatic. 'If they have, we'll know soon enough. The crows will show us.'

'And if not?' Bedyr wondered.

'Then we'll need to move soft.' Brannoc fidgeted a piece of meat from between his even teeth and flicked it away, wiping his fingers fastidiously on his jerkin. 'And fast if they sight us. Drott and Caroc in alliance are a thought to keep you awake nights.'

It was Bedyr's turn to snort laughter.

'You do not seem unduly troubled.'

'I can survive. I am less confident of your men.'

'They are fine warriors.' Kedryn heard the pride in his father's voice. 'All of them.'

'I have no doubt of that,' came the outlaw's response, the absence of mockery lending his words greater impact, 'but we speak of something no warrior has faced since Corwyn stood against Drul. I have little time for the teachings of the Lady, Bedyr Caitin, nor do I subscribe to the fancies of the forest folk, but if your suspicions are correct . . .'

His voice tailed off and Kedryn felt the chill he had experienced on that first night creep back, magnified by his father's reply.

'For the first time in my life I pray the Sisters are wrong – but I do not think they are. I think something stirs in the Beltrevan, and I must find out what.'

'If worst should come to worst, what *can* you do?'

Brannoc's tone matched Bedyr's; it was sombre.

'Bring word to King Darr in Andurel,' Kedryn heard, 'that he may alert the Lords of Kesh and Ust-Galich. Seal off the Lozin Pass to hold the Horde while Darr raises his army. Alert the Sisters in Estrevan – if they do not know already. Fight.'

'Against Ashar?'

'Against Ashar and whatever demons he may send to support his minions. What else is there?'

'Flight,' Brannoc said.

'To where?' Bedyr's tone held bitterness. 'I cannot – nor would I – flee Tamur. If the Horde is raised, then the Three Kingdoms must fight. Whether or not the Horde marches under Ashar's fell banner.'

'If Ashar leads you face more than Drott and Caroc,' Brannoc warned. 'Those two alone are mighty enough, but the full Confederation will hold also Yath and Vistral and Grymard – more fighting men than this world has ever seen.'

'There is nothing else to do,' Bedyr replied. 'Should we present the Kingdoms as a gift?'

Brannoc's chuckle held no mockery, rather, Kedryn thought, he sounded respectful. 'No, you will do what a warrior must.'

'And you?' Bedyr asked. 'What will you do when your promise is fulfilled and you have your pardon?'

'That?' Brannoc chuckled again. 'That was no more than a bait to tease Rycol. It amuses me to keep your loyal commander on his toes. And the knowledge that I walk free with Tamur's blessing will keep the old wolf hopping!'

'You avoid the question. Where do you stand if the Horde marches south?'

Kedryn stirred, turning ostensibly to find a more comfortable position, in fact to study the outlaw's face as Brannoc answered.

'My father was a riverman, his father of Tamur, his mother of Kesh. My own mother was Vistral. I have spent half my life in the Beltrevan and half in the Three Kingdoms. Wrong is not limited to the Beltrevan, nor right to the Kingdoms, but in this I stand with you – Ashar is indisputably evil and I should not wish to live in a world given over to his worship.'

The sincerity of his tone was matched by the expression on his swarthy features and Kedryn saw Bedyr smile in response.

'I am not sure you are the man to fight a siege, Brannoc. And if this starts, it will start with the siege of the Lozin Forts.'

'Do you say you have no place for me?' the outlaw demanded, pride and anger hardening his face.

'Not that!' Bedyr said quickly, reassuringly. 'I meant there may well be more profitable duties; matters more suited to your particular skills.'

'I can kill with the best of them,' the outlaw said modestly. 'I can go where few others dare. I can pass as a tribesman at the pinch.'

'Exactly!' Kedryn saw his father lean forwards to clasp Brannoc's forearm, his voice earnest. 'Between them, Rycol and Fengrif can command the Lozin Forts better than any two men. And the warriors of the Kingdoms can fight! But if the Lozins should fall – and the forest folk come through – then it will be a war such as this world of ours has never known. It is my guess that the Horde will strike for Andurel – if some minion of Ashar's does command, then I am certain – and lay siege to the city. The bulk of Tamur's men, and those of Kesh and Ust-Galich, will face the Horde in defence of Andurel. The Kingdoms themselves will be stripped of warriors: the barbarians will occupy them after Andurel falls. Should that happen, chaos will reign. That is when your skills will be most needed. If the Horde goes down the Idre river road to Andurel, such a man as you could inflict damage along the way.'

'As a horsefly buzzing about the hindquarters of a war stallion,' Brannoc grunted. 'What good in that?'

'Let the fly sting at the right moment,' said Bedyr, 'and the rider may find himself unhorsed. Men would rally to you – from what both Rycol and Fengrif told me, you are accomplished in the arts of outlawry: if my worst fears prove true, then our tactics must be to hit and run and hide to hit again.'

'You would turn me into some folk hero,' grinned Brannoc. 'Should I live long enough.'

'I would see you fight for the Three Kingdoms in a manner best suited to your talents,' said Bedyr.

'You trust me that much?' Brannoc sounded genuinely intrigued, and more than a little surprised. 'Why?'

Bedyr paused before answering, his expression thoughtful. Then, 'I am not sure of the *why*, only that I do. You could have refused to aid me now – you say the pardon means little – but you agreed, knowing that treachery must likely mean your death.'

'I believe that kyo of yours would fight Ashar himself to reach me if I broke my word,' nodded the outlaw. 'And I think your son would be close on his heels.'

Kedryn veiled his eyes as Bedyr's head turned towards him, seeing through his lashes the fond, proud smile that lit his father's face as Bedyr nodded and said, 'Yes, I believe they would. I am fortunate to command such loyalty. But as to why I trust you ... Sister Wynett found only honesty when she looked at your thoughts; I believe I see it when I look at your face.'

'You flatter me.' Brannoc sounded pleased. 'I had not expected such trust.'

'I had not expected to find such an ally,' Bedyr said.

Brannoc grunted, seeming, Kedryn thought, uncharacteristically embarrassed. He said, 'I will be your horsefly if it comes to that, Bedyr Caitin. I will sting and run until they swat me. Or we win.'

Bedyr laughed softly, studying the outlaw's face and seemingly finding what he wanted there for he thrust out his hand and Brannoc took it, sealing their understanding without further need of words. They settled to sleep then and Kedryn closed his own eyes, thinking of the morrow when he would see the Beltrevan for the first time.

He was elected to stand the final watch and woken whilst the sun still clung to the lower quadrant of the western skyline, bathing the contours of the mountains with fiery brilliance, the eastern horizon dark. Unwilling to exhibit what he felt was a childish excitement, he nonetheless hurried to take up his position, anxious to catch a glimpse of the land ahead before night overtook the waning day. He strung his bow and paced through the pines to the farther edge of the plateau on which they camped. Caution held him just within the tree line, but from there he was able to see the beginnings of the forest country.

The trees amongst which he stood ended on a long, wide slope of sunlit yellow earth where nothing grew. Then, abruptly as though some demarcation line had been drawn, the timber began again. Kedryn gasped as he peered down, across, to the sides, for there was nothing to see but trees. Trees like an ocean of wood, exhibiting more shades of green than he thought could exist. Trees that spread in limitless profusion as far as his eyes could see, blurring into darkness at the limits of his vision, climbing slopes to top ridges and roll on down the far sides. Trees that seemed to fill the world, the rustle of their foliage impressive as the murmuring of the Idre, their number far greater than he could imagine. It was as though he stood upon a cliff, surveying the ocean he had read about but never seen, an ocean of pine and oak and birch and beech. He stared, wide-eyed, vigilance momentarily forgotten under the sheer visual impact of the Beltrevan. How many barbarians might that wilderness hold? How would it be possible to find any in that vastness?

He started as a slight sound behind him caught his ear, bow string drawing tight as he drew back, turning to level a wickedly barbed shaft.

'Friend!'

He let the bow string ease as he recognized Brannoc's voice, seeing for the first time how well the outlaw's mottled tunic blended with the shades and shadows. Brannoc came forward, smiling.

'The first time you have seen the Beltrevan?'

Kedryn nodded, not sure what to say, nor why the outlaw should make a point of speaking with him.

'It's a fine, wild place.' Affection sounded in Brannoc's voice, almost a longing. 'A good place to hunt.'

'Do you think our hunting will be good?' Kedryn coughed softly, afraid that nervousness rendered his own voice high, seeking to match the outlaw's casual tone.

'Perhaps.' Brannoc went on smiling, staring out over the sea of timber with an almost proprietorial fondness. 'It will depend who does the hunting.' Kedryn frowned and Brannoc went on, 'Tomorrow or the next day we shall quit the main party. You know our purpose, but do you know the danger?'

'I am not afraid.'

'I did not think you were. Had I thought that, I should have refused to allow you to accompany us.' He raised a hand to silence the youth's protest. 'It is not a question of usurping your father's authority, but a matter of survival. This is your blooding, is it not?' He smiled as Kedryn nodded. 'It may not be as you imagine it – it may not be at all glorious. In fact, if your father's suspicions are correct, it may well be a matter of hiding and running, an affair of caution rather than swordplay. Are you prepared for that?'

'I am prepared to do my duty,' Kedryn said, staunchly. 'I shall do as I am ordered.'

'By me?' asked the outlaw.

'My Lord Bedyr has so instructed,' Kedryn agreed.

'Your father agrees that I lead in the forest because I know the Beltrevan,' Brannoc said slowly, his face earnest. 'That shows he is a sensible man, and in the Beltrevan you will survive longer showing sense rather than courage. Courage is a virtue too often confused with foolhardiness.'

The words might have come from the lips of Tepshen Lahl, whose own instructions were frequently of such bent: Kedryn ducked his head in acknowledgement.

'You must move as an outlaw, not a hero,' Brannoc continued in the same mild tone. 'Do exactly as you are told. No more; no less. If misfortune should befall, you will return to High Fort. Do you understand?'

'If you should die?' Kedryn said slowly.

'Or your father, or the kyo,' nodded Brannoc. 'Any of us, blooding or no, you will not play the hero – you will run. Do you agree?'

'Do you order it?' asked Kedryn.

Brannoc paused, eyes fastened on the youth's face, then he said, 'I ask it.'

Kedryn returned his stare: 'I agree.'

'Good!' A broad smile split the outlaw's tanned features. 'Now saddle your horse – we ride for the Beltrevan!'

Feeling strangely uplifted by Brannoc's approval, Kedryn followed him back to the meadow, where the squadron was already preparing to leave. He set his gear in place on the horse and snatched a meal while the final vestiges of the day ribboned the horizon, the larger area of the sky already conceded to the darkness. A wind had started up, blowing from the north, redolent of pine sap, a wandering, frisky wind that sent small tendrils of chill playing over Kedryn's face as he set foot to stirrup and swung readily into the saddle.

Brannoc took the lead, quitting the plateau not via their entry route, but in the opposite direction, along the shelf to its western rim, then down a steep slope on a gently curving path that kept timber between the Tamurin riders and the facing gradients. Kedryn saw how caution governed his actions even down to the smallest details: it would be difficult for any chance watchers to observe their coming.

At the foot of the slope Brannoc turned east again, setting an easy pace along a shallow valley, then swinging north to climb the valley wall and trail down the far side so that the column merged with the shadows, traversing the downswing rather than the hogback where they might have been spotted. They rode in silence, the meandering path carrying them steadily deeper into the timber. The horses' hooves made little sound, and what small noises did arise were lost beneath the susurration of the foliage. Owls hooted and twice Kedryn heard the screaming of a hunting cat, but there was nothing to indicate their presence was suspected. They rode slowly, Brannoc picking a cautious path amongst the timber, avoiding obvious trails in favour of the less noticeable ways, the dense undergrowth forcing them to move often at little more than a walk. There was a dreamlike quality to it, though Kedryn was unsure whose dream it might be, for he remained tense, his head moving constantly from side to side as he sought to penetrate the solid-seeming blackness, conscious of the animal movement beneath him, but barely aware of making any progress. No matter how long they rode, they seemed not to arrive anywhere, for the timber about them remained unchangingly dense, ominously shadowed.

Then his mount halted unbidden and he realized the column had stopped. Brannoc appeared out of the night, stepping close to warn

Kedryn to dismount. He obeyed, unable to resist the impulse that sent his right hand to the sword hilt jutting above his left shoulder, the familiar bindings comforting as he waited. Brannoc came back down the line to beckon him forwards and he led his animal after the outlaw, abruptly aware that he could now make out his father and Tepshen Lahl ahead. He glanced up and saw the sky for the first time that night, realizing that Brannoc had brought them to another camping place that afforded both cover and protection.

It was a clearing scoured by fire, ancient stumps thrusting like jagged, blackened teeth from the growth of fresh grass. A spur of rock encircled three sides, a spring splashing from the stone to gather in a bowl before trickling away into the forest. The sky above was only just paling, and before the first soft hint of sunlight touched the heavens the Tamurin were settled, guards posted and horses picketed. There was little conversation for the concentration of the night ride had left most of them wearied, and the surrounding timber – still forbiddingly shadowed – was somehow oppressive, unlike the woodlands of their homeland. It was almost, Kedryn thought as he, in turn, stretched on his cloak, as if the trees themselves spied upon the column.

That day he slept badly, dreaming of nameless things that pursued him through forests of clutching, sentient trees whose limbs tore at his flesh and sought to hold him, that whatever chased might catch and rend. He woke sweating, licking his lips and feeling ashamed of his infantile terrors. He rose quickly, going to the spring to splash cool water over the memories, finding great comfort in the sight of Bedyr and Tepshen Lahl, and – rather to his surprise – Brannoc, preparing for a fourth night of travel.

The outlaw set a faster pace this time, the nature of the forest shifting as they rode farther from the Lozins, the tall pines giving way to less sombre timber and the undergrowth becoming steadily less brambly, growing familiarity rendering the woodland less menacing. They halted earlier than usual, at the foot of a low hill, Brannoc climbing on foot to the summit, then returning to lead the rest up. Kedryn wondered if the place might have been a fort in some forgotten time, for when he topped the crest he saw that the apex of the mound was hollowed, the rim forming a natural buttress topped with a palisade of beech, and the concave declivity within lushly grassed and easily large enough to conceal and feed the horses.

While dawn began to light the sky, Bedyr called a council.

'We divide our force today,' he told the warriors circling him.

'Torim, you command. Tepshen, Kedryn and I will scout deep with Brannoc to guide us. The rest of you will base here and scout the surrounding forest. Use this place as a redoubt if you must, but avoid open fight if you can. We need to learn, not kill, and the less attention you draw, the better. See what you can see, but do nothing to attract the forest folk. By the time the moon begins to wane we should return to meet you here. If not, you will ride for High Fort and report to Rycol.'

Torim shifted uneasily on the grass, toying with his sword hilt. He was a grizzled warrior, grey in his beard and a long scar marring his features, lending them a melancholy air. 'Lord Bedyr,' he said softly, 'is this wise? Should we not remain in strength?'

Bedyr shook his head. 'My friend, I ask much of you. I have the easier part of this, for Brannoc has convinced me a small group may go where all of us should be spotted. If the barbarians fall on anyone, they are more likely to fall on you. I ask you to act as decoy, Torim.'

Torim grunted indifferently and said, 'Then we shall be a decoy, Lord.'

'Thank you,' said Bedyr, and the matter was closed.

Brannoc produced a small square of soft hide on which he had drawn a crude map of the area and the Tamurin crowded close as he indicated the contours of the land and the customary locations of barbarian settlements.

'Remember,' he warned, 'that the forest folk are likely on the move. They may well have abandoned these holdings, so you could stumble on them anywhere; or they on you. Tread warily.'

Torim nodded and folded the map into his tunic, his face dolorous as ever.

That night Brannoc led Bedyr, Tepshen Lahl and Kedryn away from the hillock. Two days later they saw their first sign of the forest folk.

The Beltrevan had so far been ominously deserted, the very absence of barbarians indicative of wrongness. As Brannoc pointed out, they should have found evidence of hunters, seen something of the Grymard, through whose territory they travelled. But there was nothing until they came upon the settlement.

They moved in daylight now and the outlaw was scouting ahead, returning to beckon the others forwards, cautioning them – unnecessarily – to maintain silence as he led them on foot through a dense stand of oak. He stopped, pointing, just inside the tree line.

Before them stood a broad clearing, obviously man-made, the

timber cut back and the grass trampled down. At the centre there was a patch of blackened soil where a central fire had once burned. When Kedryn dipped a hand in the ashes, they retained a degree of warmth. Around the fire there were the marks of lodges, post holes and discoloured grass showing where the hide structures had stood, signs of individual fires and scatterings of gnawed bones lending further weight to the impression that the place was only recently vacated. Brannoc pointed to the north.

'They left not long ago, in that direction.' He sounded more than a little worried, his dark eyes troubled as he stared at the surrounding trees. 'Why would Grymard venture north? That direction takes them directly into Caroc territory.'

Kedryn saw his father and Tepshen Lahl exchange glances, then Bedyr said, 'Let us see why.'

Brannoc nodded and they began to trail the Grymard.

It was a group of five families, moving steadily northwards without attempt to hide their tracks. When Kedryn asked why they should, Brannoc informed him that the forest folk were, by nature, secretive, the stronger tribes preying on the weaker, and that for a Grymard settlement to move so openly towards Caroc territory was unprecedented. 'Unless,' he added sombrely, 'your father is right, and they go to join the Confederation.' Kedryn nodded, storing the information, aware that he did not yet come even close to understanding the ways of the Beltrevan. He had seen the Grymard on their journey, watching from the cover of a blackthorn thicket, and thought they looked a sorry bunch, not at all like the noble savages he had anticipated. They travelled mostly on foot, the three horses they possessed were small animals, burdened under great piles of hides and poles and packs. He saw dogs dragging loaded travois and women with matted, reddish hair carrying even greater bundles while the men ranged ahead and to the sides without paying much more than perfunctory attention to the terrain. They were short, heavy-built men, animal-like beneath thick beards, unkempt hair decorated in the same fashion as Brannoc's with pieces of bone and shell, and layers of furry, hide clothing. They were all heavily armed with swords, axes, spears and bows. In a distinct group behind the leaders he saw youths of around his own age, as best he could estimate, proudly carrying the trophy poles. The grinning skulls rattled as they moved, as if conversing amongst themselves, the empty sockets where the eyes had been seeming to peer into the undergrowth, picking out the hidden observers. As Kedryn watched them go by he felt the now familiar chill creep along his spine.

'They travel as though to a Gathering,' Brannoc said after the tribe had disappeared. 'You saw the white and red feathers on the trophy poles? They are the sign of peaceful intent – like your blue peace banners – and the forest folk use them only when they gather. Yet all the Summer Gatherings are ended.'

There was no need for elaboration: Bedyr simply nodded and they returned to their hidden horses and continued their trailing of the Grymard.

The path lead unerringly northwards, and as the moon grew fatter the group they followed was joined by others until the barbarians moved in a straggling, quarrelsome column of close on a hundred souls. Most, Brannoc said, were Grymard, but there were Vistral and some Yath amongst them, and they went purposefully, as if headed for some pre-ordained destination. Their halts were brief and they ate mostly the provisions they carried with them, doing little hunting. They appeared to be hurrying.

Close on the full moon they arrived.

They were deep into Caroc territory by now and Brannoc was mightily wary. Kedryn was gripped by an excitement that bordered close on hysteria, compounded of the tension that was an almost palpable thing and the enforced waiting occasioned by the outlaw's insistence on scouting ahead. It was as Brannoc had warned him – his blooding was turning out to be a matter of hiding rather than the glorious – and triumphant – fighting he had anticipated. There was little glory to be found crouching in a thicket while barbarians with oily hair straggled by; less still in the long waiting for the outlaw's return.

'Be patient,' Tepshen Lahl counselled when the youth asked why they should not simply range ahead of the column of forest folk and precede them to wherever they were going. 'Any warrior can show courage when he faces a blade, but a wise man knows *when* to use his blade, and how to wait to use it to most effect.'

The waiting ended with Brannoc's return.

Despite the natural darkness of his features Kedryn could see that he was pale. There was nothing of his customary light-heartedness about him, but rather a haunted air, as though he had stumbled upon something he had dreaded and hoped not to find. He squatted at the base of a slender ash, twining his braids about a finger as he eyed each of his companions in turn.

'You have seen it,' Bedyr prompted when the outlaw's silence grew too much for him.

'I have seen the Horde.' Brannoc's voice was husky. 'Over that ridge. When the sun goes down you will see the fires.'

'I'll see more than that,' Bedyr said. 'I'll see the camp itself.'

Brannoc stared at the Lord of Tamur and said, 'Go back now! Go back and seal the Lozin Pass. Go tell King Darr to raise his army – he'll need every man in the Kingdoms!'

'I must see it for myself,' Bedyr told him. 'We must each of us see it, so that each one may carry the word if the others fall.'

'You may well fall,' Brannoc murmured, his voice that of a man scarcely able to credit the evidence of his own vision. 'We may all fall. The Confederation camps over that rise. Drott and Caroc and Yath set their lodges side by side. The Grymard and the Vistral join them. Every tribe in the Beltrevan camps there: the Horde is raised!'

The anticipatory excitement that Kedryn felt rise within him was immediately quashed by the expression on his father's face, and when he turned towards Tepshen he saw the same gravity. Had he not known them better, he would have thought he saw fear.

'Tonight,' Bedyr said, not really asking a question, 'can you bring us close?'

'You can see the camp from the ridgetop,' Brannoc answered. 'Any closer and the dogs will take your scent.'

'Guards?' asked Tepshen.

Brannoc shook his head, a wry smile curling his lips. 'What need? Who would be foolhardy enough to chance the wrath of the Horde?'

'We'll stay downwind,' Bedyr said, his voice firm, calm. 'Can we trust the wind?'

Brannoc sniffed the air, plucking a blade of grass and letting it drift from his fingers. He shrugged, 'I think so.'

'Good,' smiled Bedyr, though the expression held no humour, 'we shall see what we face tonight, then. We shall estimate their numbers – if the tribes join, there can be only one reason – and return to High Fort. If we are spotted, we run. There will be no stopping – should one of us fall, he is left. Do you understand? To bring word to Darr is more important than any life here.'

He looked at each one in turn. Kedryn said, 'I will not desert you.'

'You will do as I order!' Bedyr's tone was that of a commander, not a father. 'Your duty is to Tamur and the Kingdoms, boy. Remember that!'

Kedryn would have spoken again, but Tepshen Lahl's hand closed on his shoulder, locking the words behind teeth clenched in hurt.

'I am Lord of Tamur,' Bedyr said in a softer tone, 'as you will be one day. We have a duty to Tamur, and it outweighs our personal loyalties. Do you understand that, Kedryn? Should I go down – or Tepshen, or Brannoc – your duty is to Tamur and the Three Kingdoms. You *must* take word to Darr in Andurel. That above all else is important. More than my life, or yours, the safety of the Three Kingdoms is paramount. Do I need ask your word on this?'

Reluctantly, Kedryn shook his head. Embarrassed and irritated with himself, he rose as though stiff from the waiting and fetched a sharpening stone from his kit, settling to honing his sword blade, aware of the hot flush that suffused his face.

'It is no easy thing, lordship.'

He looked up as Tepshen Lahl settled fluidly beside him.

'Most men have simple duties – their family, their lord, their king. They need not think much beyond that, so for them the world is largely black and white. A lord must think in larger terms, for his family is so much more than wife and children – his people are his family, and he must think of their welfare, or he is not worthy to be their lord. Your father is worthy.'

'Would he leave me?' Kedryn demanded.

'Yes,' said Tepshen Lahl, his voice unyielding. 'It would break his heart, but he would leave you if his duty to the Kingdoms required it. As would I. As you will leave us if need be. If you cannot see that, you are not worthy to be prince of Tamur.'

Kedryn lowered his blade, studying the kyo's calm, impassive features. 'I did not think it would be like this,' he murmured, feeling unpleasantly close to childish tears.

'No,' said Tepshen, 'but it is. And if the Horde does camp over that ridge, you will have chance enough later to put blood on your blade. Be patient.'

Kedryn nodded and began to hone his dirk, not wanting the kyo to see how close he was to tears. He was grateful when Tepshen grunted and rose to his feet, clapping him on the shoulder. After a little while he followed the easterner across the clearing to face Bedyr.

'I am sorry,' he said. 'I shall do exactly as you order.'

'I never doubted that you would,' Bedyr replied. 'You are too good a warrior.'

That pleased Kedryn, and he determined to obey his father's orders, to live up to the expectations of Bedyr and Tepshen Lahl in a manner befitting a prince of Tamur. No matter what might happen, he promised himself, he would execute his duty, whatever the personal cost. Then he realized, as he thought more deeply about it, that he hoped they might all escape detection and return safely to High Fort. It was not at all as he had anticipated, and he wondered if this was a sign of maturity. He contemplated asking Tepshen or Bedyr, but decided against it for both men appeared lost in their own thoughts, as if mentally preparing themselves for what they dreaded finding over the ridge.

They remained in hiding as the sun went down and the Beltrevan was once more given over to the night. As the light faded Kedryn saw that the sky beyond the ridge glowed, as if a forest fire raged, and he realized that he looked at the reflected brilliance of multitudinous camp fires, their luminescence so great that it lit the sky itself. Further, as the stillness of evening possessed the forest he heard a steady thrumming, almost as though the Idre ran close by, and recognized it as the sound of a myriad voices rising from the great encampment. He could not imagine how many folk it took to produce so much noise, but he felt suddenly very small and more than a little frightened.

He was pleased when Brannoc grunted and climbed to his feet, announcing that if they were to risk their lives it might as well be now.

They left their horses tethered in the cover of the trees and commenced the ascent of the slope. It was thickly timbered and they reached the crest safely, flattening as Brannoc raised a warning arm and began to wriggle forwards like some great serpent. Bedyr followed him, then Kedryn, with Tepshen Lahl bringing up the rear. The outlaw led them along a rib of ground that thrust into a valley, its sides too steep to afford safe ground for tents, halting on the edge and easing forwards to peer down. As he came to the rim and saw what lay before him, Kedryn clenched his teeth to suppress the gasp that threatened to explode from his mouth.

Below his position the ridge curved gently away to the northeast, forming one side of a long, broad valley. Only a few trees grew there, the valley being mostly grassed. At least, Kedryn assumed grass grew there: it was lost beneath the mass of lodges that stretched beyond the limits of his sight. They spread in profusion across the valley bottom and up the sides, seeming, from his vantage point, like some enormous growth of gigantic mushrooms. Countless fires blazed, filling the night with light and sound that mingled with the babble of voices, the clattering of cookpots, the barking of dogs and the wickering of horses. Men and women and children, from fur-swaddled infants to bent-backed oldsters, shifted amongst the vast array of dwellings. Skull-hung poles thrust above the lodges like seed pods extruded from the squat leathern growths, overhanging the narrow alleyways between the tents, fireglow lending the bleached bones a macabre life. At first it was difficult to observe any order in the apparently chaotic arrangement of shebangs, but as he stared wide-eyed at the daunting scene, he saw that some notion of organization governed the arrangement. The height of the ridge and the contours of the terrain distorted his view, so that the outer reaches of the encampment appeared a random jumble of lodges, but closer to the centre of the enormous conglomeration a distinct pattern became visible.

A fire of epic proportions burned there, the conflagration so great that a wide circle of open ground like a plaza was left between the flames and the hide tents facing towards the blaze. These were larger than the others, and armoured warriors stood about each canopied entrance as though on watch. One, he noticed, was separated from its companions by a greater space on either side, as if accorded a degree of respect in excess of its neighbours, and as he watched, a man emerged.

Kedryn could not make out his features clearly, though he had an impression of dark hair and thick beard, beneath which a torque of some kind glittered, of powerful shoulders beneath the opulent wolfskin robe that swathed the man. He saw the armoured guards group about the figure, and then his attention was caught by another.

Later, he could not explain his impressions, for they seemed illogical and he could not understand why they were so clear. In that instant, however, he saw the figure as distinctly as if no more than a pace or two separated them. It – somehow he did not think of it as a mortal man, though he could no more explain that than he could the clarity of his perception – was taller than the wolfskinned chieftain, long-limbed and oddly angular, as though the shoulders hunched awkwardly beneath the mass of furs that draped the body. Hair like fresh-fallen snow cascaded about a face that was not quite human, the set of the bones beneath the milky skin triangular, making Kedryn think of an insect, the mouth a lipless gash under a thin, sharp nose, the eyes set so deep as to be almost invisible, as if burned into the skull. There was a predatory air to the creature, as if hawk and wolf and forest cat merged in almost-human form, and when the white-maned head rose to survey the camp, Kedryn ducked, seeking instinctively to bury himself in the undergrowth, to hide from that awful gaze. He was convinced the creature could see him, not through mortal eyes, but with a supernatural vision, for he knew with a ghastly certainty that he looked upon Ashar's Messenger. And in the same horror-chilled moment that their destinies were somehow linked.

He felt horribly cold, an awful, nauseating chill coalescing deep in his belly so that bile rose in his throat and he felt his eyes water as he fought against the compulsion to vomit out his last meal and flee panic-stricken from that impossible, threatening gaze.

He conquered the impulse with an effort that shook him physically, and when his eyes cleared again he saw the figure moving away from the lodge, accompanied by the barbarian chief, leisurely circling the bonfire, more richly robed torque-bearers forming a retinue in their wake. He wiped a hand across a face slick with cold sweat, starting in near-terror as a hand touched his shoulder and he turned to find his father's face close, Bedyr's voice soft as he called his son away.

As he descended the slope he became aware that his teeth were chattering. When he reached the horses and could see the faces of his companions he saw that each man was stunned by the enormity of the barbarian encampment. No one spoke; in silent accord they mounted their animals and rode softly away, anxious to put distance between themselves and the forest folk.

It was some time before Bedyr called a halt, and when at last he spoke, his voice was grim.

'There can be no more doubt: we face the Horde.'

'Did you see him?' Kedryn heard his voice falter as the others looked towards him.

'I saw lodges and warriors,' Brannoc said, 'of the Caroc and the Drott; the Yath, the Grymard and the Vistral. They were together, in peace. They have met in peace only once before – when Drul raised the Horde.' His voice was hushed and solemn, tinged with awe, almost with terror.

'No.' Kedryn shook his head, confused. 'There was a . . . he was not a man . . . He was all in furs, with snow-white hair. He looked . . . I thought he looked . . . directly at me. I thought he saw me.'

Bedyr's hand fell upon his shoulder, fingers tight through the leather of his jerkin. 'He could not have seen you! No man could see you!'

The urgency of his tone frightened Kedryn and for a while he forgot he was a warrior. 'I do not think he was a man, Father. He was

. . . I believe he was Ashar's Messenger! He could not have seen me, could he?' He heard the desperation in his voice and shuddered despite himself, gripped by a nameless dread.

'No!' said Bedyr fiercely. 'It was a trick of the firelight. I saw no one such as you describe.'

'Nor I,' added Tepshen Lahl, his face solemn.

Kedryn's gaze went from one to the other in confusion, his own memory so stark he could not believe that he alone had seen the creature so clearly. Then he saw Brannoc fold the thumb of his right hand against his smallest finger, the three remaining digits spread rigidly in a fan that he passed across his eyes as he stared at the youth.

When the outlaw spoke, his voice was hoarse. 'He saw Ashar's minion. He saw the Messenger.'

Bedyr glared at the woodsman, his face stricken, jaw tight over clenched teeth, the pressure of his grip increasing on Kedryn's shoulder until the youth winced beneath the force.

'We ride for Andurel! We must warn the Kingdoms!'

Kedryn stared wide-eyed at his father, Bedyr's tone curdling fresh fear inside him. He would have spoken again, asked why his description of the figure should produce such reaction, for surely it confirmed what had been already anticipated, but Bedyr was turning towards the horses, his shoulders bowed as though weighted by unwished-for knowledge and his eyes grim. Kedryn felt himself possessed by a numinous dread that halted the question stillborn and, silent, sprang to his own mount.

Bedyr waited barely long enough for the others to reach their saddles before he drove heels to his stallion's flanks and charged southwards, uncaring of the hoof-thunder, intent only on quitting the Beltrevan and whatever awful danger lay there.

Chapter Six

Though he could neither define what it was or how he knew, Borsus sensed a subtle change in Taws as the mage greeted Balandir, Ulan of the Caroc. It was not easy, at the best of times, to read expression on that corpse-milky face, and now the warrior's attention was as much on the conversation of the chiefs as on the Messenger, for on this parley rested the future of the Confederation. If Balandir should agree to throw in his lot with Niloc Yarrum, bring his Caroc thousands into the body of the Horde, then the invasion of the Three Kingdoms was certain. If not . . . Borsus was uncertain what might happen. By now he was attuned to thinking of invasion, and the possibility of Balandir refusing alliance had only now occurred to him. Not war, he thought, for the joining of Drott and Yath and Grymard and Vistral left even the mighty Caroc outnumbered; and Niloc had the mage at his back, an ally to strike fear into even Balandir's savage heart. Yet there was something wrong, and it troubled him.

He took his place in the circle, on Taws's left, his attention divided between Balandir and the Messenger. Niloc sat facing the Caroc Ulan, Vran of the Yath to his right, beyond Vran, Ymrath, leader of the Vistral, and Darien of the Grymard. The Gehrim of each Ulan stood silent behind their masters, a living wall to guarantee the privacy of this future-shaping conclave, the blazing light of the great bonfire striking brilliance from their armour and the weapons they carried. Beyond them, a second barrier to the vast mass of forest folk awaiting the outcome, stood the beribboned peace poles, thick bunches of feathers dyed red and white stirring at their tops. Borsus could not see past the Gehrim, but he knew that the woodsfolk stood there in their thousands, bar-Offas and warriors, women and children, old-sters; all silent, waiting. The night air was thick with their anticipation, settling a stillness on the vast encampment that spread down the valley, the mood silencing even the quarrelling of the dogs.

He heard Niloc Yarrum say formally, 'I bid you welcome, Ulan Balandir. I greet you in peace and fellowship.'

Balandir replied in like form, his voice thickened by the heavy scar that twisted his mouth down at one side, setting a streak of white in the fox red of his beard. He was an impressive man, shorter than Yarrum but wider in the shoulder, deeper of chest, his hair dressed in the fashion of his people, drawn to the left side in a long plait decorated with pieces of silver and colourful feathers. His furs were luxuriant, a jerkin of otter pelts gleaming in the firelight, a cape of horse hair attesting to his wealth, his boots of hog's hide, the lacings chased with silver thread. As custom demanded, he bore no weapons other than a dagger, but that was silver-hilted, the workmanship as fine as the blade at Niloc's waist, the sheath a work of art, carved from a length of redwood and inscribed with Caroc runes. Looking into his pale blue eyes, Borsus was uncertain whether he saw measured consideration there or mistrust.

'You are Taws,' Balandir grunted, turning his attention to the ominous figure beside Niloc. 'I have heard it said that you are Ashar's Messenger. Is that true?'

Borsus shifted his head far enough to the side that he could study the mage as Taws replied. He saw the snow-maned skull duck briefly, the cratered eyes steady on the Caroc's as Taws said simply, 'I am.'

The brevity of the response seemed to take Balandir by surprise, for he frowned, fidgeting with an ivory thumb ring. He glanced at Niloc as though seeking confirmation and Niloc said, 'Taws is the Messenger. He is come to raise the Horde. He will give us the Kingdoms.'

'The Kingdoms may not be easily given,' replied Balandir, his face expressionless. 'I do not think they consider themselves a gift.'

'Do you doubt Ashar's power?' asked Taws, his voice flat, cold as crusting ice on a mid-winter pool.

'No,' said Balandir in a tone that suggested reservations, adding diplomatically, 'I respect Ashar enough that I am not prepared to take unproven word of his Messenger.'

'You have *my* word,' Niloc snapped, his features darkening as he glared at the Caroc, ebony eyes swinging to the mage in silent request for some evidence that would convince the sceptic.

Borsus licked his lips, anticipating an outburst from Taws, some immediate, overt demonstration of the thaumaturgist's puissance. Somewhat to his surprise, no such display came. It seemed almost as though Taws's mind was elsewhere, as if he were anxious to have done with the meeting, yet unwilling to risk the dissolution of the Horde by offending the Ulan of the Caroc.

He saw the death-pale face rise and was reminded of a serpent rearing to strike, but all Taws said was, 'How may I prove it you, Ulan?'

Balandir's frown became an expression of confusion and he shrugged, otter pelts rustling against horse hide. He turned the ivory ring around his thumb, eyes falling from Taws's rubescent gaze.

'If you are truly Ashar's Messenger – and my doubt is born of respect, you understand – then you came from his sacred fire. My shamans say that flame is life blood to the Messenger. I . . .'

'Shall have your proof.' Taws finished the sentence, ignoring protocol to such extent that Balandir gaped, too shocked to argue or complain as the strangely angular being rose to his feet and spun around, the furs that swathed him brushing Borsus's face. Balandir's Gehrim tensed, hands clenching on sword hilts and spear shafts, that action prompting a reactive alertness in the Gehrim of Drott, Yath, Vistral and Grymard. Taws ignored them, motioning for those closest to stand aside as the Ulans rose, staring after him.

He marched past Dewan, who averted his eyes, looking to Niloc Yarrum for instruction, receiving a slight, pacifying gesture in response. Borsus moved instinctively to follow, then halted as Taws stopped just inside the ring of truce poles, turning deep-sunk eyes that now gleamed dangerously red to Balandir.

'Watch, Ulan. Watch and believe. And when you have your proof, you will give your allegiance to Ashar and the one he has chosen as hef-Ulan of the Horde.'

Balandir was too disconcerted to reply, merely nodding dumbly as Taws strode between the ribboned poles, the great mass of folk parting before him as if a maddened forest bull had charged into their midst.

The mage stalked directly towards the massive bonfire that dominated the centre of the camp. It lit the meeting of the Ulans and the surrounding lodges as though a piece of the sun were brought to rest upon the earth of the Beltrevan. Such was its heat that few could approach closer than twenty paces, and then only at risk of scorched flesh. It sent a column of raw fire high into the night, sparks like stars cascading upwards, carried on the gusting of its roaring breath. Borsus joined the Ulans as they followed in Taws's wake, stopping when furs began to singe and skin prickle beneath the onslaught of the blaze. Taws did not stop. As a man bent on some urgent mission he marched beyond the bearable perimeter of the heat, fourteen paces, thirteen, twelve. Borsus glanced swiftly at Balandir and saw the Caroc's jaw set in a taught, disbelieving line, as though he could not credit the evidence of the eyes he squinted against the ferocity of the blaze. He heard the Ulan gasp as Taws came to the very edge of the piled wood. Then even he gasped as the mage set hands to burning faggots and began to clamber up the sloping side of the bonfire.

The furs that hid Taws's body should have burned, but did not. The ashen hair should have shrivelled, the skin blackened and roasted. Eyes should have boiled, flesh melted from bone, but none of these things happened. Instead, Taws climbed the pyre as easily as though he scaled a gently sloping bank of sun-kissed grass, the burning wood he clutched affording handholds as might the roots of trees, great blazing branches secure beneath his feet until he stood atop the bonfire and raised himself to his full height.

Flame gusted about him, swirling his white mane as would a summer breeze. Sparks formed a corona about his head, a hellish halo that seemed to illumine his features as he turned slowly around, arms upraised, to survey the gathering. He opened his mouth and spoke where there was no air to breath, only hell-heat and awful death for any mortal being.

'Do you doubt?'

Borsus could do no more than stare at the impossible figure, but had he been able to tear his eyes from the flame-shrouded creature, he would have seen that every soul in the valley looked to Taws. That Balandir unwittingly shook his head; that Niloc Yarrum was smiling hugely. He had no need to turn to know that the mage's words had somehow carried through the clamour of the fire, that every one of the watching, gaping forest folk had heard them, for their reply came in full-throated answer.

'No! No! *No!*'

Taws's fleshless lips thinned back in parody of a smile and he turned full circle again, hands reaching out as though to encompass the mass.

'I am the Messenger!'

It was a statement, not a question, but it was answered nonetheless.

'*Yes! Yes, you are the Messenger!*'

Still with that awful smile on his mantis-features, Taws revolved once more as the valley reverberated with the shouting of the Horde, the roaring echoing against the sky, louder even than the bellow of the flames. Then, agile despite the curious angularity of his body, he descended the great pyramid of incandescent timber to face Balandir.

'Do you doubt?'

There was menace in the question now and Borsus was reminded of the urgency he had earlier sensed in the mage. He looked to where Balandir stood and saw the Ulan drop to his knees, head bowed in full obeisance.

'No. You are the Messenger.'

'I speak for Ashar?'

'You speak for Lord Ashar.' Balandir's head remained down, his heavy plait coiling on the trampled ground, his hands braced before him.

'And Niloc Yarrum is hef-Ulan of the Horde.'

There was no question implicit in the Messenger's tone, but still a moment passed before Balandir grunted, 'Yes, I acknowledge Niloc Yarrum as hef-Ulan.'

'Good.' Taws bent, hands that articulated in a manner not quite human locking in the Caroc's jerkin, raising the bulky man effortlessly to his feet. 'I bid you welcome to the Horde, Balandir. I shall raise you high when we have taken the Kingdoms. Your people will praise you for this night's work.'

Balandir stared at the red-pupilled eyes, his resentment of the Drott Ulan's elevation mollified by this promise. Taws's smile became gentler, and he touched fingers lightly to the Caroc's lips, ignoring the instinctive backwards step the Ulan took, seeming amused by the sudden fear in the man's eyes.

'Serve me well, Balandir,' he murmured, 'and you will be well rewarded. You have Ashar's promise on that.'

Then, abruptly as he had quit the council circle, he turned away, calling over his shoulder as if summoning a hound. 'Borsus, I have need of you.'

Surprised, Borsus hurried after his master.

'Taws!' Niloc Yarrum's shout was a mixture of amazement and more than a little anger. 'Where do you go? You are needed here.'

The Messenger slowed his pace without halting, addressing the hef-Ulan of the Horde with no more ceremony than he had used on the warrior now at his heels. 'I go on Ashar's business; yours is with Balandir: go about it.'

Niloc's mouth tightened with embarrassed fury, the same conjoined emotions suffusing his swarthy features, but he offered no further protest, merely staring at the mage's departing back before returning with a grunt to the council circle. Not daring to look back, Borsus followed Taws through the crowd to the lodge of hides occupied by the sorcerer.

Inside, the place was overheated as ever; braziers and flambeaux filling the shadowy confines with flickering light and the oppressive warmth favoured by the mage. Borsus slid his bearskin from his shoulders and even then felt his shirt plaster swiftly to his back as sweat started from every pore. Taws sucked in his breath in a manner that prompted Borsus to think again of serpents and sank on to a fur-covered chair, brusquely motioning the warrior to take the seat facing him.

For long moments he was silent, staring into the flames of a brazier, the fireglow reflecting off his gaunt face so that it assumed the colouration of a fresh-skinned skull. Then, startling Borsus with the abruptness of the words, he said, 'I need you.'

Borsus opened his mouth to reply but realized he had no idea what to say. There was no need, for Taws continued as though speaking to himself, still staring into the brazier.

'You will say nothing of this. Not to your woman, or the hef-Ulan, or whatever friends you have here. You will speak to no one. Do you understand that?'

His head lifted then and Borsus found himself transfixed by the crimson pupils, seeing on Taws's face an expression he could not fathom. There was anger in it, and determination, and something else Borsus had never seen there before, nor ever thought to see. Something that on any mortal face he would have read as fear. He nodded dumbly, not trusting himself to speak.

'There was one who watched,' Taws went on slowly, as if he found the words difficult to utter. 'One who should not have seen what he did. But perhaps that is to my advantage, because now I know he *does* live and I was not sure of that. Not until now.'

He paused as though lost in reverie, the rubescent eyes no longer focused on Borsus's face. The warrior waited in silence, the Messenger's apparent indecision somehow more frightening than any forthright display of rage.

The eyes focused again and Taws said more definitely, 'I sensed him. He is young. I knew he would be. Perhaps that makes it easier, too – you will seek the young one. Ignore the rest – they are nothing – but find the young one and kill him if you can. If not, put my mark on him. Do not fail me in that!'

The final words were spat with such venom that Borsus started back, almost toppling his chair, sweat that was not a product of the heat beading his forehead. He drew a shirtsleeve across his face, forcing words from a mouth gone dry with tension.

'Shall I have Dewan search the camp, Master?'

'*You will speak to no one of this!*' snarled Taws, his expression such that Borsus locked his teeth in jaw-aching effort to prevent them from chattering. 'You ride alone. *Alone*, do you understand?' His tone softened a little as he saw the naked terror stark on the warrior's bearded features. 'He is not to be found in the camp. He is from the Kingdoms. He would not have come alone, but the others are unimportant. Only the young one matters; and you are the only one I can trust in this.'

'Master?' Borsus heard his own stutter, no longer able to hold back the castanet clattering of his teeth. 'The Kingdoms? How?'

'It does not matter,' rasped Taws. 'What has happened in the Beltrevan cannot have gone entirely unnoticed by the Kingdoms. Doubtless they have spies; doubtless the movements of the southern tribes have been noted. Most probably they sent a scouting party – perhaps warded by some grammarye of the Ashar-damned worshippers of Kyrie. Yes! That would explain much. Warded by such glamour they might have escaped my attention, but he could not. No! Not he, not linked by destiny to what I do.' He chuckled then and Borsus shivered afresh, for that diabolic laughter was the raw material of terror, the stuff of nightmares, infinitely worse than any whispering of the quadi who called to men at night from the other-world. The sweat that now drenched Borsus's body was suddenly chill as winter rain and he was glad when the chuckling ceased.

'He will return now.' Taws was abruptly purposeful. 'He will be riding for the Kingdoms. Towards the westernside fort, I imagine. You will take the finest horse here – it does not matter whose – and pursue him. You can ride?'

Borsus nodded, not daring to point out that only recently, and only because he was favoured by the Messenger, had he experienced that luxury reserved for the highest of the tribes. At that moment it seemed far preferable to take his chances on a horse.

'Good,' said Taws promptly, 'then you will ride for the edge of the forest. He will likely be slowed in his return by the Grymard and Vistral still coming in to join us, so you will likely get ahead of him. Lay in ambush and as I say – kill him if you can; if not, then mark him. Wound him! That will be enough. Now – quickly! – fetch me your arrows.'

His talon-nailed fingers flicked in dismissal. Needlessly, for Borsus was already on his feet and moving thankfully for the hide-curtained exit, glad of any excuse to be gone from the stifling lodge and the strange mood of his master.

He did not have far to go, his own lodge standing close beside Taws's, empty now, for Sulya was with the other women thronging the spaces about the truce circle. He was grateful for that – he had no wish to hear her questions about the mage's orders, or face her irritation when he refused to answer. He found his good yew bow in its wrapping of doe skin and wound a second string about his forearm, then slid two hands of wickedly recurved war arrows into his quiver, instinctively checking the fletching of each as the hard ash shafts were dropped into the stiffened hide container. Then, aware of his heart drumming nervously against his ribs, he returned to Taws's lodge.

The Messenger snatched the quiver from his outstretched hand and spilled the arrows carelessly on to the fur-covered floor.

'Bring the horse!'

It was a command and a dismissal: Borsus hurried to obey.

He ran, using Taws's name to clear a way, to the stockade built to hold the Drott horses. There were no guards save the prowling dogs and these he kicked from his path, oblivious of the fangs that snapped at his heels. He ducked beneath the poles of the corral, too intent on obedience to allow his usual wariness of the horses sway, snatching a length of plaited rawhide from the fence as he went. He already knew which animal he would need if he was to reach the High Fort road before whatever quarry he pursued: Niloc's own great grey beast. And let Taws explain to the hef-Ulan! He fashioned a loop in the rope, which gave him time to remember how the animal lay back its ears and snapped its huge yellow teeth even at Niloc, but his fear of the Messenger's anger was greater than his dread of the stallion and he went in amongst the beasts, ignoring their snickering and the stamping hooves as he stalked the grey.

He threw the rawhide noose over the plunging head as the animal reared up, feeling his feet leave the ground as the lariat drew tight and he hauled himself hand-over-hand towards the horse until the sweet, sharp odour of its sweat was in his nostrils and he could clamp fingers in its mane. He used his weight to bring the head down to where he could clasp an ear and fight the animal to the corral gate. His sudden expertise amazed him as he kicked the gate pole clear and brought the stallion out of the stockade, shouting for the warriors now gaping at his daring to close the gap behind him, yelling for more to help him saddle the angry beast.

'Would you embrace the eagle?' gasped a startled Drott.

'Would you anger Taws?' Borsus shouted back, halting the man's escape. 'I act on his orders!'

He was known as Taws's man and mention of the mage's name brought him the help he needed to set the rawhide halter about the snorting muzzle, the padded leather saddle on the back. Still he needed three men to bring the stallion to Taws's lodge.

Taws stood outside, Borsus's quiver and bow in his hands, his expression irked as he saw the company the warrior brought with him. Unspeaking, he took the halter from Borsus and handed the Drott the bow and the quiver. He stared at the horse, then moved his right hand in a shifting pattern that drew cold light from the night air, reaching out to touch the flared nostrils. The witchfire bathed the stallion's head and it calmed instantly, breath soughing noisily, neck dropping. Taws nodded to himself and turned towards the staring warriors. He beckoned them closer and set his hands on the shoulders of each in turn, staring deep into their eyes as he had once stared into Sulya's. And, like Sulya, the men assumed slack expressions, the tension draining from their bodies. Taws murmured something to each and motioned them away.

'They will not remember,' he told Borsus, 'and the horse will carry you.'

Borsus slung the quiver on his back and laced the wrapped bow beside the saddle, too busy with his preparations to wonder what spell Taws had woven that not one of the great mass thronging the avenues between the lodges seemed to notice him.

'The youngest!' Taws's voice was urgent as he faced Borsus. 'Remember that – the youngest. Any others if you can, but put a shaft into the youngest.'

'Master,' Borsus asked nervously, 'what if there is more than one? What if they are all young?'

'Then take them all!' snapped the mage, the ferocity in his voice sending the warrior back a step. 'But do not fail me. Fail me and you face the wrath of Ashar!'

Borsus nodded, licking dry lips, thinking that if he should fail he had best flee the Beltrevan and take his chances against the Lozin walls alone.

As if privy to the thought, Taws said, 'You have no choice between success and such eternal suffering as you cannot imagine. Fail and you are lost! You cannot hide from me, Borsus. Nowhere can you hide from me. Remember that, too – and do not fail me.'

'I shall not,' responded the warrior, hoping he sounded more confident than he felt, no longer sure that even clean death could forestall the Messenger's vengeance.

'Go now,' ordered Taws, and Borsus set foot to stirrup and climbed into the saddle, urging the now-docile stallion through the unseeing crowd, feeling like a quadi as he left the camp and climbed the valley side, out into the moonlit Beltrevan.

He rode cautiously at first, for as he went from Taws's presence all his wariness of the animal returned, but when the beast made no attempt to unseat him he grew steadily more confident. Whatever magic Taws had used on the stallion, it appeared to do more than merely render the animal docile. Borsus found himself sitting the simple saddle with a greater ease than he had ever experienced, his legs gripping the ribs as though he had sat a horse all his life, like some Keshi plainsman. The jarring, spine-tingling clash of buttocks with bony spine was gone, replaced by a fusion of purpose that rendered his movement one with the horse. He was surprised to find that he was comfortable, and as that realization dawned he chanced a greater speed, finding that of no more moment than if he were running on foot, so that he drove his booted heels against the flanks and gave the stallion its head.

Great trees flashed by him and he ducked, avoiding their branches with a casual expertise that brought a whoop from his lips, the night gallop becoming a thing of pleasurable excitement. He coursed game trails and the main forest paths, utilizing all his knowledge of the woodlands to make the best speed possible.

The last time he had travelled this far south he had been on foot, a warrior commanded by the bar-Offa Dewan, part of a raiding party led by Niloc Yarrum after Vistral slaves. Now he was riding the stallion of the hef-Ulan, still a warrior, but no ordinary man, rather – to judge by Taws's admonishments – a man entrusted with a task vital to the success of the Horde. He wondered if he would dare – if the Messenger would allow him – to speak of this to Sulya. Surely, it would increase his standing in her eyes.

But Taws, he recalled abruptly, had sworn him to secrecy, and that remembering set him to wondering afresh what urgency gripped the mage.

Whoever the youth he was riding to kill might be, he appeared to represent some threat to Ashar's purpose. Certainly, Borsus had never seen the sorcerer so perturbed. It was unlike him, but then the whole affair contained an element of mystery beyond the comprehension of a simple warrior. Why had Taws not announced his knowledge of the spy when it came? Why not alert the camp and set the entire Horde to scouring the forest? Surely that was the more certain way to apprehend the mysterious youth, to guarantee his death. Could it be that Taws did not wish Niloc Yarrum and the Ulans to know what transpired? Could it really have been fear Borsus had seen on that terrifying visage?

He did not know. He was a simple warrior, albeit favoured of the Messenger. What he did know, with a surety that brought a sudden coldness to the pit of his belly, was that he faced an unimaginably horrible fate if he failed his master. With that thought in mind he urged Niloc's grey horse to even greater speed, intent on reaching the egress of the High Fort road ahead of his unknown quarry.

He slowed his pace when the stallion began to labour, though not stopping until the sun was well up. Then he rested for a while, chewing on the dried meat he had thought to snatch as the animal munched grass. He continued through the remainder of the day, the novelty of his new-found horsemanship wearing off so that he maintained a more even speed, aware of the danger of exhausting the beast and finding himself afoot. He was accustomed to going without sleep on war marches and after the second day time blurred. He dozed, sometimes in the saddle and sometimes as he stretched on the ground, allowing the horse to rest, but never for long, preferring to kill the animal if he must rather than fail to set his ambush. And in time he came to the place where the timber of the Beltrevan gave way to the stone of the Lozins.

He reined in, staring at the massive peaks, the great blue ribbon of the Idre to his left, glimpsed through a fence of pine. It was close on the middle of the day, the sun almost directly above him, warm on his back, the air lazy with the sound of insects and the song of birds. Before him the High Fort road began, a wide, rocky avenue that rose steadily steeper into the cut that divided the mountains. If he was in time – and he prayed fervently to Ashar that he was – he would spot his target from here. He set about finding a suitable place.

He found it where the forest thinned and stone began, a borderland belonging properly to neither mountains nor woodlands. Grassy hummocks boundaried the road, the friendly timber of the Beltrevan to the north, the knolls thick with bushes and small, almost stunted trees, naked rock showing in places as if the bones of the land thrust out from the earth of its skin. He found himself a monticle that commanded a clear view of the road, looking down and to the north, close enough to the forest that he could escape there when his task was done, the Idre not far behind him. The hillock was almost completely encircled by dense bramble thickets, the thorn-crusted twistings a living barrier against cavalry, the few small trees that grew there pleasantly reminiscent of his familiar greenwood. He tethered the wearied stallion between the vantage point and the river, hidden by more copious timber, and ascended the knoll.

Bracing the bow against his knee he bent the yew wood, sliding the string securely into its fastening notches. He tested the pull and then drew an arrow from his quiver. It was the first time he had held the shafts since Taws had taken them, and when his fingers touched the ash he experienced an odd tingling sensation, almost as though the arrow was possessed of a life of its own. He licked his lips, studying the head, but saw nothing different, only the familiar metal, pointed and honed, the edges glittering where he had applied the whetstone, the recurved tails ugly in their threat of lodgement. Whatever ensorcellement Taws had set on the arrows was invisible, only that slight vibrancy indicating whatever power they held. Borsus notched the shaft and settled down to wait.

Fear that he had come too late was starting to stir before he heard the riders.

They were approaching fast, giving no heed to caution if the clatter of shod hooves on stone road was any indication. Borsus rose to his feet, camouflaged by brambles and trees, bowstring taut before they came into view. He held the red-dyed goose feathers of the flight against his cheek as he sighted down the shaft, dark eyes scanning the approaching party for the one Taws had not quite described.

There were a few more of them than he had fingers, dressed in motley tunics of brown and green and russet leather, mounted on big, deep-chested horses such as he knew the Kingdomers rode. They were armed with bows and swords, but the weapons were sheathed and they appeared more intent on speed than vigilance. He studied them with the swift eye of a natural hunter.

Four stood out immediately. One looked almost to be a tribesman, his hair plaited and decked out with feathers and shells, his features dark as any woodlander's; another was unlike any man Borsus had seen. He was shorter than his companions, a single oiled queue streaming behind a face strangely yellow in hue, with slanted eyes that shone a gleaming black against the sallow skin. The remaining pair looked to be father and son, such was the likeness of them, their faces cut from the same proudly handsome mould, the shoulder-length brown hair they wore in loose ponytails identical, save for the touch of grey that streaked the older man's. There were no other youths, and Borsus knew he saw the one Taws had told him to kill.

He moved a pace out from the tree and felt the fletchings of his shaft touch his lips. The arrowhead was steady on the young man's chest, sighted to pierce the heart. Borsus loosed the arrow.

It was Brannoc who gave warning.

He rode a pace or two behind Bedyr as the Tamurin scouting party thundered southwards, all caution forgotten in the need to bring word of the Horde's raising to the Kingdoms. He saw no more than a slight movement on the hummock to their left, a shifting that was not occasioned by wind or animal movement. He was not sure what moved there, only that even on the edge of the Beltrevan any unexpected movement was dangerous. He bellowed over the pounding of the hooves.

'Ware ambush!'

It was Tepshen Lahl who saved Kedryn's life.

Perhaps only the kyo could have moved so fast.

He flanked Kedryn, their horses racing side-by-side, Torim a head behind and to his right, the remainder of the men at their back. He heard Brannoc's warning cry and looked to where the outlaw pointed, his action simultaneous with the sighting.

His reins came over, turning his mount against Kedryn's even as he rose in his stirrups, hurling himself at full gallop from the saddle to crash against the youth. He struck Kedryn, pitching his charge sideways and forwards, Kedryn's horse wickering in surprise and faltering in its stride. One hand clutched the saddlehorn, the other Kedryn's shoulder, and the kyo was plunging between the animals, dragging Kedryn down.

Borsus's arrow struck, not the heart it was aimed at but the shoulder. Kedryn felt the twin shocks of kyo and shaft together, yelling in pain and confusion. Instinctively, he held his seat, clenching teeth against the fire that burst abruptly down his left arm, hand loosening on the reins so that his mount veered off to the right, dragged by the weight of Tepshen Lahl. It seemed the roar of the Idre filled his head, but through it he heard his father echo Brannoc's scream.

'Ambush! Ware ambush!'

Then all was confusion as Torim rode in close to reach down and fasten a hand on Tepshen's shoulder, hauling the smaller easterner up from between the animals that threatened to crush him, and the men behind were charging wild for the hillock.

Two went down with red-fletched arrows in their chests, and the horse of a third screamed and began to buck madly, reaching its head back in a vain attempt to snap at the shaft that protruded from its neck. Bedyr spun his stallion in its own length, putting his own body between his son and attack, his sword flashing bright in the afternoon sunlight. Brannoc raced on, circling the mound as the Tamurin charge broke against the bramble thickets and the warriors turned back, grouping around their lord and their prince. Kedryn shook his head, staring aghast at Tepshen Lahl's empty saddle.

'Tepshen!' he screamed. 'Ward Tepshen! Tepshen is down!'

Then a hand clamped on his good arm and he heard the familiar voice say, 'I am here, Kedryn. Look to yourself.'

He stared down, pain momentarily forgotten as he saw Torim lower the kyo to the ground, the long-bladed eastern sword already in his hands. A smile flashed between them and then Tepshen Lahl was gone, charging on foot up the hummock, a wordless battle shout erupting from his snarling mouth.

Men and horses obscured Kedryn's view, and he realized with some embarrassment that the Tamurin set themselves between him and the hidden archer. Past them he saw Tepshen reach the thorny barrier and crash through. Then pain flooded his body and he moaned, only dimly aware of Bedyr's shouted orders that the Tamurin take him clear.

He struggled to draw his sword, but the action drew the shoulder latchings tight against the protruding arrow and he groaned, kicking angrily at the man who moved to take his reins. Instead, he took the leathers himself, allowing the warriors to drive him forwards, bunched protectively about him. Turning in the saddle, he saw Bedyr and Torim, the one still with blade in hand, the other holding a bow, standing rearguard. Tepshen Lahl came back into sight, sword sheathed now, left hand moving flat across his chest to indicate the knoll was empty. Then the Tamurin had Kedryn in amongst the broken ground farther up the road and halted.

A warrior called Sylar bellowed orders and the men formed a circle about their prince, bows out with shafts notched to the strings. Sylar issued a fresh string of commands and six men dismounted, clambering to the nearest vantage points to cover the trail north. Kedryn used a sleeve to wipe sweat from his face and looked down at his wounded shoulder. Dark wood flighted with red feathers stuck at an almost vertical angle from his tunic, the leather darkening as it absorbed blood. He touched the shaft gingerly, seeking to test the depth of penetration, and winced as sharp pain brought bile to his throat. Even so, he could see it was not a killing wound: Tepshen Lahl had dragged him down so that instead of piercing the heart, the arrow had lodged between shoulder-blade and collar-bone.

'Can you ride?'

He recognized the concern in Sylar's voice, but pain and anger made his reply irritable. 'Of course! Should a flesh wound prevent me?'

Sylar smiled grimly. 'Good. Mayhap we shall need to. And fast.'

Kedryn nodded, his face apologetic. 'I can ride, Sylar. Forgive my temper.'

The Tamurin chuckled, making a dismissive gesture, and turned his mount to face down the trail.

Bedyr and Torim came back with Tepshen Lahl. The kyo's tunic and breeks were scored by thorn marks and scratches stood bloody on his face, but he ignored them, riding straight to Kedryn's side. Bedyr shouted for the men to regroup, his expression troubled.

'They have gone?' Kedryn asked.

'There was no one,' grunted Tepshen.

'One bowman,' Bedyr said, and his tone told Kedryn that this fact troubled him more than had it been a full scale ambush. 'Dismount.' Kedryn frowned his confusion and his father added, 'I must remove the shaft.'

Torim, his grizzled features angry, asked, 'Where is Brannoc?'

No one was sure, but when a warrior suggested the outlaw had fled, or perhaps deliberately taken them into the ambush, Bedyr shook his head saying, 'No, I do not think so.'

Kedryn swung awkwardly from the saddle, finding that any movement of his left arm set the arrowhead to grating painfully against the bone and watched with more than a little nervousness as his father unsheathed his dirk and Tepshen Lahl sprang lithely to the ground.

'Sit,' Bedyr ordered, and Kedryn obeyed instantly.

Tepshen Lahl squatted behind him as Bedyr used the dirk to slit the tunic around the arrow, then put both his arms around Kedryn, pinning the youth's to his side. Bedyr smiled briefly and took the shaft in both hands, the left hard against his son's shoulder. He said, 'This will hurt you,' and as he spoke broke the arrow. Kedryn gritted his teeth, determined not to whimper.

'I have been truly blooded,' he said instead, pleased with the grunt of approval that elicited from Tepshen and the smile Bedyr gave him.

'Thanks to Tepshen it is not serious,' Bedyr told him. 'Unless it was poisoned. I had best remove the head, though; and that *will* hurt.'

Kedryn shrugged as best he could, effecting nonchalence. Bedyr shouted for Torim to start a fire, fetching a whetstone from his saddlepack and drawing the sharpener along the cutting edges of his dirk. When the blade was honed to his satisfaction he passed it a few times through the flames and nodded to Tepshen. Again, the kyo encircled Kedryn with his arms, this time locking his fingers so that the youth was braced rigid.

'There is no pain,' he murmured in Kedryn's ear. 'There is only honour and dishonour.'

'I choose honour,' Kedryn replied, hoping that he could make good the boast as he saw his father bring the blade towards him.

It hurt horribly, but he did not cry out. He wanted to, but that would have shamed him and he was determined to show that he was as much a man as any here. He was glad for Tepshen's arms about him and the supportive strength of the kyo at his back. He stared fixedly as Bedyr cut into his flesh, opening a wound large enough that the barbed head might be withdrawn.

It came out bloody. Bedyr sniffed at it, then set it aside. He said, 'This will be worse.'

Kedryn wondered what could be worse, then found out when Bedyr set his dirk in the flames until the metal of the blade grew red before he pressed it to the wound. Then it was very hard not to scream, for Bedyr seemed to hold the heated metal against his flesh for a long time and the smell of scorching was accompanied by an agony so intense that the muscles of his jaw ached from the pressure of holding the cry inside. His vision blurred and he realized he must have fainted, for when he opened his eyes he was resting on his back and Brannoc had returned.

He heard the outlaw saying, 'There was one man. I chased him but he reached the forest, so I let him go. He waited in ambush and I do not understand that – why would just one man wait?'

Bedyr offered no answer, but passed the woodsman the arrow shaft. Brannoc studied it and said, 'Drott. A lone Drott. That is very strange.'

Kedryn sat up then and they helped him to his feet. Bedyr said, 'We must ride, Kedryn. Can you sit a horse?'

'Yes,' nodded the youth, noticing for the first time that cloth swathed his shoulder and his left arm was bound across his chest. 'If I can be helped into the saddle.'

They got him mounted and when he was astride the horse, he saw the two bodies and the carcase of the wounded animal, its throat slit to grant it a more merciful death. He said, 'I am sorry.'

'For taking a wound?' Bedyr asked. 'There is no shame in that.'

'No.' Kedryn shook his head. 'Because they died for me.'

'They died in battle, defending their prince,' said Tepshen Lahl, seeing no point in adding that such death was honourable.

Kedryn stared at the kyo and was about to protest that he had not meant that; that he was not certain what he meant. Only that he sensed somehow the ambush was intended for him alone. But Bedyr interrupted briskly, cutting off his explanation.

'There is no time for discussion. We ride!'

There was understandable urgency in his father's voice, but Kedryn sensed something more behind the words, saw something in Bedyr's expression that told him he should say no more on the subject. Dutifully, he fell silent, falling in behind Bedyr, Tepshen Lahl and Torim flanking him like broody hens warding a vulnerable chick.

Brannoc and three Tamurin ranged out ahead now, but there was no further attempt at ambush and they camped that night in the foothills of the Lozins, giving their dead decent burial, where their final resting place would not be disturbed by barbarians.

Kedryn wanted badly to ask Bedyr why the Drott had singled him out, for by now he was certain that had been the case, but he became feverish and could not find the proper words. Instead, he tossed in troubled sleep, his feverish dreaming filled with a corpse-pale face framed with snow-white hair, eyes that glowed like the blade his father had pressed to his shoulder transfixing him malevolently, a gash-lipped mouth whispering over and over, 'Die, Kedryn, die.' He started into wakefulness several times, to find Bedyr or Tepshen Lahl seated beside him, bathing his sweated face, murmuring encouragement, but when he tried to shape his question the words got lost and he fell back into disrupted slumber.

He was relieved when dawn came and he had only the throbbing of his shoulder to contend with. He could still sit a horse well enough, but the pace Bedyr set was fierce and he was forced to concentrate on riding to the exclusion of all extraneous thoughts, and when they camped again he was simply too weary to attempt any investigation of his suspicions. He decided to let them lay until the gates of High Fort were locked behind him.

But still he dreamed of that awful face.

It was there whenever he closed his eyes, as though he stared again at the great barbarian encampment and saw the creature turn towards him, seeking him through fire and distance and darkness. It filled him with a numbing dread akin to the dull throbbing of his shoulder, for he knew – without knowing how – that the dreams were somehow real, that if the creature could not actually *see* him, then it at very least knew him, and sought him. And that was, perhaps, the most frightening thing of all: that the creature sought him.

He was mightily glad when the north gates of High Fort came in view and the pace slowed, archers showing on the battlements, the catapults and mangonels armed ready for attack.

Bedyr rode out ahead then, right arm raised and his shout echoing off the Lozin walls.

'Open the gates for Bedyr Caitin! Tamur bids you open!'

The portals creaked back and the Lord of Tamur reined in his mount alongside his son's, his face anxious. 'The Sisters will tend you now, Kedryn. Their care will end the dreams.'

'You know?' Kedryn gasped.

'You spoke in your fever. I would have explained – as much as I am able – but I deemed it wiser to bring you safe to High Fort before I set it out in words. Forgive me, I was afraid.'

'Afraid?' It was not an admission Kedryn had expected to hear from his father.

'Aye.' Bedyr ducked his head in agreement and apology. 'After you are tended I will tell you everything I know. And hope you understand.'

Confusion gripped Kedryn more firmly for that, but there was no opportunity to question Bedyr further, for they were passing through the gates and Rycol was coming, grim-faced, from his vantage point on the wall, wearing half-armour, as though he anticipated forest folk on their tail.

'You are wounded!' He halted, staring at the bandaging of Kedryn's arm, then spun on his heel, shouting for men to aid the Prince of Tamur from his horse and carry him to the Sisters hospital.

Kedryn allowed the soldiers to assist him from his horse, but pushed them, one-armed, away when they would have lifted him like a helpless child. 'I need a guide, not a litter-bearer,' he grunted.

'He took an arrow,' Bedyr told the High Fort commander. 'Have a man escort him to the Sisters, and see my men fed – we've ridden hard. I'd speak with you instantly.' To Kedryn, he added, 'I'll join you once I've told Rycol of your exploits.'

'The Horde?' asked Rycol, unable to contain his curiosity.

'Is raised,' said Bedyr. 'And worse.'

Rycol's gaunt features paled. 'The Messenger?' His tone was hushed, almost fearful.

'In the privacy of your chambers,' Bedyr said. 'We need plan to our defence.'

Kedryn followed the serjeant Rycol charged with his care across the flagstoned plaza and into the maze of corridors that ran like a warren throughout the fort. Walking seemed strange after the long hours in the saddle, and to his irritated embarrassment he needed several times to halt, shaking his head to clear it of the mists that seemed to fill it, grunting his apology to the solicitous officer and finally allowing the man to lend strong arms to his support. He was pleased there were no questions, the serjeant more concerned with bringing his prince to the wards occupied by the Sisters, and returning to a post he clearly thought under threat of imminent attack.

Blue-robed hospitallers surrounded the young man as he entered the wards, parting as Wynett approached, her pretty face drawn by worry. For all her youthful appearance she was obviously in command, her orders obeyed unhesitatingly, issued with a calm confidence. Kedryn was led to a small, white-walled chamber, a single window attesting to the lateness of the day, sweet-perfumed plants with bright red flowers suspended in hanging baskets from the walls to cheer the otherwise plain plasterwork. He found himself blushing as his clothes were expertly removed and the redolence of his sojourn in the forest laved, his protests ignored by the women who viewed his naked body with the concerned indifference of midwives, or – he reminded himself – nurses. They settled him on the narrow wooden bed, the sheets pleasantly cool, and bustled out as Wynett reappeared, carrying a tray on which he saw pots and mortars and small surgical instruments. She set the tray down on a table beside the bed and used scissors to snip the bandages from his shoulder.

'How were you hurt?' she asked as she cut.

'An arrow,' Kedryn answered, suddenly aware that her fair hair smelled of apple blossom. 'My father cut it out. And cauterized the wound for fear of poison.'

Wynett frowned as she studied the ugly searing that marked his otherwise unblemished flesh. 'How long ago?'

'Two days,' he replied. 'At least I think it was two days ago – I grew feverish.'

Wynett nodded, turning from her perch beside him to bring a

phial from the tray, spilling three or four drops into a cup already filled with water.

'Drink this.' She passed him the cup and he smiled his gratitude, as much for the fact she made no move to feed him the potion as for her solicitude.

There was a faint bitterness to the draft, and when he had drained the cup Wynett pushed him gently back against the pillows and stared into his eyes. Gently, she eased the lids back, her fingers soft and delicate on his skin, her eyes very blue as they gazed into his. Whatever she saw there appeared to reassure her, for she smiled, nodding to herself.

'I do not think the arrow was poisoned, but I should like to examine it. Is that possible?'

Kedryn remembered the way Bedyr had set the head aside, rather than tossing it away, and said, 'I think my father may have it.'

'Good.' Her smile reminded him of summer dawns and he thought again that it was a pity she had chosen a celibate life. 'Now let me see the wound.'

Her hair brushed his chest as she bent close and he felt a fresh source of embarrassment stir beneath the sheet that covered his lower body. Wynett, however, appeared oblivious of the reaction, sniffing at the wound, then touching it gently. Kedryn winced at the slight pressure and Wynett made a small noise deep in her slender throat. Without saying anything more she took a pot from the tray and smoothed a greasy salve over the burned flesh, then motioned for him to sit up so that she could apply fresh bandages.

'You had best remain here tonight. You must not bathe, or move your arm. Tomorrow you can go to your own quarters, but you must return here each morning, and you must not remove the bandages.'

Kedryn nodded.

'Now,' Wynett smiled, 'tell me everything that happened.'

Kedryn told her, starting with their trailing of the barbarians to the great gathering and ending with Bedyr's removal of the arrow. As he recounted the tale she began to frown, the lines that showed between her eyes deepening as he spoke of the figure he had seen with such clarity.

'The others did not see him?' she asked.

'No,' Kedryn shook his head, 'they saw only distant men. Barbarians. We were too far away – I do not understand how I saw him. But I dreamed of him, after.'

'When?' she demanded, the sharpness in her previously soft voice alarming Kedryn.

'After I was wounded,' he replied. 'I dreamed of him. I saw his face, speaking to me, telling me to die.' He licked his lips, no longer sure, here behind the walls, safe, of the certainty he had felt on the Beltrevan road that the ambush was intended for him alone.

'Go on,' Wynett urged, 'tell me *everything*.'

'I cannot be sure,' he said slowly, 'but after the ambush – after I learnt there was only one man – I became convinced he was there to kill me. No one else, though he slew Daffyn and Ardor. I believe my father thought that, too, though he said nothing of it at the time. He promised to explain after you had tended me.'

'I think he will,' said Wynett thoughtfully, her eyes clouded now. 'I think he had best.'

'You know something of this.' Kedryn raised himself from the pillows, awkward with his tight-bound arm. 'Tell me.'

'I know a little,' Wynett murmured. 'I am a Hospitaller, not a far-seer or a sibyl, but all the Sisters know of the Messenger.'

'Brannoc said I had seen the Messenger,' Kedryn murmured.

'Where is your father now?' Wynett glanced round, as though expecting Bedyr to come through the door, but all that showed in the room beyond was a Sister busily crushing herbs with mortar and pestle.

'With Rycol, planning our defence,' he said.

Wynett pursed her lips, her face troubled. Then, surprising Kedryn with the apparent irrelevance of the question, asked, 'Do you know the Estrevan road?'

'Of course.' Lyassa's tutoring had included geography and he had found that interesting: his grasp of the Three Kingdoms' territory was reasonably comprehensive. 'I have never been there, but I have studied the maps. Through the Morfah Pass. Why?'

'It may be useful to you.' Wynett shrugged, seeming suddenly uncertain of herself. 'Perhaps . . . But I think we should wait for your father. Meanwhile, you must rest. Will you permit me to help you?'

'Shall I recover sooner?' he wondered.

'Rest will aid recovery,' she promised, 'and I can wake you when Bedyr comes.'

'Then yes,' he said, and allowed her to press him back against the pillows, watching as she cupped his face, enjoying the sensation of her hands on his skin, staring into her eyes. They were so blue, like the sky above Caitin Hold at midsummer, and her voice, murmuring softly, was like the gentle babble of a brook. A lassitude gripped him pleasantly and the room became dim.

He heard his father's voice and realized he had slept. The room was lit by torches now, their glow reminding him unpleasantly of the barbarian fires, the window shuttered against the night. He opened his eyes, seeing Bedyr and Wynett on stools beside the bed, the Sister holding a bloodied arrowhead with obvious distaste.

'It was not poisoned,' he heard her say, 'but it remains redolent of magic. I believe the intention was to mark him.'

'He would have died had Tepshen Lahl not acted so swiftly,' Bedyr responded, and Kedryn saw pain on his father's face. He said, 'Father?' and Bedyr turned.

'You are awake.'

'He is stronger than I thought,' said Wynett. 'Strong enough to hear what you should tell him, Bedyr Caitin. For his sake, and the Kingdoms'.'

'Aye,' Bedyr nodded. 'I owe you that explanation, Kedryn.'

Wynett rose, smoothing her gown, and smiled at her patient. 'I will have food brought.'

'Thank you,' Kedryn murmured, recognizing that she wished to leave him alone with Bedyr, feeling suddenly apprehensive.

Bedyr turned his stool to face his son as Wynett closed the door, his handsome features drawn with worry. He swept a hand through his long hair, and Kedryn saw that he had not yet changed from his riding gear.

'I had best tell this straight,' Bedyr began with uncharacteristic awkwardness, 'and after, I shall answer whatever questions you put to me. Are you thirsty?'

Kedryn nodded and Bedyr poured wine, passing his son a cup and taking one for himself. He drank deep, as might a man about to embark on a long or difficult story. Kedryn waited patiently, sipping his own.

'Your mother and I were agreed that you should hear this when you came of age,' Bedyr commenced. 'We had hoped to tell it together, for I am not sure I can explain as fully as she, much of it being to do with Estrevan. But you are blooded now and come of age, and circumstances dictate the telling should be different than our plans would have it, so . . .

'Yrla chose to quit the City of the Sisters because she read a text extracted from the Book of Kyrie by the Sister Alaria. As you know, the Sisters believe the Book foretells the future of the Three

Kingdoms – or at least indicates *possible* futures, possible threats. One such was found by Alaria.

'Her interpretation has it that one day Ashar would send his minion to raise the Horde and bring the forest folk southwards, their own might fortified by the magicks of the one called the Messenger. As in all things, there was a balance to this – counterweighting the powers of the Messenger would be one born of the Kingdoms. Out of the joining of Tamur and Andurel. Yrla, as you know, is of Andurel High Blood; I am Tamurin: you share our blood.

'You may be the one – the only one, if Alaria's text is correctly translated – able to defeat the Messenger.

'The Sisters saw the Messenger's coming some time past, but not until now was there any sign of the Horde. Now it is raised. We saw it. And you saw the Messenger. Wynett believes that only you *could* see him because your destinies are linked, and for that same reason he was able to see you. The arrow that wounded you was ensorcelled – I do not understand why only one man was sent, but I believe the intention was to kill you. Or, if that proved impossible – as, thank the Lady and Tepshen, it was – to mark you so the Messenger may find you at some later date.

'Wynett has set what barriers she can on that spelling, but we must seek the aid of Sisters more adept in such matters. There are such in Estrevan, of course, but also in Andurel, and that lies closer. And it is vital I warn Darr of these events.

'When you are healed, we must take the Idre south to Andurel. I shall send Tepshen to Caitin Hold with word for Yrla, but you must accompany me south. And Kedryn – whatever should transpire, you must at all costs avoid confrontation with the Messenger until we have got the advice of the Sisters. Do you agree?'

Kedryn did not notice the request: his head was spinning with the import of Bedyr's words.

He was the saviour of the Kingdoms?

The coming of age he had longed for so desperately no longer seemed so attractive. He felt very young again. And very frightened.

Chapter Seven

For long moments Kedryn stared at his father, confused and more than a little frightened by the magnitude of Bedyr's announcement. It was as though his world had turned suddenly on its head, catapulting him to a prominence he neither sought nor understood. He had ridden out from Caitin Hold a youth intent on proving himself a man, anticipating excitement and adventure, and he had found himself delivered of a responsibility he could scarcely comprehend, without any idea how he might dispense the duty Bedyr had so abruptly laid upon him. He drained his cup as if the wine might provide him with answers, but when none came he turned again to his father.

'How . . .' he began, then found he did not know exactly what he wanted to ask, and said instead, 'I do not understand.'

'Nor I fully,' said Bedyr, his brown eyes troubled. 'I know only what your mother has told me, and she is uncertain of the true meaning.' He rolled the plain earthenware cup between his hands, a frown lining his face. 'That she had to quit Estrevan for the world was all the plain fact she felt she could extract from the text – as you know, the Sisterhood places great emphasis on free will, so beyond that she was guided by her heart. She married me when she might have had her pick of the nobles of Ust-Galich or Kesh, the High Born of Andurel. For that I can only be glad, but beyond . . .' He paused, lifting the jug to pour wine into both their cups. 'Even when you were born – and no more children came – we were not certain. How could we be? It was all so vague. The seers of Estrevan foresaw the fire burning in the Beltrevan, but could not put time or location on the flames, only warn that the Messenger walked abroad. There was no sign of the Horde's rising and so Yrla and I decided we should say nothing. We debated long on that, but in the end it seemed too great a burden to lay on any child.

'Then the word came down. Warnings from Estrevan and Andurel, messages from Rycol, more from Fengrif, and we could only – is hope the correct word? I am not sure, but even then it seemed inopportune to tell you what we could only suspect – we hoped it might be no more than a stirring of the tribes.

'But then you saw what I and Tepshen and Brannoc could not, and I could no longer doubt. Nor any longer hope to save you this destiny. I would have told you then. By the Lady, Kedryn, I swear I would have told you had I not feared the knowledge might render you vulnerable to Ashar's minion! The ambush – your wounding – convinced me further. You were right in thinking that bowman waited for you alone, but when you *were* wounded I feared to speak lest that somehow should lay you open to the Messenger's designs.'

'My dreams,' Kedryn said softly. 'They were not dreams, were they?'

'They were dreams and not dreams, both,' Bedyr murmured. 'The mark that arrow set on you left you open to some sending of the Messenger.'

'He told me to die.'

The fear he heard suppressed in his son's voice brought Bedyr from the stool to Kedryn's bed. He set a hand on the good shoulder, the other clasping Kedryn's.

'A lesser man would have succumbed. And now the walls of High Fort and Wynett's ministrations will fend those fell sendings. Perhaps in Andurel the Sisters may have the means to remove the magic altogether. If not, then mayhap we shall go to Estrevan.'

'With the Horde at the gates?' Kedryn asked, feeling strengthened by his father's use of the simple word *man*. 'Tamur will have need of you, father.'

Bedyr smiled grimly. 'Tamur – the Three Kingdoms – may have greater need of *you*.'

'But I am nothing,' Kedryn objected. 'How can I be whatever it is the text says I am? How can I save the Kingdoms unless I fight? Even fighting, I am merely one more warrior, and not even very experienced.'

'I do not know.' Bedyr shook his head. 'I know only that somehow you hold the key to the Messenger's defeat.'

'Surely the text says more,' Kedryn protested. 'Surely the Sisterhood must know what I am to do.'

'No,' said Bedyr. 'The text is vague. Free will is all to the Sisters, and it would appear that in this matter even some small measure of guidance is too much, that any indication of the course you should take would be tantamount to outlining your path, the directions shaping your decisions and thus limiting your choices. I can offer no guidance other than the obvious advice that you should avoid the Messenger.'

'But how may I defeat him if I am to avoid him?' Kedryn wondered.

'You are a man now,' his father said gently, 'but still a young man. You have courage, and your skill with weapons is, perhaps, second to none, but the Messenger has all the fell power of Ashar at his beck, and I think that is more than you could handle. I do not say hide, only that you should exercise caution.'

'Advise me,' asked Kedryn, his grip on Bedyr's hand tightening. 'What should I do?'

'In view of what has happened,' Bedyr said carefully, 'and given the Sisterhood's concern with free choice I think I can only *advise*, but I would suggest that you rest here until Wynett considers you able to travel safely and then accompany me to Andurel. There we shall seek out Darr's Sisters. Beyond that I do not know.'

'You are Lord of Tamur,' Kedryn said loyally, 'and my place is at your side, in battle or in peace, though I think we shall know little of that in the days to come. I shall go with you to Andurel.'

Bedyr smiled then and Kedryn felt relief in the pressure of his hands. 'There is no one else knows this,' he said, 'other than Yrla and the Sisterhood. Not even Tepshen, though I believe he suspects, as does King Darr. For your own safety, it might be best you say nothing of it.'

'No,' Kedryn agreed, 'I think that the wisest course. If people knew what the text suggests they might expect from me what I do not know how to give. I am not sure what *is* expected of me, so I think it best I remain what I am . . . what I have been,' he added warily.

'Well said,' Bedyr applauded.

A discreet tapping at the door interrupted them then and when Bedyr invited entry, Wynett appeared, bearing a loaded tray from which appetising smells wafted. She set it down and glanced at Bedyr.

'You have told him?'

'Everything,' said the Lord of Tamur.

'And how do you feel about it?' she asked Kedryn, her blue eyes enigmatic.

'Frightened,' he said. 'And . . . proud? I have done nothing to be proud of, but I am pleased I may be of service to my land. However that is to be.'

'You have become a man,' she told him, smiling so that he felt his chest swell with genuine pride. 'I am not versed in these matters, so I can offer little advice other than to live your life in accordance with the teachings of the Lady and your duties as a prince of Tamur. Do what you believe is right, Kedryn: no man can do more.'

With that she left them, and Kedryn found that the odours emanating from the tray were the most pressing thing on his mind. He was mightily hungry and as – he decided with blunt pragmatism – there appeared to be no way he could define the course his life was to take other than by living it, he had best apply himself to matters in hand.

He filled his belly, and with Bedyr's help drained the fresh wine jug, after which he found himself pleasantly sleepy.

'Rest,' advised his father, 'there will be no dreams, and the sooner you are recovered, the sooner we shall be on our way.'

Kedryn nodded drowsily, then raised himself from the pillows. 'The defences! What of those?'

'Rycol has sent word to Low Fort,' Bedyr assured him, 'and Fengrif attends a council on the morrow. Wynett says you may be there, so you will be privy to whatever is decided. There is little we can do for now, though, other than seal the gates and man the walls. In any event, there is time – that large a mass cannot move fast, even with Ashar's minion at the head. So sleep – you have earned the rest.'

He rose, bestowing a fond, proud smile on his son, and left the room. Kedryn settled back against the soft sheets, only to find Wynett returned, offering him the slightly bitter medicine again. He drank it and fell almost instantly into a deep slumber. He dreamed, though not of the Messenger, but of a girl with golden hair and blue eyes who took his hand and led him through sun-kissed meadows where birds sang and deer watched their passing with gentle gaze, unafraid, for they knew no harm was threatened.

He woke as the dream was entering a most interesting stage involving the fastenings of the girl's dress, feeling mildly disappointed that he could not linger a while longer to discover what lay beneath the clinging blue gown. He stretched, yawning, then sat up, aware that he felt much recovered. The throbbing was gone from his shoulder and although he could not move the arm for the securing bandages, he felt certain it was becoming usable again. He pushed back the sheets and rose, crossing to the shutters to pull them back and let in the sun. The air was cool on his face, hinting at the proximity of autumn and sweet with scents. He stared out of the window, seeing that his room looked on to a walled garden where Sisters were already busy tending the shrubs and flowers that grew there. One glanced up, catching his eye and waving. Kedryn waved back, smiling, thinking that if all this was what he was to save then it would be easy to find a sense of purpose.

'I am glad to find you so recovered.'

He turned at the sound of Wynett's voice, then blushed as he realized he was naked, covering himself with his good hand as he darted back to the bed, where sheets afforded him modesty.

The Sister hospitaller smiled mischievously, setting down a breakfast of fresh-baked bread already spread with creamy butter, eggs and cheese, with thick slices of cold meat, and a large mug of aromatic tisane.

'You are not the first naked man I have seen.' She chuckled at his reddened features, adding to his somewhat confused pleasure, 'But few have been so handsome. All over.'

Kedryn stared at her departing back, wondering if Sisters ever changed their minds to forego their vows of celibacy. Then appetite became paramount and he devoured the food, clearing the tray before Wynett returned to mix more medicine and dress his shoulder afresh.

'It is healing well,' she told him. 'You may go to your own quarters today, though I imagine you will want to attend the council first. Fengrif is on his way now.'

She indicated the clothes she had brought with her and left him alone. Kedryn found undergarments and breeches secured by clasps so that he was able to don them one-handed, a knee-length tunic of soft, dark blue cloth that had no fastenings other than a belt again secured by a simple clasp. He dressed as swiftly as he was able and went looking for the council.

It was held in Rycol's private chambers, the fort commander's wife herself ushering Kedryn towards a door of polished oak, delaying his entry with murmured condolences on his wounding and genuine concern in her green eyes. He smiled his thanks for her felicitations, remarking to himself on the disparity between husband and wife. The Lady Cador na Rycol was small and round, with abundant red hair coiffed about a plump-cheeked face aglow with maternal concern. Kedryn assured her politely that his wound was healing rapidly, thanks to the ministrations of High Fort's excellent Sisters hospitaller and this seemed to mollify her, for she allowed him to reach the door and go through into the room beyond.

He was surprised by the books that lined one wood-panelled wall, for Rycol seemed too much the stiff-backed soldier to give much time to literature, and he saw that many of the texts had nothing to do with matters military. Ducking his head, he bade formal greeting to the men seated about the long table that dominated the centre of the chamber, their sombre countenances a contrast to the sunlight streaming in through the high windows lining the wall facing the shelved books.

Bedyr sat at the head, his borrowed tunic marked with Tamur's fist, Rycol to his left and Fengrif to his right, the Keshi's rotund cheeks seeming hollowed by the import of Bedyr's news. Tepshen Lahl sat beside Rycol and Brannoc faced him across the dark wood, his decorated hair exotic against the simpler styles of his companions. Kedryn followed his father's prompting gesture to the high-backed chair at the far end, realizing that he arrived on the tail end of a discussion that was not entirely to Rycol's liking.

'He gave loyal service,' Bedyr was saying, so that Kedryn guessed the subject was the impudently grinning Brannoc – no longer, he assumed, to be considered outlaw, 'and I gave Tamur's word that he would be pardoned any offences. He will be useful, old friend.'

Rycol's thin mouth pursed, his gaze hard on Brannoc's face, doubt in his eyes. Brannoc smiled back and shrugged. 'You need not swear undying friendship, commander, but for whatever you consider it worth, I give you my word I *am* loyal. What I saw in the Beltrevan persuades me that any sensible man must oppose what is coming – and you know me for a sensible man.'

Rycol was about to reply when Tepshen Lahl interjected: 'He saved Kedryn's life.'

The gaunt face swung to study the kyo uncomprehendingly. 'The way I heard it told, *you* did that. Your action brought our prince clear of the arrow.'

'I did not see the bowman,' grunted Tepshen, his usually impassive features registering self-disgust. 'Had Brannoc not cried out, the shaft would have taken Kedryn in the heart.'

Rycol digested this news, stroking his fresh-shaven jaw, and looked again to where Brannoc lounged as though he were daily privy to these councils. Rycol grunted once and said, 'I apologize.'

'I accept,' grinned Brannoc, and turned to Kedryn. 'How are you, Prince?'

'Well, thank you,' Kedryn responded, answering the grin with one of his own, 'and better still if you were to use my name.'

Brannoc nodded and Bedyr tapped the table lightly.

'Now that is settled, let us discuss our strategy. Brannoc, you know the Beltrevan better than any here – give us your thoughts.'

The former outlaw straightened a little, reflectively twisting a plait between the fingers of his left hand. 'The tribes are joined in the great Confederation. The Drott have migrated southwards, which means they crossed Yath land – which in turn means the Yath are with them. We saw Grymard and Vistral moving to join the Horde under truce poles, and I saw Caroc in the camp. I would estimate the entire forest is raised against the Kingdoms. Exactly how many warriors that may be, I cannot guess. But more now even than in Drul's time.

'There is more,' he added when Fengrif moved to speak, 'and worse. It was not just a warrior camp – *all* the forest folk were there! The entire Beltrevan is on the move. Old men and children, women. Do you comprehend what that means?'

'Migration,' murmured Rycol.

'Aye,' said Brannoc, 'a migration that leaves nothing behind. *Nothing*! They have quit their traditional territories to come south. If I know the woodlanders, that means they intend to come through the Lozin gates or die on the walls. There will be no turning back.'

'How many?' asked Fengrif, licking his lips nervously.

'More than may be counted,' said Bedyr. 'From where we watched, the camp spread farther than the eye could see. I believe Brannoc is correct, and that means the Three Kingdoms are outnumbered. The Beltrevan is larger than Tamur, Kesh and Ust-Galich together – we face horrendous odds.'

'Corwyn built the Lozin Forts against that eventuality,' Rycol grated, his voice harsh, 'and Drul's Horde broke on our gates. Even aided by the Messenger, can they succeed?'

All eyes turned towards Bedyr. He stared back, his jaw set firm in a grim expression. 'I do not know,' he said honestly, 'but if the Book is correct, the Messenger wields unimaginable powers. I believe they may be strong enough to breach the gates.'

'Against men our defences are impregnable,' Fengrif offered. 'We boast twenty centuries between us. Catapults; mangonels; the river barriers; the signal towers, even, when their lenses are directed into the chasm. Surely if we decimate the Horde, the Messenger himself must go down. How can he win if we destroy his army?'

'I do not know.' Bedyr's hand clenched in a fist that thudded dully against the table. 'I know only that the Book foretells such danger as is unprecedented in all the history of the Kingdoms.'

'They can approach only along the roads,' Fengrif continued doggedly, 'and there we have them bottled. Whatever their strength, we can pick them off. The roads will block with their dead. The river? We loose the booms and any boats they use can be burnt where they float; sunk by the catapults.'

'Ashar thrives on fire,' murmured Brannoc, the comment stilling the Keshi commander's flow. 'It is said his Messenger is born of fire. I do not think fire would be a wise weapon to use against him.'

Fengrif's plump face became dolorous. 'Would you limit our advantages, Brannoc?'

The dark-skinned man shrugged, shaking his head, his smile gone now. 'No, Lord Fengrif, I would give us every advantage we can dream of, but I do not believe we may number fire amongst them. I believe the balefire of your catapults, the burning of your lens, may serve to strengthen the Messenger, not weaken him.'

'How?' Fengrif protested, unwilling to relinquish the point.

Brannoc shrugged and said, 'I do not know how. I know only what I believe. Certainly, it is what the forest folk believe.'

'There may be sense in it,' Bedyr interposed before the Keshi could speak in argument. 'Like Brannoc, I do not know. Perhaps we should ask Kedryn for his opinion: he has come closer – if that is the right word – to Ashar's minion than any other here.'

Kedryn swallowed, self-consciously straightening his back, aware of a reluctance to even discuss his paranormal encounter. But, he reminded himself, it was his duty; and if he truly was the one Alaria's text described, then sooner or later he must surely face the enemy. Whatever the outcome.

'I saw him *through* fire,' he began. 'The blaze at the camp's centre lay between us, but still I saw him. And when I dreamed of him, he was surrounded by flame. More than that I cannot say.'

He glanced apologetically at his father, feeling that he added little of any use, but Bedyr smiled, nodding thoughtfully. The others studied him curiously, as if wondering why he should have been so singled out, though he thought he saw in Brannoc's eyes something more, something that might have been suspicion, or perhaps pity. He was grateful for Bedyr's next words.

'It would seem we cannot be certain. I would suggest, therefore, that fire be used with caution. We cannot afford to forego the potential advantage of balefire and lens, but let their use be sparing until the effects may be known. And cease instantly on the first sign of . . . what, Brannoc?'

Again Brannoc shrugged. 'I know not, Lord Bedyr.'

'Riddles,' snapped Rycol. 'Riddles piled on riddles.'

'We face an unknown foe,' Bedyr said gently. 'We know only that the Book says he is strong, therefore we must exercise caution.'

'I am a soldier,' Rycol answered, not straightening, for he was ramrod stiff from the start. 'I know how to fight and I know how to hold a fort. I can do either of these things, and if Ashar himself stands with the Horde I will fight him!'

'Your courage is unquestioned,' Bedyr responded politely, though Kedryn could see he fought a degree of irritation, 'but what we face is the unknown. Courage may not be enough.'

Fengrif cleared his throat, his dark eyes troubled. 'I am persuaded we must be wary in our use of fire, but if – as – we face an opponent whose powers are beyond those of plain soldiers such as Rycol and myself, should we not seek the aid of those with matching strengths? I mean the Sisterhood, of course.'

'I intend to ask whatever aid the Sisterhood can give,' Bedyr promised. 'As you know, I travel to Andurel once we are done here, and I shall seek audience with the Sisters there. But I am by no means sure they can help.' He paused, waiting for the startled expressions to fade from the faces of his comrades before continuing, 'The teachings of Kyrie do not seem to lend themselves to warfare. No doubt Sisters will come to both forts to succour the wounded, and their powers will doubtless increase the morale of our men, but I am not certain they will be able to lend active help.'

'You say we must face Ashar's minion unaided?' Fengrif gasped.

'I say I do not know what assistance the Sisterhood may give in battle,' corrected Bedyr. 'They will doubtless speed the healing of wounds – as Kedryn's presence testifies – but if you are looking for magicks to counter magicks, I do not know.'

'Is anyone sure of their powers?' asked Brannoc.

'I know them as healers, as far-seers,' said Rycol. 'Sibyls and spiritual guides. Wynett has often aided me in judging men. I have had no need of their aid in battle before.'

'We need it now,' grumbled Fengrif, tugging on his long moustache. 'By the Lady, we need all the help we can get!'

'Aye,' said Bedyr, 'and I have no doubt the Lady *will* help us, though I do not pretend to know how.'

'You offer us little hope, Bedyr,' Rycol said. 'It seems all we can do is lock the Lozin gates and fight. And hope Estrevan has the power to aid us.'

'That is,' Bedyr admitted, 'the shape of it.'

Rycol smiled then, fiercely. 'In that case,' he said, seeming almost relieved by the absence of options, 'I will do what I am good at – I will fight.'

Fengrif touched beringed fingers to the horse head of Kesh that was picked out in gold on the chest of his green robe. 'We shall both fight, my friend: I think we shall have little choice in that particular matter, but there is more to it.' He paused, his round face thoughtful, as though he marshalled his words, seeking those that would best express his concern. 'Were we facing only the Horde I should be as sanguine as you, but we are not. We face the Messenger and my Lord Bedyr has made clear that his powers are unguessable. I trust no one will consider me a doomsayer if I ask – what if we cannot hold them?'

There was silence in the sunny room. Kedryn studied the five men, seeing four faces that spoke of an inner wrestling with a consideration hitherto uncontemplated, now to be confronted no matter how distasteful. Only Tepshen Lahl's features remained impassive, as though the kyo had known such an option before and accepted it now with complete fatalism. Brannoc's smile was gone, his visage graven as if the enormity of the concept robbed him of all humour. Rycol appeared aghast, his expression giving mute answer: *then I shall be dead*. Fengrif blushed darkly, seeming embarrassed by his own question. Bedyr's cheeks hollowed, his eyes narrowing. Finally, breaking the leaden silence, he said, 'You force us to the point, Fengrif.'

The Keshi raised apologetic shoulders and Bedyr made a placatory gesture.

'It is a point we had to reach eventually. Now is as good a time as any: we must plan for every contingency. So,' he turned grave eyes to the fort commanders, 'as Lord of Tamur and representative here of King Darr, I give you orders I know are not necessary, for they are what I believe you would give yourselves. But let any blame fall on me. You will hold your forts to the last man. Whatever sorceries Ashar's minion may bring against you, *you must hold!* The Kingdoms need time and you may be the only men able to buy it.

'I would remain here with you, but I believe the Kingdoms are better served by my departure for Andurel. There I shall secure Darr's ear to the gravity of the situation. I have no doubt that the King will instantly mobilize the full strength of the Kingdoms, and if you can hold out that strength may tell.

'I shall – as I have said – seek the advice of the Sisterhood and bring back to you whatever aid may be found there. But I fear the Horde will be upon you before I can return, so I say to you – hold the

Lozin gates to the last man, for the future of the Kingdoms may well rest on the siege.'

'We shall hold!' barked Rycol, seemingly pleased by a situation he could readily understand. 'You need not doubt, Bedyr.'

'I did not,' assured the Lord of Tamur, his smile grim. He looked to where Tepshen Lahl sat. 'You will not accompany us to Andurel, my friend. You will lead our Tamurin back to Caitin Hold and apprise my lady of the situation. Listen to whatever advice she offers! I shall give you letters for Estrevan, and you will dispatch them instantly. I . . .'

He broke off, surprised, as Tepshen Lahl shook his head and said, 'My place is at Kedryn's back. I took oath on that.'

Kedryn stared at the kyo with amazement writ large on his features. Never before had he heard Tepshen question an order: obedience was integral to the easterner's code of honour. That he should take such exception now was an unprecedented statement of his regard for the young man, and it filled Kedryn with a poignant tenderness.

Bedyr understood, for he ignored Rycol's snort of anger and smiled sadly at the slant-eyed man. 'Tepshen, Tepshen, look to your own teachings in this,' he murmured, his voice mild. 'Kedryn is Tamur and while he is in Andurel he will have his back to the danger – you will ward him best from Caitin Hold. I would trust no other with this. Do you not see? Let Tamur fall and Kedryn stands landless. And do not forget the Sandurkan! Our Tamurin will be employed against the Horde, and that will weaken our defences along the Kormish Wastes – I have little doubt the desert nomads will seize that advantage, and then I shall need your wisdom.'

Kedryn spoke then, ignoring what little protocol existed and careless of what Rycol or Fengrif might think of his interruption. 'Tepshen, you are my father in spirit, but in this I believe the father of my flesh is right: go back to Caitin Hold and guard my mother. I ask you to do this.'

The jet eyes turned towards him, a smile in which both pride and regret mingled, creasing the pale features. Tepshen Lahl said, 'Do you order this?'

Kedryn's face was solemn as he replied, not sure where the words came from, but knowing what he should say, 'I *ask* it, but if I must order it, then an order it shall be.'

'Now I know you are truly a man, my Prince,' Tepshen responded, 'I do not like it, but I will do as you say. I will go back and hold your kingdom for you.'

'Thank you,' Kedryn said, the words too small to encompass the gratitude and the love he felt for this enigmatic man who had chosen to devote his life to Tamur.

'What of me?' asked Brannoc.

Bedyr's attention was focused on the exchange between his son and the kyo, but he answered promptly: 'Be the horsefly we discussed. May I assume you were not alone in your previous ... occupation?'

'You may,' said Brannoc, his smile returning for an instant.

'And since you enjoyed the confidence of our loyal Fengrif, I imagine you may well have equal sway with your fellow freebooters.'

This produced a chuckle from Brannoc; an embarrassed clearing of the throat from Fengrif.

'There are some who have listened to my advice on occasion.'

'Go to them,' Bedyr said, 'seek them out and persuade them that their own best interests lie in the defence of the Kingdoms. If the Horde comes through the Lozin gates, sting. If it moves south, sting. Take this,' he drew a ring from the second finger of his right hand, passing it to Brannoc, 'show that and the paper I will give to you to any official of the Kingdoms and it will be accepted as my word. When I come north again with Darr's army, join us. But meanwhile, should it prove needful, strike where you may inflict the most damage.'

Brannoc nodded, turning the ring between his fingers, staring at the seal engraved on the raised boss. It was the badge of Tamur.

'You had best have a title,' Bedyr said, waving down Rycol's snort of protest, 'perhaps ... Commander of Auxiliaries?'

'It will be a change from wolfshead,' nodded Brannoc, grinning again now, as if even the threatened cataclysm was insufficient to dampen his spirits for long. 'Does it mean I stand equal to my lords Fengrif and Rycol?'

Kedryn found it difficult to suppress a laugh at that, especially when he saw Rycol's face.

'Perhaps not quite,' Bedyr responded tactfully. 'Let us say that you command in matters auxiliary, independent of the forts. But within the boundaries of High and Low Forts you come under their command.'

'I had better stay in the field, then,' smiled Brannoc.

'That might be wiser,' agreed Bedyr. 'Now, may we assume we are in accord?'

One by one they nodded.

'Good.' Bedyr rose. 'Then perhaps we can eat and be on our way – there is little enough time.'

It seemed to Kedryn, as they left the chamber, that he had contributed little other than to persuade Tepshen Lahl to return to Caitin Hold. He wondered if Alaria's text might be wrong, or wrongly interpreted, though it felt close to blasphemy to consider such a possibility, but he could not see how he might be of any benefit to the Kingdoms other than as a warrior. Were he manning the walls of High Fort he would, he felt, be of some use. Or returning home with Tepshen to rally the men of Tamur, either against the barbarians from the north or the desert raiders out of the Kormish Wastes. He could understand the need for Bedyr to journey south to Andurel, but saw little value in his accompanying his father. His shoulder, he felt certain, would be healed well enough to raise a shield or hold a bow by the time the Horde reached the gates, but by that time – it seemed – he would be far away in Darr's city. He felt almost as though he was running away, turning his back on the fight, but Bedyr was clearly intent on taking him south and he could see no alternative. Having persuaded Tepshen that the kyo must obey even so clearly an unpalatable command, he did not wish to contradict his own advice. And, he was forced, albeit reluctantly, to admit, were he to remain in High Fort he would be merely one more warrior, his presence unlikely to make much difference to the outcome.

Kyrie's Book was enigmatic: he wished it were more obvious, for then he would at least have some clearer notion of what he was supposed to do. As it stood, it seemed he could only continue to obey orders and allow his father to make the decisions as Lord of Tamur, and that – for all it was the way he had lived his life until now – was frustrating. If he was in some unexplained way the hope of the Kingdoms, it seemed he should have some greater degree of instruction. Perhaps, he decided, such enlightenment would be found in Andurel.

These thoughts occupied him through the meal so that he paid less attention than he would usually have accorded to the excellent venison or to the conversations surrounding him as he sat at the high table. He listened with half an ear to the string of orders Rycol issued to the officers he summoned, calling up missiles from the armouries, organizing the strengthening of the watches, generally putting High Fort in a state of battle-readiness. He responded politely to Fengrif's farewells when they had done eating and the Keshi announced his departure for Low Fort, a half-formed notion taking shape in his head. Bedyr announced that they would take passage downriver at dawn and returned to his quarters to draw up papers for Brannoc and write the letters he wished Tepshen to carry back to Caitin Hold and send on to Estrevan. There seemed little profit in watching as his father wrote, and with one arm still unusable he could offer little help to the squads bringing catapult missiles and stocks of arrows to the battlements, so he went looking for Sister Wynett.

She greeted him with a smile as he entered a room whose walls were lined with shelves on which stood the paraphernalia of her art: jars and jugs and phials and bottles ranked in colourful rows. As she looked up from behind a simple table littered with parchments, sunlight from the window behind her rendered her hair a brighter gold, so that her face seemed haloed.

'I thought I might see you,' she told him, motioning towards a chair before the makeshift desk. 'How is your shoulder?'

'Mending,' he said, 'but that is not why I came.'

'No.' Her smile remained, but it changed subtly, becoming more serious. 'You came about your . . . responsibilities?'

'How did you know?' Kedryn sat, frowning.

'It is not difficult to guess,' she laughed. 'Yesterday you were Kedryn of Tamur; today you learnt the fate of the Kingdoms may rest upon your shoulders. You feel no different. You have not changed. You wonder why not. Am I right?'

He nodded. 'I do not know what I should do. What is expected of me?'

'Your duty, no more,' she said, serious now as she saw the doubt in his eyes. 'It is, mayhap, harder that way, but I believe it is the only way. It would be easy if the Book set down rules for your conduct – told you what you should expect, how you should conduct yourself, but that is not Kyrie's way.'

'I might wish for clearer instructions,' he muttered, more than a little morose. 'I am told the fate of the Kingdoms may rest upon my actions, but even that is not definite. My father believes it is so, but he admits he is not absolutely sure. And nothing tells me what to do.'

'I told you before that I am a Sister hospitaller,' Wynett replied, gently pushing the papers aside so that she might rest elbows on the table, her eyes steady on his face. 'We of Estrevan follow the callings of our natures, which means we tend to specialize. Oh, I know people consider us all to be gifted of the Lady, which we are, though not in the way most folk believe. We develop our talents in the City of the

Lady; we learn what they are, and when we know we go out to practise them. Mine proved to be the art of healing, not that of the far-seers or the sibyls or the interpreters, or any of the myriad other more subtle skills. I was blessed with the ability to help the hurt – and I am thankful for that – but I cannot intepret the teachings of Kyrie beyond the simplest form. For that you need the Sisters you will find in Andurel, or perhaps Estrevan herself. I cannot tell you what to do, Kedryn – that is something you must find out for yourself.'

'Free will,' he grunted, dissatisfied.

'Free will,' she confirmed, 'for without free will there can be no choice, and without choice there can be no true loyalty, no true purpose.'

'Tepshen Lahl might argue with that,' Kedryn grumbled, feeling she talked in circles that brought him ever back to the beginning of his confusion. 'He might argue that obedience is all, and how can there be obedience without clear instruction, without leadership?'

'Tepshen Lahl chose that course,' Wynett answered. 'I cast no doubt upon his worth, but he is from the east, and there people obviously hold different beliefs. Does he believe in the Lady?'

Kedryn found himself startled by the question: it was not a subject he had discussed with the kyo, but when he thought about it, he shook his head. 'I do not think so. I think he respects the teachings, but gives them no great heed. His loyalty is to his chosen master.'

'You said *chosen*,' Wynett pointed out. 'May I assume you agree with me?'

Kedryn chuckled then, for her blue eyes sparkled as she smiled and her lips were red and full. He shook his head. 'A Hospitaller? You weave words as skilfully as any.'

'I speak from what I know. From what I learnt in Estrevan. We all choose, even if our choice is not to choose. Do you not see it? The Lady has it that we are all masters of our own destinies, that our lives are a series of choices. Without that we are but puppets.'

'I would choose to serve the Lady as best I may,' Kedryn affirmed, frowning again now, 'but I should welcome some clarification of my options.'

'If you have faith,' Wynett assured him, 'that will come. You must do what you believe is right. I cannot advise you better.'

'Do you think I should go to Andurel?' he asked bluntly. 'It seems almost as if I run from the battle.'

'I do not think you would do more good remaining.' Wynett leant forwards, so that he caught a waft of the apple blossom scent of her hair. 'Rycol and Fengrif will hold the forts as well as any man. What do you think?'

The point was turned and Kedryn shrugged. 'I had considered that, but I think you are right – one more warrior will not sway the outcome of the siege.'

'You see?' she said, eyes twinkling. 'You are already making choices. You could have stayed – Bedyr would not have prevented you.'

Kedryn paused: she was right. His father had only advised, leaving the ultimate decision to him, and he had opted to travel south. It dawned on him that he had not considered returning to Caitin Hold, and that – in a way – was another free choice. He nodded.

'I think I begin to see.' Then he added, 'But I should still welcome some hint as to what I must do.'

'And I cannot give you that.' For an instant a sadness passed across the pretty features of the Sister. 'Perhaps you will find it in Andurel.'

'It appears increasingly obvious that I should go there,' he allowed.

'It does,' Wynett agreed. 'And against that choice, I have prepared medicines for your shoulder. Before you arrive, your arm should be fully healed.'

'You never doubted I would go,' Kedryn gasped, protestingly, though he smiled as he said it.

'I felt sure you would see it as the wisest course,' she smiled. 'And given the urgency of our situation, I felt it best to prepare in advance. May I show you what you must do?'

He nodded and she rose in a soft swirl of blue, fetching a small satchel from a shelf, lifting her arms so that he could not help but gaze at the thrust of her breasts beneath the simple gown.

'This,' she told him, bringing a phial of dark brown glass from the bag, 'is to be taken at dawn and dusk until it is used up. Apply this ointment for the next four days, and change the bandages each time. By then the flesh should be healed and you will be able to use the arm again. But avoid too much exertion of the muscles and consult any Sisters hospitaller you encounter on the journey.'

She replaced the containers in the satchel and handed it to him, the action bringing their fingers into contact. Kedryn fought the impulse to take her hand. Instead, he weighed the bag and smiled.

'Do these things also ward me against the Messenger's sorcery?'

Wynett's brow darkened on mention of the name. 'They will, as will distance. In this I concur wholeheartedly with your father – until your way becomes clearer to you, it is undoubtedly the wiser course to stand well clear of Ashar's minion.'

Kedryn nodded, then asked, 'And you? What will you do when the Horde reaches the gates?'

'My duty,' said Wynett simply. 'I am Paramount Hospitaller to High Fort: I shall have plenty to do.'

'High Fort may fall,' said Kedryn, the words heavy on his tongue. 'What then?'

'Then I expect the forest folk will kill me,' she answered with a fatalism worthy of Tepshen Lahl.

'I should not want that,' Kedryn mumbled, blushing.

'Nor I,' Wynett said before he could speak further, 'but I cannot leave while my skills are needed, so I have made my choice.'

'I hope King Darr's army will arrive before that happens,' he murmured.

'So do I,' Wynett smiled, then gestured at the littered table, 'but meanwhile I must prepare, so perhaps we should say farewell now.'

'I wish,' Kedryn faltered, afraid of giving offence, but finding it impossible not to say something of what he felt, 'that . . . if you did not wear the blue . . . then . . . perhaps . . .'

'But I do; I chose it.' Wynett looked into his eyes with a fond understanding. 'But if I did not . . . Well, you are a very handsome man, Prince Kedryn. All over.'

He felt the flush climb upwards from his throat to engulf his face, then saw her smile and began to chuckle. He wondered if it was a sign of growing maturity that he was able to execute a most courtly bow, bidding formal farewell in a manner that would doubtless have delighted Sister Lyassa.

He also wondered, as he left the peaceful chambers that constituted the wards of the Sisters hospitaller, how many more farewells he would need to make before his world settled again to its normal course. If ever it was to settle.

He carried the satchel to his chambers and stowed it with his gear. His bow and quiver were racked there as before, the sword he had not yet used in battle alongside, fresh clothes for the journey down the Idre set out in readiness: undergarments and three shirts, a soft leather tunic bearing the crest of Tamur, and breeks, boots with corded twine woven into the leather soles that they might find purchase on the deck of a riverboat, and his cloak, laundered after the nights spent spread on the ground of the Beltrevan. He found his dagger belt and succeeded after several attempts to fasten it about his waist, drawing the long-bladed Tamurin dirk. The honed steel shone deadly bright in the sunlight that now filled the chasm of the Idre, spilling throught the window as if in defiance of the looming darkness to the north. He studied the weapon, recalling the lessons given by Tepshen Lahl in its use, both alone and as counterpart to the sword. There was a lethal beauty in its pure functionality, the cannell blade edged on both sides, the quillons flattened to guard the wielder's hand, slightly arched that an opposing blade might be blocked and turned, the scale cross-strapped with leather to afford a secure grip, the pommel weighty enough to deliver a stunning blow. He slid it back into the plain leather sheath, thinking of what Wynett had said to him and promising himself that he would do his best to adhere to her advice: like the dirk, he would remain sheathed until he knew he was needed.

He crossed to the window and looked down towards the Idre. The murmur of the river still filled the canyon, but the water was visible now, no mist rising, so that the great blue-silver ribbon stretched like an artery below him, pulsing and coursing towards the heart of the Three Kingdoms. Above it loomed the walls of High Fort, busy now as soldiers checked the ballast of the catapults, the cording of mangonels, while squads toiled along the catwalks bringing ammunition to the war machines, great blocks of stone and the leather sacks that held the balefire. Across the chasm he could see the fluttering brilliance of Low Fort's watchtower sending heliographic messages to her companion bastion, and he wondered what effect the great lenses would have should their power be turned on the river. Or would that – as Brannoc had suggested – merely fuel the flames of the Messenger's strength?

There was so much he needed to know and, it seemed, so little time to find the answers.

Impatient, he went to his father's quarters.

Bedyr sat at the plain table, a quill in his hand and a frown on his face as he wrote busily upon a sheet of yellow parchment. He looked up as Kedryn entered, smiling wanly.

'I address your mother: is there anything you would have me add?'

'That I hold her in my heart; that she should not worry about me; that I shall attempt whatever duty it is the Lady asks of me.' He thought for a moment and added, 'Tell her that I miss her, father.'

Bedyr nodded and began to write again. Kedryn saw that his attention was focused on the letter and decided to seek diversion elsewhere. As he turned to go Bedyr said, 'Tepshen prepares to leave. You will find him in the ostlers' yard.'

The slamming door punctuated the sentence. Kedryn ran, awkwardly with his bandaged arm, along the corridor, oblivious of any princely dignity in his haste. It would be typical of Tepshen Lahl to depart without indulging in any farewells. It would not mean the kyo was unfeeling, only that he placed duty above all else and now considered it a priority to reach Caitin Hold as swiftly as possible. He was pounding down a winding staircase chequered with alternating blocks of light and shade from the narrow embrasures cut into the deep stone before he realized that the letter he had seen his father writing must be handed to the kyo, and so Tepshen could not leave unknown. Even so, he wished to have a little time to say his farewells, for it occurred to him that there there was a possibility he would not meet Tepshen again for some time. Or even, not ever.

He gasped an apology to the captain of bowmen he came close to spilling on his back as he hurtled though the door opening on to a catwalk and hurried along the colonnaded passage as the officer muttered something about princes and pride. After that he was a little more careful, weaving his way amongst the men who now seemed to fill High Fort like busy worker ants.

The stables were built hard against the Lozin wall that formed the west side of the fort, long, tile-roofed structures redolent of hay and the companionable odour of the animals. An exercise yard of packed earth fronted the covered stalls, surrounded by grain stores and tack houses and the quarters of the ostlers themselves. These latter were split by a tunnel giving access to the interior, and Kedryn trotted down the passage to the far gate.

Tepshen Lahl was standing there, watching as the Tamurin squadron saddled their mounts, his own tall roan gelding already accoutred. He was out of the motley he had worn in the forest and dressed in Tamurin riding gear again, his longsword latched on his shoulder, his gloved hands thumb-hooked to his belt. He turned as Kedryn approached, slowing his pace for he knew the emphasis the kyo placed on correct behaviour.

'You are ready to go,' Kedryn remarked, unnecessarily.

Tepshen nodded, permitting a slight smile to curve his lips.

'Would you have gone without so much as a farewell?' Kedryn chided.

'I knew you would come,' the kyo returned calmly. 'Unless some duty prevented it.'

'No duty could be more important than to bid you farewell,' responded Kedryn with mock formality, 'and to ask that the Lady bless your going.'

'Thank you.' Tepshen ducked his head in acknowledgement. 'I also ask that the gods you believe in look with favour upon *your* journey.'

Kedryn gave thanks for this, then, remembering his conversation with Wynett, asked, 'Tepshen, do you believe in the Lady? Do you believe in the Book?'

The kyo studied the young man's face and shrugged. 'I believe there is much of sense in the Book. I believe it provides guidance, and that is good. As for the Lady, I do not know.'

'But if you do not believe in the Lady,' Kedryn frowned, 'how can you believe in Ashar?'

'Do I believe in Ashar?' asked the kyo innocently.

'You must!' Kedryn insisted. 'How else explain the Horde? What I saw in the Beltrevan?'

'I believe in magic,' Tepshen Lahl said. 'I believe you saw something in the forest that was denied to my eyes. That does not confirm the existence of Ashar.'

'But,' Kedryn began, then hushed himself as Tepshen raised a hand.

'Kedryn, I have known you since you lay in swaddling cloth; before that I knew your father. You both believe in the Lady, and therefore in Ashar, and I respect your beliefs as I must respect those of any honest man, even though I do not share them. I believe in myself and my sword, and both are at your disposal. Is that not enough?'

'Yes,' Kedryn nodded, 'but if I *am* chosen by the Lady it would help me greatly to know that you, too, revere her.'

He saw from the frown that creased the unlined yellow brow that Tepshen was not privy to the knowledge, and experienced a flush of embarrassment that this information should be withheld from the one man as close to him as his own father. 'You should have been told!' he exclaimed.

'It is not important,' Tepshen murmured. 'Were it important, your father would have told me.'

Kedryn shook his head and blurted out an account of Alaria's text and his own doubts. 'I had hoped you might advise me,' he concluded.

Tepshen Lahl reached up to slip the binding thong from his scabbard, allowing the eastern sword to drop to battle-readiness at his waist.

'A sword,' he said, right hand caressing the diamond-patterned grip as might a lover's fingers stroke beloved flesh, 'is a length of metal safe in its scabbard. Until,' and the blade flashed bright, sweeping up, over, and down so fast the movement was a blur, ending with the beak point level on Kedryn's belly, 'it is drawn. How useful it may be then depends on the skill of the swordsman. That skill depends on natural talent and on the teaching received by the swordsman. You could be kyo in my land.'

It was the highest compliment he had ever voiced in Kedryn's hearing, and it brought a smile of appreciation that faded slowly as the greater impact of the words sank in.

'I have been your teacher in many things,' he continued, the blade sliding with equal grace back into the scabbard, 'but in others I cannot guide you, in those things you must look to your beliefs.'

'You say I should go to Andurel,' Kedryn murmured, a sense of relief creeping through his doubts, 'as did Wynett and my father.'

'You may well be this thing the text spoke of,' nodded Tepshen, 'but you are like a fine sword honed to readiness, needing the hands of a kyo to use it well.'

'And the Sisterhood may be the kyo.'

'Perhaps,' Tepshen smiled. 'Or perhaps you alone will find the way, but I think Andurel will set your feet upon the path.'

'I thank you, kyo.' Kedryn bowed in grateful acknowledgement, as Tepshen had shown him it was done in the east. 'I go south with lighter heart, knowing you think it best.'

'I am pleased that I am able to lighten your burden,' responded Tepshen with equal formality. 'If it may be lightened further, know that I shall be dead before harm comes to Tamur or your mother.'

Kedryn nodded, feeling his new-won manhood slipping a little as his eyes watered. He put his arm to Tepshen's shoulder, hugging the smaller man against his chest, grateful for the responding embrace.

'Look to your father for advice,' Tepshen urged when they broke apart, 'and to your own heart for what is right.'

'I will,' Kedryn promised.

A discreet cough echoed then down the stable passage and they both turned to see Bedyr approaching, a leather wallet wax-sealed with Tamur's stamp in his right hand.

'Give these to Yrla,' he asked the kyo. 'They explain the situation and grant you authority to speak in my name. Send the documents for Estrevan to the Sisters as swiftly as possible. And, old friend – guard yourself. Tamur has need of you.'

Tepshen took the wallet and slid it into his tunic. Bedyr put out his hand and the kyo's locked against it, his slanted eyes grave on Bedyr's face.

'We shall meet again,' he said. 'Somewhere.'

Then he spun and shouted for the waiting Tamurin to mount. He climbed astride his own horse and raised a hand in farewell. As he clattered down the paved tunnel Kedryn wondered if it had been moisture he saw in the jet eyes, or merely reflected sunlight. The squadron trotted after him, calling their adieux, and the stable yard grew abruptly silent.

'A fine man,' Bedyr remarked.

'Aye,' Kedryn agreed.

Together they went down the passageway, catching a final glimpse of the Tamurin as the column rode out through the southern gates.

'What of Brannoc?' Kedryn asked, thinking that he wanted to speak with the newly appointed Commander of Auxiliaries before the ex-outlaw slipped away.

'Busy counting his purse.' Bedyr smiled, adding when this brought an expression of disappointment to his son's face, 'He pointed out that not all his fellows might be as patriotic as he, and that the purse I promised him might well be useful in securing their loyalty.'

Kedryn nodded, pleased that his faith in Brannoc was not spoilt, and walked with Bedyr to the treasury.

Brannoc was grinning hugely as a dour officer spilled coin into an already weighty satchel, his scowl telling of his disapproval.

'I had never thought to find High Fort's gold at my beck,' Brannoc remarked, smiling as the almoner announced the counting done.

'Use it wisely,' Bedyr said, smiling back.

'I will,' promised Brannoc, more solemn. 'As I promise my loyalty.'

'That is worth more than gold,' Bedyr returned sincerely. 'The Kingdoms stand in need of good men.'

Chapter Eight

Borsus's return to the great encampment was less eager than his departure. The exhilaration of the ride out was gone, due both to a growing familiarity with the stallion and the knowledge that he must face Taws with the news that he had failed to kill his quarry. The mage had told him, he reminded himself, that should killing prove impossible, then a wound would suffice, but that did little to reassure him. At the best of times, Taws was not one to accept failure lightly, and his mood of late had been strange enough that Borsus began to fear for his life, or – worse – his soul.

By Ashar! How had the renegade guide spotted him? And even then, with his arrow unleashed and flying true, that odd slant-eyed man had moved faster than any mortal had right. At least he had succeeded in putting a shaft into the young warrior, and perhaps time would bring death; but would Taws understand? Would he accept?

Borsus rode with a heavy heart and more than once contemplated turning aside, losing himself in the woodlands. Perhaps Taws might not find him; perhaps the Messenger would be too occupied with the Horde's advance to concern himself with one failed tribesman.

Or perhaps not – and that seemed the more likely, for Taws was not the kind to forgive or to forget. So Borsus continued northwards, though at an easier pace, his apprehension growing as he came steadily closer to the gathering. There was little point, he decided, in attempting any kind of subterfuge, for Taws would merely fix him with that rubescent stare and draw the information from him. He did not like to contemplate what would happen then. Better to report what had happened and trust to luck, hoping that the mage would be satisfied. With that decision made he pressed resolutely onwards, as might a warrior approach a battle from which he had little expectation of emerging alive.

He came in sight of the camp at noon. He had expected to find it sooner, the Horde drifting south, but it was not moved yet, although he had been gone several days, and he wondered if the advance waited on his return, or on the decision of Niloc Yarrum as to how the attack should be pressed. He reined in, ignoring the anticipatory snickering of the stallion as the beast scented its fellows, to survey the scene below his vantage point.

The great fire still burned at the centre and the lodges stood in their rows, but the truce poles were down, indicating – as he could see no sign of battle – that accord was reached and Niloc Yarrum accepted as hef-Ulan. The sky above was black with crows and after the clean forest scents of the woodland, the valley assaulted his nostrils: smoke from the cookfires joined the rank odour of human sweat, mingling with the reek of the offal that filled the charnel pits, fought over by the myriad dogs that, in their turn, added to the stench. It seemed strange that he had not noticed the smell before; stranger still that he saw no scaffolds giving victims to the blood eagle. A testament, he supposed, to the unity of the Horde. Nervously, he heeled the stallion forwards, down the slope.

He was approaching the lodges when a warning shout went up, the sound of his name surprising him. He saw folk staring at him as he rode by, though few would meet his eyes when he looked towards them, and then a familiar figure blocked his path, armour glittering in the noonday light.

'Borsus,' Dewan said, 'get down off that stolen horse and follow me.'

Borsus gaped at the bar-Offa of Niloc's Gehrim, trying to see past the concealing cheek plates and nasal of the helmet to the man's eyes. Dewan gestured and two Gehrim came forward, one snatching the reins from Borsus's shock-slackened grasp, the other raising the butt of his spear to knock the rider from the saddle. Borsus dismounted before the blow could land and faced Dewan.

'I rode on the Messenger's business,' he protested. 'Taws told me to take the animal.'

'I go about the hef-Ulan's business,' Dewan announced, adding softly that only Borsus might hear, 'I am sorry, old friend, but I have no choice.'

Borsus shook his head in confusion, barely feeling the spear that prodded his back as Dewan spun about and began to march through the lodges to the inner circle where the Ulans' dwellings stood. He followed dumbly, wondering what went on, gazing hopefully at Taws's dark tent, protesting all the while that he had ridden on the Messenger's instructions and surely Taws had – would – explain.

Dewan, however, remained intractable, refusing to say more, and the Gehrim he led moved silent and stolid as automata, herding Borsus as they would drive a reluctant hog to the slaughter. Fear grew as they approached the lodge of Niloc Yarrum, and Borsus felt certain he heard mocking laughter rustle from the bleached bone of Merak's skull as Dewan halted before the bull hide curtain and shouted the name of the hef-Ulan. Borsus stared wildly about, but all he saw were curious faces staring at him, the eyes indifferent to his fate, no sign of Taws or rescue as a hoarse shout from within the lodge bade the Gehrim bring him in.

He was stripped of weapons and pushed through the entry to the ante-chamber, blinking in the sudden dimness. Niloc lounged in an ornate chair of carved wood and bone, a silver-chased drinking horn spilling dark beer over his right hand, Balandir seated to his left, Vran to his right, Darien of the Grymard and Ymrath of the Vistral lower down the table. The air was heavy with incense and spilled beer, the torches smoking untended, filling the chamber with shadows rather than light, and the reddened eyes that fastened on Borsus showed the traces of the mushrooms that had filled the carved wood bowl at the table's centre.

'Leave us,' Niloc ordered, motioning for Dewan and his men to quit the tent.

Borsus felt sweat run cold down his spine, an ugly knot of fear clamp tight fingers on his belly, prompting an unconscionable desire to urinate. He fought it, locking knees that threatened to tremble as the hef-Ulan glowered at him as though already marking the outline of the eagle on his torso.

'So, you thought to take my horse.' Niloc's voice was harsh, the words slurred by the potency of the ale and the effect of the mushrooms. 'You *dared* to take my horse!'

Borsus opened a dry mouth to protest, to explain, but Niloc Yarrum made an impatient gesture that sent beer flooding over the table and he decided that silence was the wiser course.

'A warrior,' Niloc informed the Ulans, 'a lowly warrior who stole the horse of the hef-Ulan. What punishment should he receive?'

'The eagle,' said Vran, so promptly that Borsus, even in his fear, remembered how the Yath had looked at Sulya. 'No less.'

Balandir grunted impatiently, reaching across the table to select a mushroom, chewing it noisily as he mumbled, 'Cut him down if that's your wish, but let's be done.'

'Aye,' said Ymrath, moodily, his features sour with impatience. 'My people grow restless.'

'And mine,' added Darien, thudding a fist against the table top for emphasis. 'The Horde is raised, Yarrum – we should march, not delay for trivial slights.'

'The theft of my horse is no trivial slight, Grymard,' Niloc snapped angrily, lurching a fraction more upright. 'I am hef-Ulan of the Horde. How do I lead the Horde without my horse?'

Darien turned a face flushed with rage and narcotic fungus towards Niloc, his right hand dropping to the hilt of his dagger, and for a moment Borsus thought he might attack the hef-Ulan, but he regained control and muttered, 'By Ashar, man! Are we to sit in this valley until winter overtakes us? I brought my people to you that we might take our part in the Confederation, not squabble over some warrior. Kill him and be done with it.'

Borsus stared in amazement, gaping as Balandir leant heavily on the table and said, 'Brothers, do we fall to quarrelling amongst ourselves? Should we fight when the Kingdoms await our blades? I say settle this and let us be on the move.'

'How can we move when we wait on the Messenger?' snarled Niloc, and Borsus's puzzlement grew apace, a frown forming on his bearded features as the hef-Ulan turned towards him again.

'You are his man, you tell us.'

'Tell you what, hef-Ulan?' Borsus stuttered, bewildered now. 'I do not understand.'

'*Ashar's blood!*' Niloc shouted, half-chewed shreds of mushroom exploding from his mouth, tangling in his beard. 'Tell me why you stole my horse!'

'I,' Borsus fumbled, 'I did not *steal* it. I . . .'

'Did you ask my permission then?' Niloc demanded, his tone dangerous, his eyes red and wild.

Borsus shook his head, forcing words from a dry mouth in a rush that he hoped would forestall the temper of the Horde's leader and its bloody outcome. 'I did as the Messenger told me to do, hef-Ulan. No more. He told me to!' And he halted, a greater fear impinging as he recalled Taws's words: *You will speak to no one of this.*

'Well?' Niloc prompted irritably.

Borsus licked his lips, his eyes shifting from one face to another, seeing no sympathy nor any hope there. He was wrapped in a quandary that he did not understand: he had done as Taws bade him, but now it seemed he was accused of theft, of taking Niloc's horse, and he could not explain without engendering the mage's anger. For an instant he thought it had been better had the renegade who pursued him put a shaft between his shoulders; it would have been easier than this.

Finally, mumbling, he managed, 'The Messenger will explain, hef-Ulan.'

'The Messenger,' Niloc informed him with a deadly ponderousness, 'has shut himself away in his lodge since the night of the council. The Messenger receives no one. The Messenger does not respond to my requests that he guide us. The Messenger does not appear disposed to explain anything, so I turn to you. *Tell me what goes on!*'

Borsus felt a pit opening beneath him. A yawning chasm that flickered bright with Ashar's fire. It seemed the heat cloaked him, sweat pouring down chest and back, running free from his hair into his beard. It became very difficult to control his bladder. He shook his head hopelessly, dragging a despairing hand across his face.

'I did only as I was bidden,' he muttered.

'And I have only your word on that,' snarled Niloc. 'Why did you take the animal?'

Borsus came close then to blurting out the reason, but fear of Taws remained greater than fear of Niloc: the Messenger's kiss outweighed the embrace of the blood eagle, and all he could say was, 'I was told to, hef-Ulan.'

'Kill him,' urged Vran. 'Messenger's man or not, I say you should kill him.'

Borsus cast a poisonous glance at the Yath and suggested desperately, 'Might you not inform the Messenger of my return? Perhaps he will speak then.'

'When he ignored *my* entreaties?' rasped Niloc. 'You set yourself high, warrior.'

'No, Lord,' Borsus returned, raw terror lending him a frantic eloquence, 'you are hef-Ulan of the Horde, no man stands higher than you. I am a worm; I am nothing – I do only as I am bid, and I followed the orders of the Messenger.'

He paused as Niloc eased back into the chair, wiping moist gobbets of mushroom from his mouth, his dark eyes intent on Borsus's face. With fear sending adrenalin in a flood through his system, Borsus found himself thinking with abrupt clarity. Thinking that something was weirdly amiss, that he had never seen Niloc Yarrum so disturbed, for there was more than rage in those glittering orbs. There was doubt, too. He let his gaze flicker over the others, seeking some clue. Vran looked merely spiteful, but both Darien and Ymrath were frowning as though they wrestled with some inner conflict, and Balandir was staring at him with open curiosity.

It was the Caroc Ulan who spoke next: 'You say you took the hef-Ulan's stallion on the word of the Messenger, but you cannot – or will not – tell us what that word was. Will you tell us what you did?'

'I cannot!' Borsus gulped. 'On my soul, Lord Balandir, I cannot. I am sworn.'

'The blood eagle takes little heed of oaths,' Vran said with an evil smile.

'I went on Ashar's business!' Borsus cried.

'You went on my horse,' grunted Niloc, though Borsus thought there might be a fraction less anger in his tone. 'And I would know the reason why.'

'Hef-Ulan, I returned the horse!' Borsus said, not sure how much longer he could control his bladder.

Niloc stared at him for horribly long moments before speaking again, and when he did, his voice was low and harsh, ugly with menace.

'I am minded to see how long you can hold your tongue after I begin to cut the eagle on your carcase.'

Self-control became impossible then, and Borsus groaned as warm liquid spilled down his legs.

'He pisses himself like a cringing dog,' sneered Vran, earning in that single sentence Borsus's undying enmity. 'Let the eagle loosen his tongue!'

'Wait,' urged Balandir, stroking at his silver-streaked beard, 'it may be the wiser course to do as he suggests.'

'What?' Vran pantomimed excessive surprise. 'Does the Ulan of the mighty Caroc bow to the wishes of a mere warrior?'

Balandir turned in his chair, fixing the Yath with a threatening gaze that brought a flush of pink to Vran's tanned features. 'I bow to the wishes of the hef-Ulan, Yath, and those of the Messenger. We have all seen the power of the Messenger – would you risk his wrath?'

Vran's flush grew deeper. His eyes fell away from Balandir's steady gaze and he reached for his drinking horn, hiding his embarrassment in its contents. Balandir returned his eyes to Niloc's face.

'You are hef-Ulan, Yarrum, chosen by the Messenger, but it may be that Taws will take amiss the slaying of his man, so – for the sake of the Confederation – I suggest we *do* inform him.'

Niloc chewed on his moustaches for a while, then nodded, glancing to the silent Ulans of the Vistral and Grymard.

'How say you?'

Darien shrugged, tugging at the gold hoop hung from his left ear. 'It may be as well to heed Balandir's advice. At the least, we might see an end to this waiting.'

Ymrath worked a piece of mushroom from between his teeth and spat it on to the furs covering the floor. 'Perhaps,' he allowed. 'I'd lief avoid the Messenger's anger.'

'So!' Niloc's attention returned to Borsus. 'It would appear you may be saved. Dewan!'

The leader of the Gehrim came through the curtain, right hand slapping his chest in salute. 'Hef-Ulan?'

'Go to Taws's lodge and inform him that the horse thief is returned,' ordered Niloc. 'Ask that he attend me.'

Dewan ducked his head in acknowledgement and pushed the hides apart. Borsus watched the smoke swirl as he went out, voicing a silent prayer to Ashar that the mage should hurry to his rescue. His breeches clung clammy to his legs, aggravating the soreness imparted by the hectic ride. His whole body was damp, his shirt heavy with sweat, and he felt abruptly weary, his limbs leaden and stiff, a dull ache beginning to pound inside his skull. Incongruously, he wondered where Sulya was, whether she waited for him, as he waited for his fate. He wanted to walk away, go to his own lodge and strip off his soiled clothing, have his woman lave him and bring him sweet wine to drink, sink with her on to soft furs. Instead, he held himself rigid, knowing that if he relaxed, he would begin to tremble, perhaps disgrace himself further by falling to his knees. He stared fixedly ahead, locking his gaze on one of the flame-pots suspended from the tent's roof, watching the aromatic smoke curl upwards and break against the hide ceiling, drifting slow and thick towards the single hole. He did not dare turn as he heard the bull hides at his back slap apart and felt a gust of fresher air wash over him: if it was Dewan, he thought he might begin to weep.

It was not: it was Taws, and the mage was angry.

He moved past Borsus with a curious, gliding step, the red-lit gloom of Niloc's lodge seeming to enlarge him as he halted, fur-swathed shoulders hunched, before the table and stared at the leaders of the Horde.

'You delay my man.'

Cold accusation iced his voice, lending it an awful menace. Borsus could see only the curtain of white-silk hair that draped his skull, but he could readily imagine the gaze that transfixed the Ulans. He saw

Vran lick nervously at fleshy lips, lashes dropping over lowered eyes, as if the table had suddenly become of immense interest. Ymrath's fingers moved instinctively in the warding gesture, then clenched in a fist, Darien locked both hands about his drinking horn and began to blink furiously, swallowing as though a mushroom lodged in his throat. Balandir retained a degree of control, ducking his head and murmuring throatily, 'Welcome, Taws.' Niloc Yarrum essayed a smile and said, 'My thanks, Messenger.'

'Your thanks? Your welcome?' Taws's voice was the crackle of frost on the breaking earth of a grave pit. 'For what? For delaying my man?'

'He stole my horse,' Niloc muttered, his eyes refusing to meet Taws's.

'On my order,' the thaumaturgist replied in a serpent's hiss. 'Did you think he took the beast of his own choosing?'

'I did not know what to think,' grunted the hef-Ulan, aware of the others watching him, knowing they felt grateful the Messenger's attention should focus on him, not them; resenting it. 'Had you but informed me . . .'

'Am I to request your permission for my actions?' Taws's voice dripped mockery. 'You forget who made you, man! I go about Ashar's business, and that takes no heed of your petty wants.'

Niloc's dark features reddened. Borsus saw Balandir stifle a smile, then become solemn as the mage's eyes swung towards him.

'Do any of you believe the Horde can succeed without me?' Taws demanded. 'Are you grown foolish in your pride?'

'No!' Niloc hurried to assure the fur-bedecked creature. 'We bow to Ashar's will, to you. But how am I to lead if some plain warrior may take my horse at will?'

'At *my* will!' It was said in a tone that sent the hef-Ulan back into the depths of his chair as might a cornered animal retreat defensively into a hollow. The drinking horn toppled, beer spilling unnoticed, ignored, over the table. 'Must I remind you of my power?'

'No!' Borsus forgot his own discomfort as he saw Niloc Yarrum squirm in something close to terror. 'No, Taws! I assure you.'

'*I* assure you,' Taws responded, his voice softer, but no less threatening, 'that what this man does, he does at my bidding. You will never again question that.'

'I will not,' Niloc muttered sullenly.

'No.' There was awful promise in the one barbed word. 'You will not.'

Borsus saw the hef–Ulan's face grow pale, then felt his own skin crawl as Taws turned towards him and he saw the stark fury on the mage's taut-fleshed visage. The sunken eyes sparked bright, as if fire burned within the sockets, and the craters of the cheeks seemed deeper, as though rage sucked them in to meet the grinding teeth. For a moment Borsus thought the Messenger's wrath would fall on him, but then Taws smiled, and that was somehow more frightening.

'The horse,' he rustled. 'Bring me the horse.'

Relief lent Borsus speed. Knowing only that he was saved from the blood eagle and not the object of Taws's anger, he hurled himself through the curtaining hides, anxious to be gone from the lodge. Dewan stood there, his eyes wary beneath the concealment of his helmet, moving to halt Borsus as the warrior exploded into the outer chamber.

'The stallion! Where is it?' Borsus ignored the Gehrim who moved to block his path, making himself a way with the announcement, 'I go about the Messenger's business!'

'There.' Dewan hiked a thumb past the entrance and Borsus saw the beast tethered beyond the skull-hung trophy poles, munching oats. The saddle and bridle fittings had been removed, and someone had draped a blanket over the horse's back. Borsus hauled the cloth away and dragged the halter loose, paying no heed to the irritated wicker as the big head was yanked away from the fodder.

'What are you doing?' Dewan was alarmed. 'Ashar's blood, man! Niloc will kill you!'

'No,' Borsus replied with the first confidence he had felt since returning, 'I think not.'

He tugged the protesting animal down the avenue between the poles, seeing Taws emerge, Niloc Yarrum and the Ulans behind him, their eyes narrowing as the light hit them, Vran shaking his head as though to clear it of the mushrooms' effects. He halted as Taws raised a hand.

'This animal you prize so much,' the mage said, his voice cut silk, 'is nothing. My purpose is everything. I give you one last lesson, Niloc Yarrum. And you others – Balandir, Vran, Darien, Ymrath – you learn the lesson equally, for what I do to this beast, I can do to you. Any of you! Watch and learn.'

He set his red-eyed gaze on the stallion and beckoned Borsus towards him. When the warrior let go the halter the animal made no move, stilled by that rubescent glare. He raised one fur-clad arm, long, angular fingers extending, moving in a swift pattern, crimson light dancing at the tips. His lips moved and the witchfire lanced towards the horse, enveloping it.

The stallion screamed then, rearing up with flattened ears and wide, terror-filled eyes as its mane and tail, every bristle of extraneous hair, began to burn. The smell of scorching hide filled the air and the great hooves thudded down, the hindquarters bucking, crashing against the trophy poles so that skulls rattled and fell loose. Flame issued from the orifices of the body, the rolling eyes boiling and melting down fire-blackened cheeks like obscene tears. The hide itself cracked and split, peeling from the framework of the skeleton beneath to fall in charred pieces to the ground. Throughout the camp dogs began to howl, as though sensing the ghastly fate of the stallion and sharing its agony, for the animal did not die. Instead it remained horribly, impossibly, alive as the internal organs burst and burnt, their reek far worse than any charnel pit. It seemed contained within a confined area established by Taws's magic, for it continued to kick and rear even though it was now a flaming outline of charring bones, dripping melted innards. Then sinews and ligaments grew brittle and snapped, and the bones fell apart, clattering, still burning, to the earth. They smouldered for a while, then were calcified, leaving no more than a smoking dust and the reek of burning.

Borsus watched with gaping mouth, barely aware of the horrified gasps that came from the Ulans, seeing only dimly the shocked faces of the crowd that watched, the horror of the stallion's fate magnified by the wanton destruction of so highly-prized a symbol of status. He looked to where Niloc Yarrum stood and saw the hef-Ulan's jaw set tight over clenched teeth, a nerve pounding on his forehead. Behind, him, the Ulans stood white-faced with shock.

Taws said, 'Never again question my designs,' and stalked away.

Borsus followed unbidden, taking care to skirt the grey ash that lay before the lodge. None moved to halt him and he did not look back.

Taws strode directly to his own tent, pushing the heavy flap aside and entering without waiting for the warrior on his heels. Borsus caught the thick hide and ducked through, experiencing a fresh wash of sweat as the heat inside struck him. It seemed the interior was hotter than before, the air stifling and difficult to breath. His hair plastered against his skull, the bronze of his torque becoming un-comfortably warm against his throat. Taws pointed at a fur-covered settle and motioned him down. Borsus sat, not sure he could find the strength to rise again as the mage lowered himself into a second chair, sighing as though he luxuriated in the overpowering atmosphere.

'Well?' he demanded. 'Why did you not kill him?'

'I wounded him,' Borsus said quickly, deciding that a straightforward account was his safest course, no longer surprised that the mage should know the outcome of the ambush. 'It was the best I could do. My shaft would have killed him had one of them not dragged him down.'

Crimson points flickered dangerously in Taws's eyes and Borsus held his breath. But then the mage grunted deep in his throat and said, 'But the arrow stuck?'

'Aye!' Borsus nodded enthusiastically. 'It would have taken him in the heart had one who looked to be of the forest not given warning, and the other – I have not seen his like – acted so swift. It took him in the shoulder. Here.'

He tapped the upper part of his own left shoulder, adding, 'It went deep, I think. I might have put a second into him had they not shielded him and charged me. I killed two, but then I was forced to flee. I thought it better I bring you the news, Master, than die uselessly.'

Taws made no comment on this, which Borsus took as approval.

'Describe him. Tell me everything you know of him.'

Not stopping to wonder why description was necessary, Borsus ransacked his memory for details. 'He was the youngest – as you told me. Dressed like them all in motley leather, as spies might wear. He wore a sword and there was a bow on his saddle. His hair was brown and long, cut as the Tamurin wear it. They shouted his name, which was Kedryn. There was another – old – who might have been his father, so alike were they. I think they were nobles.'

Taws nodded. 'So, he is called Kedryn. What else? What happened then?'

'They put their bodies between us, Master, and charged my hiding place. I killed as many as I could, then I ran for my horse. The woodsman came after me, but I escaped him and returned here.'

'Where Niloc Yarrum grows restless,' Taws muttered, more to himself than to the nervous warrior. 'Well, it might have been done better, but at the least I can find him now.' He laughed suddenly, a high-pitched yapping sound that chilled the sweat on Borsus's back. 'So that is what I must do. And that will give Niloc Yarrum all the blood he wants. Come!'

He rose to his feet, towering over Borsus, who rose less steadily on uncertain legs, and thrust the entrance flap aside. Borsus trailed after, his head reeling, wondering why Taws had delayed the Horde's advance and why the young man called Kedryn was so important to the Messenger. There seemed no reason, certainly not one he could think of, for surely Taws's power was too mighty to take account of one young Tamurin. And why must the knowledge be kept from Niloc Yarrum? Such matters, he decided, were not for the likes of him: better that he should simply follow orders.

Returning to the hef-Ulan's lodge pleased him little, but he had no choice in the matter, for Taws progressed directly there, ignoring the Gehrim as he entered the inner confines of the tent.

Niloc and the others were again seated about the table, but the effects of the mushrooms appeared to be negated by Taws's demonstration. Impatience was replaced by fear as the mage strode in.

'Strike your tents,' he said without preamble. 'The Horde marches.'

'Now?' Despite his earlier restlessness, the hef-Ulan was surprised by the sudden announcement.

'We have business in the Three Kingdoms,' Taws said briskly. 'Ashar's business. Let us go about it.'

Without awaiting a reply he turned and left the tent. Borsus went with him, but not before he saw the expressions of shock and delight on the faces of the chieftains. It was as though they had begun to lose faith in the great dream, and now that faith was rekindled so abruptly they could scarcely dare believe it. He did not delay to see their further reactions, but hurried after the mage.

'Master?' he dared ask, 'Have you further need of me?'

Taws paused, staring at him as if seeing him for the first time, and shook his head briefly, 'No. Make whatever preparations you must. Swiftly.'

As Borsus hurried to his lodge he was reminded of his soiled breeks, for by now the leather was drying and stiffening, chafing his thighs as he ran. He cursed when he saw that Sulya was not waiting for him and decided, despite Taws's admonition to hasten, that he would cleanse himself: the stink of his own urine reminded him too much of the terror that had induced it. He unlaced his jerkin and tugged his shirt over his head, noticing as he tossed the garments aside, that his weapons had been replaced, wondering if that was courtesy on Dewan's part or mute acknowledgement of his position as Taws's man. That he was, there could no longer be any doubt, though he was still by no means certain he relished that status, whatever privileges it brought him. He flung himself down on the bed of furs and loosened the thongs of his boots, dragging the soft moccasins from his feet so that he might untie the cords of his breeks and remove the fouled leathers. Outside, he could hear the camp criers shouting warning of impending departure, the responding shouts of the forest folk gradually filling the afternoon as word spread along the valley. He unwrapped the linen that covered his loins and poured water into a copper bowl, setting the receptacle to heat over the hearth fire. He was reaching for the cloths beside the water tub when Sulya appeared.

Her blonde hair was dishevelled with haste, her blue eyes wide with curiosity, opening wider as her nostrils crinkled at the smell of his discarded clothes.

'What happened?' she asked. 'Where have you been?'

'On the Messenger's business,' Borsus snapped, not willing to admit he had fouled himself in naked terror. 'Lave me.'

'We are on the move,' she protested. 'I must ready the lodge.'

Borsus experienced a sudden rush of fury. It was as though the confusion attached to his solitary ambush, the secrecy, Taws's delay, the fear he had felt as Niloc contemplated giving him to the eagle, the startling, horrifying, destruction of the stallion, even the sudden announcement of the long-awaited advance, coalesced in a wash of blind rage. To the Messenger, to the hef-Ulan, he was no more than a puppet, jumping on their bidding, and now his own woman questioned him. He struck her hard across the face, sending her reeling back against the wall of the lodge. She slid down the hide, rubbing at her cheek with tears forming in her eyes.

'Do not question me,' Borsus warned.

Sulya stared at him, her eyes travelling over his nakedness, then she smiled. 'As you say, warrior.'

Without further ado she took the cloth from his hand and dipped it in the heated water, began to scrub the sweat and drying urine from his body. Borsus began to smile as her hand moved over his thighs: it was so simple to control a woman. If only he had that control over his life.

He felt himself grow beneath her ministrations, and fought the impulse to take her, knowing there was not enough time. Sulya, in turn, began to tease him, using the cloth artfully, murmuring as she worked.

'What did you do? What task did the Messenger set you?'

'I cannot say,' he gasped, thinking that this was a more subtle interrogation than Niloc Yarrum had employed, and far harder to resist. 'I am sworn to secrecy.'

'I am your woman.' She looked up, blonde hair brushing his naked loins, her hands still moving gently. 'Surely you can tell me?'

'On my soul, I cannot,' he groaned. 'I am forbidden by the Messenger himself.'

Sulya pouted, turning to rinse the cloth. When she brought it again against his body it was warm, and resistance, like Borsus himself, became harder.

'They say you were summoned by the hef-Ulan.'

'I –' he paused to gasp, '– was.'

'They say he was angry.'

'He –' Borsus moaned, '– was.'

'And that because he threatened you Taws destroyed his stallion.'

'Yes!' was all Borsus could manage.

Sulya replaced the cloth, smiling, and washed him. 'The one you took.'

Borsus was about to tell her that was only on Taws's order, but then recognized the admiration in her tone and said, 'Aye, I did.'

'No other would dare that,' she whispered, beginning to dry him.

'I am the Messenger's man,' he told her, pride in his voice now.

Sulya nodded, a degree of caution entering her voice as she said, 'Niloc Yarrum would kill any other man who dared take his horse.'

Borsus stretched, at ease now, and said, 'He did not dare kill me because I stand beneath the Messenger's wing. He threatened it, but he could not.'

'Is that why,' she asked innocently, 'your breeks are fouled?'

Borsus kicked at her, but she avoided his foot adroitly, laughing, saying, 'Better piss than blood, warrior.'

Borsus began to laugh with her, taking her in his arms as relief washed through him, putting his face in her hair as he murmured, 'There'll be blood enough when we reach the Kingdoms. I'll have skulls then to weight the lodge. And you'll have silks to wear. Perfumes! I'll put gold on you then and we'll live high as Ulans.'

'Not if the Horde moves without us,' she remarked with feminine practicality. 'And the lodges come down already.'

Borsus grunted and let her go, waiting as she brought him fresh apparel from the small trunk of carved wood that contained almost everything he owned. He dressed, strapping his sword across his back and hiking his buckler to a comfortable position between his shoulders, then went outside to whistle up their dogs. He owned four now; big, powerful hounds given by Drott seeking to impress the warrior who stood so close to the Messenger. Sulya fetched the harnesses and he kicked the snapping canines into submission, leaving the woman to strike the lodge and load the beasts as he went to saddle his horse.

After riding Niloc's stallion he felt easier around the big equines and he got his tack in place with less difficulty than usual, leading the small, hairy mare back with his head high as he caught the envious glances of less fortunate folk. He saw Niloc's lodge coming down and wondered which of his several horses the hef-Ulan would ride now that his prized stallion was gone. He did not linger to find out, for he had no wish to remind the leader of the Horde of his part in the animal's destruction: despite Taws, he remained wary of Niloc's black and unpredictable temper.

Sulya had their lodge spread over the tent poles when he returned, and he lashed the travois to the mare's saddle, leaving the loading to the woman as he set to stowing the smaller items in place on the frameworks the dogs would drag. Sulya was – sensibly – wary of the hounds, who took little pleasure in this ignominious duty and expressed their dissatisfaction with snapping teeth and surly growls. As he loaded the travois he could see Taws standing silent, watching his shebang struck and packed. The mage made no move to assist or instruct, seeming once more lost in his own thoughts, as if he communed with some internal spirit, and the business of removal was merely a necessary delay to his final purpose. As Borsus mounted the mare and Sulya took his stirrup, he saw the Messenger settle himself comfortably on the piled furs that covered one frame, the poles lashed to a fine, deep-chested gelding that appeared to need no guidance beyond the presence of its backwards-facing passenger.

Then, at the centre of the camp, Dewan raised a trumpet fashioned from the horn of a forest bull to his lips and blew one mighty blast that was echoed by the clarions of the Caroc and the Yath, the Vistral and the Grymard, and the Horde began to move.

Niloc Yarrum led the way, mounted on a grey mare, his Gehrim spread in a loose formation behind him. Then Taws, and behind the mage, delighted to be so close to the head and thus free of the dust and stink that would envelop the rest, came Borsus and Sulya, behind them the great mass of the Drott. Balandir led his Caroc out next, followed by Vran and the Yath, then Darien and his Grymard, and finally the Vistral, with Ymrath at their head.

The vast column straggled along the valley, following the line of the ridge until it flattened, affording less difficult ascent, and began to climb towards the rim. Borsus turned there, looking back from his vantage point at the enormity that was the Horde. Even more than the great sprawl of tents, this movement testified to the magnitude of the confederated tribes. It seemed that the earth itself shifted, flowing in a massive river that defied gravity, spreading out as the way became easier and the walls of the valley no longer confined its passage, moving inexorably up the valley sides, covering the grass, setting the very trees to trembling. The afternoon was filled with the thunder of the migration, the pounding of uncountable feet, the thud of hooves, the faster pattering of the hounds' paws, the myriad voices lifted in song and shouting and boasts. Dust rose in a sun-dulling cloud, hiding even the blaze of the central fire, and above, lending their own stridency to the mind-numbing roar, whirled the crows, black omens against the pall of grey.

'Ashar!' murmured the warrior, part in prayer, more in stark wonderment at the sheer weight of moving forest folk. 'Surely there is nothing that can stop us now.'

He felt Sulya's hand grip his booted ankle, her fingers tight, and looked down to see an expression of disbelief on her face as she stared back and shook her head and said, 'Nothing!'

And Borsus raised his spear to the dust-grimed sky and the screaming crows and shouted, 'Ashar!'

And this time it was a cry of pride and challenge and bloodlust.

Through the remainder of the day and into the twilight the Horde moved. The creatures of the forest fled before it, even the predator cats and the proud, horned bulls, for nothing like this had ever marched the Beltrevan, not even in the time of Drul. Never had the world seen the like of this Horde, and surely there was nothing that could halt it.

A squall of grey, rain-laden cloud blew down from the Lozins as Kedryn and Bedyr prepared to embark for Andurel, prompting them to draw their cloaks tight about their shoulders as they hurried into a tavern in the riverside district of the settlement below High Fort.

On Bedyr's suggestion their last farewells had been said behind the fort's mighty walls, the Lord of Tamur preferring to depart with little ceremony lest too many questions be asked. Better, he had convinced Rycol, that the forts complete their preparations and gain reliable news of the Horde's imminence before alarming the civilian population with talk of war. Unsure as to how long the forest folk might take to arrive at the gates, or how long they might be held there, Bedyr hoped to alert King Darr and return with the full might of the Three Kingdoms at his back before panic spread – as spread it would, he was certain, should word of this new Confederation and its frightful leader get out.

Even so, the tavern – filling steadily as the rain began to pound out of a leaden sky – was alive with gossip. The shimmering of the signal towers as they flashed messages back and forth across the Idre could not be hidden, even by the lowering cloud, and as rivermen and the dockside labourers took shelter from the squall, they wondered aloud what was going on up at the forts. Kedryn had heard numerous opinions, ranging from the purely imaginative to the more sensible: King Darr was planning a royal progress; Tamur and Kesh stood poised for war; the Idre threatened to flood; barbarian raiders had approached the walls. The one thing no one mentioned – presumably because it was considered so utterly impossible that it fell beneath even the wildest speculation – was the likelihood of barbarian invasion. Several approaches were made to the two warriors who sat in the farthest corner, for they both wore surcoats emblazoned with the fist of Tamur over their tunics, and the blades sheathed beside them had a business-like, military look suggesting they were something to do with High Fort, but each enquiry was deftly fended by Bedyr. He was not curt – he owed his people better than that – but he had a way of adroitly turning the questions back on themselves, so that finally they ended and the questioners found a fresh source of speculation, assuming the two men were couriers, their lips sealed by the oath of the mehdri.

Kedryn listened more than he spoke, marvelling at his father's diplomatic talents even as he wondered if it were not better to make a general announcement and thus alert all of Tamur to the impending danger.

'Not yet,' Bedyr told him softly, toying with a near helmet-size flagon of mulled red wine. 'They have known peace too long to accept the notion without panic breaking out. A word spoken here will travel the length of the Idre, changing all the way, until by the time the river breaks on the Andurel cascades it will be the destruction of the forts and wholesale slaughter throughout the north. If worst should come to worst, we'll need every man, not towns emptied by rumour. Not nomad bands of frightened folk seeking refuge.'

'But surely the Tamurin would not flee,' Kedryn argued. 'They would rally to the defence.'

'Aye, they will,' nodded Bedyr, ladling fresh measures into both their tankards, 'given a rallying point and leaders. Those are what we must provide, and to do that we must reach Andurel and inform Darr.'

'Brannoc goes abroad already,' said Kedryn, thinking of how the newly-appointed Commander of Auxiliaries had slipped stealthily from High Fort the previous night. 'When he recruits his freebooters will they not talk?'

'I think not,' smiled Bedyr. 'Brannoc is a sensible man, and he knows what we face. He understands the need for caution in this, and I believe I impressed on him the need for quiet preparation. Besides, if freebooters cry doom, will they be credited?'

'So he serves secretly?' Kedryn grinned.

Bedyr nodded, sipping the hot wine before he spoke again. 'Let us say that King Darr and the strength of Andurel is one column of our army. Tamur, Kesh and Ust-Galich provide the second, third and fourth. I hope that so far as the Messenger is concerned he will see only those columns. Brannoc and his freebooters will be the fifth. A secret column.'

'Your horsefly,' Kedryn murmured.

'You sleep with your ears open,' Bedyr smiled.

'And a blade to hand, these days,' nodded Kedryn grimly.

'I think there will be little need of blades for a while,' Bedyr said. 'Not on the way to Andurel.'

'Shall I find my answers there?' wondered Kedryn.

But before his father could reply the tavern door opened to admit a gust of wind and a portly man whose bulk was magnified by the voluminous cloak he wore.

'Refreshing weather,' he announced cheerfully, shaking dense droplets of moisture from his mantle, 'after so warm a summer.'

The derisive cries this statement prompted were answered with a beaming smile that made Kedryn think of the moon's full face. The newcomer was round in every way. As he pushed back the deep hood of his cloak a head devoid of any trace of hair was revealed, twinkling eyes shining from beneath craggy, naked brows surveying the scene, white teeth gleaming from between thick lips. He shed the cloak, exposing a tent-like jerkin on which the trident badge of the River Guild glittered, small against the surrounding expanse of water-proofed leather. He hiked a belt that might have girded a horse higher on his ample belly and shook both high-booted feet as delicately as a cat. Then he shouted for evshan, the fiery spirit favoured by rivermen – who claimed it was needed to keep out the damp of the Idre – and tossed a coin to the smiling landlord.

He took the liquor down in one swallow, sighed contentedly, and waited for his mug to be refilled, surveying the tavern before marching purposefully across the room to the corner where Kedryn and Bedyr sat.

'I am Galen Sadreth,' he exclaimed, 'May I sit?'

Bedyr motioned at a nearby settle and the riverman hiked it to the table and lowered his bulk down on to the wood, leaning forwards on both elbows so that his huge body served as living screen against the curious stares turned towards the corner.

'I understand you seek passage down my river.' His voice was softer now, a deep bass rumble.

'We seek passage to Andurel,' Bedyr nodded.

'If you are the two Lord Rycol mentioned, you have it,' beamed Sadreth.

'And what did Lord Rycol say?' Bedyr enquired mildly, seeing the second mug of evshan disappear as he spoke.

Sadreth smiled and bellowed over his shoulder for a refill, waiting until a serving wench arrived with a pewter jug, patting her buxom behind as she departed, before answering. 'That two gentlemen of Tamur have business in the Queen of the Kingdoms and would welcome the services of an honest riverman.'

'Which, of course, you are,' Bedyr murmured, smiling.

Kedryn, too, began to smile as the massive man pantomimed surprise that such a question should be addressed him. 'Not only honest,' Sadreth exclaimed, 'but reliable. The very best, in fact. The swiftest and the safest, captain of the finest barque to ply the Mother of Waters.'

'Such exemplary services must demand a high price,' opined Bedyr.

Sadreth shrugged and it was like watching a mountain move. 'There are times,' he said, 'when purpose determined the price.'

'And did Lord Rycol speak of our purpose?'

'Only that swift, safe passage is required.' The riverman beamed again, tapping a fleshy finger to the side of his broad nose. 'But I am able to smell trouble when it comes floating down the Idre.'

'Trouble?' asked Bedyr.

Sadreth nodded. 'The signal towers are mightily busy and while I do not read the military codes, I am familiar with the more usual messagings, which these are not. So – trouble. Beyond that, well, I am a travelled man. Once I even visited Caitin Hold ... Lord Bedyr.'

Kedryn tensed, unsure what reaction this would bring from his father, but Bedyr made no move, merely sipped his wine and stared at the riverman as though judging him. Finally he said, 'I should prefer you did not make my name public.'

'As you wish,' smiled Sadreth, his bald pate gleaming as he ducked his head. 'May I ask, though, if this young man is Prince Kedryn? Amongst my many superlative qualities, I admit to the weakness of curiosity.'

'He is,' Bedyr agreed. 'And like me, travels incognito.'

Sadreth nodded some more, studying Kedryn. 'He favours you, my Lord. And both your identities are safe with me. You may trust my crew, too.'

'If Rycol sent you, I do,' said Bedyr, 'which leaves us only your fee to negotiate.'

The riverman grinned amiably and said, 'The honour of carrying both Lord and Prince of Tamur is too high that such trivial matters need mention. Passage is free.'

'Thank you,' Bedyr murmured, echoed by Kedryn. 'When do we depart?'

Sadreth glanced towards a window, indicating the rain that leaked between the tight-closed shutters. 'When this fret is done, my Lord. My Lord? Should I call you that, or do you prefer some pseudonym?'

'I am called Bedyr,' came the answer, 'and my son is Kedryn. Or will your men recognize the names?'

'Some may know them for what they are,' shrugged the riverman, 'but they'll assume – aided by my suggestion – that you are merely named after yourselves.'

Kedryn thought about that for a moment and saw that it was unlikely any would think the Lord of Tamur and his heir would travel unannounced, whilst the use of real names would make communication easier.

'How long will this last?' he wondered, pointing to the leaking window.

'Not long, I think,' replied Sadreth. 'Summer is over and autumn announces her presence, no more. This is just a little warning, though I'd lief embark dry if you're agreeable.'

'I am no riverman,' Bedyr admitted. 'We'll be guided by you.'

'Excellent,' beamed the big man, 'so we'll wait a while in this pleasant place and quaff a little more fortification. Wench!'

His mug was refilled a third time and Bedyr ordered more wine. Kedryn began to feel mildly tipsy, relaxing in the warmth of the tavern and the riverman's company as Sadreth regaled them with endless anecdotes of life on the Idre, making no further mention of their purpose in journeying to Andurel or the events that had brought them to High Fort. Bedyr called for food and they ate, the fresh-baked bread and the spicy stew soaking up the alcohol, but inducing its own soporific contentment so that he felt almost reluctant to leave when Sadreth cocked an ear and announced the squall was dying.

He was not sure how the riverman could tell, but Bedyr rose and fastened his cloak about his shoulders, tossing the pouches that contained what little clothing he carried over his left shoulder, carrying his sheathed sword in that hand. Kedryn followed suit and Sadreth led the way out of the tavern, collecting his own cloak en route.

Outside, the pelting rain had died to a drizzle that in turn faded away as they progressed to the waterfront. The cloud dispersed and an unseasonably pale sun emerged, transforming the sky to grey metal. The tail end of the wind that had brought the squall still blew, but weaker now, twisting and turning on itself, rattling shutters open and setting the rigging of the craft visible along the riverbank to flapping and creaking. The Idre was a sullen grey, matching the colour of the sky, her surface wrinkled with wavelets that splashed fretfully against the stone of the moorings.

Sadreth indicated a barque close-moored to the river wall, pride in his voice as he said, 'The *Vashti*, the finest craft on the river.'

Kedryn's experience of boats – which, Sadreth hurried to explain, were things carried on larger craft – was minimal, and his knowledge less, but the *Vashti* looked impressive. She sat low in the water, a good twenty paces from the figurehead carved in antique image of a watersprite to the long sweep of the tiller, her lines sleek, suggestive of speed. Her stern was raised three steps from the rain-wet planking of her deck and overhung with a canopy striped in bright green and yellow. She carried double masts, the main with furled squaresail, and a smaller, forward stem that the riverman said was used for tacking in difficult weather. Long oars, ten in all, were stowed along her gunnels, heavy brass rowlocks indicating where the sweeps would be fitted when rowing became necessary. Her hatches were battened against the storm, but from the way she rode the river, Kedryn guessed the holds were already filled. She looked well-kept, sleek and polished, her sides golden over-lapping planks, topped with a bright red rail that contrasted with the azure of the figurehead.

'Is she not the loveliest thing you have set eyes on?' asked the riverman. 'And blessed by the Lady – she'll ride the fiercest floodtide and run swifter than a charger. You'll not find a sweeter vessel in all the Kingdoms.'

195

'She's beautiful,' Kedryn agreed, gulping as he crossed the gang-plank and found his world transformed into a place of uncertain footing as what had seemed mere ripples from the security of the wharf became great surging waves that raised and dropped the deck beneath his feet.

'You'll find your legs soon enough,' chortled Sadreth. 'Now, stow your gear here.' He indicated a low, chest-like container set between the masts, adding, 'Your swords, too, I suggest – they'll be mere encumbrances on board.'

Kedryn glanced at Bedyr, then relinquished his blade to the locker when his mute enquiry was answered with a nod. Looking around, he saw that the crew were coming on board, eleven men dressed in a variety of tunics and breeks that bore no resemblance to any kind of uniform save for the trident symbol on each chest. They glanced incuriously at the newcomers, falling into their places with the prac-tised ease of men long accustomed to their duties. Sadreth beamed at them and marched to the stern, beckoning Bedyr and Kedryn to join him.

'We have passengers,' he announced, his voice carrying easily down the deck and beyond. 'Two gentlemen bound for fair Andurel. Mehdri, so there's only time wasted in asking questions. They're called Bedyr and Kedryn – named, they tell me, for our gracious Lord of Tamur and his noble son. They're on King's business, so set your backs to it!'

With that he settled himself on the tiller seat and wrapped both meaty arms about the boom. Two men, fore and aft, sprang ashore and loosed the moorings, tossing the thick ropes on board and leap-ing after them with an agility that Kedryn envied: as the *Vashti* slid clear of the wharf he found himself staggering back against the rail, clutching the bright-painted wood to steady himself. He was saved from embarrassment by the sight of Bedyr clasping a canopy stay and lowering himself to the narrow bench that ran around the stern, his face suddenly losing its tan to become a green-ish colour.

Sadreth shouted an order and the squaresail came down, filling with the remnant of the wind and bringing the craft leaping from the dockside to midstream, white water churning beneath her prow.

'She flies, does she not?' laughed the riverman.

'She does,' Kedryn agreed, forgetting his discomfort as the *Vashti* gained speed with startling alacrity, racing the river – as her captain had promised – faster than any steed.

'Ugh,' moaned Bedyr, and hung his head over the side to donate his meal to the Idre.

'Bedyr!' cried Sadreth cheerfully. 'You did not tell me you have no stomach for the water.'

'No,' grunted the Lord of Tamur. 'I did not.' He clutched miserably at the pole, watching the banks hurtle by with a dolorous expression that spoke louder than any words could of his dislike of this mode of travel. Kedryn grinned sympathetically and then, for the first time since the arrow had struck him, he began to laugh with genuine humour.

Chapter Nine

By the time the *Vashti* docked at Gennyf Kedryn was in better shape than his father. The preparations Wynett had supplied were healing both the damaged muscle of his shoulder and the scar of the cauterizing burn. He was able to use the arm again, perhaps less adroitly than before, but certainly with far more agility. Bedyr, on the other hand, succumbed to river sickness and spent the greater part of the time either stretched on a pallet or crouched over the side. He was denied even the temporary comfort of nights spent on dry land for he urged Galen Sadreth to maintain full speed and the riverman complied by setting running lights each dusk and foregoing the usual anchorages, holding to midstream and easing the pace only a little. As Gennyf hove in sight, however, he insisted on docking, explaining that the Sisters there would provide a remedy for the sickness, overcoming Bedyr's opposition with the blunt observation that a man wasted by illness would be of little use to whatever purpose they had in Andurel. Kedryn added his own voice to this persuasion and Bedyr, finally, agreed.

The *Vashti* consequently moored a little after dawn and Bedyr, his uncertain steps supported by Sadreth, allowed himself to be escorted to the hospice.

It was an attractive building in an attractive town, roofed with blue tiles, the walls of washed blue stone, surrounded by a pleasant garden in which Sisters were already working as the trio approached. The sight of a riversick traveller was apparently a commonplace, for Bedyr was rapidly administered a draft that calmed his churning stomach and returned his features to a hue closer to his normal tan. Kedryn, obeying Wynett's instructions, asked that his shoulder be examined and was delighted to hear the pronouncement that the healing process was, indeed, well under way, and that full mobility would return to him within days, certainly before he disembarked at Andurel. His only disappointment – though small, in view of the urgency of their journey – was that he did not have more time to explore Gennyf.

From the river it had seemed a pretty place, full of picturesque edifices that had none of the hard practicality of the more northern settlements. But speed was of the essence and the knowledge that the Horde must be drawing daily closer to the Lozin Forts made it easy to forego the indolent pleasures of sightseeing. There would be – he hoped – time enough for that later; perhaps none if they delayed, for then Gennyf might cease to exist. They set off again while the morning was still young.

It passed swiftly into afternoon, the *Vashti* leaping, as usual, from her moorings to cleave rapidly to midstream, the smaller craft that were becoming steadily more numerous as they travelled south giving way before the barque, Sadreth's mate – a grinning, well-muscled Galichian called Ivran – blowing a warning through the bugle mounted cunningly between the hands of the figurehead. The crew, somewhat disgruntled that their customary ports of call were ignored, busied themselves with running repairs or lounged about the deck tossing knucklebones against the promise of the wages they would receive at journey's end. Sadreth spent his time at the tiller, doing his best to instruct Kedryn in the ways of the river, and by late afternoon Bedyr was sufficiently recovered that he, too, listened to the impromptu education imparted by the sailor.

Kedryn found himself intrigued by the enclosed life of the rivermen, for although Sadreth had boasted of visting Caitin Hold, it became rapidly apparent that such landbound journeying was far in his past and far less frequent than he had at first implied. The River Guild held sway from the Lozins to the Andurel cascades, guildsmen manning the vessels that transported freight and passengers up and down the Idre, seldom straying out of sight of the wide water, sometimes settling in one spot to operate ferries, but never dabbling in what they considered the less consequential business of fishing or – the captain informed his audience with considerable disapproval – the frivolous pastime of boating for pleasure.

'Why do you go no farther?' Kedryn asked. 'The Idre does not end at the cascades. Has no one sailed farther south?'

'Portage,' Sadreth replied. 'Have you seen the cascades?'

Kedryn shook his head.

'They are murderous,' the riverman announced. 'Rocks and white water that would spill even the *Vashti*. Smash her like matchwood. Besides, who needs travel farther? Look about you.'

Kedryn turned full circle, studying the river. He could not see the banks, only a distant merging of sky and water, ahead a small island showed, a thin plume of smoke rising on the still air indicating that it was inhabited. Flocks of white-winged birds swooped shrieking about the barque and great fishes jumped from the water as though daring the avians to attack.

'You see her on a fine day,' Sadreth said, 'for summer lingers as we move farther south. Tomorrow she will be different. A week later, different again. Her currents change, the safe passages shift, she is always different, never predictable. See her in winter and you'd not know her. And in spring! When the northern snows melt and fill her she's a torrent. It's as much as any guildsman can do to keep pace with her, so why look farther south?'

The answer that sprang to Kedryn's lips was simply because it was there, but he recognized that Galen Sadreth was married to the Idre as surely as any man wed to mortal woman, and he kept his mouth closed, merely nodding, thinking that he, who had barely ventured out of Tamur, was hardly in a position to question one who daily plied so magnificent a waterway.

And magnificent the Idre undoubtedly was. The river had seemed wide where she cut through the Lozins, but now he saw that was the natural funnelling of the mountains. Here, so much farther south, she broadened to the proportions of a lake. The islands they passed seemed as isolated as any ocean-girt atoll, the towns as ports on unknown shores. One day, he promised himself, I shall take this journey at leisure and see those places Galen describes: Farol and Issinar, Lemantin, Tuerol, Fuengiras, Palamir and Marena. And those only on the Tamur side; more – so many more – to explore where the plains of Kesh rolled down to the water.

'But,' he exclaimed as a thought struck him, 'the Idre divides below Andurel. Ust-Galich is boundaried by ust-Idre and Vortigern. Surely there are boats on those waters?'

Sadreth sniffed dismissively. 'Fishermen, no more. The Galichians – save for a few like Ivran – have little taste for water. Their trade is land-bound: they freight their wares overland to Andurel and consign shipment to the Guild there. The Keshi are much the same: they fish the banks of the Vortigern, but send few of their sons to apprentice with the Guild. That's why so many of us are Tamurin, and those mostly born on the river.'

Another thought struck Kedryn then, but he kept it to himself until he found a chance to be alone with Bedyr, for it bore strongly on the task in hand. He waited until darkness had fallen, the Idre assuming a ghostly phosphorescence as the red and yellow running lights were lit and the night look-outs posted, the remainder of the crew settling in hammocks slung about the deck. Neither he nor Bedyr had found themselves able to adapt to this strange mode of sleeping and so had arranged their bedding on the solid oak of the hatches.

'Galen says it will be eight days more before we reach Andurel,' he murmured, pitching his voice low so that only his father might hear his concern, 'and we have been on the river twice that already. By now the Horde must surely approach the Lozin Forts, and King Darr must still raise his forces. How can we hope to return in time?'

In the faint light of the newly-risen moon Bedyr's face was solemn as he nodded.

'It is something that concerns me, too. I – we – can only hope that the far-seers of Andurel have, at the least, alerted Darr to the extent that he has set plans in motion. Sent word to Hattim and Jarl to stand ready. Mehdri can take word overland near as fast as Galen transports us south, and – the Lady willing! – the forts will hold long enough.'

'But the armies must surely travel by land,' Kedryn protested, 'and armoured men cannot travel with the speed of the mehdri.'

'No,' Bedyr acknowledged, 'but some can take passage on craft such as this. Perhaps sufficient to sway the outcome.'

'Up river?' Kedryn wondered. 'Against the current?'

'Aided by the Sisters, perhaps,' said Bedyr. 'They can sometimes use their powers to drive a vessel, though I understand it is a talent possessed by few, and mightily taxing, for it involves the contradiction of natural laws.'

'If such gramaryes tax the strength of the Sisters,' Kedryn queried, 'then does the same not apply to the Messenger?'

Bedyr shrugged, his face becoming grim. 'I do not know. Not for sure, though I doubt it. The Sisters prefer to live within the boundaries established by the natural order. As you already know, they place great emphasis on free will and consider any disruption of nature to be contrary to that belief. Thus, while they can sometimes effect weather changes, or lend speed to a vessel, they are weakened by the process. Sometimes destroyed. It is something to do with the nature of their talents, the manner in which those skills are used affecting the users. In a way I suppose it is a matter of belief.

'I do not believe the Messenger suffers any such qualms. He is, I think, a living contradiction of the natural order, and would not hesitate to go against it should such action further his foul purpose. Indeed, I suspect that it may be his purpose to bring about just such disruption.'

Kedryn experienced a chill such as he had not felt since quitting the Beltrevan, for Bedyr's words implied a greater enormity than barbarian invasion, something beyond conquest.

'What do you think his purpose is?' he asked, aware that his voice had become huskier as a sense of doom settled on him.

'I am not sure,' Bedyr admitted. 'The destruction of the Kingdoms, certainly. But that, for all it is undoubtedly monumental, is still no more than a long-cherished dream of the tribes. Since Drul raised the forest folk back in Corwyn's time the woodlanders have dreamed of looting the south. The Sandurkan hold much the same desires: it is not so unusual. What seems different now is that the Horde is led by Ashar's minion, and that suggests a purpose beyond pillage and rapine. Though just what that may be I cannot guess. Perhaps he seeks to destroy the world. I do not know, Kedryn, and that is one more good reason for seeking the counsel of the Sisters in Andurel.'

'I had thought,' Kedryn said slowly, 'that when you spoke of my being the one Alaria's text foretold, I should be called on as a warrior. Now I wonder if it means something more.'

Bedyr rose on one elbow, reaching out to grasp his son, to reassure him with the simple, plain pressure of his grip as he knew he could not do with words.

'Perhaps it does,' he said softly, 'but I should lie to you if I gave you answers I do not have: I do not know. I know only that I believe with all my heart we must go to Andurel to seek the answers. Perhaps beyond Andurel, to Estrevan itself.'

'If there is time,' Kedryn murmured.

'Aye, if there is time.'

Bedyr's voice was grave, the wan moonlight imparting planes and shadows to his features that lent further solemnity to the statement, almost belying the strength he had so far shown. Kedryn was constrained to place his own hand over the one that grasped his forearm, seeking in his turn to reassure his father, their roles momentarily reversed.

'We shall,' he announced firmly. 'And if we believe in the Lady and the Book, then surely we must – why else Alaria's text?'

Bedyr smiled then, the firmness of his purpose regained. 'You grow apace, Kedryn. I thank you.'

Kedryn smiled back, proud that he could aid his father, watching as Bedyr recomposed himself for sleep with the pragmatic commonsense of an experienced campaigner. He, too, stretched on the pallet, but sleep eluded him for their conversation had once again set astir the confusions in his mind. He could not see how he might be so important to the defeat of the Messenger, nor how – even aided by magic – King Darr might bring his armies to the defence of the Lozin Forts in time. The vast camp he had seen in the Beltrevan had surely contained sufficient barbarians that the forts might be overwhelmed by sheer weight of numbers, even without the sorcerous assistance of Ashar's minion. And with such aid, could even the Sisters prevail against the evil? Of that alone he was confident – that the Messenger was the very quintessence of evil. He had sensed that as he looked across the fire at that unearthly visage and felt the knowledge settle inside him like a sickness.

He was not much given to praying, few Tamurin were, though their respect for the Lady was tacit, but now he whispered the reverences instilled by Sister Lyassa, asking the Lady to bless their purpose and speed their arrival, adding a plea that – should it be her will – answers might be granted him.

None were just then, but he felt the breeze freshen and heard the braces of the foresail crack as the canvas bellied, the *Vashti* starting under him as does a willing horse forcing itself to greater speed in compliance with its rider's urging. He heard Galen Sadreth call softly from the stern, wondering if the riverman ever slept, and saw two of the nightwatch pad softly on bare feet to check the ropes. Above, the moon remained an enigmatic sliver of silver against the blue-black of the sky, attended by a panoply of stars, the Idre a great softly gleaming ribbon stretching away to the south. He listened to the wash of water against the prow and in a while slept.

In the morning the breeze grew stronger and both sails were set, the barque plunging swifter than a courser towards her destination, prompting Kedryn to wonder if his prayer had been heard. It kept up throughout the following days and Galen's estimate of their arrival time was cut by more than a day. Close to dusk on the sixth day out of Gennyf Andurel hove in sight.

Kedryn had seen nothing like the city. Not even the grim magnificence of the Lozin Forts could compare with what he saw illuminated by the waning light of the setting sun, for in size and splendour Andurel dwarfed even his wildest imaginings.

He clung to the figurehead, deaf to the braying of the great horn as Ivran gave warning of their approach, his eyes wide as he stared, turning his head from side to side and still unable to encompass the full glory of the place. It spread across the Idre in a great barricade of towers and palaces, houses piled like boxes, one atop the other, down to the water's edge and across to the far banks. Bridges arched over waterways, jetties thrust out like beckoning fingers, wharves and warehouses stood along docks against which bobbed a multitude of vessels large and small, the river lapping against their planks. Rooftops of tile and marble, slate and wood, coruscated colour against the amber glow of the sun to the west, while to the ceast lanterns blinked a kaleidoscope of brilliance in the encroaching darkness. As they drew closer, Galen shouting for the sails to be furled as he slowed the *Vashti*, Kedryn saw that the city was built on a whole series of islands linked by bridges and catwalks, some wide, some narrow, some almost flat, others rainbow arches set with multi-coloured stone, seeming too steep to climb even though he saw people watching from the apex of the curves. There were gardens amongst the buildings and as the barque eased closer to the docks he saw that what had at first appeared a random jumble of structures was, in fact, a city laid out on planned lines. Wide avenues ran down to the waterfront, interconnecting streets and alleyways criss-crossing between them, the avenues spreading back, rising, directing the eye to the highest point of the largest, central island. There stood a building of such simple grandeur that without ornamentation it still could not help but dominate all of Andurel. It was white, though the western wall was painted red by the sun, square, with a great dome at the centre of the roof and tall, narrow windows along all the sides he could see. A low wall surrounded it, a gate facing him with an avenue running down to the closest structures, trees and grass visible between. It bore no insignia, no flags or pennants, but he knew instinctively that this must be the fabled White Palace, ancestral home of the Three Kingdoms' elected monarch.

Then it was lost behind the lower edifices as the *Vashti* hove to, Galen throwing his considerable bulk against the tiller to bring the barque round smooth and sweet to dock gently against a jetty of dark blue granite.

The crew busied themselves mooring the craft as Galen came down the deck, beaming at his passengers.

'Did I not say she is the swiftest vessel on the Idre?' he enquired happily.

'You did,' Bedyr replied, answering the smile, 'and you were right.'

'And now you have business to attend,' said the riverman, 'as do I. But before you depart, may I ask a question?'

Bedyr nodded and Galen said, 'Would you have me wait? I can

doubtless find a cargo to transport up river, but if you prefer I remain, I can do so.'

Bedyr thought for a moment, then said, 'Friend Galen, you have served us well, and I thank you for that. I would not rob you of your livelihood, but it may well be that swift passage north will be required.'

'Then I wait,' beamed the huge guildsman. 'My lads will welcome the opportunity to carouse awhile and,' he tapped his nose ponderously, 'I sense the urgency of our journey south may well be multiplied on the return. You'll find me here, or in the tavern of the Golden Horn.'

'My thanks.'

Bedyr thrust out his hand and it was engulfed in the riverman's grip. Kedryn did the same. Galen said, 'Fare thee well, young Kedryn. And remember you've a friend on the river should such be needed.'

Kedryn smiled, extracting his hand from a fist that threatened to crush it, almost sorry to leave the guildsman.

'Come,' Bedyr set his scabbard on his belt and tossed his satchels to his shoulder, 'we'll go a-visiting.'

They turned, moving towards the avenue that disgorged between two low warehouses of red stone, then halted as a double column of eight mounted soldiers trotted into view. They rode matched horses, roan paired with roan, grey with grey, black with black, chestnut with chestnut, the rear brought up by two superb riderless whites. The warriors were clad in plain round basket helms burnished to a silvery sheen, each one emblazoned with a golden three-pointed crown, dully shining suits of link-mail beneath surcoats of dark blue against which the same insignia glittered, leather breeks of a matching blue colour, and high, black boots. They wore sheathed swords, but no other weapons, though one man held a small golden rod in his right hand, raising it as he espied Kedryn and Bedyr.

'Darr's far-seers have been at work,' Bedyr murmured.

Kedryn could only stare, for he was accustomed to the motley trappings effected by Tamurin warriors, not this opulent display of uniform armour.

'My Lord Bedyr Caitin!' The column halted, the officer – closer, Kedryn could see that the crowns on helm and breastplate were marked with a small, central diamond – slapping clenched right fist to his chest. 'Prince Kedryn! King Darr bids you welcome to Andurel and requests that you attend him.'

Behind him, Kedryn heard Galen chortle and could not resist

turning to grin at the riverman, who waved and pantomimed a massive bow.

'My thanks,' he heard Bedyr say. 'We are honoured that the King sees fit to send an escort.'

'Your mounts.' The officer gestured and the two white horses were brought forwards with the precision of a drill exercise. Kedryn mounted, wondering if everything in Andurel was done with such formality. He hoped not: he was more used to the freedom of Tamur and, despite Lyassa's lessons, unsure of the correct procedures.

'My Lord? Prince?'

The officer waited as though uncertain that they could control their animals. Kedryn resisted an impulse to drive his heels against the charger's flanks and race the column up the avenue, instead he watched Bedyr nod and brought the horse in line as they set out at a sedate trot.

At least the pace gave him a chance to study Andurel at closer quarters, and he found it as marvellous as it had seemed from the river. Initially they rode past warehouses that, despite their size and obvious opulence, were much the same as warehouses anywhere, but then they began to pass taverns and bazaars displaying a bewildering variety of goods from gaily dyed cloths to full suits of battle armour, kiosks selling sweetmeats and bangles, jewellery, scarves, leatherware, and all the streets thronged with people. He lost count of the multiplicity of available purchases as they passed an area of more sober emporiums whose goods were displayed discreetly on counters overhung by canopies so that browsers might not be disturbed by sun or rain, and then houses. Such houses as he had never seen. All brilliant tilework and mosaics of tiny coloured stones, with ornate balconies and roofs hung with lanterns and pennants and metal cylinders that chimed as the breeze blowing off the river struck them. There were the gardens he had seen from the deck of the *Vashti*, but looking this close more like small parks, with colonnaded walkways and little gazebos, fountains and plazas, birds singing in the trees as they bade farewell to the day.

Then they passed between two massive pillars of white and gold and the avenue ran straight, rising towards the palace. It was, he saw, encircled by an area of parkland that ended at the wall. This was low, formal rather than defensive, though it would break any cavalry charge, and past it he saw that the earth was dug out to form a deep trench invisible from the outer side, running almost to the walls of the palace itself. This was broached by the gate, an arch of white stone surmounting two great portals of dark, red wood set with massive bronze fittings. It was open and they trotted through into a flagstoned courtyard.

Kedryn gasped as he saw that his first impression of a single great block of a building was, in fact, a cunning architectural trick. What had appeared to be the main wall of the structure was in reality a high screening wall enclosing the actual palace buildings. Darr's stronghold was as solidly defendable as Caitin Hold itself, the deceptive screen hiding ramparts and catwalks, stables and barracks and armouries. The great dome he had seen was the cupola of the palace proper, rising from what appeared to be a single gigantic block of white from which windows and balconies looked down on the yards, arched doorways affording entrance.

He was barely aware of the groom in white and gold livery who came forward to take his reins, smiling as Kedryn tore his gaze from the magnificence about him and dismounted. He was given no more time to study his surroundings for the officer requested that he and Bedyr accompany him and marched briskly across the courtyard to a door guarded by two plate-armoured halberdiers.

Bedyr seemed at ease, and Kedryn reminded himself that his father had visited Andurel more than once, whilst he, seeing the palace for the first time, felt vaguely like a country bumpkin. He effected an air of nonchalance, but nonetheless gazed around in wonder as they were led across a tall-ceilinged room with a floor of striated red marble and walls hung with massive, ancient tapestries to a second guarded door. Past this there were fewer sentinels, and the rooms became smaller, set with alcoves in which stood statuary in stone and marble and metal. These alcoves were linked by corridors where windows of stained glass reflected dazzling patterns of colour in the light of flambeaux burning in ornate receptacles seeming too delicate to support the weight of the torches they carried. They progressed steadily inwards until their escort reached a stairway that curved up towards the higher storeys. He began to climb, Bedyr and Kedryn following, until they came to a gallery lit by the windows of the great dome and he halted at a door inlaid with brass plates moulded in the shape of faces. He pounded once and when a voice called from inside, saluted and pushed the door open, his back rigid as he announced, 'The King awaits you.'

Bedyr entered without hesitation, Kedryn following a pace behind, trying hard to remember the protocols Lyassa had struggled to instil in him.

It was not necessary, for the man who came towards them as the door closed opened his arms and embraced Bedyr as might an old friend, unmet for too long a time. Bedyr in turn tossed his satchel aside and returned the embrace with enthusiasm, leaving Kedryn the opportunity to study the monarch.

Darr was a fraction shorter than Bedyr and some years older, his face thin and homely. His soft, yellowish hair was cropped to neck length, more grey in it than showed in Bedyr's, bound with a plain circle of gold, a short, square-cut beard decorating a chin that was saved from weakness by the wide, firm set of his smiling mouth. About his neck hung a heavy gold chain from which was suspended a silver medallion on which, in bas relief, stood the three-pointed crown that blazoned the tunics of the palace guards. It was the most opulent thing about him, for his robe was plain grey, unadorned, and the belt about his narrow waist was of simple black leather, the sheathed dagger no finer than the Tamurin blade Kedryn wore. When, finally, he released his grip on Bedyr and turned towards Kedryn, the young man saw that his eyes were blue and tired, the pleasure that shone there contrasting with the deep creases lining his cheeks and brow.

'By the Lady, Bedyr,' he smiled, studying Kedryn, 'is this the child I saw so long ago? He's a man, and he favours you.'

Kedryn gaped, not sure how he should respond: Lyassa's instruction had not included lessons on the informality of kings.

Darr made it easy for him by clasping his shoulders as he began to kneel and saying, 'Kedryn – Prince Kedryn! – welcome to Andurel. I only wish your arrival presaged happier times.' His voice was light, echoing the weariness that showed in his eyes.

'My Lord,' Kedryn began, then broke off as Darr raised a negligent hand, saying, 'Darr. Call me Darr in the privacy of my own chambers. There'll be time enough for formal address later, and you're too much a younger version of this old warrior for such tiresome correctitude.'

Kedryn nodded, turning the motion into a bow, raising his head to find Darr beaming, asking, 'And Yrla? She is well?'

'When last I saw her,' Bedyr said. 'Though that seems long and long ago.'

'Aye.' Darr's expression grew solemn and he stroked at his grey-streaked beard. 'Since then much has happened. Tell me. Sit down and tell me everything. You'll take wine?'

Without awaiting an answer he crossed to a spindle-legged table and lifted a jug of blue crystal, filling three goblets with a pale, golden vintage that sparkled as he passed the cups as casually as though they drank in some tavern. He motioned towards chairs set about a window recess, their backs and arms inlaid with gold, the seats of some soft, blue material. Kedryn sat, sipping the wine as Bedyr recounted their adventures in the Beltrevan and beyond.

As he spoke, Darr turned to Kedryn, his eyes no longer laughing, but thoughtful, nodding occasionally as if Bedyr's words confirmed suspicions held but not welcomed.

'The Messenger,' he murmured when Bedyr was done, so softly that it seemed to Kedryn he must speak to himself, vocalizing his thoughts. 'As we feared. And Alaria's text. But what to make of it? How to use it?'

'Has the Sisterhood not suggested some means?' Bedyr asked, the question bringing a shaking of Darr's head.

'Not here. Not to me. The far-seers spoke of your coming, but were not able to penetrate the Beltrevan. Estrevan has sent no word. So, what to do?'

Kedryn found himself perplexed by the monarch's curious mode of speech. He had thought that the King would be firm, positive as Bedyr, not vague as Darr appeared, but his father seemed accustomed to it and shrugged as he answered.

'Raise your army and march north. Use the River Guild to transport a spearhead and ask the Sisterhood for help. Before long – if not already – the Horde will attack the Lozin Forts. If the Messenger is able to breach the defences the barbarians will flood south. Literally – they'll doubtless come down the Idre.'

'And storm Andurel,' Darr nodded. 'Take her, perhaps. Cut off the head. Then what? Spread? Strike out from here. So many, you say. They could take the Kingdoms one by one. Unless . . .'

'Unless we halt them at the Lozins,' Bedyr finished for him. 'My Tamurin can muster and march from the west. Let Jarl's Keshi strike from the east and we'll mayhap crush them between us. Hattim's Galichians will form the reserve, for it will take them longer to come north to join us.'

'Hattim,' Darr murmured, his tone thoughtful, dubious. 'Hattim doubts the veracity of my reports. Why I needed you here. Hattim does not trust the abilities of the Sisterhood. Hattim does not believe as we do.'

'He'll believe readily enough if he sees the Horde rafting down the Idre,' grunted Bedyr ominously. 'But Jarl? Is he firm to our purpose?'

Darr raised a hand, turning it from side to side. 'Not certain, but not opposed. He'll listen. Hattim is the problem.'

'Command him,' Bedyr snapped, his tone one Kedryn had never thought to hear addressed to the monarch.

'Easier to suggest,' responded Darr mildly. 'Hattim feels safe. Hattim does not enjoy the notion of war. Ust-Galich lies so far to the south.'

'I do not *enjoy* the notion of war,' answered Bedyr, 'but sometimes it must be fought. By the Lady, Darr! Are you King here, or not?'

To Kedryn's amazed eye Darr appeared embarrassed. He toyed with the medallion about his neck, his lips pursing before he shrugged and said evasively, 'Peace sometimes softens. Hattim is soft. Ust-Galich is too far removed from the forests. The Beltrevan is a child's bogeyman there. And Hattim plots. He would see the Sethiyan line established in Andurel. He covets my crown. The Lady knows why – it's a heavy thing to wear. But Hattim: Hattim wants it. He may see a way in this.'

'You speak of treason!'

Such rage sounded in Bedyr's voice that Kedryn started, coming close to spilling the wine he held. He stared from his father to the King, wondering how Darr – weak, it seemed – retained his position, a treasonable thought crossing his own mind: that Bedyr Caitin seemed more regal than the bearer of the crown.

Darr shrugged and murmured gently, 'He is not that obvious. I dare not confront him. For the sake of unity. And we need him. There is strength in unity. Face Hattim with such an accusation and civil war might be the result.'

Kedryn saw his father's hand tighten on the goblet until he thought the crystal must shatter. Bedyr composed himself with an effort and asked, 'Do Tamur and Kesh fight alone then?'

'No,' Darr answered slowly, 'Hattim can be played. Perhaps a Galichian force to guard Andurel.'

'I doubt that Tamur and Kesh alone are enough,' Bedyr retorted, his tone bitter.

'*If*,' said Darr, emphasizing the word, 'the Horde should break through, the Idre is the way, is it not?'

'Aye,' Bedyr nodded, his tone brusque and more than a little angry, 'I believe it must be. The tribes are numerous enough that they can spread west and east, but the main force must surely strike for Andurel to take the head – as you so rightly pointed out.'

'Bedyr, Bedyr,' murmured Darr, 'I *am* still King. Hattim may delay if ordered into the field. But to guard Andurel? That he would agree to. And guarding Andurel he stands directly before the Horde if worst comes to worst. Tamur and Kesh to west and east, harrying. A trap? The Horde along the Idre?' He drove his right hand forwards, blocking the movement with his left. 'The army of Ust-Galich before.' He steepled his fingers, touching thumb to thumb at the base of the triangle, bringing his hands together. 'Tamur and Kesh closing from the sides? From behind?'

'It would not work,' Bedyr said bluntly. 'They are too many. Darr, you did not see them! They could hold Tamur and Kesh at bay and still come down the river to seize Andurel. Hattim's force could not hold them. They'd take the city.'

Darr sighed. 'A thought, no more. A pity it cannot work. So, Hattim must be persuaded?'

'If the Three Kingdoms are to survive,' nodded Bedyr.

'Well, we must see what we can do,' said Darr thoughtfully. 'Jarl will listen to you. He'd sooner not, but he will. Hattim will argue. We must convince him.'

'Has it changed so much then?' asked Bedyr, frowning. 'Can the King not command?'

'Times change,' Darr replied wearily. 'Peace changes men. Hattim has not known war as we have. This kingly business is complicated.'

'He'll know it soon enough,' Bedyr grunted.

The King nodded, sighing, tugging at his beard as he stared into the darkness beyond the window.

'But Kedryn?' He changed the topic with an abruptness that caught Kedryn by surprise, the discussion fascinating him to the extent that he had forgotten the part he might have to play. 'Alaria's text. What can it mean?'

'I had hoped the Sisters here would advise us,' Bedyr said, glancing moodily at his son. 'Yrla can do no more than suggest, and I have no inkling.'

'Nor I,' said Darr, and smiled at Kedryn. 'You appear an enigma, young man. What shall we do with you?'

'I can use a blade,' Kedryn offered stoutly, emboldened by the monarch's casual attitude. 'And you'll need every warrior you can muster. My father speaks the truth, my Lord – Darr – when he says the barbarians are uncountable.'

'I do not doubt it,' agreed the King. 'I have never known Bedyr Caitin to speak less than the truth. Not Bedyr. But you are more than a blade. You are – what? I must introduce you to Grania. The

Paramount Sister here. She heads the college. Yes. Perhaps, face to face, Grania may perceive the meaning of the text.' He nodded to himself, then beamed and said, 'But you are tired, no? And would welcome baths? And clothes? Rest if you will. Tonight we dine with Jarl and Hattim. Formally, alas. Until then I must ponder your father's words. And your place in all this.'

Kedryn was unsure of the correct response to this musing, but Bedyr seemed in no doubt.

'Are we to discuss invasion as a dinnertime topic? Or are we to defend our lands? For the Lady's sake, Darr, you *must* take action!'

Darr smiled wanly and spread both hands in a supplicatory gesture. 'I shall,' he promised, 'but in my own way. Recount what you have told me. Convince Jarl. And curb your temper where Hattim is concerned. Please? Leave him to me.'

Bedyr nodded with obvious reluctance and without further ado rose to his feet, beckoning Kedryn to follow him. Kedryn began to bow, but Darr waved, smiling, and he turned to follow his father from the room, confusion rampant.

Outside, liveried footmen waited to escort them to their quarters, explaining that baths were drawn up there, ignoring Bedyr's grim expression with the neutral discretion of skilled retainers, bringing them through more resplendent corridors to adjoining chambers from which emanated the scented steam of the tubs, condensation moistening high windows that overlooked an inner courtyard where fountains played, the spouting water silvered by the now-risen moon.

Rather than entering his own quarters, Kedryn followed Bedyr inside, standing silent as sword and satchel were flung irritably on to a bed large enough to accommodate three people. The Lord of Tamur stalked to the window and stared out, hands on hips, fists clenched, more angry than Kedryn had thought.

'Father,' he ventured, 'surely Hattim must listen. Surely the King will command him.'

Bedyr turned, fumbling with the buckles of his surcoat, dragging it off and sending it to join his blade before he answered.

'Times change,' he mimicked roughly. 'More than I had suspected, it seems. The Lady knows, Valaria's death took Darr hard – and Hattim was ever a schemer with too much ambition – but this!'

Kedryn watched as he unsnapped the metal fastenings of his jerkin and shrugged out of the toughened leather, aware that he knew nothing of Andurel's politics, for like Bedyr he could see only one response to the threat from the north and found it near impossible to countenance the likelihood of Ust-Galich failing to join with Tamur and Kesh in defence of the Kingdoms.

'He must surely see the danger,' he suggested. 'No matter what schemes he lays, he must surely see that Ust-Galich will suffer should the Horde prevail.'

'Darr appears to think so,' Bedyr sighed, rubbing the stubble that now covered his chin. 'But Darr has changed. He was stronger when his wife lived. Some said she gave him his strength – and she *was* a woman of iron purpose! – but to prevaricate now is more than I can credit. We must convince them, Kedryn! Perhaps that is the meaning of the text – that you are the one to fuse the Kingdoms.'

'I?' Kedryn returned doubtfully. 'If the King cannot command Hattim, then how may I persuade him?'

'I do not know.' Bedyr shook his head and for a moment he looked as weary as Darr, older than his years and oppressed by the weight of his responsibilities. Then he grunted, essaying a smile as he looked at his son. 'We have come a long way, you and I. And there remains a long way to go, towards some destination I cannot see. I would have you know that I am proud of you.'

Kedryn smiled. 'Ust-Galich or no, we shall defeat the Horde. Even with the Messenger at the head, we shall defeat the forest folk.'

'Bravely said,' Bedyr returned. 'Now bathe and prepare yourself for the first of our battles – against an ally!'

Kedryn nodded and went to his own chamber. He looked about him, thinking that the soft, silken draperies and the luxurious carpets that hid the floor were too soft, weakening the men who used them. Better the rough simplicity of Caitin Hold if scheming and prevarication were the price paid for such fineries. He unhooked his sword and set it carefully in the armoire of carved oak, then divested himself of clothes and entered the inner room containing the tub. The water was hot and he lay in it, idly scrubbing, aware that the marks of arrow wound and burn were almost gone now, healed by Wynett's talent, wondering how he could persuade Hattim Sethiyan to go to war when even the nominal ruler of the Three Kingdoms appeared doubtful of achieving the same end.

Like Alaria's text it seemed an imponderable, and after a while he gave it up and allowed the water to drain away, standing to turn the brass spigot of the fish-headed spout above the tub and drench himself in cold, fresh water.

Towelled vigorously dry, he explored the contents of the wardrobe, finding clothing of a nature to match the luxury of the room. There were soft breeches of doeskin and linen shirts finer than any he had seen, boots more suited to treading carpets than honest earth, and a knee-length over-robe of some russet material, the Tamurin fist emblazoned on chest and back. He dressed, cinching his own plain belt about the waist and setting an unadorned silver fillet about his lengthening hair. Then, feeling more princely than ever he had at home – and considerably more nervous – he went to find his father.

Bedyr was dressed in similar fashion, though his over-robe was of dark blue and his hair was drawn into a tail, emphasizing the stern set of his features. He nodded, smiling as Kedryn entered and clapping a hand to his son's shoulder.

'This may be harder than sword work,' he remarked with grim humour, steering Kedryn down the corridor in the direction of a staircase.

'I'd as lief work with my sword,' returned Kedryn. 'I'd sooner be with Rycol on the Lozin walls than here.'

'And I,' Bedyr agreed, 'but we have a duty here and we shall do our best to acquit that task with honour, so let's be about it.'

'What if they will not listen?' Kedryn asked.

'We return north with Galen,' promised Bedyr. 'To High Fort if we're in time, to Caitin Hold if not. Whatever Jarl and Hattim may decide, Tamur will oppose invasion.'

Kedryn nodded, heartened, and strode more purposefully to the winding stairwell that disgorged into a spacious room where people in silken finery stood conversing as servitors filled wine cups from crystal jugs and minstrels strummed garitas, their subtle melodies a counterpoint to the steady murmur of voices.

The two newcomers were saved from the duties of polite conversation by Darr, now dressed more regally in purple silk, a golden crown on his thinning hair and a formal smile on his lips.

'My Lord Bedyr Caitin of Tamur,' he cried as though greeting his guests for the first time, 'and the Prince Kedryn, heir of Tamur. Welcome!'

Bedyr went down on one knee and Kedryn followed suit, finding that he could, after all, remember his lessons.

'My Lord King,' Bedyr responded, echoed by his son.

'Rise,' said Darr. 'Let us eat.'

As he moved to the head of the column that formed on this announcement he was joined by a young woman of such startling beauty that Kedryn found himself unable to resist staring at her. She was as tall as the King, the silk of her gown so fine that the burgeoning contours of her figure were clearly outlined, the purple a dark contrast to the golden glory of her hair, drawn back in a mesh of silver filigree that exposed a slender neck circled by a chain of blood red stones linked on a rope of gold. Her features were proud, the mouth wide and full-lipped above a firm jaw, her nose aquiline, the eyes large and incredibly blue, fringed with lashes of deepest black. It was almost too strong a face, yet sensuous, the mouth inviting kisses, the eyes that caught Kedryn's amused. He had thought Wynett lovely, but this woman – girl, he saw as she turned her head – was more than that. She was magnificent. He could no more resist staring at her than he could fight the impulse to ask his father who she was.

'Ashrivelle,' answered Bedyr, 'Darr's daughter. She was a child when last I saw her, but she has grown. She takes her mother's place at times.'

'She is beautiful,' murmured Kedryn, feeling his heart quicken as they entered the dining hall and he realized that he would sit close to her. 'She is lovely.'

'Aye, she is,' Bedyr agreed. 'But I've heard she's also wilful. And we've more important matters to attend. Besides, I understand she looks with some favour on Hattim Sethiyan, so try to hold your mind to the less beautiful lords of Kesh and Ust-Galich.'

Kedryn nodded dutifully, but still felt disappointed when he found himself seated to his father's right, and thus denied clear sight of the Princess by the interposed bodies of Bedyr and Darr. More so when the position to Ashrivelle's left was taken by a softly handsome man some several years older, who addressed her with a casual ease that brought a rustle of laughter from her lushly smiling mouth.

'Hattim,' Bedyr informed his son.

Kedryn studied the Lord of Ust-Galich and decided he was more suited to such surroundings than the battlefield. Hattim was, he supposed, attractive to women, though to his eyes the man seemed weak, his features too regular, almost vacuous. His mouth was soft and his eyes a fraction too limpid, set with overlong lashes of the same white-gold hue as the hair he wore so carefully parted and combed, held back from a smooth forehead by an intricate weaving of gold and silver and some red metal. His robe was a pale green, the sunburst emblem of Ust-Galich picked out in silver and black, and both wrists bore bracelets of the same colours in which blue gems sparkled as he moved expressive hands. A belt of silver links encircled a waist that, to Kedryn, looked thickened by soft living, a sheath of red leather worked with gold supporting an ivory-hilted dagger bossed in silver.

He liked the look of Jarl better, for the Keshi Lord appeared more the honest warrior. He was seated to Kedryn's right and he greeted the young man as an equal. He was, Kedryn thought, the same age as Bedyr, though his hair was purest black, oiled and plaited as Fengrif's had been, similar rings decorating his fingers, though there comparison ended. Jarl was short and bow-legged, his features hawkish, the nose a curving, broken beak above straight, moustachioed lips, his eyes green and bright, like a falcon's, his belly flat beneath a black robe on which the horsehead of Kesh stood out red from a disc of white. His dagger belt was black, too, as was the scabbard and the hilt of the long knife sheathed there. To Kedryn's eyes he looked the kind of man who bore battle scars, whilst Hattim's body would be soft and smooth as the smile he bestowed upon the Tamurin visitors as he leant forwards to speak across Ashrivelle and Darr.

'My Lord Bedyr, Prince Kedryn, I understand you bring alarming news.'

Kedryn was surprised: he had not anticipated so direct an approach from the ruler deemed least likely to lend his support to their cause.

'We do, my Lord Hattim,' Bedyr responded, going bluntly to the point. 'The Horde is raised again and this time led by Ashar's Messenger. We must arm and march in defence of the Kingdoms.'

Kedryn watched Hattim nod thoughtfully, his face bland, whilst beside him he heard Jarl grunt softly.

'And how, my Lord, do you reach this conclusion?' demanded Hattim, toying idly with a silver knife.

'We saw the Horde.' Bedyr indicated Kedryn. 'We entered the Beltrevan and saw the tribes in parley. The truce feathers were up: Drott, Caroc, Yath, Grymard and Vistral were all in attendance. And Kedryn saw the Messenger.'

Hattim favoured Kedryn with a glance before returning to Bedyr. 'But you did not?'

'No,' Bedyr admitted, 'but my son did.'

Kedryn heard Jarl mutter, 'By the Lady!' and Hattim give a sound part chuckle, part snort. Between them, Darr glanced from one to the other as though anticipating fiercer argument, while Ashrivelle remained impassive.

'Only the boy?' Hattim twirled his knife as though the motion dismissed the veracity of the statement, questioned Kedryn's integrity.

'The *man*, and his eyes are good,' Bedyr said tightly, and Kedryn recognized that he held his temper in rein. 'And there is Alaria's text . . .'

'That?' Hattim laughed openly and the sound was contemptuous. 'Not even the adepts of Estrevan can interpret that text. Do you suggest that your son is singled out by the Book?'

Muscles tautened along Bedyr's jaw, but he forced politeness into his answer. 'My wife interprets it so, my Lord, and her belief is enough for me. Further – there was an ambush of which Kedryn was the target.'

'An ambush!' Hattim's eyes widened mockingly. 'Do tell us of this ambush, Lord Bedyr.'

Bedyr recounted the details and Kedryn blushed as he caught Ashrivelle's blue gaze fastened on him, wishing there were more of an heroic nature to the account, that he might appear more the warrior in her eyes.

'And you take this as proof?' Hattim smiled. 'Some renegade forester and the word of an hospitaller more accustomed to tending bruises?'

'I do,' said Bedyr. 'And I believe the King shares my belief.'

Darr appeared little pleased to be thus drawn into the discussion, clearing his throat noisily and stroking his beard as Hattim's eyes turned to him alight with questions.

'We can ill afford to take such news lightly,' he began. 'No man here can doubt the word of my Lord of Tamur, and consequently it behooves us to discuss our reaction.'

'Arm,' snapped Bedyr. 'And march!'

'You forget the Lozin Forts, my Lord,' said Hattim.

'Forget?' Bedyr controlled his temper with obvious difficulty. 'I do not forget the forts, Lord Hattim.'

'They held the Horde in Drul's time,' responded Hattim with insulting negligence. 'They will do so again.'

'The Messenger marches at the head!' Bedyr barked, no longer tactful. 'Can you not understand what that means? Drul attacked unaided by magic, but now Ashar's minion lends his evil to their cause!'

'My Lord of Tamur waxes wrathful,' smiled Hattim, his tone silky. 'Must I remind him that we are allies here? We serve the single purpose.'

'Do we?' Bedyr demanded. 'Then why prevaricate?'

'My Lords,' said Darr, raising his hands, 'hold your tempers. We are, as Lord Bedyr says, faced with a threat from the north; and we are, as Lord Hattim points out, allies. Let us not quarrel amongst ourselves, I beg you. And we have not heard from my Lord of Kesh. What have you to say, my Lord Jarl?'

Kedryn turned as the Keshi ruler spoke, his voice flat, left hand resting on the hilt of his dagger as if anticipating its use.

'I was doubtful when you summoned me, King Darr. Like Hattim, I believe the Lozin Forts are strong enough to repel barbarian attack, but I have received word from Fengrif that suggests this may be no ordinary sally. Now I hear a warning from the mouth of Bedyr Caitin – and I know that Tamur speaks true – and I say we should march.'

He encompassed both Bedyr and Darr in his glance, a grim smile on his hawkish features. Bedyr responded with a nod of approval; Darr with a wan smile.

'You would raise Kesh to defend the Lozin gate?'

'I would,' averred Jarl. 'What Bedyr Caitin tells us cannot be ignored, not if we are to fulfil our duty to the Kingdoms. The risk is too great.'

'The Lozin Forts are great,' murmured Hattim. 'Great enough to repel Drul and his Horde. Strengthened since then, they must surely be greater still. Surely great enough to hold out any number of forest folk.'

'You refute the existence of the Messenger?' queried Bedyr, his tone marginally softer now that Jarl appeared to have swung to the cause.

'On the word of a boy – my pardon, a *man* – I am . . . shall we say, dubious?'

Bedyr turned in his high-backed chair that he might look directly at Hattim. 'My Lord of Ust-Galich, it is as Lord Jarl says – too great a risk to ignore. Kedryn and I entered the Beltrevan and saw the Horde. The forest folk have multiplied since Drul's time: their numbers are unimaginable. I believe they are led by the Messenger – and surely even you must know what the Book says of him – and whether or not you accept that, *can you afford the risk of ignoring the danger*? Suppose,' he continued as Hattim opened his mouth, allowing the Galichian no chance to reply, 'that I am right. Suppose Kedryn did see the Messenger. Suppose the Horde is led by Ashar's minion. His magic may well be great enough to bring down the Lozin Forts, to open the way for the Horde. What do you suppose would happen then, my Lord Hattim?'

Again he went on before Hattim could interrupt. 'The barbarians will come south, my Lord. South down the Idre. They may well spread across Tamur and Kesh, for their numbers are such that Tamur and Kesh alone cannot withstand their onslaught – of that you have my word – but they will not halt there. No, they will come down the river to Andurel and the city will fall. Do you think Ust-Galich will be safe then? Not Andurel, not Tamur, not Kesh will stand between you and the Horde then, Hattim. The Three Kingdoms will be a wasteland, Ust-Galich trampled down with the rest, and all your dreams burned in Ashar's fires. Will you risk that? Can you?'

Hattim seemed unruffled by this, though Kedryn caught a glint of anger in his green eyes, and when he answered his voice was sharper, edged with malice.

'A fine speech, my Lord of Tamur. Indeed, a speech to stir the blood, or run it cold. But it still hangs on the one thread – that your son saw the Messenger. Without that, my point remains: we likely face only the Horde, and the Lozin Forts are strong enough to defeat that threat.'

'Blood of the Lady!' rasped Jarl, clenching a fist as though to pound the table. 'Bedyr is right – you prevaricate! I repeat, we cannot afford to ignore the risk!'

Hattim shrugged, effecting a patently transparent apologetic tone. 'I do not wish to prevaricate, Lord Jarl. Nor do I intend any offence to Tamur. I seek only to discuss the matter in reasonable fashion. You ask me to summon my commanders, to raise the forces of Ust-Galich and march north to a battle that may never happen. What if I am right? Shall we turn about and march back, explaining to men who have left their farms, their vineyards, their families that it was all a mistake? That Prince Kedryn thought he saw something that was not, in fact, there?'

Kedryn felt a hotter flush of anger than any he had experienced in all the tiresome debating. Unthinking, all notions of protocol forgotten, he slammed a fist against the table, ignoring the wine that spilled from his overturned goblet as he ignored the curious faces of the diners on the lower tables, turning angry eyes to Hattim.

'I saw him!' he said fiercely. 'Whether or not you believe that is of no consequence to me. I know what I saw, and that *was* the Messenger. There was magic in the arrow that struck me – Wynett said so! – and though I do not know what the text means, I do know what I saw. The Messenger is there and he will bring the Horde to the Lozin Forts and if the forts fall because we fail them – because you waste time – then the blood of warriors will be on your head and the Lady damn you for a coward!'

He broke off, torn between rage and embarrassment, barely hearing Jarl's murmured, 'Well said, lad,' aware of his father's startled smile. King Darr swallowed in seeming nervousness, while Ashrivelle stared at him with an expression he could not fathom. Nor had much time to, for Hattim answered promptly, 'A man, you say, Caitin? Then do I take it that a man accuses me? Should I take it as a challenge?'

'As you will!' Kedryn retorted.

Hattim's face grew hard and cold, the softness gone. 'You should not have dubbed him *man*, Caitin. I might have taken that from a beardless boy, but not from a man.'

Bedyr began to speak, but Kedryn grasped his arm, shaking his head and saying, 'No, Father. This is my quarrel.'

'There will be no bloodshed,' said Darr. 'I will not permit bloodshed.'

Hattim exaggerated surprise, 'A *man* accuses me of cowardice and you refuse me the right to answer?'

Kedryn was not sure where his reply came from for the words sprang unbidden to his lips. Perhaps the Lady answered his prayers: he did not know, only that he was on his feet, glaring at Hattim as he said, 'My Lord of Ust-Galich, I will fight you. But if I win, I want your promise that your army will march with us to the Lozins.'

'You have it,' said Hattim, laughing.

'No bloodshed,' Darr repeated, sighing. 'If fight you must, you will fight with kabah.'

'I accept,' Hattim said.

'And I,' Kedryn nodded, uncaring that in the hands of a skilled swordsman the kabah might easily cripple and maim, kill if the user so desired.

Softly, that only Kedryn might hear, Jarl whispered, 'Careful, lad, Hattim is not so soft as he appears: he has killed three men with the kabah. He enjoys it.'

'I have killed no one,' responded Kedryn, 'but I shall beat him.'

'Prince,' said the Lord of Kesh, smiling grim admiration, 'I believe you might.'

Chapter Ten

'This is madness! You allow civil war to foment while the Messenger himself knocks on the Lozin gates!'

Bedyr glared at his king, incomprehension behind the anger shining bright in his brown eyes, only the anger showing on his handsome face as he towered over the seated figure of Darr.

'Do I? Or do I forestall it?' The pale-haired man made a small gesture with his right hand, partly apologetic, partly an invitation for the Lord of Tamur to seat himself. Bedyr ignored it, his own hands clenched tight on his belt, as though he needed to hook them there or fasten them on Darr. He shook his head.

'I do not understand.'

'You saw how Hattim wriggled,' said the King. 'As I warned, he is loath to commit himself. Indeed, I rather suspect his intention was to prevaricate long enough that Tamur and Kesh were committed to battle without Ust-Galich. Oh, he would have raised his forces – slowly. Slowly enough that he might see the outcome before his own fief was threatened. Let the fist and the horse take the brunt, and if victorious, there would be Hattim marching to guard the rear. Should the barbarians succeed, then Hattim might seek truce – he, after all, had not opposed them.'

Raw rage suffused Bedyr's features at this and when he spoke his voice was harsh. 'Call him to account! Brand him traitor!'

'And foment civil war?' Darr asked innocently. 'What else could happen were I to face him with such accusations? He did not refuse to join us, merely expressed doubts. And Kedryn did call him a coward.'

'Coward he is,' snapped Bedyr, pacing to the window to stare into the night, out over the rooftops of Andurel. 'But Kedryn has not duelled, whilst Hattim is accomplished.'

'They will fight with the kabah,' said Darr carefully. 'I achieved that at least. Perhaps much more.'

Bedyr turned from his study of the silent city, a frown creasing his brow as suspicion dawned. 'Did you plan this, Darr? You know as well as I that the kabah can kill. And if Hattim Sethiyan harms my son I'll challenge him myself. With steel, not kabah.'

'Do you believe Hattim will win?' Darr asked. 'I do not.'

'Darr.' Bedyr crossed the carpeted floor in long strides to face the King, his voice cold, fresh anger ominous in his eyes. 'If this is some devious plan, then mayhap it will be you I challenge. You had best explain while my temper holds.'

'Bedyr,' Darr said gently, his eyes as weary as his tone, 'it is no easy thing to rule these lands. The Kingdoms go largely about their own business without reference to me. What am I? Little more than a figurehead! A lawgiver when such is needed; an arbitrator. I cobble things together, Bedyr, and if my cobbling fails to please I am deposed. We face the greatest threat ever to descend upon the Three Kingdoms – of that I am without doubt – and I find I must organize a defence with one vital element loath to commit. I could not afford to allow Hattim the time to delay further lest his delaying bring us all down. Surely you can see that? We *must* face the enemy together, unified. I sought advice on the matter, and I acted on that advice.'

'You did plan it!' Bedyr cried, his hands lifting as though to strike the monarch.

Darr did not flinch: he sat staring at his friend with sadness on his face as he nodded. 'Perhaps not *planned*. Allowed might be the better word. Now hold your temper a while longer and I will try to explain.

'I have spoken at length with Grania concerning the text, and she is of the same opinion as Yrla: Kedryn is the one referred to. Quite how he will aid the Kingdoms I do not know, though I suspect it happens already. Neither you nor Jarl would have thought to challenge Hattim in that way – you are both too conscious of our tenuous unity, and being both loyal and honest men you perhaps do not perceive Hattim as do I. A command would, as I have told you, produce only pro-testations of loyalty and further prevarication. But Kedryn? He brings a fresh viewpoint, an innocence that perceives only what must be done. I believe the Lady guided his tongue just as she will guide him in the duel.

'I believe that Kedryn will win, Bedyr. And in winning, force Hattim to act without delay, bound by a debt of honour rendered too public to forget. I believe that, thanks to Kedryn, he will be forced to join us; and it was the only way I could see to achieve that aim.'

'He is still my son,' Bedyr said doubtfully, though much of the anger was gone from his face.

'He is more than that,' Darr countered. 'He belongs to the Kingdoms now, my friend.'

Bedyr's hands clutched and opened. 'I must speak with Grania,' he muttered. 'I would hear what the Sisterhood has to say.'

'I expected as much.' Darr smiled wanly. 'Grania awaits my summons.'

He rose from his chair and crossed to where a tasselled cord of pale blue silk hung down. He tugged the cord once and resumed his chair, pouring wine that he sipped slowly, motioning for Bedyr to help himself. The Lord of Tamur shook his head, resuming his position at the window as though seeking answers in the darkness. He turned as he heard the door open, offering respectful obeisance to the diminutive, grey-haired woman who entered. The Sister Grania was tiny, her face creased with a myriad wrinkles, apple-red cheeks round as dumplings below bird-bright black eyes. Her gown, the blue of the adept, was crumpled and she smoothed it casually as she studied the two men.

'You have told him,' she murmured, then to Bedyr, 'and you do not like it.'

'I fear for my son,' said Bedyr bluntly.

'You should not: he will win.'

The reply took Bedyr aback with its brusqueness, his shock magnified by Grania's downing of a full measure of wine, followed closely by a second.

'He was wounded,' he protested.

'And the wound is full-healed,' said Grania before he could go on. 'Sister Wynett is an excellent Hospitaller. And I am an excellent seer. I have studied Alaria's text as carefully as your wife, Bedyr Caitin, and I am convinced beyond any doubt that your son is the one spoken of there. I cannot interpret beyond that, but I am certain that Kedryn is the saviour of the Kingdoms – therefore he cannot lose.'

'He could suffer hurt,' grunted Bedyr, awkward with the position in which he found himself; unaccustomed to arguing with one of the Sisterhood. 'Hattim might cripple him.'

'Does your kyo not proclaim him the finest swordsman in all Tamur?' Grania asked, producing a square of white linen with which she dabbed at her lips before sipping her wine again.

Bedyr nodded. 'But . . .'

'But what? You took him into the Beltrevan where he was threatened with far worse than a kabah. What do you think the Messenger might have done to him? Or was that different because you and

223

Tepshen Lahl rode with him? You could not have stood against the Messenger, and that one is infinitely worse than Hattim Sethiyan. Indeed, it is Hattim you should fear for – you might warn Kedryn against giving him permanent hurt.'

She filled her glass again and settled into a chair, so small that her slippered feet dangled above the carpet.

'It has come suddenly, I know, but we all anticipated the arrival of the Messenger, of the Horde. That is why Yrla quit Estrevan. Why she married you. Of course,' she added, smiling, 'there were personal reasons: free choice is all, but that was how Kedryn came into the world, and no life is without a purpose. Some are greater than others, that is all. Kedryn's may well be the greatest.'

'Did you know this would happen?' asked Bedyr, finally taking wine, that gesture mute acceptance of the web of destiny he felt forming about his son.

'Not *knew*,' replied the petite woman, 'but I suspected it might. The Book indicates something of the sort and I knew that Hattim would act as he did. How Kedryn would react, I did not know; only that honour would prevail.'

'I feel as I did on Galen's barque,' muttered Bedyr. 'Helpless in the stream.'

'Not helpless,' countered Grania, shaking her head, then smoothing back the strands of grey that broke loose from her snood. 'You chose to take the river road.'

'To reach Andurel as swiftly as possible,' Bedyr grunted.

'And to raise our army as swiftly as possible it is necessary for Kedryn to teach Hattim a lesson,' said Grania firmly. 'As Darr has no doubt pointed out, the Lord of Ust-Galich has little stomach for war and a great appetite for scheming. Kedryn cuts through all that.'

'It appears that I have little choice,' Bedyr retorted, his tone ironic.

'You have several choices,' the Sister told him. 'As Lord of Tamur you can forbid Kedryn to fight. Or you can leave Andurel. Or you can parley with Hattim. You could threaten Darr with the withdrawal of your support if he refuses to prohibit the duel. You might hire an assassin. Or kill Hattim yourself.'

Bedyr stared at the tiny woman, whose dark eyes sparkled challengingly over the rim of her wine cup. He felt trapped within a net of implacable logic, for he could see that he might have done any of these things. Were he prepared to act without honour; or Kedryn to heed such a ban. Finally he smiled, though the expression held little humour.

'Kedryn will fight,' he said. 'I would not forbid him – nor he listen if I did – and the other options are unpalatable.'

'But they *are* options,' Grania pointed out.

'Aye,' Bedyr nodded.

'And you should not hold this against Darr,' she warned. 'He had little liking for my prognostication, and believed he acted in the best interests of all.'

'No, I will not.' Bedyr glanced at the King, who sat silent, answering his friend's stare with an expression of helpless apology. 'Though I would sooner he had told me of his suspicions before Kedryn issued his challenge.'

'That would have influenced the outcome,' Grania said, somewhat testily. 'Surely you can see that. What happened, happened freely; nothing influenced Kedryn's choice. That was important.'

Bedyr's agreement was reluctant, but it came nonetheless, prompting a satisfied smile from the Sister.

'Then we are in agreement? Good. Now perhaps I may go back to bed. No doubt there will be much work to be done after the duel has secured Hattim's promise, and it will be tiring work to speed our boats north.'

'You intend to give that aid?' Bedyr asked, surprised.

'Why should I not?' Grania frowned as though the question were foolish.

'I had thought the Sisterhood exercised a prohibition of such distortions of the natural order,' Bedyr responded. 'And that the thaumaturgy was draining; even unto death.'

'What the Messenger does is a distortion,' snapped Grania, distaste in her voice, 'and what he will do is worse. I have consulted with my Sisters and we are in agreement that such deviation from our usual constraints is justified. As for the danger, are you not prepared to die in defence of the Kingdoms?'

Again, Bedyr nodded, his eyes expressing the admiration he felt for the tiny woman.

'So, now that is settled I need to sleep.' She wriggled forwards in the chair until her feet met the floor and she stared up at Bedyr. 'The Sisterhood will do all it can to defeat this threat, my Lord of Tamur. Do not doubt it. And do not fear for your son: Hattim is the least of the dangers Kedryn may face.'

With that she bustled from the room, leaving the two men staring after her. Bedyr drained his glass, turning to Darr.

'Forgive me.'

'There is nothing to forgive,' Darr responded, smiling more warmly now. 'Rather, it is I who should ask your forgiveness.'

'You are my king,' Bedyr said simply.

'And your friend,' said Darr. 'Sometimes that renders my duty difficult.'

Bedyr smiled, setting down his glass. 'Does she truly read the future?'

'Not as a sibyl,' the King replied, 'at least so far as I can understand it. Rather, her talent is to foresee the possibilities, to trace out each thread of likelihood and from that maze perceive the most advantageous path. Her advice is invaluable.'

'As will be her aid in speeding us north.'

Darr's expression told him that doubt attached to this and his eyes flashed a question.

'The Sisters will do all they can,' said Darr, his voice weary again, his features dour, 'but still it may not be enough. That particular talent is possessed by only a few, and there are not many here in Andurel. At best we can transport three thousand north in what Grania believes to be sufficient time. The rest must travel by normal means.'

Bedyr felt his heart sink as cold dread crept into his soul. Carefully, he poured a glass of wine, vaguely surprised that his hand did not shake.

'Three thousand is not enough. Even if the forts hold we must enter the Beltrevan to destroy the Messenger, and to do that we need every man.'

'I know.' Darr's face was grave, the lines on brow and cheeks deep-sunk, and in the light of the flambeaux there were dark shadows beneath his eyes. 'But it is the best we can do. That, and pray to the Lady that three thousand may fortify the Lozin gate until the rest arrive.'

'May the Lady bless our purpose,' Bedyr murmured solemnly.

'If she does not,' said Darr, his voice quiet, 'we may see the Kingdoms fall.'

'No,' Bedyr shook his head, 'for I shall be dead.'

Darr offered no argument: he knew the Lord of Tamur would sail with the first boat north.

'I pray it will not come to that,' he whispered, 'As King, but more as friend.'

'I know,' said Bedyr, rising, 'but let us not dwell on that. As Grania said – it is time to sleep.'

'Aye,' sighed the monarch, 'sleep well, my friend. I shall stay here a little while.'

Bedyr bowed and left the room, where Darr still sat, lonely, staring into the dregs of his wine cup, the weight of kingship heavy on his narrow shoulders.

In the corridors of the palace sleepy servants stirred, but he waved them away, preferring to be alone with his thoughts, unpleasant though they were. How many forest folk had inhabited that vast encampment? How many thousands of blades were even now sharpened to carve the Kingdoms? And the Messenger at the forefront of the Horde. What gramaryes might he use against the forts? What powers would Ashar lend the barbarians? Lady, he said inside his head, if you love the Kingdoms, be with us! Help us! We need you now as we have never needed you before.

Had he been a man given to formal prayer he would have knelt and made the rituals, but he was not, so he closed the door of his chamber behind him and prepared himself for sleep, his last waking thought of his son, who in the morning would fight his first duel against a full-grown man already accomplished in the deadly skills of the trajea.

Kedryn suffered no such forebodings. His challenge issued, he had found himself feeling somewhat embarrassed to have created such commotion in the dining hall. His words – and Hattim's responses – had been passed rapidly down the tables until every man and woman there knew of the forthcoming trajea, and after them the servants had taken word into the palace until, he felt certain, all of Andurel must know he had accused the Lord of Ust-Galich of cowardice. The embarrassment, however, was offset by genuine anger at Hattim's prevarication, and when he had caught Ashrivelle studying him with a greater interest than before he had squared his shoulders and smiled, determined to prove himself the better man.

The dinner had ended on a subdued note, terminating not with the customary dancing, but with King Darr's announcement that the combat would be fought in the morning and the suggestion that all present retire early. As the hall emptied, he had been aware of the glances cast his way, and several times overheard the comments of the nobles, mostly that it would be a pity to see such handsome features battered by Hattim's kabah. It had not occurred to him to think of that, for it had not occurred to him that he might lose. It was not vanity, nor the foolhardiness of youth, but rather a deep-seated conviction that he *must* win, for he had been trained by Tepshen Lahl and remembered the kyo's parting words. More, it was the certainty that by winning he would determine Ust-Galich's unhesitating participation in the coming war, and that was so vital to the Kingdoms' cause that he felt the Lady must grant him the victory.

His purpose was further strengthened by the slight smile Ashrivelle bestowed upon him as she rose to follow her father from the hall.

Consequently, Kedryn slept soundly, *his* final thought of the Princess, who was, he decided, without doubt the loveliest woman in all the Kingdoms.

He woke well-rested, dismissing the servant who came to help him dress, bathing alone and selecting clothes he felt suitable for the occasion. Dressed in soft buckskin breeks overset with high boots of sturdy leather and a simple linen shirt, he repaired to Bedyr's room, where food was set.

His father was accoutred in similar fashion, though wearing a sleeveless tunic bearing Tamur's fist on chest and back, his dagger at his waist.

'Hattim will choose the short kabah,' Bedyr advised, 'and perhaps a buckler. The Galichians fight mostly on foot. I understand he favours the thrust. Low.'

Kedryn nodded calmly. He would have preferred the long practice sword, being more accustomed to the length of the Tamurin blade, but he felt that he could match most men with either.

'You are not afraid?' Bedyr asked, the question rhetorical.

'No,' smiled Kedryn.

'Good. Then let us eat – but sparingly.'

It was, Kedryn knew, wise, – if needless – advice; a food-filled belly was more prone to suffer from the stabbing blows of the short kabah, and even with the light armour they would wear, such thrusts could be excruciatingly painful. It occurred to him that Bedyr was unusually concerned. In Caitin Hold his father had shown no reservations about his taking part in the mêlées or the individual practice combats, but here he watched carefully as Kedryn sipped the tisane that accompanied the bread and fruit he chose to break his fast, offering advice on the techniques Hattim was likely to employ until Kedryn was constrained to ask that he cease lest his concern undermine confidence.

'I am sorry,' Bedyr smiled, 'as Lord of Tamur I know you are his match, but I am still your father. I forget that you are a man.'

Kedryn nodded, realizing that their relationship had been changing in subtle ways since first they entered the Beltrevan. He had gone into the forest a youth anxious to win his status as a man, respectful of his father and totally willing to acknowledge Bedyr's precedence in all things. Now, though he could not define exactly when or how it had happened, he *had* become a man. It was more than the blooding of the barbarian arrow, more like some internal change, some growth of confidence and self-awareness. He remained respectful, continued to acknowledge Bedyr as his liege lord, but he was now prepared to argue with his father, to make his own decisions and hold to them even though Bedyr might disagree. It was, in many ways, a strange feeling, but one that he enjoyed.

'Aye,' he said, 'I am. And you *are* still my father, but now I must fight my own battles. Hattim Sethiyan will be my first.'

Bedyr stared at him then with something like sadness in his eyes, then ducked his head once and began to smile. 'Then go and fight it,' he said. 'Trounce that popinjay soundly. But, Kedryn – do not damage him permanently.'

Kedryn laughed, pleased that Bedyr should express such confidence. 'No,' he promised, 'just bruises enough to teach him a lesson.'

They rose together and marched to the King's audience chamber, where by tradition participants in the trajea met prior to combat.

Darr was already settled on the throne there, his slender form amplified by the formal robe of green and crimson, the enlarged shoulders lending him stature, the heavy crown concealing the sparseness of his hair. Ashrivelle sat beside him on a lower throne, dressed in pure white embroidered with gold thread, her hair ribboned with more gold, the gown drawn in by a golden belt. Kedryn again felt his heart quicken as he gazed at her, wondering if it was concern he saw in her eyes, realizing that they were somehow an even purer blue than Wynett's. When she smiled at him he experienced an unfamiliar sensation, as though they were the only two in the chamber save for some hidden choir whose voices rose in a song only he could hear. It was a pleasing experience and he smiled back, gazing openly at her beauty, finding in it another reason to defeat Hattim, for he recalled the familiar way the Lord of Ust-Galich had spoken with her in the dining-hall, though he did not realize that what he felt was jealousy.

Her father's voice returned him to the reality of the moment and he tore his eyes away, seeing Jarl of Kesh and numerous other nobles entering the chamber, Hattim amongst them, accompanied by adherents in the livery of Ust-Galich.

'My Lords and Ladies,' Darr announced in formal, regal tones, 'Prince Kedryn of Tamur has issued challenge to our Lord of

Ust-Galich, whose honour demands that he requite the imputation, though at my command the trajea will be fought with the kabah, not naked steel. Further, Prince Kedryn has elicited from our Lord Hattim the promise that should he prove victorious, Ust-Galich will arm and march to the defence of our realm on the instant. Is this understood?'

There was a murmur of assent from the watching crowd and Darr beckoned the combatants forward.

Hattim stepped up to face the King with a smile on his lips. Kedryn saw that he was dressed in similar clothing, though his wrists were bound with leather and his boots sewn with metal links.

'Do you, Prince Kedryn,' Darr asked, 'repeat and maintain your challenge?'

Kedryn realized abruptly that Lyassa's teachings had not included the protocols attaching to a duel so he simply ducked his head and said, 'I do.'

It appeared sufficient, for the King nodded and said, 'And do you, Lord Hattim, accept this challenge and the promise that appertains?'

'I do so accept,' Hattim smiled, his voice confident, 'and I give word now, in the hearing of all, that mehdri stand ready to take my orders to my liegemen should the Prince of Tamur best me. Let there be no doubt that Ust-Galich stands ready to fight!'

This brought some cries of approval from the onlookers, but a sour expression from Bedyr, beside whom Jarl stood with unconcealed contempt on his dark features. Kedryn allowed his eyes to wander to Ashrivelle, but her face was impassive.

'As challenged, you have the choice of instruments, Lord Hattim,' Darr said. 'How do you choose?'

Hattim beckoned and two men in Galichian livery came forwards, one bearing a selection of short kabahs, the other bucklers. Hattim bowed mockingly, inviting Kedryn to take first pick. The younger man studied the practice blades, hefting them and checking the wood for weaknesses. Each one was roughly the length of his forearm from blunted tip to hilt end, constructed of straight hardwood shafts carved flat, with blunt-rimmed metal discs dividing the facsimile blades from the leather-bound hilts, those bulging in semblance of a boss. He made his selection and turned to the bucklers. These were not much larger than his spread hand, circles of fire-hardened wood overlaid with hide, held by a single wooden grip. He chose one and stepped back.

Hattim began his selection, turning as Jarl, a frown on his face, demanded, 'And armour? Where is the armour?'

The question brought a response from the crowd and an innocent smile from Hattim.

'I agreed to fight with the kabah, my Lord of Kesh. No mention was made of armour.'

'It is customary,' said Bedyr, echoed by Jarl.

'My Lord of Tamur fears for his son,' Hattim said, still smiling though his eyes were cold. 'Perhaps he should have taught his son better manners in order that he might avoid such fatherly concerns.'

Kedryn saw Bedyr take a step forwards and cried out, 'There is no need of armour! I shall not hurt my Lord Hattim – too much.'

Hattim's smile froze on his face as laughter echoed in the chamber. The eyes he turned towards Kedryn flashed a stormy green as his hand tightened on the hilt of the weapon he had chosen, knuckles whitening as his teeth clenched and he hissed, 'And I will teach you respect, boy.'

'My Lords,' said Darr, 'are you sure of this? I would have neither one of you hurt.'

'I am sure,' Kedryn promised before Hattim could speak, leaving the Galichian only the chance to nod his agreement, his weakly handsome features flushing with rage and embarrassment.

'So be it,' the King agreed doubtfully. 'And the terms?'

'Who first cries enough,' said Hattim, glancing spitefully at Kedryn, 'loses.'

'Aye.' The younger man answered the stare undaunted. 'So be it.'

Ashrivelle looked to her father then, leaning back to whisper in his ear, Darr nodding assent before straightening and saying, 'As monarch I retain the right to call a halt should I deem one man the victor. Is this acceptable to you, my lords?'

Hattim nodded with obvious reluctance. Kedryn ducked his head once.

'Then let us repair to the practice ground,' said Darr.

The assembly followed the King from the chamber, Bedyr and Jarl moving to flank Kedryn.

'Be careful, lad,' warned the Keshi. 'Hattim looks to break some bones.'

'Ward your manhood,' Bedyr murmured.

Kedryn thought of Ashrivelle, and wondered if it had been concern for his safety that had prompted her whispered intervention. 'Does the Princess truly favour Hattim?' he asked.

Bedyr's face expressed surprise; Jarl bellowed a laugh that turned heads around them.

'At a time like this he thinks of a woman!'

Kedryn flushed, grinning, but undeterred. 'Does she?'

'There has been no formal declaration,' grunted Bedyr. 'But for the Lady's sake, Kedryn! Think of the trajea, not the Princess.'

'Mother favoured Estrevan until she met you,' Kedryn said, his voice thoughtful.

Bedyr shook his head in exasperation. 'Remember the teachings of Tepshen Lahl for now. You'll have time enough to dream of Ashrivelle after.'

'Aye,' Kedryn agreed. 'But she is not promised, is she?'

'No!' Bedyr snapped. 'She is not promised, but if you allow your mind to wander Hattim will leave you unattractive to even the poxiest whore, let alone a princess.'

'Good,' said Kedryn, and fell silent as he began to prepare his mind in the way Tepshen had taught him.

As they entered the practice ground he was ready. His limbs were loose, his concentration focused on the duel; he was aware of the audience watching from the surrounding tiers of seats only as an extension of the arena itself, not even sure where Ashrivelle sat, feeling the firmness of the packed soil beneath his booted feet, noting the shadows cast by the palace buildings and the areas of light where the early sun might blind him.

The practice ground was designed for footwork, not cavalry practice. It was large enough that combatants might circle, but not so large that they might avoid one another for long. Circular, it was walled by the palace – faces showed as pale blurs in windows – with the tiered seats rising five high all around. Between seats and sand there was a chest-high barrier, intersected on the quadrants of the compass with narrow exit points. Hattim Sethiyan stood at the centre, swinging his kabah in whistling arcs. Kedryn moved to face him.

He did not turn as he heard Darr call out, 'May the Lady bless you both. And may she elect the rightful victor. Let the trajea commence.'

Hattim's kabah thrust forwards to punctuate the sentence, a low, straight strike propelled by the full weight of his shoulder, directed at a point midway between Kedryn's belt buckle and groin. He grimaced as the blow was deflected, turning faster than Kedryn had expected to counter the answering swing.

'I will not hurt you too much,' he parodied, circling, his left arm extended to present the buckler, his kabah held low. 'I will just change your shape a little.'

Kedryn said nothing, studying his opponent, seeing how Hattim moved his feet, how he balanced himself. He held his own buckler closer in, the kabah out to the right, waiting, assessing the older man's technique, unwilling to commit himself until he was sure of a stroke that would not leave Hattim crippled.

He did not wait long: his silence seemed to infuriate the older man, for Hattim made a sudden feint, thrusting forwards at the waist, then losing the strike to ram the buckler at Kedryn's face as he brought his blade up and over, anticipating a blow to Kedryn's neck.

The kabah scraped Kedryn's side as he turned, deflecting the buckler with his own blade and punching the Galichian hard in the belly. It was less soft than Kedryn had thought, but still Hattim gasped, dancing back in time to avoid the upswing of his opponent's weapon. He continued backwards, crouching with his buckler protective over his midriff as Kedryn advanced, knees bent, feet moving in short, shuffling steps that suddenly became larger as he drove forwards, parrying Hattim's defence to make a cut and reverse that snapped that man's head back, then down, leaving an ugly welt along his jaw and a swelling bruise across his cheek.

Had they fought with swords Hattim's blood would have spilled; had Kedryn struck with full force, the man's jaw would have broken. As it was, Hattim staggered, eyes glazed, while Kedryn waited, kabah lowered, for him to recover. When he did, raw rage blazed in his green eyes and he roared an inarticulate cry as he hurled himself forwards, kabah criss-crossing the air before him. Kedryn parried the blows, allowing Hattim to drive him across the arena until he sensed the barricade at his back. Before Hattim could pin him there, while triumph flowered in the man's eyes, he ducked under the blade, spun to avoid the jab of the buckler, and kicked Hattim's legs from under him.

The Lord of Ust-Galich crashed face-first into the wooden fence. His kabah was flung from his hand and he went down. Kedryn stood patiently, allowing him to rise, then stooped to flick the fallen blade to the panting, furious man.

Hattim snatched it from the air and turned again. Blood oozed from a cut lip, staining the fine linen of his shirt, the swelling purple bruise that disfigured his mouth combining with his anger to render him ugly. He advanced slowly, buckler to the fore, right arm bent at the elbow to hold the kabah on a straight line, more cautious now, aware that he faced an opponent more formidable than he had anticipated. Kedryn let him come, seeing murder in the green eyes now, extending his own buckler, his kabah alongside.

They fenced – as best as the short weapons allowed – for long moments, Kedryn again familiarizing himself with Hattim's style. He turned two thrusts, then felt his shirt tear as Hattim swung his buckler in a slashing motion across his chest, closing fast. A foot lashed out to hook his knees as the kabah drove at his face. He pushed the blade away, but felt his legs go as Hattim slammed a shoulder against his breast, toppling him off-balance. He landed on his back, legs lifting in time to send the downswinging blade to the side. Then he was rolling as Hattim stabbed, driving the blunted tip into the earth in a torrent of blows that would have broken ribs or burst his stomach sac had any landed. Voices shouted from the audience, expressing disapproval but neither combatant paid them heed, Kedryn because he was too intent on staying alive, Hattim because he was too lost in fury.

Then Kedryn felt the kabah drum earth close by him and reversed the direction of his roll, turning his body back to trap the blade and force it down flat against the dirt. Hattim's buckler slammed hard against his shoulder, jarring his arm and bringing an unwilling grunt of pain, but he ignored it, turning again to lift his legs and thrust his feet into the man's stomach.

Hattim was lifted up, then hurled back by the double kick. He tottered, arms flailing, then sat down heavily. Kedryn sprang to his feet and kicked the fallen blade towards the Lord of Ust-Galich.

'Your kabah, my lord.'

He could not resist it.

Again he waited until Hattim was on his feet, flexing his shoulder to ease the bruise he felt forming. Hattim spat and screamed and charged, technique lost beneath the surge of embarrassed anger that transformed his whole face to a purple hue, as though consumed by one enormous bruise. Kedryn backed away, deflecting blows, letting his opponent tire himself, circling the arena with buckler and kabah working in joint defence. He went round once, then a second time, then turned a thrust that would undoubtedly have ruined his manhood had it landed, dodging inside the punching buckler to ram his own kabah into Hattim's belly.

The Galichian grunted, doubling over, and Kedryn swung his buckler against the side of his jaw. He saw Hattim's eyes cross as the head snapped sideways, and straightened it with a short swing that laid the flat of the wooden sword in a line from temple to chin. Hattim went down on his knees. Then he leant forwards until both hands rested on the earth. His head drooped, lowering until it touched the soil. Kedryn stood back.

'Enough!' he heard Darr cry. 'I pronounce Prince Kedryn the victor.'

'*No!*'

With monumental effort Hattim lurched to his feet. Both cheeks were welted now, and blood ran freely from his lips, but he advanced, moving awkwardly, bent from the pain in his belly, stumbling towards Kedryn.

'It is done!' shouted the King. 'Lord Hattim, cease!'

Hattim shook his head, sending bloody spittle in an arc, and continued his advance.

'My lord, please,' Kedryn urged.

'The Lady damn you,' snarled Hattim, and drove forwards.

Kedryn shifted to the side, easily avoiding the lumbering attack, driving his buckler against Hattim's left arm just below the angle of the shoulder. The Galichian yelped, staggering sideways as deadened nerves sprung his fingers loose from the kabah, then swung to stab at Kedryn's face with the buckler. Kedryn took a half pace round and sideways, the wooden disc moving past his head as he rapped down with his blade, catching Hattim on the base of the thumb. Again, Tepshen Lahl's lessons served him well, for he caught the nerve cluster he aimed at and Hattim's left hand was involuntarily opened to drop the buckler. Kedryn paced one stride back and levelled his kabah on Hattim's throat.

'My lord, you are beaten.'

Hattim snarled and reached up to clasp the blade, but Kedryn snatched it back, seeing berserk madness in the man's eyes now. He took a second pace back as Darr shouted again, echoed by the crowd.

'My Lord Hattim, I command you to cease!'

Hattim made a sound deep in his throat and lunged barehanded for Kedryn's weapon. Kedryn stepped to the side, raising the kabah to his left shoulder. He swung it down as Hattim came level, using the boss, placing the blow carefully, measuring its force as Tepshen Lahl had instructed him. It landed against the base of Hattim's neck and the Galichian jerked abruptly upright, his head lifting as his eyes opened wide, staring sightlessly. Then snapped shut as his body went limp and he fell, nerveless, to the dirt of the arena.

Kedryn stood, blade and buckler lowered, but this time Hattim made no attempt to rise and when Darr's voice rang out in announcement of Kedryn's victory there was a shout of approval that echoed from the walls about the arena. Kedryn turned to face the King and bowed. As he straightened he saw that Ashrivelle was studying him carefully, but when he smiled at her she lowered her eyes, avoiding his gaze.

Then Bedyr and Jarl, attended by Keshi, were crossing the arena as men wearing the sunburst of Ust-Galich on their robes moved to lift the unconscious Hattim, bearing him away to the hospitallers as Kedryn was surrounded, compliments loud in his ears.

'You fought well,' Bedyr told him, smiling proudly.

'And taught that braggart a lesson,' added Jarl.

'And held him to his promise,' grinned Kedryn. 'Do the mehdri ride now?'

'Darr will see to that,' his father said. 'You did the Kingdoms a service today.'

That pleased Kedryn and he let them lead him away to where the King and Ashrivelle sat.

'The undoubted victor,' Darr smiled, leaning forwards to add more softly, 'I am in your debt, Kedryn – Hattim has no choice now, save to act in concert.'

Kedryn bowed low, finding Ashrivelle's eyes on him again, a slight smile playing about the corners of her mouth. He wanted to say something gallant, something about her beauty inspiring him, but before he could form any suitable words she spoke.

'Should the Prince of Tamur not attend our hospitallers, Father? He did not emerge entirely unscathed.'

Her voice was low and melodic. Kedryn smiled carelessly, dismissing his small hurts. 'I am unharmed, Princess, though I thank you for your concern.'

This time Ashrivelle smiled back, and that alone made the trajea worthwhile, but she shook her head. 'If you are to defend the Kingdoms, Prince Kedryn, you will need a sound shield arm.'

Kedryn summoned all Lyassa's teachings in a courtly bow that would have surprised and delighted the tutor Sister, saying, 'Your smiled negates any hurt, Princess.'

Then he blushed as she laughed, and allowed Bedyr to steer him away through the thronging nobles who called praises for his conduct, blushing afresh as the ladies' whispered praises reached his ears. Jarl's Keshi made a path, forming an honour guard about him, Bedyr smiling proudly at his side as they entered the palace.

He was taken to the hospital, seeing Hattim stretched on a couch with several Sisters attending his damaged face. He was conscious again, but when Kedryn paused by his bed to courteously offer apologies, the Galichian snarled and turned his head away.

'Ungracious cur,' Jarl muttered, sending a venomous glance at the wounded man. 'Must I fight alongside such as that?'

'You must,' said Bedyr. 'We all must. But Kedryn, tread wary about Hattim – I believe you have an enemy there.'

Kedryn shrugged. 'Surely he can find enemies enough to the north.'

It did not occur to him that Hattim would harbour a grudge until Bedyr said, 'A man like Sethiyan does not take kindly to defeat, and you have bested him in both the duel and his scheming. I think he will remember that.'

'Let him,' said Kedryn, easily, still basking in the warmth of Ashrivelle's smile.

'Heed your father's words!'

Sister Grania emerged from a side chamber, bustling to Kedryn's side as she waved the attendant Keshi back. 'Leave us be, Jarl: I wish to talk to the Prince alone. You, too, Bedyr Caitin. I'll send him to you when I'm done.'

Kedryn watched with amusement as the Lords of Tamur and Kesh beat a retreat from the diminutive woman, following her into the chamber, where she slammed the door and bade him sit. Her manner was one that commanded instant obedience and he settled on a plain wooden chair as Grania fetched ointments from the array of pots lining three sides of the simple, white-washed room. She told him to remove his shirt, kneading his bruised shoulder and grunting when he winced, applying salve to the hurt muscle.

'You were wounded here?'

Kedryn touched the spot where the arrow had entered. There was only a slight discoloration of the flesh now, and no pain at all.

'I thought so. I can feel the magic.'

She began to rub salve on to the spot, talking all the while. 'I am no hospitaller, but this will take out the bruise. And this will perhaps dull the gramarye. But he's tricky, the Messenger, and he'll be looking for you, so – as your father said – tread wary. Beware of Hattim, too, for he's not one to forgive or forget, and much rests on your shoulders.'

'The text?' was all Kedryn managed to get in between her flow of words.

'Aye, the text. You're the one Alaria guessed was coming, though don't ask me what you're to do because I don't know. Go north and fight. You'd do that anyway, of course, you don't need to tell me, but take care. As best you can. It's my suspicion that he'll be looking for you, so ware ambush and archers, for I think he'll put hounds after you. Darr will have the army of Andurel raised within days and we'll be sailing north. I'll have a finer perspective when we reach the forts, so mayhap I can offer better advice then.

'For now, stay away from Hattim and avoid any more duels. You've a greater trajea before you than any you might find here.'

'I have no wish to fight *any* trajea,' Kedryn objected, taking advantage of Grania's need for breath. 'I had no wish to fight Hattim, but I could not avoid it.'

'It was your destiny,' said the tiny Sister. 'The Lady put the words in your mouth. Hattim needed a lesson.'

'Can you read the future?' Kedryn asked.

Grania smiled, her round face wrinkling like a winter apple. 'Perhaps.'

'But you will not tell me what I must do?'

'You must do what you think best,' she said firmly. 'That is as much future as I can read for you.'

'Sister Wynett said as much,' Kedryn protested. 'I thought to find out more here in Andurel.'

'Would you have it set out for you?' Grania faced him, her eyes serious. 'How would our lives be if we knew what steps to take down all the road of life? Free will is all, Kedryn.'

'So I am confirmed as the one the text mentions, but that is all?' He was disgruntled.

'That is all,' she agreed cheerfully.

'That is not much help,' he grumbled.

'Did you need help when you challenged Hattim Sethiyan?'

'No,' he allowed, 'but then I spoke without thinking.'

'Sometimes it is better to speak without thinking. Sometimes that is the more honest way. Sometimes the Lady speaks through us.'

'But I am not of Estrevan.'

'Do you believe the Lady speaks only through the adepts? Not so! We learn in Estrevan how to interpret her teachings; we learn what our talents are; we learn how to use them. But the Lady is not the sole prerogative of Estrevan: she belongs to all.'

'But to use your talents you must remain celibate,' he ventured.

'We must,' Grania agreed. 'I am not sure why, save that such state appears to focus latent powers that become lost when we depart that condition. I suspect it is something to do with concentration.'

'I . . .' Kedryn paused, embarrassed.

'Are yet celibate?' Grania chuckled. 'It is nothing to shame you. In time you will not be; or perhaps you will be. You will decide. It does not matter.'

'But if I am the one spoken of in the text, surely I must remain celibate?'

Grania detected the doubt in his voice and emitted a trill of laughter, shaking her head vigorously. 'It is something you will decide for yourself,' she repeated. 'When the time comes you will know what is right for you.'

'So I could marry?' he wondered, half to himself.

'You could bed every whore in Andurel, though I doubt you'd find that much to your taste. Do you have someone in mind? Our Princess, mayhap?'

Kedryn felt his face flush as he nodded.

'She would make you an excellent wife – if she would have you.'

'Would she? Have me, I mean?'

'Perhaps.' Grania smiled at him, dark eyes twinkling. 'The only way you will ever know is by asking.'

'I barely know her,' Kedryn murmured.

'But you think you love her?'

'I,' he chose his words carefully, 'I am not sure. She is the loveliest woman I have ever seen, but I should like to know her better.'

'Already you show sound judgement,' Grania applauded. 'It is one thing to bed some maid who takes your fancy, another to set your cap at the King's daughter. Though the High Blood does flow in your veins from your mother's side, and the Caitin line is fine as any.'

Kedryn thought carefully for a while, finding Grania's brisk, matter-of-fact manner conducive to frank questioning, thinking besides that the Sister would know as much about palace politics as anyone.

'Would I be considered acceptable?'

'By whom?' she asked with the bluntness he found pleasantly reassuring. 'Darr or Ashrivelle?'

'Both. After all, the Princess could not marry without the King's permission.'

'No,' Grania acknowledged, 'Though the girl has a mind of her own, as did her mother, and she'd not allow herself to be forced into any political alliance unless it pleased her. That's a thing Hattim Sethiyan has learnt.'

'He wants to wed her?' Kedryn frowned, the news irritating him. Ashrivelle joined with that – what had Jarl called him? – *cur*? 'Does she . . . favour him?'

'No more than any of the other candidates.' Grania chuckled as his face darkened. 'Come now, did you think you were the first to find our princess appealing? Hattim finds her mightily attractive – not only for the obvious reasons, but also because such a union would further his ambitions by linking the Sethiyan line with Andurel. And that thought has crossed other minds, I assure you. Jarl has sons he would not be sorry to see enthroned.'

'I had not thought of that,' Kedryn protested. 'I mean, I have no wish to be a king.'

'You will be Lord of Tamur someday,' Grania told him. 'That is much the same thing.'

'No!' His reply was fierce, bringing an approving smile to her face. 'Tamur serves the Kingdoms and neither my father nor I hold any ambitions to take the throne of Andurel. It is for Darr to elect his successor – with the approval of the three lords.'

'But whoever has Ashrivelle's hand weights the odds in his favour,' Grania said. 'Do you not think so?'

'I suppose,' he allowed, 'but that was – is – not in my mind.'

'No, I do not believe it is.' The Sister capped her salves, motioning for him to put on his shirt. 'So what – should you find your dreams are fulfilled – would you do with your bride?'

'Take her home to Caitin Hold.' Kedryn shrugged, realizing as he did so that his shoulder no longer throbbed. 'What else?'

'Ah, now that is yet another question.' Grania settled into a chair with shortened legs, built to accommodate her lack of stature. 'Mayhap Ashrivelle would not wish to dwell in Tamur. What if she wished to remain here, in Andurel?'

'Then,' Kedryn said forlornly, 'I suppose she would not be the woman for me. I could not live here: Tamur is my home.'

'You would give her up for that?' Grania's eyes twinkled, studying his face, and it occurred to him that he was subjected to some kind of examination.

'I should have to,' he nodded. 'I shall be Lord of Tamur one day, as you say, and then I shall have a duty to my people.'

Grania smiled. 'You will do, young Kedryn. And do not despair – I believe the King would look upon a proposal with favour.'

'And Ashrivelle?' he wondered.

'Ashrivelle will make up her own mind, and as she barely knows you I cannot forecast how that decision might fall. At present it is her intention to study in Estrevan, for a while. Indeed, had the Queen not died she would be there now.'

'I am glad she is not,' Kedryn said quickly.

Grania nodded. 'But Darr might well send her now that barbarian invasion threatens. There will be many who flee beyond the Gadrizels if the forest folk break through.'

'Will they?' Kedryn asked.

'I do not know.' Grania's merry face clouded, her mouth turning down. 'There is a darkness in the Beltrevan that obscures our vision. The very presence of the Messenger seems to fill the place with magic so that our powers of far-seeing and foresight are both limited. It is possible. It is also possible he will be defeated at the Lozins, but that is something we shall not know until we are there and it has happened. That is why I shall accompany you on the first boat.'

'Galen holds the *Vashti* for us,' he said, wondering if she already knew that, 'but it is small – a barque, not a troop carrier – and it may be dangerous.'

'No matter,' Grania snorted, 'the important thing is to get there as swiftly as possible. Mayhap we can counter the glamours he will doubtless bring against the forts.'

Kedryn shivered, remembering the ominous dreams that had plagued him as he fled the Beltrevan. The notion that he would face the dark cantrips of the Messenger rather than warriors in honest battle had been pushed to the back of his mind, but now Grania's flat statement forced him to consider that likelihood and he found it unpleasant. The axes and the arrows of the forest folk were things he could understand, things he could contemplate without fear; the idea of eldritch powers was infinitely less palatable. He shook himself, forcing a smile to his lips.

'Whatever fell magicks he may use, we shall face them,' he vowed.

'I know you will.' Grania's smile was sympathetic. 'And you should feel no shame for fearing them – you would be foolish to do otherwise. But always remember that the Lady is with you.'

Kedryn nodded, setting aside that momentary rush of near terror, telling himself that the stab of pain he experienced in his shoulder as he thought of the Messenger was no more than the twinge of a healing nerve.

'Now,' said the Sister, brusque again, 'let us find Darr and the others. I would know what plans they form.'

She rose from her minuscule seat and led the way through the quarters of the Sisterhood to a chamber set high beneath the palace dome, guarded by soldiers in the silver mail and three-pointed crown of Andurel who parted ranks unbidden as she approached, opening the door to announce her as they would any noble of the High Blood.

Kedryn followed her into the chamber, where sunlight illuminated a round table set with food and wine, suits of antique armour and displays of weapons around the walls emphasizing the military nature of the council in progress. King Darr was seated farthest from the door, smiling as Grania and Kedryn came in, Bedyr to his right, Jarl on his left, the others unknown to Kedryn. He was surprised that he did not see Hattim Sethiyan there; and disappointed that there was no sign of Ashrivelle. He held a chair for Grania and settled himself next to her, wondering what had been, and what would be, decided.

'Welcome,' said the King, 'I trust you have suffered no serious hurt?'

'No, my Lord, thanks to Sister Grania I do not have even a bruise to show.'

'Which is more than can be said for Hattim,' murmured Jarl, just loud enough that the Galichians present could hear, the comment bringing a frown of disapproval to Darr's face.

'What have you decided?' asked Grania, as though attendance at war councils was an everyday event, the question deflecting angry response to the Keshi Lord's slur.

'Our Lord of Ust-Galich presents his apologies,' said the King. 'He has elected to travel south in person in order that his promise be honoured without delay: he raises the Galichian forces, and will march north immediately his army is mustered.'

Jarl muttered, 'He hides his bruises,' effecting an innocent smile when the statement elicited surly glances from those wearing the insignia of Ust-Galich.

'Mehdri ride at this instant for Kesh and Tamur,' Darr went on, 'whilst my lieutenants commandeer transport vessels for the army of Andurel, which even now girds for war. Our plan is to meet the Horde at the Lozin gates.'

He looked at Bedyr and Jarl, motioning for them to speak.

Bedyr said, 'I have sent word to Tepshen Lahl that he is to send the war banners through all of Tamur. We leave a token force in each of the border forts against the threat of Sandurkan raids, but our main force will ride for High Fort with all haste.'

'My Keshi will meet us at Low Fort,' said Jarl. 'The Horde will find a bloody welcome when it reaches the walls.'

'We hope to meet and match the barbarians on the Lozin walls,' Darr added. 'If Rycol and Fengrif can hold out long enough we shall, I pray, bring a sufficiency of men that not even the Messenger may overcome the forts. If we cannot defeat them there – should the armies of Tamur and Kesh not arrive in time – then they will find the banks of the Idre lined with warriors, whilst Hattim's Galichians will block their path south. They will be caught between the three armies.'

'If you reach the forts in time,' Grania said.

'There we look to the Sisterhood for help,' Darr told her. 'Can it be done?'

'Perhaps.' Grania sounded less certain than usual. 'We shall do our utmost, but meanwhile I will travel with Kedryn and Bedyr on the *Vashti* – I would see our enemy as soon as possible, and you need not argue with that, Darr. My Sisters will attend the other vessels, which I imagine will take some time to provision and load.'

Darr nodded dubiously. 'Is that the wisest course?'

'I believe so,' Grania replied. 'You do not need me to raise your army and the more I can learn of the Messenger, the better I shall be equipped to help when your full force arrives.'

'So be it,' the King agreed.

'Then,' announced the Sister, slipping from her chair to the floor, the tabletop almost hiding her as she stared around the watching circle of faces, 'I suggest we depart now. There is little more Lord Bedyr can do here, whilst he – and Kedryn – may do much at High Fort.'

Kedryn was surprised by this prompt suggestion of departure, but Bedyr came readily to his feet.

'Sister Grania speaks sense,' he announced. 'With your permission Darr?'

The King nodded. 'I bow to Sister Grania's advice. Go with my blessing, Bedyr. Fare you well, Prince Kedryn, may the Lady be with you.'

Kedryn bowed, impressed by Darr's conviction. The hesitancy he had seen in the King was gone: the battle plan was laid with alacrity, and with Grania's aid the *Vashti* would bring him north to face the Horde swifter than she had come downriver. Despite the malign threat of the Messenger the prospect excited him. It would be a battle that would go down in the chronicles of the Three Kingdoms, and he was to be a part of it, perhaps an integral part. His blood sang, and the sole regret he felt was that his departure looked to be so abrupt that he would have no chance to speak with Ashrivelle.

That, he decided, was a pleasure he would put aside for some future date, for with all the Kingdoms girding for war no other suitors would find opportunity to woo her, and if he survived he would be a full-fledged warrior, perhaps even a hero in her eyes. He left the chamber with high hopes, an eager smile on his face.

Chapter Eleven

Rycol stared into a night that seemed somehow composed of a denser blackness than mere absence of light might impart. The season turned, the departure of Bedyr and Kedryn seeming to mark the transition from summer to autumn, and since they had gone south on the *Vashti* the days had grown gradually shorter, the sun falling steadily earlier behind the looming rimrock of the western Lozins. But the waning of the year could not account for this darkness; he felt in the marrow of his bones that something more, something fell, lay behind the occultation. A wind blew down the canyon of the Idre from the north, strong enough to set the torches and braziers mounted along the ramparts of High Fort to flickering, tongues of flame streaming southwards as though the fires directed themselves at the fort, hungering. It was a chill wind, gusting about the crenellations of the wall and whistling over the rocky surfaces of the cliffs, prompting him to draw his heavy cloak tighter about his armoured shoulders, his face and ungloved hands tingling with the numbing rawness. It was strong enough to shift any cloud, yet no stars were visible, nor moon in the impenetrable obfuscation of the sky: there remained only darkness.

He rested his elbows on frigid stone, craning forwards as he attempted to penetrate the blackness, but could see nothing. Below, invisible, he could hear the rumble of the river as it poured down from the Beltrevan and he looked towards it, startled that no reflection of firelight showed on the surface. He shivered, less from the cold than from a pervading sense of dread, and walked towards the closest watch station.

Two sentinels stood patiently beside a brazier, wrapped in the winter-issue cloaks he had ordered broken out, the cowls drawn up so that they appeared faceless, ghostly figures in the light of the flames. They came to attention as he approached, saluting, and he greeted them with more cheeriness than he felt, aware that they, too, suffered the demoralizing effects of the unnatural night.

'It is like watching a fog, Chatelain,' the one he remembered was called Demiol responded when he asked how went the watch. 'They could be on us before we see them.'

'We should hear them, though,' ventured the other, whose name Rycol thought was Gandar, the exhalation of his words steaming the air, 'should we not?'

Rycol nodded and said, 'The forest folk seldom attack at night, anyway.'

'Is this night?' Demiol asked.

'What do you mean?' Rycol demanded, hearing the note of doubt – or was it fear? – in the man's voice.

'It is . . .' Demiol shrugged, his cloak rustling as his shoulders moved, seeking words that might explain what he felt, '. . . unlike night.'

Rycol stared at him, studying his face in the glow of the brazier, seeing hard-etched planes, a beard in which grey showed, knowing him now for an experienced warrior long-used to night watches, a cordor entrusted with a command of twenty-five men, the complement for this section of the wall. He was not, the chatelain knew, a man given to night fears, yet now he could see something close to that in the soldier's eyes.

'It is unseasonably dark,' he agreed, 'but nothing more.'

'The wind,' Demiol gestured at the streamers of flame that dribbled from the brazier, the motion of his hand continuing to encompass the canyon and the sky, 'should clear this . . . darkness.'

'A freak condition,' Rycol offered, knowing the explanation sounded feeble. 'What else?'

Demiol answered his commander's gaze with a stare of his own, then licked his lips before he said, 'A sending, Chatelain. Of the Messenger.'

Rycol stifled the sigh that threatened to escape his guard. He had been afraid of this, arguing with Bedyr when the Lord of Tamur had instructed him to inform his command of the likelihood of the Messenger's presence amongst the barbarians at the first sign of glamours, that such announcement would serve no purpose other than to put unnecessary fears into his men. But Bedyr had insisted, pointing out that even the little-known was preferable to the utterly unknown, and that if gramaryes were brought against the forts it were better the defenders had at least some idea of what they faced than find themselves beset by unexplained magicks. Rycol had disagreed, but obeyed, making public announcement three days previously, when the sky had filled with crows that swooped and swirled about both bastions, their raucous croaking making a tumult of the day from dawn to dusk, flooding in a dark tide out of the north until the weight of wings hid the sun and men demanded an explanation of their coming. He had summoned his captains then and informed them that High Fort – and her sister across the river – faced more than the Horde: that Ashar's minion was thought to march with the forest folk. They had taken it well, largely because few gave much credence to the news. They knew they faced a massing of the tribes, but that was something they could understand, a thing for which they had waited through their years of service. And they knew that Bedyr Caitin rode the Idre south to bring reinforcements from Andurel, to bring the massed warriors of the Three Kingdoms to the defence of the Lozin gates. They could look forward to such honest battle, and the handful who had muttered doom at the thought of the Messenger had been shouted down.

Then, on the second day, a storm totally out of character for the time of year had raged. No sooner had the sun risen than a great swathe of night-black cloud had formed above the Beltrevan and moved steadily south until it hid the golden orb, obfuscating light so that the forts were shrouded in gloom. Peals of deafening thunder had reverberated from the walls of the river canyon while lightning, like some multi-legged insect, had stalked the earth. Seven men had been struck and seared unto death, weapons and armour melted to their charred bones; and from Low Fort had come the news of nine more deaths. Sixteen men out of the twenty centuries that manned the forts was no insupportable loss, though it was odd that all were of rank – cordors or tellemen – and those who had at first dismissed the Messenger began to listen to those who gave his presence weight.

The storm had ended at sunset, replaced by a steady downpour that, in its turn, was unseasonable, filling the gutters and water spouts with torrents of foaming grey, pooling in courtyards and plazas, driving rats from flooded basements and cellars while not a man in either fort walked dry and the armourers broke out stocks of oil that would not usually have been needed until the winter rains began.

The sky-born flood had continued until some hours after dawn on the third day, ceasing reluctantly as lowering cloud the colour of rotted flesh bloomed over the canyon, the air becoming stifling, sodden clothing steaming as it dried, a fetid odour hanging over the forts as if the heavens themselves decayed. Rycol had ordered stocks of winter fuel brought up from the store rooms and set braziers laden with juniper and sprinkled with aromatic oils to burning, in an attempt to counteract the stench, but they had done little good and gloom had filled his command. He had called on Sister Wynett, who had produced potions that went some way to restoring flagging spirits even as she reported an increasing number of men complaining of minor – and mostly inexplicable – ailments.

Rycol himself had begun to experience doubt then, for while he could cheerfully face an enemy he could see, one he could fight, he knew that if this assault continued he would command a demoralized force. Even he felt the leaden oppression that hung, miasmic, over the citadel, found himself irritable, snapping at his wife and struggling to contain his anger when officers reported men complaining of sickness. He had ordered a double ration of evshan to be issued to the men and called for an impromptu banquet at which he had served stocks of Galichian vintage to his officers, knowing that across the Idre Fengrif did the same, for the signal towers had informed him that the Keshi chatelain suffered the same problems.

The sooner Bedyr returned with help from Andurel, the better.

'And if it is?' he asked the cordor, forcing a lightness he did not feel into his voice. 'Would you permit some forest shaman to overcome you?'

Demiol shook his head, 'No, Lord Rycol; though I'd sooner face the tribes.'

'You may have that wish granted ere long,' Rycol told him.

'Will they attack?' asked Gandar, turning to peer into the stygian blackness. 'Or will this keep up?'

'They attack already,' answered the commander. 'This is an attack, as was the rain and the crows – all of it. Think of it as such and hold your defence strong.'

'Then . . .' Gandar broke off, his eyes wandering from Rycol's face to the darkness, back to the gaunt features of his chatelain, 'You think this *will* continue?'

'I know not lad.' Rycol twisted his mouth to what he hoped was a credible smile, reaching beneath his cloak for the flask of evshan he had thought to latch to his belt. 'But I know I command sturdy warriors who will not fail me, whether the attack be from blade or blackness. And I know the night watch is the longest – and that the stoutest heart may need a little fortification. Here, take a swig; it will keep out the cold and mayhap more.'

Gandar stared in amazement at the proffered flask. The Lord Rycol was, he knew, a fair man and a staunch warrior, but this was unprecedented. He glanced at Demiol, not sure if he should accept.

The cordor winked from the depths of his cowl and Gandar transferred his spear to his left hand, taking the leather bottle.

Rycol watched as the soldier – a youth, he saw as the cowl fell back – raised the flask and swallowed, gasping as the fiery liquor traversed his throat. When the young man moved to return the flask he motioned at Demiol, his smile a little more genuine now.

'Your cordor feels the cold, too, lad.'

Demiol grinned, taking the bottle and tilting it to his lips, thinking that for all his stiff-backed authority, the chatelain was one who knew a soldier's needs.

'Thank you, my Lord,' he murmured, returning the flask. 'That sits well.'

'Aye, it does.' Rycol held the flask to his own lips, working his throat even though he allowed none of the liquor to go down, knowing that word would be passed along the wall of how the commander himself shared a drink with honest soldiers. Knowing it would be good for morale. 'And while our bellies are warm let me promise you something – our Lord Bedyr will even now be travelling north with the full might of the Kingdoms at his back. King Darr himself will lead, and all of Kesh – Ust-Galich, too – close behind. The Sisters of Andurel will doubtless travel with the army, and when that strength arrives we'll teach the forest folk and their black-hearted shaman a lesson. You have my word on that!'

He smacked his lips and stoppered the flask, offering the two sentinels a crisp salute that, he was pleased to see, was returned with equal precision.

'And now I'll continue my own watch. Stand firm.'

'Aye,' promised Demiol, echoed by Gandar, 'That we will, Lord Rycol.'

The evshan or his presence, he did not care which, had driven the doubt from their voices and he felt cheered as he proceeded along the wall towards the glow that marked the position of the next watch station, the brazier no more than a faint beacon in the encompassing gloom. He halted there and held much the same conversation, again offering the flask of liquor and making the same promises, hoping they would not prove false. What little doubt had lingered in his mind concerning the presence of the Messenger was dispelled now for there could be no questioning the unnatural nature of events, only curiosity as to what would come next. He ended his patrol with an empty flask and, weary, found his own chambers.

It was late, the candle melting slowly within its carved crystal container indicating an hour after midnight, and his wife was not yet abed, but dozing beside the fire that glowed welcoming in the deep stone hearth. She woke as he entered, fussing about him as he unclasped his cloak and slumped in a chair, staring morosely at her greying hair as she knelt to unfasten his boots.

He experienced an irrational irritation at her ministrations and fought it down, guessing that, like the darkness, this was another aspect of the Messenger's sorceries. His temper was frayed of late, and while he hid it from his men he found it increasingly difficult to control his vexation in the privacy of his own quarters. Remorse took the place of anger and he bent forward to stroke her hair, smiling as she turned her face into his palm, her own eyes tired.

'How goes the watch?' she asked, aware of the responsibilities that weighed heavy on his ageing shoulders, anxious to share, and thus lighten them.

'Slowly,' he replied. 'The night seems longer without moon or stars. It seems that time has ceased, but the men stand it well enough.'

The Lady Marga Cador na Rycol set his boots aside and fetched a covered pan in which coals smouldered from the bed, placing it that he might rest his feet upon the surface as she turned to the latchings of his armour.

'How long will it last?' she wondered, and although he knew the question was rhetorical he could not help the flush of anger that abruptly filled him.

'How should I know? Blood of the Lady! Am I a seer?'

Instantly, he was once more remorseful, beginning an apology which she dismissed with a shake of her head, massaging his shoulders, where tension knotted muscle.

'Today I nearly struck Katina for dropping a comb.' Her fingers worked skilfully on the taut cords, the art learnt long ago during her time with the Sisters in Estrevan. 'It was not her fault, but still I shouted at her. Raised my hand to her. This,' she gestured towards the shuttered window, 'affects us all.'

'Nonetheless, Marga, I am sorry,' he told her, taking her hand and kissing it.

'I know,' she said, continuing the massage. 'It is hard to maintain a cheerful face while we wonder what gramaryes will next afflict us.'

Rycol nodded, sighing as he felt his shoulders ease. 'Honest attack would be preferable to this, but I think the Messenger seeks to soften us.'

'He will not!' She released her grip and began to unfasten the lacings of his undercoat. 'He cannot!'

'Can he not?' Rycol murmured. 'He turns the year to winter, sends rain to soak our souls, fills the air with the stench of decay – what will the dawn bring? There is a limit to what men can stand.'

His wife drew herself up to her full height, standing before him to place her hands on his shoulders, forcing him to look up into her eyes, her voice firm as she said, 'We have not reached our limit yet, Bevan Rycol. We have a way to go before that comes, and before it does Bedyr will be returned with Darr and the army. Then we shall show Ashar's creature the mettle of the Kingdoms – do not doubt it!'

'Oh, my love,' he smiled, circling her waist with his arms, burying his face against the warmth of her robe, 'had I but a century or two with your strength.'

'You have me,' she answered. 'Now come to bed and sleep. We'll worry about tomorrow when it comes.'

But it seemed that tomorrow was not to come, for when Rycol woke he saw no light through the shutters, though when he looked to the time candle he saw it almost burned away, indicating the hour of dawn, and long years of service had accustomed him to waking then. He rose, feeling his skin pucker in the chill that filled the chamber, pulling on a fur-lined robe as he strode to the window and threw the shutters back. Darkness met his gaze, barely alleviated by the torches he saw flickering dimly below, and when he looked up to where the sun should be he saw nothing.

Dread filled him then, a numbing, soul-deadening emptiness in which hope had no place for there was no room left for optimism or confidence, only the beckoning void. He heard voices crying in bewilderment and raised in curses as men stumbled against obstacles hidden by the gloom, a dog howled mournfully, its cry taken up by others until High Fort was filled with the keening. Despite the warmth of the thick robe he shivered, his teeth tight-locked against the chattering he knew would come should he relax. Turning slowly from the window he saw his wife's face a pale blur and moved towards her, seeking the reassurance of her arms.

'Find Wynett,' she advised. 'Seek the counsel of the Sisterhood.'

Rycol shuddered, feeling himself lose his struggle against despair.

'You are Bevan Rycol, Chatelain of High Fort,' Marga declared firmly. 'You guard Tamur's border and you will not allow this to deflect you from your duty.'

He nodded, not speaking, and rose to thrust fresh logs on the waning fire. The glow cheered him a little, but then the dancing flames reminded him of Ashar and the Messenger and he shuddered afresh, sinking to his knees.

'Here, drink this.'

He turned to find a cup of evshan offered him and took it, emptying the vessel in a single swallow, gasping as the liquor inflamed his empty belly. For a moment his head spun, then the warmth spread, rekindling hope and with it, anger.

'Aye,' he said fiercely. 'I'll seek Wynett.'

'And you'll show no great concern,' Marga warned. 'You'll laugh this off. Why, if darkness is all the Messenger can send against us, we have little to fear.'

Rycol nodded and began to dress with clumsy fingers. There was more than mere darkness to this new sending: the stygian gloom that filled the fort sank soul-deep and he feared for the spirit of his command, knowing that the staunchest warrior might succumb to this onslaught of bleak depression. If he, the chatelain, could feel such despair, how must it afflict the soldiery? Fight it, he told himself, just as you told your men to fight it, and thank the Lady that you have a wife stout as Marga.

Only when he was gone from their chamber did his wife allow herself to weep, for she, too, felt that awful despair.

It lay heavy on her husband's soul, though he did his best to hide it as he made his way down corridors lit by flambeaux, expressing a barely-felt confidence to all who questioned him, pausing to speak with the officers who demanded instructions, calling for fresh stocks of torches and inflammables for the braziers to be set along the walls and about the courtyards, anxious to reach Wynett and learn the Sister's thoughts. An atmosphere close to panic gripped the place, as though the darkness seeped into souls, and only the discipline of which he was so proud maintained any semblance of normality, and that was hard won for so dense was the blackness that the torches and flambeaux and braziers made little dent on its almost palpable solidity. Familiar walkways became confusing mazes, plazas and courtyards through which he would normally have strode in moments were hazardous, time and distance meaningless, direction confused by the obfuscation, panic lurking like some prowling beast in the unnatural night.

He found Wynett busy in the hospital wards, administering medicaments by torchlight to men more confused and frightened than sick. Curbing his irritation, he waited while bruises and sprains were tended, listening to the calm reassurances of Wynett and her fellow adepts.

'They are frightened,' she said when she was done and they stood in her small chamber, their faces shadowed, 'they face the unknown.'

'I feel it,' Rycol admitted. 'When I woke and saw no light I knew panic.'

'It is only natural,' Wynett replied. 'All men fear something. Most fear the darkness – it is in us from long and long ago. We are creatures of the light and the Messenger has given us night.'

'What can you do?' Rycol asked. 'If this continues I'll not have a man fit to fight.'

Wynett studied the gaunt-featured chatelain and felt a surge of pity. She could sense the tension he struggled to control and the rigid hold he maintained on his emotions. Her own were held in check by the training of the Sisterhood, awareness that the bleak despair prowling the edges of her perceptions was an emanation of the Messenger enabling her to establish mental barricades, transforming fear to a righteous anger that denied the power of Ashar's minion.

'There are preparations I can administer,' she suggested. 'Given to the men, they will raise spirits. But the quantities must be carefully measured lest they become careless. I sense the power growing, and I suspect the real attack will come soon, in which event you will need alert warriors.'

'Anything,' Rycol said helplessly. 'Anything is better than this.'

Wynett smiled. 'I will do what I can, but you must be careful they do not take too much. This sending is a part of the Messenger's design and he may well anticipate our countermeasures. If he has guessed what I shall do, then he may plan his attack when my remedies have calmed the men, hoping to find them overly tranquil. Or mount his attack whilst our hope is at its lowest ebb.'

'You think he will strike soon?' Rycol demanded. 'By the Lady, Sister, I'd welcome open battle.'

'I think he will keep this up a while yet,' Wynett said. 'Though I doubt even he can maintain such a sending for much longer – it must drain him mightily. For now, I suggest you light the fort as brightly as possible and I will prepare my potions. Also, it might be well for you to address your command. But first . . .'

She rose to fetch a phial from the collection shelved about the room, measuring a few drops into a cup, adding a little water before passing it to Rycol. The chatelain drank the mixture and frowned.

'I feel no different. Is this what you would give the men?'

'In larger quantity,' Wynett confirmed. 'It will take a little while to work, but when it does, you will find yourself strengthened.'

'So be it.' Rycol climbed to his feet, folding his cloak about him as might an old man wearied by years and cares. It was, Wynett thought, the first time she had seen him look his age. 'I will do as you say. Thank you, Sister.'

He went out into the unnatural night, bumping into a young halberdier as the soldier stumbled towards the light of the hospital. Both men cursed, the youngster not recognizing his commander until Rycol threw back his hood.

'Forgive me, my Lord, I did not see you,' the soldier muttered, then turned a haggard face towards the chatelain. 'Lord Rycol?'

'What?' Rycol only just succeeded in preventing the word coming out as a bark of anger as he heard the fear in the man's voice.

'Can we fight this? Forgive me, but I am afraid.'

It was not an admission Rycol expected from one of his men and in other circumstances he might have answered it differently. Now, however, he set a hand on the youth's arm, feeling it tremble beneath his grip, and asked his name in paternal manner, wondering as he did so if this was an effect of Wynett's draft.

'Ranulf,' said the soldier forlornly. 'Of Cordor Gryffin's brace.'

Rycol tightened his grip reassuringly, smiling grimly as he said, 'Well, Ranulf, you are not alone in your fear. We all fear the unknown, but we are also warriors sworn to the defence of the Kingdoms, and this is an attack on our charge. You would face the forest folk in battle, and you will face them in this – I have no doubt of that, lad, for I know I command good men. Fight your fear, Ranulf, and we shall win. This will not last forever and when it ends I'll need good men beside me. Now see the Sisters and then return to your post – I rely on you, Ranulf.'

He was surprised to find the speech heartened him, and saw that it had the desired effect on the halberdier, for Ranulf squared his shoulders and saluted.

'Aye, Chatelain, I'll do that. I'll not let you down.'

'Well said,' Rycol exclaimed, clapping the warrior on the back as Ranulf turned to leave.

He watched until the man was gone into the welcoming light of the hospital and then faced the blackness again. Across what he knew was a cobbled yard with a well at its centre, but now seemed a midnight pit, he could make out the faint glow of torchlight. The distance was at most twenty paces, but the glow was dim, as though seen from far off. He heard a man cry out, shouting in anger and pain as he stumbled against some unseen obstacle, and thought that if the barbarians should attack now his defences would be pitiful, his archers unsighted, his catapults firing blind. In this gloom the entire population of the Beltrevan might be massing below the walls – he needed light. He needed bonfires lit on the approaches, the forest road ablaze – but he remembered Brannoc's warning that Ashar's minion thrived on fire, and cursed afresh: the Messenger tied his hands.

Slowly, unpleasantly aware of the disorientation he felt, he made his way across the courtyard to the brazier, then onwards to the dining hall. That, at least, was brighter and he shed his cloak to gulp a hurried breakfast that was constantly interrupted by the arrival of officers seeking instructions or reporting men injured in falls and collisions. He was preparing to leave when his seneschal announced a deputation from the town. Rycol sighed, realizing that it had to come sooner or later, but not sure how to handle it. Blessing Wynett for her calming potion, he rose to courteously greet the three men who entered.

Orgal Leneth was the spokesman, a miller whose establishment enjoyed a lucrative contract with the fort. He was a plump, jolly-faced man, sensible and humorous, though now his red cheeks were pale and his eyes furtive, the cap he held in his thick fingers turning nervously. With him were Talkien Drass, an innkeeper, and Beriol Seren, owner of several warehouses. Drass was tall and thin, with a penchant for finery, whilst Seren dressed as though he were one of the town's poorest inhabitants. Like Leneth, they were both nervous.

'My friends, please sit.' Rycol smiled, motioning to the empty chairs that lined the long table. 'Have you eaten, or may I offer you something?'

'An explanation,' said Leneth directly, lowering his considerable bulk on to a seat. 'What is happening?'

'Aye,' Drass added before Rycol could speak. 'What magicks are afoot, Chatelain? I've seen three men wounded in needless brawls even though my tavern remains near empty. There's a mood abroad none of us can understand.'

Seren said nothing, but his eyes radiated questions as his fingers fiddled with the frayed edging of his ancient cloak.

Rycol took a deep breath, wondering what he could say that would not foment panic. So far the sendings had appeared limited to the confines of the forts, but now it seemed they were spreading and he was uncertain how the townsfolk might take news of imminent attack;

less confident of their holding firm should he mention the Messenger. Yet he could see no way to avoid such announcement: these were intelligent men who would not be fobbed off with excuses.

'Tell me what happens,' he prevaricated.

'Darkness,' said Leneth, 'a foul darkness that seeps like some malign fog down from the forts. I see it is worse here, but it shrouds our town and seems to make men mad. The ferrymen refuse to cross the river; dogs howl in the streets; there is confusion. I feel . . .' He broke off, shaking his head, wiping at eyes that suddenly moistened.

'Frightened?' asked Rycol, deciding abruptly to take the bull by the horns. 'Lost? Despairing?'

'All that,' Leneth nodded, his voice close to breaking. 'What is it?'

'A sending.' Rycol set his hands flat on the table, fixing each man in turn with a clear gaze, hoping that he did the right thing. 'The Horde is raised again and this is the first move against us.'

'The Horde?' Beriol Seren's voice was a fear-stained whisper. 'Aided by sorcery?'

'The Messenger marches at the head,' Rycol announced, modulating his tone to what he hoped was the correct level of confident disregard, continuing before any of them had further chance to speak, 'But you need have no fear. What you feel is a ploy to weaken us – but it does not! My Paramount Sister already prepares countermeasures and within a few days you will see King Darr himself arrive with the full might of the Three Kingdoms behind him. Our Lord of Tamur has already sped to Andurel with word, and when he returns we shall trounce the forest folk more soundly than in Corwyn's time.

'I trust you with this information because you are loyal citizens and I know you will not allow sway to these fell magicks. I had not thought they affected your domain, but now I learn they do I put my trust in you. You must maintain order in the town – I rely on you for that.'

The three men exchanged glances, their faces paling further to a waxy hue. Seren swallowed, covering his mouth with a trembling hand as if he feared he might vomit. Leneth said softly, 'The Messenger?' Drass shook himself as if to wake from a nightmare, the gaily-coloured tassels that fringed his cloak waving wildly.

'I put my faith in you,' Rycol reiterated, 'and I will give you all the help I can. Sister Wynett has a draught that will help you, and if sufficient may be produced, I will distribute what I can in the town, but meanwile I ask that you keep order.'

'It may not be possible,' Leneth said helplessly, the words coming slow and thick from his fleshy lips. 'Already people demand explanations. If we tell them the Horde is raised – and the Messenger with it – there will be panic.'

'There must not be!' Rycol answered swiftly. 'We can withstand these sendings. My men stand firm and we anticipate the arrival of Bedyr Caitin and King Darr. No matter what foul sorceries are sent against us, we shall defeat them. Listen to me – the Kingdoms need you! Do not betray that trust!'

Leneth sighed, wiping a hand across his face, his voice dull as he said, 'We shall do what we can, Lord Rycol, but what can we tell them?'

'Tell them that they are Tamurin and that they have a duty to the Kingdoms,' Rycol answered, seeking to instil in them the same purpose he struggled to plant in his men, unpleasantly aware of the chaos that might erupt should he fail. 'That their king is on his way with an army such as we have never seen, and that the forts will hold. Tell them the barbarians shall not set foot on Tamur's soil while I command this bastion.'

'And the Messenger?' asked Drass. 'What should we tell them of him?'

'As little as possible,' said Rycol. 'Nothing at all if you can avoid it, but if you cannot – well, tell them he is a forest shaman with a little more power than most. And tell them there are Sisters coming from Andurel, perhaps from Estrevan, whose strength will outweigh any magicks he may send.'

'You are confident?' demanded the innkeeper.

'I am,' Rycol lied.

'It is bad for business,' murmured Seren.

'Panic will be worse,' the chatelain responded. 'If necessary, I shall proclaim military law.'

The man's face paled further and he began to shake his head. Drass, a little sharper, said, 'How can you afford the men?'

'I have sufficient,' Rycol answered, effecting a casual air he did not feel. 'I should prefer not, but . . .'

'It will not be necessary,' Leneth said. 'If you are confident, Lord Rycol, then we share your optimism. We shall do as you ask. Perhaps a proclamation.'

'An excellent idea,' Rycol nodded. 'And now I suggest you attend the hospital. Sister Wynett will supply the medicament I spoke of and it will, I assure you, help. If you will excuse me?'

'Of course,' the miller nodded, and Rycol climbed to his feet, thankful to see a telleman he knew to be reliable nearby.

Rather than have the trio overhear his intructions, he crossed to the officer's table and put his mouth close to the soldier's ear.

'Varun, you see the burghers? Take them to the hospital and tell Wynett to feed them whatever draught she gave me. Get one yourself, too. And Varun? You will behave as though you know exactly what you are doing. Give them no cause for concern. I want no panic in the town.'

The telleman nodded and rose to his feet, wiping crumbs from his tunic. Rycol was pleased to see him smile as he bowed to the three townsmen and asked that they come with him, pausing to summon a squad of five men to accompany him with torches.

When they were gone Rycol sat a moment, thinking. If the townsfolk panicked his problems would be doubled, for they would either come knocking on his gates in search of protection – and thus encumber his quartermasters with extra duties whilst cluttering his fort with useless civilian bodies – or flee, which would spread the panic. He grunted, more angry than despairing now, seeing the enormity of the Messenger's design, for these ensorcellements denied the military strategies he understood, giving him no clear enemy to fight whilst he faced the onslaught of nameless fears engendered by the dark glamour. At least – he hoped – he had succeeded in reassuring Leneth and the others, and they would return to the town in better spirits. He shouted for his seneschal to bring quill and paper and prepared a list of instructions, commencing with a message to Sister Wynett that she should let him know immediately her remedies were prepared and arrange to administer them as swiftly as possible, first to his troops, then, if sufficient quantity existed, to the townsfolk. He ordered all available men to be mustered at noon, when he would address them, and asked if any news had come from Low Fort.

The seneschal shook his head. 'The signal towers cannot penetrate the darkness, my Lord.'

Rycol hid the anxiety this news brought and dismissed the man. For a while he sat alone, thinking hard. Without the signal towers High and Low Forts would be forced to operate independently, unable to plan a joint strategy. Was that the Messenger's design? To divide and thus conquer, perhaps to bring the might of the Beltrevan against only one fort? If that should happen he was not sure either bastion could withstand the siege, for the sheer weight of numbers must tell in the end, and if one fort should fall, the way south would be open. Whether through Kesh or Tamur made little difference for either way led ultimately to Andurel.

An ugly knot of fear curdled in his soul, then became replaced by harsh anger. Not the niggling irritation he had felt before – Wynett's draught seemed to have put paid to that – but a righteous ire that distilled into a cold determination to fight no matter what the odds. He had promised Bedyr he would hold the fort and by the Lady he would do that!

Abruptly he rose and swung his cloak about his shoulders, shouting for a captain to bring a squad with torches.

He waited as the men were assembled and then strode from the dining hall into the blackness outside. Familiarity aided him a little as he led the procession to the battlements, glancing up towards the tall column of the signal tower, unable to prevent the useless hope that he would see some flash of light answering the fulgurations of High Fort's heliographs from across the Idre. There was no answer, the radiance of his own tower was dulled, as though the pervading darkness swallowed the signals, and he turned away, dismissing the hope as wasted.

The fires along the north wall had been trebled so that as he moved along the rampart he walked in roseate light, as though through a tunnel, armour burnished by the flames, the blackness beyond thick and menacing, scarcely held back by the radiance of the braziers and torches. He spoke encouragingly to the men there, repeating promises, studying the faces that watched him for sign of breaking spirits. As best he could tell, they were holding up, though most voiced the same complaint that the fort was vulnerable so long as the sending lasted.

When he reached the central point of the wall, where ramparts supported a heavy catapult, he came to a decision. Beyond, where normally the low tower would have commanded a clear view along the Beltrevan road, he could see nothing: he ordered the mangonel loaded with balefire. The telleman in command shouted for the removal of the stone and Rycol watched as it was replaced with the leather sack containing the flammable liquid. The fuse was lit and the telleman knocked the latch down, the great weighted arm swinging up to strike the crossbar and send the missile hurtling ino the darkness. Within seconds the sparks trailing from the fuse were lost. Rycol waited, silently counting off the range. Then he heard the dull thud of impact. And gasped as the anticipated flare refused to materialize. Where brilliant flame should have splashed there was nothing: the darkness remained impenetrable. The telleman stared at the chatelain. Rycol smiled dourly and shrugged.

'If they come,' he said, loud enough that his voice would carry to all the nervous, listening men, 'we'll hear them. And they'll be massed thick enough you'll not need to see them.'

He hoped it gave them some encouragement. He felt little himself.

Not far from the hummock that had marked his ambush of the Tamurin scouting party, Borsus watched the cloud that filled the canyon of the Idre. It hung as though painted upon the sky, a stark blackness that stretched across the river like a curtain draped from the Lozin walls, still, unmoving even though a wind blew eerily amongst the dwindling trees, its whistling almost drowning out the steady thud of axes and the shouts of the forest folk as the timber came down.

There was activity all about him, and only Taws's instructions had saved him from the labour of tree-felling, for the Messenger had said he wanted his man close these past days in case he should be needed. The rest, from bar-Offas to warriors, were set to bringing down the trees and hauling them to the road. There they were stripped of branches and cut to the measures dictated by Taws, his designs etched with dye on numerous smooth-scraped hides. The final shapes were not yet assumed, but from his own studies of the designs, Borsus could see how the lengths would fit together, becoming towers and catapults, rams and moveable shelters.

Niloc Yarrum had at first objected to this further delay, for his plan of attack was simpler; indeed, it was the traditional battle strategy of the tribes: to mass and charge, seeking by sheer weight of numbers to force an entry, careless of lost lives.

'You would climb the corpses of your warriors to the ramparts?' Taws had demanded, the contempt in his voice bringing a dark flush to the hef-Ulan's swarthy features. 'How many would be left? Enough to take the Kingdoms?'

Niloc had clenched his jaw, a rage that had fomented since they reached the edge of the forest and he had begun to scent the impending battle close to boiling over in dismissal of the mage's exhortation.

'Listen,' Taws had said, looking from one face to the next as the Ulans sat about the table of Yarrum's lodge, 'you do not attack some forest stronghold now. You go against the mightiest forts in all the Kingdoms. The Lozin gates! Do you believe you can simply throw your men against them and overcome? If you do, you are fools!'

'Will you not aid us?' Balandir had asked, ignoring the insult. 'Will your magic not bring down the walls?'

'In time,' Taws had responded, 'I could do that. But there is more beyond the gates.'

'The Kingdoms lie beyond the gates,' Niloc had rasped then. 'Open them for us, Taws, and we will do the rest.'

The mage's red eyes had fastened on the hef-Ulan's and Niloc had looked away, unable to meet that rubescent stare. 'I will give you the Kingdoms,' Taws had promised, 'but the Lozin gates are but the first step. Past them you must face the armies Darr will bring against you. By now they will be massing – Tamur and Kesh and Ust-Galich. You outnumber them I know, but still they will fight hard, as cornered rats will fight, for you threaten everything they hold dear. I can open the gates for you – and I shall! – but in my own way. And without wasting men whose blades will be needed when you enter the Kingdoms.'

'How else do we fight?' Vran had asked.

'With war engines,' Taws had answered.

'War engines?' Niloc Yarrum's tone was incredulous. 'What do we know of war engines, mage? We fight with sword and spear, bow and axe. Do you ask us to change the ways of our forefathers?'

'Your forefathers could not take the Lozin gates,' Taws said softly, menace in his voice.

Balandir had set a restraining hand on Niloc's arm then and asked, 'What is your plan, Taws?'

'I will send magicks against them,' the mage had promised. 'Sorceries that will weaken their spirit and confuse them. While I do that, you will construct the engines I shall show you. Towers to mount the walls; catapults to threaten their defences; shelters that will enable your warriors to approach the gates and use battering rams.'

'Weapons of the Kingdoms,' Niloc had protested scornfully. 'Why can you not bring down the gates with your sorceries?'

'Would you question Ashar's will?' the mage had snapped. 'I have promised you the Kingdoms, but they are not some ripe fruit that I shall pluck for you, and peel that you have no labour of it. You must work for this, man! Ashar demands labour of his subjects.'

'Show us,' Balandir had said, ignoring the furious glance Niloc threw at him for that usurpation.

Taws had ordered skins brought then and dye, and sketched the designs that were now duplicated by the craftsmen of the forest, reproduced so that the carpenters and workers in wood might each command a team of men as the engines were constructed.

Niloc Yarrum had not enjoyed this further delay, and while the trees were felled and stripped and dragged to the clearings about the trail he had remained in his lodge, emerging only occasionally to study the results, expressing his impatience in bouts of random anger. Borsus had been glad of the opportunity to avoid him then, for his fury was shown in the reappearance of the blood eagle and Taws had been preoccupied with his own preparations.

He had commanded a fire to be built just out of sight of the fort on the western bank, a blaze almost the size of the conflagration that had marked the great gathering of the tribes. It had burned for three days as the mage sat before it, unmoving through the days and nights, staring into the flames, untouched by their heat even though he positioned himself closer than any human man dared go. On the evening of the third day, as the sun sank behind the great wall of the mountains, he had risen and lifted his arms, crying out to Ashar. And the smoke from the bonfire had become a column of roiling blackness, darker than night, lifting towards the stars and then shifting, stirred by a wind that seemed to come from the mage himself, turning and coiling in thick, oily tendrils that reached like questing talons to the south. It had gathered, massing, and all the forest folk had watched as the darkness spread, drifting along the canyon of the river until it hid the Idre and the mountains and everything between. Even Niloc Yarrum had emerged from his lodge then, to study that weird cloud, and when Borsus had glanced at the hef-Ulan he had seen awe on the man's face.

Taws had turned his back on his creation then and gone to his lodge, beckoning for Borsus to join him.

The warrior had followed him into the tent of hides and waited, surprised by the weariness he saw etched on the skeletal features of the mage.

'Do you think me limitless?' Taws had asked, smiling as might a wolf wearied by a hard kill. 'There is a price to everything, Borsus, and we must pay it if we are to win our desires. I have laboured hard for this and now I hunger.'

Borsus had stared at the Messenger, not knowing what he meant, for he had never seen Taws take sustenance and did not understand.

'Go outside,' the mage had said, 'and tell the first warrior you see to attend me. Bring him to me.'

The light that flickered in the deep-sunk eyes then had kindled fear in Borsus's soul, for there was a part of him that knew the mage's hunger was for more than flesh, and he had hurried to obey.

Outside he had encountered a Yath, a bar-Offa, returning from the task of tree-felling. The man had gaped when Borsus told him the Messenger required his presence, and demanded to know why.

'He wants you,' the Drott had said. 'I do not know why, but if you value your soul you will obey.'

Frightened, but more frightened still of incurring the Messenger's wrath, the Yath had followed Borsus into the lodge.

As they entered, the mage rose to his feet, his eyes glowing a fiercer red as he studied the wary Yath, his lips curving and peeling back from pointed teeth in ghastly approximation of a smile. The Yath had taken a step back, only to find Borsus behind him, blocking the exit. Taws had stepped forwards and the Yath had set a hand about the sword sheathed on his hip. Then the hand had frozen and the cry of protest forming in the man's throat died stillborn as Taws's gaze locked upon his face. Borsus had wanted to close his eyes, to shut out what he now knew was coming, but could not. He had no wish to see what followed, but was unable to resist the compulsion that fixed his attention on the scene as Taws raised hands that suddenly seemed scaled and taloned to cup the Yath's cheeks with an awful tenderness, easing the head back so that the terror-paled features were turned upwards as might be those of a lover about to receive a kiss.

He could not tear his eyes away as the mage did kiss the Yath, his face descending over the man's, lips closing on lips, the obscene caress going on and on as the Yath's hand fell from his sword hilt and his limbs shuddered, a hideous palpitation wracking his body. Finally it was done and Taws let go his grip, the Yath pitching lifeless and somehow deflated to the floor of the lodge. The mage murmured in satisfaction, a tongue that was a startling red in contrast to his milk-pale skin emerging to flick over the fleshless lips.

Borsus started as the carmine gaze turned in his direction, but Taws made no move towards him, merely waving a dismissive hand and saying, 'Take this thing away.'

He stooped to grasp the dead Yath by the latchings of his mail shirt and dragged the corpse from the lodge, ignoring the fearful glances that came his way as he hauled the body over the stony ground. He felt that he should alert the man's clan brothers to his fate, that they might grant his remains honourable disposal, but was afraid of their reaction, thinking that while Taws remained in his lodge there was little to prevent a vengeful warrior from slipping a knife between his ribs. So he brought the body to his own lodge and stripped it of armour, piling that with the man's weapons some little distance away, and whistled up his dogs.

The hounds came running out of the growing twilight, growling as they scented the fresh meat. Borsus left them to eat, staggering into his own lodge with hollowed eyes and visibly shaking hands.

'What ails you?' Sulya looked up from the food she was preparing, stroking a strand of wheaten hair from her forehead.

'Beer!' Borsus threw himself on to the furs that served them as a couch, wiping at the sweat he felt beading his face.

Sulya hurried to obey, lifting the hide sack from its peg and spilling the dark liquid into a mug of carved wood, raising her skirts to wipe away the spillage that frothed over the rim. She handed the mug to Borsus and watched her man drain it in a single, shuddering swallow. Refilled it as he thrust out his arm, then stooped to smooth his tangled black hair.

'You have been about his business?'

There was no need for her to define whom she meant and Borsus nodded, thinking that the spell Taws had summoned to ensure her affections had left her without memory of Andrath's fate. He drank the second mug without speaking, then began to talk as she filled him a third measure.

'He hungered.'

'Hungered? Taws does not eat or drink.'

'Not flesh, nor ale. But he eats.' He shivered, beer spilling from the mug on to the furs, unnoticed. 'Oh, he eats.'

'What?' she asked, frowning her curiosity.

'Souls.' Borsus shook his head. 'I do not know. He said he hungered and told me to bring him someone. Anyone.'

Sulya's frown deepened as he broke off, swallowing ale, her blue eyes questioning. She turned to stir her cookpot and then settled herself beside her man, placing a hand she hoped was comforting on his shoulder, feeling the tension there.

'I saw a Yath. A bar-Offa by his torque.' Borsus stared into the flames of the cook fire. 'I told him to come with me, or face the Messenger's wrath. I brought him to Taws's lodge.'

He paused again, wiping at his mouth as though to eliminate the memory. Sulya tightened her grip on his shoulder, staring at his face, seeing the horror there, the self-disgust; hearing it in his voice.

'Taws embraced him. And the Yath died. I dragged his body out and it was like some insect drained by a spider. I gave it to the dogs.'

'His embrace kills?'

Her voice was hushed and Borsus nodded. 'Aye, it kills. It does more than kill, I think. He takes the soul, the essence of life.'

'You had no choice,' Sulya told him. 'What else could you do? He is the Messenger.'

'Aye,' Borsus grunted, 'he is the Messenger and his word is law. Niloc Yarrum bows before him; Balandir dare not argue with him. The Ulans tread carefully about him. What else could I do?'

'Nothing,' she said firmly.

'Will the dead Yath's clan understand that?' Borsus emptied the mug; Sulya refilled it swiftly. 'Or will they proclaim blood debt?'

'Of the Messenger?'

'Of me!' Borsus looked at her then and she saw fear in his dark eyes.

'How can they? You obeyed the command of the Messenger. You are his man – all the Horde knows that. Who would dare stand against you? Not even Niloc Yarrum, not after Taws's destruction of his horse. All the forest folk know that to cross you is to cross the Messenger.'

'Aye,' Borsus sighed, his voice bitter. 'I am raised above my fellows, am I not? Dewan and his Gehrim dare not question my coming; the hef-Ulan himself walks carefully where I am. But what price do I pay, woman? Am I a warrior or a puppet? I feel Taws's strings on me, twitching me this way and that like some doll of straw. I feel I am no longer my own man.'

'You are a warrior,' she said loyally, not comprehending, 'you do Taws's bidding as do we all to greater or lesser extent. Niloc Yarrum himself – the hef-Ulan of the Horde! – does Taws's bidding. And when the hef-Ulan questioned your taking of his horse, did Taws not demonstrate his trust in you? What greater honour can there be than to stand so close to the Messenger?'

'Battle honour,' Borsus muttered sullenly. 'To win skulls in honest fight. As it was before Taws came.'

Sulya gasped at this, glancing to the covered entrance of the lodge and shaping the warding sign as though she feared the Messenger would appear to condemn this blasphemy.

'There will be skulls enough when we attack the Kingdoms,' she said quickly. 'There's honour to be won on High Fort's walls.'

'And perhaps Yath vengeance, too,' Borsus grunted, refusing to be mollified.

'They would not dare!' Sulya was shocked by the notion, cupping Borsus's cheeks in both her hands and turning his head to face her.

'If Taws demanded that you bring him someone you had no choice but to obey. Better a Yath than one of our own Drott. Better some bar-Offa than you.'

'Think you so?' he asked, smiling wearily, despite his misgivings, for the way she held his face reminded him of the way Taws had touched the dead man.

'I do,' she confirmed. 'You are my man, Borsus, and I am proud to be your woman. I should be proud were you no more than a lowly warrior, but to know you are the favoured of the Messenger, that doubles and redoubles my pride.'

Borsus laughed hoarsely, thinking that she had indeed forgotten Andrath, forgotten the manner in which she came to be his woman. And Sulya took the laughter for confirmation and pressed her lips to his.

For a moment, Borsus stiffened against her embrace, the memory of what he had so recently witnessed rekindled, but then the press of her body lit a different fire and he put his arms around her, drawing her down on to the furs beside him.

That evening their meal was eaten burnt, but neither cared.

And the following day, and for nineteen more after that, the great fire had continued to burn, sending out its pall as the axes and adzes and planes worked on the timber and the war engines took gradual shape.

There were three great catapults built, each one mounted on a wheeled platform, the throwing arms fashioned from single trunks, weighted at one end with massive blocks of stone, powered further by twinings of plaited rawhide at the fulcrum, the pulleys Taws designed, drawing the arms down that the baskets might be loaded with missiles, each ballista capable of hurling huge boulders high and far.

Three assault towers rose above the trail, also mounted on wheeled platforms, pyramidal in shape, tapering to their tops. Each framework was walled with planks, and the planks were covered with uncured hides, stinking but less likely to take fire. Inside, ladders rose to a series of shelves, the topmost with a wall that fell down to form a bridge that would span the gap between tower and fort.

Three wheeled shelters were constructed, like moveable longhouses, the roofs of solid timber covered with hides, designed to protect the men inside from missiles hurled from above, ropes hanging down from crossbeams to support the battering rams that ran half the length of each structure.

No mention was made of the dead Yath and by the time the

engines were completed Borsus had relaxed, grateful that Taws made no further demands upon him, save, on the twentieth day, to inform Niloc Yarrum to stand ready.

The hef-Ulan was mightily pleased by this news, even offering Borsus sweet wine as they awaited the appearance of the mage.

It was dawn, though to the south night still reigned. Balandir, Vran, Darien and Ymrath came to the hef-Ulan's lodge, their eyes fierce, gleaming with battle lust. Then Taws entered.

'Prepare yourselves,' he told them. 'Sound your war horns. We approach under Ashar's spell and soon the gates will fall.'

'Praise Ashar!' Niloc bellowed, his fist thudding hard and heavy against the table. 'Praise his Messenger!'

'Aye,' echoed the rest. 'Praise Ashar! Praise the Messenger!'

Taws smiled his vulpine smile. 'Set warriors to the engines,' he instructed, 'I will send the darkness before us that we shall be on them before they know of our coming.'

Yarrum's teeth showed, his smile predatory, and he shouted for his armour, for Dewan to inform the Drott. The Ulans of the Caroc, Yath, Grymard and Vistral yelled for their own Gehrim to spread the word.

By mid-morning the Horde was armoured. Niloc Yarrum stood atop a hummock, a silvered battle helm concealing his face, his breast plate glittering in the sun, the Ulans at his side. He raised the sword that had taken Merak's head and Dewan blew the war horn, the clarion ringing over the uncountable mass of forest folk.

Taws stood before the fire and gestured with both hands. Like a fog blown by a strong wind, the darkness began to clear, daylight sweeping slowly southwards. As the trail ahead grew light the war engines began to move. Hundreds manned the ropes spread before the great constructions, more hundreds pushed from behind. Creaking and groaning, the catapults and towers and shelters were shifted down the trail, towards High Fort, hidden from the defenders' view by the sweeping darkness, propelled by the eager strength of the forest folk.

Throughout the remainder of the day they laboured, then again for half the next, always with the darkness before them, until Taws ordered a halt, announcing the proximity of the fort. Then the carts loaded with missiles were brought up and their contents piled about the ballistae as the massed ranks of forest folk waited with drawn swords and ready bows.

At noon the battle commenced.

Chapter Twelve

The cordor Demiol, of Varun's hundred, was the first to perceive the commencement of the onslaught, and that but briefly.

He was alone on the ramparts of the north wall, his eyes red-rimmed from the effort of attempting to pierce the yet-impenetrable blackness that lingered about the fort, though his spirits were high thanks to the preparations Wynett had provided. He had paused whilst patrolling his section to rest against a buttress, seeking – even though he now knew it was futile – to see into the murk, wondering if he might hear something.

What he heard was a whistling sound that had him cocking his head to one side. Then, in the final instant of his life, he saw the source of that sound as a boulder came out of the darkness to shatter against the buttress and crush him as it caromed off, smashing down on to the stone walkway to bounce over, into the darkness below. Demiol did not hear the screaming of the second or third warriors to be struck by the missile, nor the shouting that instantly followed as tellemen and cordors bellowed for their commands to stand ready and the soldiery yelled in confusion, most of them not knowing what had happened.

A second missile reduced a catapult to ragged fragments, killing four of its crew, then a third exploded against the wall, sending a shrapnel burst of jagged rock splinters scything over the ramparts, fresh screams ringing through the unnatural night as men were cut and maimed. High Fort's mangonels responded, firing blind into the darkness, their missiles landing unseen and unheard. Archers loosed shafts, then ceased as the tellemen recognized the uselessness of such retaliation against an enemy that remained invisible, that might, for all they knew, not even be there.

Rycol, eating a midday meal, left his food unfinished as he heard the sounds of attack. Snatching his sword and latching the scabbard to his belt as he ran, he hurried from the dining hall in time to see a stone smash down on to a brazier, spilling burning coals in spark-trailing arcs across the limitations of his vision. Instantly he was running for the steps leading to the north wall, cursing as he careened into men near-lost in the occultation, using all the strength of his powerful lungs to shout for order, sending warriors fumbling for their battle stations as he grabbed a torch and began to climb the angulated stairway.

He reached the wall and bellowed for the watch commander to attend him, hearing more stones thud against the battlements as Varun came running out of the dark.

'We cannot see them!' the telleman gasped. 'We have no targets! We cannot hear them.'

Rycol heard men screaming farther along the wall, then ducked as a missile landed close by, crashing on to the stairs below.

'No matter,' he told the officer, 'they are there. Range your catapults for the maximum distance, then shorten each volley to the minimum. And pray!'

Varun nodded and disappeared into the gloom. Rycol cursed afresh as stone chips shaved his cheek, and paced along the ramparts as more boulders descended in a nightmare hail. He found a squad of archers crouched beneath the shelter of the wall and took their cordor by the shoulder, telling him to organize the removal of the wounded. Frustrated by their uselessness, the bowmen were glad to be occupied, and Rycol found himself alone, swathed in a blackness that was filled with the sounds of hurt men and falling stones. He fought the threat of panic, making himself listen to the missiles, counting them as they fell, and came to the conclusion that no more than three ballistae were ranged against his fort. Spaced along the north wall were ten mangonels, five more commanding the river, though so far as he knew no attack was mounted from that direction. It appeared, as best he could tell, that the barbarians massed on the Beltrevan road, though how many, he could not estimate. Nor did he know if Low Fort came under fire, for the darkness still filled the river canyon and he had no word from Fengrif, the obscurity having defeated all attempts to get a boat across.

It was unusual – indeed, it was unheard of – for the tribes to employ catapults, and he guessed the Messenger's hand in their use. Whatever the source, it was unimportant now: what counted was the demoralizing effect of the attack. It was as he had feared: his own men had no targets on which to sight, not even the satisfaction of hearing their missiles land, and he could recognize the frustration in the shouting that filled the wall and the cries that echoed from the yards below.

He moved towards the glow of a brazier, finding himself close to a shattered mangonel, the archers with whom he had spoken lifting wounded men from the wreckage and carrying them, awkwardly in the obfuscation, to the stairways, stumbling and cursing as they negotiated rubble, the wounded screaming as unsighted men dropped them. He moved on, encouraging the soldiers who crouched nervously against the wall, their only warning of descending stones the abrupt whistling that accompanied the blocks as they tumbled out of the darkness. It was a nightmare and he saw that his defence stood in terrible danger should the occultation continue. He could not tell if the countering barrages found their mark, nor how many tribesmen massed along the road. For all he knew, the forest folk crouched below his walls even now; and what other war engines they brought against him he could only guess. He continued along the ramparts, taking his own inventory of the damage and finding two of his catapults demolished, the remaining eight firing as he had ordered. Eleven men were dead, and seven wounded too severely to remain at their stations. There were more hurt by flying chips, but they applied their own bandages, preferring to stay on the wall in readiness for the assault they felt sure must soon follow.

He found Varun again and ordered all but two of the mangonels to stand down, wary of deplenishing stocks of missiles in futile response to the Horde's barrage. The telleman asked if they might use balefire, but Rycol refused, remembering both Brannoc's warning and his own experiment.

Then a cordor appeared to inform him that a ram was brought against the main gate.

Leaving Varun in command of the wall, Rycol hurried to a point directly above the gate.

He craned over the battlements, but below he could see nothing, though he heard a dull thudding, as might come from a fist pounded against a far-away door.

'Stones!' he yelled. 'Bring stones, by the Lady!'

Men came, pleased to find some positive response to the attack, and rubble was lifted to be dropped into the stygian gloom below. What effect it had, Rycol could not tell, and he quit the wall, leaving orders for the bombardment to continue until he should command otherwise.

A torch in one hand and the other on the familiar stone of the wall, he descended the stairs and made his way to the courtyard facing the gate.

The telleman in command of that area, a young officer called Istar, waited by a brazier with drawn sword. His hundred was spaced about the yard, strengthened by two cords of archers, who crouched with strung bows and fletched shafts beneath the colonnades flanking the yard. It was a classic defence, the bowmen ready to open fire should the gate give way, Istar's swordsmen poised to charge should the attackers break through the aerial volley. But in the pervading darkness, Rycol doubted the bowmen would find clear targets – from their positions the gate was near-invisible, despite the braziers set there.

Istar's face was drawn as the chatelain approached, concern for his command etched deep upon his youthful features.

'How can they see?' he wondered aloud. 'We move as blind men, but they have reached the wall. What magicks do they command?'

'None that we cannot defeat,' Rycol snapped. 'How do you know they are there?'

The telleman beckoned in answer and Rycol followed him around the walls of the yard to where the gate stood, high and solid, stout oak timbers set with bronze castings, four massive hinges to each wing, the crossbar thick as a man's waist and resting on great hooks of metal bolted deep into the wood. As he came close he heard a steady, rhythmic pounding, and when he set his hands upon the timbers, he felt them vibrate beneath his palms, as might some massive heart. From above he could hear the shouting of his own men as they spilled stone upon the attackers, and between the thuddings of the ram he caught the clatter of the missiles, guessing that the barbarians manning the ram were protected by some defensive construction.

'They are doubtless there,' he acknowledged, smiling encouragement at Istar. 'But we are behind the strongest gate in all Tamur and it will take them too long to break that down.'

'Too long?' Istar queried. 'Surely they have all of this endless night to accomplish their task.'

'Bedyr Caitin will be here soon,' Rycol promised. 'And King Darr with him.'

'Can we not use fire?' asked the young telleman. 'Spilled from above it would roast them where they stand.'

'And mayhap fire the gate,' Rycol pointed out. 'Or lend strength to the Messenger's ensorcellements. No, Istar, our walls can withstand them.'

'But if they do break through . . .' the officer said softly, doubtfully.

'Then have your bowmen range on the flames of the braziers,' said Rycol. 'Leave two men here to shout a warning. At the first sign of the gate giving way pull them back, and instantly they are withdrawn, loose your archers. Those bowmen can flight five shafts before a single barbarian crosses our portals. After that it will be sword work. Should it come to that, send a runner and you'll be reinforced with a second hundred.'

Istar nodded, reassured by his commander's apparent confidence, and Rycol left him in the darkness of the yard, listening to the heartbeat pounding of the ram.

His own heart beat faster as he retraced his steps, for although he would not allow it to show, or yet admit it to the men who looked to him for inspiration and command, he doubted even High Fort could withstand the sorcerous attack indefinitely. The rain of missiles continued and while few men were harmed now, save those needed upon the ramparts, the fabric of the bastion suffered constant damage. The steady barrage would eventually weaken his walls, or destroy his own catapults, and then, he felt certain, the forest folk would storm the walls. Unless the battering ram was disabled, it must eventually break down even those strong gates. And if the barbarians were able to penetrate the fort under cover of the darkness, his plight would be dire: the Horde Bedyr had reported would overrun High Fort like a storm-raised flood.

These dour thoughts in his mind, he made his way to his command chambers, exchanging a few tersely reassuring words with his worried wife as he doffed his helm and took the goblet of wine she poured him.

'Wynett has care of the wounded,' she told him, 'and I am busy in the kitchens. You need not concern yourself with food, nor worry for the hurt.'

'Thank you,' he said, smiling grimly. 'Let us hope the walls hold.'

'They will,' said Marga. 'At least until Bedyr arrives with the army. The Lady will not desert us.'

'I pray not,' Rycol grunted.

He drank the wine as he dispensed orders to the officers who came to him, proud of them for the discipline they showed, surprised when he glanced to the candle melting at his elbow and saw that the hour stood close on what should have been twilight. The supernatural darkness robbed the senses of chronological assessment and as he spoke with his commanders he realized that few knew whether it was day or night, only that the attack continued, the barbarians seemingly equipped with an endless supply of missiles.

'Of course,' he remarked, a trifle irritably, to a telleman, 'they have all the stone of the Lozins at their disposal.'

And most of it, he remarked to himself, falls against my walls. He did not voice that thought, but concentrated on ordering his defence as best he could. Half the men manning the north wall were stood down and a series of positions organized that word of frontal assault might be shouted from man to man while the remainder were grouped in barracks and dining hall to rest and eat, waiting in reserve. He maintained a full hundred, complemented by archers, at the north gate and reinforced the positions along the river for fear the forest folk would attempt a water-borne assault. From Sister Wynett he received word of the wounded, learning that thirty men were maimed beyond usefulness and a further seventy temporarily incapacitated. There were sufficient supplies of the fear-deadening potion to last five more days, but after that it would be gone, and little chance of gathering fresh stocks while the attack continued. His signal tower remained useless and there was no word from Fengrif on the east bank.

Finally there were no more orders to be issued and he found himself alone. He poured more wine and drank it slowly, wondering what he might do to counter the assault. Were he able to see his enemy, he might have sent a force out through the postern to flank the barbarians on the battering ram, but without knowing what numbers he faced, it seemed too dangerous an exercise. He sighed, stroking his chin as he voiced a silent prayer that Bedyr or Darr would arrive as he had promised with Sisters from Andurel who might drive back the awful obscurity that so hampered his defence.

That aid would come when it came, he decided, and brooding on it was of no use. He rose and set his helm upon his grey hair to inspect the wall again.

There was a little more damage, though not yet sufficient to occasion real alarm. What was of more concern was the morale of his troops, for the hour was shouted up from the yards below and his men knew that true night must grip the Beltrevan. Yet there was no cessation of the bombardment. It slowed a trifle, but the missiles still came whistling out of the now-real night, whilst the two catapults answering the barrage fired only sporadically for fear of needless waste. Archers and swordsmen occupied themselves with dice, or the tending of their weapons, the strain of frustration showing on faces lit by the dim red glow of the torches and braziers, or the sudden arguments that erupted amongst men rendered helpless by the Messenger's sending.

Rycol did what he could to cheer them, knowing that what they needed was honest battle against an enemy they could see. Then, with the promise of evshan to hearten them, he went down again to the dim interior of High Fort.

The yards were empty, men moving beneath the cover of colonnaded passages, or hugging the walls of buildings, and he realized that in the time it had taken him to descend the stairway the barbarian catapults had shifted range. Where before the fire had been concentrated against the north wall, it was now directed at the interior. At least one ballista still maintained its assault on the ramparts, but the others now sent stones crashing on to rooftops or into the deserted yards. It was doubly unnerving, for the forest folk seldom fought at night and the very fact that they utilized catapults to strike at the interior of the fortress suggested a strategy never before employed.

Rycol huddled instinctively against a wall as he heard the now-familiar whistling of an incoming missile. Then gasped as the roof before him exploded inwards, shards of broken tile and chunks of masonry rattling through the shadows. He heard, but could not see, the impact, though he felt pieces of broken stone rattle against his breastplate and helm and staggered beneath the onslaught. From the darkness ahead he heard a man scream, and broke into an awkward run, halting as a knee crashed against something solid.

The screaming became an agonized whimper and through squinted eyes he made out the shape of a boulder surrounded by fragments of the roof. Using his hands more than his sight, he moved around the block and found a halberdier pinned beneath the rock. Both the man's legs were crushed and as Rycol bent to succour him, he felt warm blood on his hands.

'Kargen?' The halberdier's voice was hoarse as he clutched at Rycol's hand. 'Is that you, Kargen?'

'No,' said the chatelain, 'it is Rycol.'

'My Lord, forgive me,' moaned the dying man.

'For what?' Rycol asked gently. 'There is nothing to forgive.'

'I should not have been here. I was lost.'

'No matter.' Rycol cushioned the man's head.

'I was afraid. I did not think it would be like this.'

Fear mingled with the pain in the halberdier's voice and Rycol wondered briefly, cynically, why he should still feel afraid: the bombardment could no longer threaten him. He said, 'You are forgiven.'

'Thank you,' said the halberdier, and coughed and died.

Rycol lowered the lifeless head and rose to his feet, hearing more stones thud down some distance off. Surely, he thought, they cannot keep this up. Surely it must cease soon, at least for the night.

It did not. Throughout the night the barrage continued with a mind-numbing regularity. Sleep was disturbed by the steady thunder of the missiles and the irregular screaming of stricken men. It seemed that the Lozins themselves rained stone upon High Fort and even in those parts not affected by the bombardment, men lay restless, listening, waiting for death to crash from the obfuscated sky.

At the hour the candles said was dawn there was no change, only a quickening of the barrage. The ram, silent through the night, began to pound again and though he put a brave face on it, Rycol felt a bleak despair creep into his soul, for he knew that his men could not withstand much more.

On the deck of the *Vashti*, bathed in autumnal sunlight, Kedryn felt the wind whip his face, sending his hair in a streaming mane that fluttered in the near-gale propelling the barque northwards at a breath-stealing pace. Beside him, Bedyr sat in silence, his proud features solemn as he studied the tiny figure clutching the central mast, too small to stand in danger of the boom that swung beneath the billowed sail. For the seven days, and as many nights, since they had departed Andurel, Sister Grania had held that position, and as best either of the Tamurin could tell, she had neither slept nor rested, taking only the food and wine brought her where she stood, and that silently, automatically, as though her hands raised it to a mouth that chewed and swallowed independent of the mind that cast the weather spell.

Galen Sadreth had readily agreed to the Sister's announcement that she would utilize her powers to speed their northward passage, and settled himself at his tiller as Grania moved about the craft while it slid from its moorings and tacked into the stream. Once at the centre of the Idre, the Sister had begun to chant softly, her head bowed, her right hand upon the thick stem of the mast, her left raised palm-outwards to the sky. A wind had started then, slight at first, but growing momentarily stronger until it filled both sails and Galen shouted for his crew to stand down from the complex work their counter-current passage involved. There had been little for the men to do after that, for the wind gained strength and the *Vashti* sped over the water, foam surging in twin waves from her prow, her wake spreading in a roiling vee behind, setting those craft they passed rocking with its force. She flew, driven by Grania's magic, faster than mortal vessel could sail, cleaving the Idre swift as an arrow from dawn to dusk and on, while the tiny Sister held to her post and murmured her spell, unsleeping, unmoving.

'We'll make the Lozin harbourage by nightfall at this pace,' the captain remarked, glancing towards the sun. 'But what price does she pay?'

'I know not.' Bedyr's voice was fraught with concern, his eyes troubled as he studied Grania. 'I fear she exhausts herself to bring us there. I pray it will not prove wasted effort.'

'Wasted?' Kedryn asked. 'How can it be?'

Bedyr shrugged, drawing his cloak closer about his shoulders, for the wind of their passage was chill. 'This takes a toll, and I doubt the Messenger waits on our coming. By my estimation, the Horde has now had time to reach the walls of High Fort and the attack may well have begun. What sorceries he will employ I do not know, but they will be powerful – they will doubtless demand powerful counter-spells, and if Grania devotes all her strength to this, she may well have none left for the greater battle.'

'The Sister surely knows her own strength,' Galen suggested. 'She must be aware of her limitations. If she has any.'

'Aye,' Bedyr allowed, 'but I fear the urgency of the situation compels her to the task in hand. And even Grania does not know the full power of the Messenger.'

'If she felt such was the case she would surely bring us there more slowly,' Kedryn said, expressing a confidence he would not have felt scant weeks before. 'I place my trust in her.'

'As do we all,' agreed his father, 'but still I am concerned for her.'

'There is nothing you can do,' said Galen, phlegmatically. 'That trance she holds remains unbroken. When Mennim took her food this morning he said she ate it without seeing it. Her eyes are far away: she neither sees nor hears us. She communes with the Lady.'

'Would that all the vessels might travel as swiftly,' Kedryn said. 'If Darr's fleet were with us, and Hattim's close behind, we might not need the Sister's magic to defeat the Messenger.'

'Perhaps not,' Bedyr nodded, 'but it takes time to raise an army, and time is one thing we have in short supply. Hopefully the re-maining Sisters will bring the King's force north with equal alacrity, and Hattim's Galichians after, but for now it is Grania we must rely on.'

Kedryn looked forwards, past the blue-clad figure and beyond the carven prow to where the Lozins lay across the horizon, a dark line spanning the edge of his world. There, perhaps, lay his destiny, for there the Horde lay, and the Messenger. Unconsciously, he rubbed at his shoulder, where the Drott arrow had struck.

'It pains you?' Bedyr enquired, seeing the motion.

'No.' Kedryn shook his head. 'Wynett's care ended the pain, and Hattim's blows are memories, but I feel something. No more than a memory, but something I cannot describe.'

His father's face became grave, clouded with foreboding.

'A glamour,' he murmured. 'Mayhap you should have remained in Andurel.'

Kedryn smiled, shaking his head. 'I have a duty, Father, as do you. As do all loyal to the Kingdoms. Mine rests there, I believe.' He pointed to the north, along the shining line of the river. 'Where the Horde threatens. And it is a duty I cannot – nor would not – avoid. Could I serve the Kingdoms better elsewhere, then Grania would have told me.'

Bedyr nodded without speaking, for there was little to say, though much to hope for, and so much of that rested on the small shoulders of the Sister.

Kedryn, in turn, fell silent, continuing to study the northern sky-line, exhilarated by the *Vashti*'s passage despite the tingling sensation he experienced in his shoulder. It had not been there when they commenced their journey, nor had he been aware of any discomfort until the outline of the Lozins became more distinct against the haze. Now he realized it was stronger, as though his approach amplified the feeling, the increasing proximity of the Messenger magnifying the spell laid on the arrowhead. Grania, he thought, would have some remedy for that, but Grania was unapproachable, lost in the trance of her casting. He dismissed the mild animus, relegating it to the back of his mind as the line of the mountains grew ever darker, steadily larger.

Galen's estimation proved correct, for as dusk transformed the blue silver of the river to cerulean the settlement below High Fort hove in sight. Off to the west the sun still lit the edge of the sky, but to the east, over Kesh, the heavens were dark, the moon risen half full. Lights shone in the town, hazy, as though seen through a fog. Grania let go her hold on the mast and slumped to the deck, the wind she had conjured dropping, leaving the sail limp in the abruptly-still air.

Instantly, Kedryn was moving forward, even as Galen shouted for

277

the crew to reef the sail, using the barque's dwindling momentum to bring her in towards anchorage. Kedryn knelt beside the Sister, who turned a face no longer rosy, but pallid with the expenditure of effort, towards him, her lips moving. He needed to put his ear close to her mouth to hear her say, 'There is magic here. More powerful than I anticipated. Get me ashore.'

'Take her, I'll bring our gear.'

Bedyr's voice was urgent and Kedryn lifted the tiny Sister in his arms as his father fetched the armour Darr had provided from the lockers. She seemed to weigh nothing, her body light as a bird's, and he stood easily, cradling her as the gangplank was run out and men leapt ashore to moor the vessel. Only when he had reached the stability of the dockside did he glance towards High Fort, and then he gasped, his eyes widening in shock.

The moon that bathed the river to the south cast no light on the fortress, and little on the town. What he had taken to be some river mist now seemed a pervading darkness that hung in an almost palpable cloud about citadel and settlement. Had he not known better, he might have taken the hour for midnight, so deep was that obfuscation. And about High Fort it was deeper still: he could not make out the walls he knew were visible from where he stood. He halted, trying to pick out landmarks, hearing his father's sharp intake of breath behind him.

'They have come,' said Bedyr, his tone grim.

'Aye,' Grania whispered from the cradle of Kedryn's arms, 'and we have arrived none too soon. Get me to an inn. I must warm myself, and eat.'

'Tears of the Lady!' Galen joined them, leaving Ivran in charge of the *Vashti.* 'What goes on?'

'A sending.' Bedyr turned to the riverman. 'Can you find your way through this?'

Galen nodded. 'To fort or tavern?'

'Tavern,' Bedyr said, 'and swiftly.'

The sailor looked about him, shaking his massive head in bewilderment, then pointed and began to stride into the gloom. Kedryn hurried after him, realizing that within a few paces, he could find himself lost, for the occultation robbed him of direction as surely as might a blindfold. Bedyr flanked him, bulky beneath the weight of his armour, and they followed Galen to where a lantern gleamed fitfully above a closed door.

The riverman thrust the portal open and held it as the two Tamurin entered, pausing as faces turned towards them, the eyes that studied them oddly hostile.

A tall, thin man dressed in a tunic of scarlet embroidered with gold that matched the lacings of his boots came forward, hope and fear mingled on his narrow features.

'My Lords,' he murmured unctuously, 'welcome. I am Talkien Drass. Are there many of you?'

'We are four,' Bedyr said.

'Four?' The innkeeper's tone was shocked, resentful. 'Are you not the promised army?'

Kedryn pushed past him, moving to the fire that burned in the open hearth. Five men sat there, turning sullen faces towards him, but when he looked at them they shifted without speaking, making space. He settled Sister Grania close to the fire and said, 'Food. Quickly.'

Drass nodded, rubbing his hands nervously, and called for victuals to be brought.

'And wine,' Grania murmured. 'Mulled wine. Galichian red, for preference.'

'Chatelain Rycol promised an army.' Drass addressed himself to Bedyr, a note of accusation in his tone. 'Where is the army?'

Bedyr glanced about the tavern, aware that all there waited for his answer. 'It follows,' he said. 'King Darr sails from Andurel, Hattim of Ust-Galich close behind. Jarl raises Kesh, and my Tamurin march e'en now.'

He swept his cloak back as he spoke, revealing the fist emblazoned on his dark green tunic. Drass stared at it, his expression uncomprehending.

'Do you not recognize the Lord of Tamur?' barked Galen. 'You speak with Bedyr Caitin, man! And that is Prince Kedryn by the fire.'

'My Lords!' Drass bowed low, long hair falling about his sallow face. 'Forgive me. I had thought . . . we all thought . . . you would come with the full strength of the Kingdoms, as Lord Rycol promised.'

'We come ahead,' Bedyr responded. 'Lord Rycol promised true — the army follows. But for now there is only us and the Sister.'

Close by Kedryn's seat a man uttered, 'What good is one Sister? What can she do?'

'Much,' Kedryn snapped, turning angry eyes on the spokesman. 'Let her but regain her strength and she will show you.'

279

The man opened his mouth to speak again, but the expression on Kedryn's face persuaded him to think better of it, and he fell silent.

A wench appeared with mulled wine, a platter of steaming meat and a bowl of vegetables. Her eyes were troubled as she set the food before Grania, frightened and hopeful at the same time. Kedryn saw that all there held the same look, as though fear curdled into animosity, the hope of Rycol's promise persuading them of some instant salvation that they now doubted.

'This darkness,' he asked a man nearby, as Grania took a mug of wine and sipped carefully, 'how long has it lasted?'

'Thirty days!' The man counted them off on his fingers. 'Or thirty long nights, rather. There is no sunrise – only this! And the barbarians wait beyond the walls like wolves in winter.'

'Lord Rycol bade us remain,' Drass added. 'Else many would have fled. We waited in hope of his promise, but now . . .' He glanced at Bedyr, at Kedryn, his pale eyes expressing his doubt.

'But now you have your Lord here,' Bedyr said firmly, 'and I give you *my* promise that the army follows. This Sister is Paramount in Andurel, and she brought us here with white magic that we might face the barbarians with her power.'

'Will that be sufficient?' Drass murmured. 'A single Sister?'

'The Paramount Sister,' Kedryn corrected.

'Even so,' Drass began, but found himself interrupted by Grania, who had finished her second mug of wine and was chewing heartily on a thick slice of roasted meat.

'I can throw back this darkness,' she promised. 'And when I do, your spirits will lift. Has Wynett not provided you with remedies for the malaise I sense?'

'She did,' said Drass, 'but not enough. She could not produce sufficient for all of us. Not fort and town, both.' Bitterness entered his voice, 'Chatelain Rycol said his soldiers need it more than we.'

'As indeed they do, for they face the brunt. But no matter.' Grania's customary brusqueness began to return as she ate. 'I need a little rest, and then I shall apply myself to lifting this sending. I imagine the defenders cannot see their enemy?'

Drass shook his head.

'I thought not,' murmured the Sister. 'And you cannot see that this despondency I sense in you is exactly what the Messenger seeks. This is a time when you must show courage, for there will be wounded in the fort who might fare better here, and Rycol will need supplies. Do you provide such?'

Drass shrugged, his face suddenly guilty. 'Not since the third day. It is hard enough fending for ourselves. River traffic has ceased with this accursed darkness and the farms go untended. Besides, the fort comes under constant bombardment – it is dangerous to approach.'

Grania nodded, turning to Kedryn, beckoning Bedyr closer.

'This darkness robs the spirit. Of itself, it is hard enough to bear, but there is more to it than mere lack of sight. It induces hopelessness, resentment, fear.'

'I see that,' Bedyr nodded.

'Let me but finish this,' Grania indicated her food, 'and then we shall go to the fort and see what we can do.'

'Meanwhile,' said Galen, cheerfully shoving two men aside so that he might seat himself, 'I find this obscurity puts a chill in my bones that only evshan can lift. Innkeeper?'

'I have only a little evshan left,' said Drass. 'Lord Rycol has commandeered so much – evshan, fuel, even building blocks.'

'What little you have left you may bring me,' Galen informed him. 'And I suggest you wipe that sour look from your sorry features: doubtless Lord Rycol's need is greater than yours. Indeed, you should be proud to serve Tamur as best you can.'

'I am, please believe me.' This was addressed to Bedyr, rather than the riverman. 'But it is not easy.'

'It will change,' Bedyr promised, though Kedryn noticed with cynical amusement that he did not specify whether for better or worse, 'but meanwhile, I suggest you do as my companion asks. In fact, bring evshan for us all.'

'Instantly, my Lord Bedyr.' Drass executed another sweeping bow and beckoned a serving wench.

A flask of the fiery liquor was brought and Galen filled the three mugs. 'A toast,' he suggested. 'To the damnation of barbarians and the victory of the Kingdoms.'

'Do not damn them,' Grania murmured, colour returning to her cheeks as she sank another mug of hot wine. 'They are misguided. Let us drink to victory, though.'

'To victory,' nodded Bedyr, echoed by Kedryn and Galen.

'And now,' Grania said, 'shall we seek out our enemy?'

She slid from the settle, only to clutch at the table as she staggered, shaking her head as though to dispel a vapour, her rubicund features suddenly pale once more. Kedryn moved to take her in his arms again, but she pushed his hand away, murmuring, 'No. Let me walk out of here,' and he stood aside, watching with concern as she moved slowly towards the door, a strained smile fixed upon her lips. He followed close behind, anxious lest she fall, as Galen and Bedyr distributed the packs between them.

'You will need torches.' Talkien Drass made no offer of guidance, but he provided them with lengths of wood, the ends wrapped in pitch-soaked cloth, and lit both flambeaux.

Kedryn swung the door open and they went out into the eerie night, the air chill after the warmth of the tavern. He heard the door thud shut behind them, and when he turned he saw that faces watched from the windows, but none ventured out.

Grania took a few short steps into the murk, those sufficient to hide her from the onlookers, then halted, turning to Kedryn. 'I need your strength.' She swayed as she said it, close to toppling, and he stooped quickly, sweeping her up as Bedyr and Galen held the torches close.

'I did not want them to see how weak I am,' she murmured. 'They are frightened enough already. We face a powerful foe, my friends, and hope will be a potent weapon against him.'

'Can you lift this?' Kedryn asked, looking about.

'In time,' came the faint response, 'but I need rest, and Wynett's care.'

'Then let us go,' said Bedyr, raising his torch high as he moved into the blackness.

'Follow the sound of the river,' Galen suggested. 'So long as that lies to our right, we move towards the fort.'

It was sound advice, for as they drew farther from the tavern the darkness grew denser, all sense of direction fading, buildings invisible until torch glow lit on walls so close a stretched hand might touch the stone. The air was colder, too, as they approached the glacis leading to the southern gates, and Kedryn felt a hint of the numbing despair that gripped the townsfolk.

'We should have commandeered that flask of evshan,' Galen muttered. 'It would warm against this damnable chill.'

'There is evshan in High Fort,' Bedyr said, his voice deliberately cheerful. 'Something to look forward to.'

'Aye,' said Galen, then cursed volubly as he stumbled against a hidden wall.

'Do we move in the right direction?' wondered Kedryn, following the light of his father's torch, Bedyr's figure no more than a faint shape ahead.

'I hear the Idre,' came the answer, 'I think so.'

They moved slowly, from building to building, occasionally aided by the dim glow of lanterns hung before doorways, or the filtered radiance from shuttered windows, until the houses ceased and they faced total blackness.

'The land rises,' Bedyr announced, 'towards High Fort, I believe.'

Beneath his booted feet, Kedryn felt the cobbles become flagstones and surmised that they climbed the glacis. It seemed to last forever, but then faint illumination pinpricked the darkness and the sweeping rise of the glacis flattened.

'Wait!' Bedyr urged as Galen pushed forwards. 'A fort under siege is likely to answer a stranger's knock unkindly. Use that voice of yours.'

Galen promptly issued a stertorian bellow, announcing the arrival of the Lord of Tamur and his party.

From the darkness ahead a cry came back, 'Approach and show yourselves.'

They went forwards, halting abruptly as the torches lit the tall gates of the fort's south wall. Above, they heard the rattle of armour against stone, then to their right flame shone and the same voice ordered, 'This way. Slowly – else my bowmen bring you down.'

They moved towards the light, finding a cordor standing by a low gate, flanked by archers.

'Lord Bedyr!' he saluted as he recognized the Lord of Tamur. 'Thank the Lady you have come.'

Bedyr stood aside, making way for Kedryn to carry Grania into High Fort, the cordor standing confused, watching as the quartet entered.

'The rest, my Lord?'

'There are no others yet,' Bedyr told him. 'The army follows.'

The cordor's face was lined with weariness and grew more haggard at this news. 'How soon, Lord? We are hard pressed.'

'Soon enough,' Bedyr promised, looking about him, seeing a court-yard ringed with braziers that glowed like distant beacons in the all-pervading obscurity, 'but for now we need your Paramount Hospitaller.'

The cordor nodded and shouted for a serjeant to escort them to the wards.

'Send word to Lord Rycol that we are come,' Bedyr commanded. 'I would confer with him once the Sister is attended.'

A second man was despatched and they followed the serjeant

along the perimeter of the yard, moving from brazier to brazier, hearing the clatter of missiles from the northern reaches of the bastion.

'Catapults?' asked Bedyr.

'Aye, Lord.' Fatigue rang hollow in the man's voice, but still he smiled. 'Catapults with an endless supply of stone. Much more and the forest folk will have the Lozins brought down and go around us.'

'They'll meet the army of Tamur then,' Bedyr said firmly. 'What of Low Fort?'

'No word,' the serjeant shrugged. 'The signal towers are useless in this foul night.'

'The Sister will end that,' promised Bedyr confidentially. 'And then we'll have honest fight.'

'I'd welcome that, Lord. Let me but see my enemy. This, though . . .' He gestured at the surrounding gloom, 'this seeps into the soul.'

Kedryn shivered as he heard the dejection that crept into the serjeant's voice and glanced down at Grania. The Sister appeared asleep, her eyes closed and her mouth open, her breath faint. He experienced a momentary rush of panic as the ugly thought that she had expended all her strength on bringing them north at so breakneck a pace and was now wasted crept into his mind.

'I have a little life left yet, do not fear.'

He could not be certain whether she spoke, or if the words formed in his head, voiceless, but he felt a surge of hope, smiling at the diminutive woman, so light in his arms.

'The hospital,' the serjeant announced, and Kedryn saw that they stood before the entrance.

'Take Grania in,' Bedyr suggested. 'I shall await Rycol. Join us when you have seen her settled.'

Kedryn nodded and carried Grania in, pausing as he saw the beds occupied by wounded men, Sisters setting splints, bandaging maimed limbs, soothing men who moaned in pain, others who lay without limbs. He had never seen the effects of artillery fire and it horrified him. To be struck down by some chunk of stone that hurtled out of the darkness was somehow far worse than the notion of sword cut or arrow wound, a random thing that seemed to deny individuality. And to be unable to retaliate must render it far worse. His face grew sombre as he stood there, recalling the ward as he had seen it before. Then, for all that his shoulder was afire with the pain of the arrow, it had been a bright place, cheerful and full of hope.

Now there was a grimness to it, shadows pooling despite the torches set along the walls, the faces of the Sisters wearied by their labours, the eyes of the wounded empty, haunted by shadows deeper than those that fell between the beds, as if the darkness through which the missiles that had struck them had come had tainted the stone with the Messenger's fell glamours, imposing more than fleshly wounds on their victims.

He saw Wynett coming towards him, and the change he saw in her was painful. Purple shadows ringed her care-filled eyes and her cheeks were hollowed, her hair drawn tight back, emphasizing the thinning of her face. There was blood drying on her blue gown and her shoulders slumped as though weighted by the empathic pain that etched her features.

Yet she smiled, albeit wanly, and said, 'Kedryn, it seems wrong to say I am glad to see you.'

'It goes hard?' he said, not really meaning it as a question.

'Aye.' She nodded, frowning as she recognized Grania in his arms. 'What has happened? Quickly, bring her.'

'She exhausted herself with the travel spell,' he said, following Wynett along the chamber to the side room he had previously occupied. 'She brought us north swifter than I thought possible.'

'She was ever thus,' Wynett murmured. 'Set her down while I fetch remedies.'

He set Grania gently on the bed, standing as Wynett returned with a tray that she placed on the small table. As she worked on the unconscious woman he looked about, barely recognizing the chamber. The plants that had flourished so cheerfully were withered, hanging limp in their baskets, and the single lantern seemed to cast less light than he recalled. He looked at Wynett's bent head, seeing that the hair he had admired was lank now, as though in long need of washing.

'She will sleep,' the Hospitaller promised, rising to face him. 'I have given her a potion that not even her will may overcome. We need her help, but she needs sleep more, lest she destroy herself. Tell your father that — and if need be, tell him I forbid any disturbance until she wakes.'

'Aye,' he said. 'But you — how fare you?'

Wynett smiled, smoothing a tendril of loose hair back. 'Tired, but that is a common complaint. The wounded are, in a way, the least of our problems. This sending is the greater, for it sets a despondency on the soul and that is harder to fight.'

'In the town they said you had remedies.'

'In ever shorter supply, and what we have is given to those manning the walls. They cannot see their enemy – only hear the missiles – and the sending is mightily powerful. We join in prayer to the Lady, and that helps a little, but we are essentially hospitallers, not casters.'

'Grania said she will lift it,' he murmured, looking to the sleeping Sister.

'And she will,' confirmed Wynett, 'of that I have no doubt. Her talents are powerful, but there are limits even to Grania's strength, and she is closer to those limits than she would admit.'

'You know her?' he asked.

'Of course. I was of Andurel once.' Wynett turned tender eyes on the elder Sister, stooping to smooth the covers over her supine form. 'It was Grania who persuaded me of my vocation. She saw it in me before I recognized it in myself, and much of my training was under her tutelage.' She laughed softly, and beneath the griming of bloody surgery and lack of sleep, Kedryn saw the beauty that had entranced him shine through. 'It was a matter of some irritation to my mother – she saw more use in a well-planned marriage than the ways of Estrevan, but with my father's support Grania prevailed.'

'You might be safer now had she not,' he remarked.

'Perhaps,' Wynett shrugged, 'though if the Horde breaks through, not even the White Palace will be safe.'

'The palace?' Kedryn saw her suddenly in a new light, aware of similarities he had not noticed before. 'You are of High Blood?'

'My mother was the Queen Valaria,' said Wynett, carelessly. 'King Darr, my father.'

Kedryn's mouth gaped open, occasioning a chuckle from Wynett. 'Then Ashrivelle is your sister.'

'Indeed. You met her?'

'Briefly.' Now he could see how much alike they were, and was surprised that he had not seen it before. 'She is beautiful. You are both very lovely.'

'Thank you.' Wynett parodied a curtsey. 'Though I do not feel it at the moment. Was she well? And my father?'

'Aye,' Kedryn nodded, 'but do you not know that?'

'We have no contact,' murmured Wynett, shaking her head. 'I foreswore all else when I embraced the way of the Lady.'

Kedryn was about to ask her more, but a shout from the entrance called his attention to Bedyr and with a murmured apology he left

286

Wynett, striding to where his father waited with Galen and a grey-faced telleman.

'Rycol awaits us,' Bedyr said by way of explanation. 'Is Grania tended?'

'She is,' Kedryn confirmed as the telleman led them away into the gloom, 'and Wynett says she is to remain undisturbed until she wakes. And father? I learnt that Wynett is the King's daughter.'

'Aye.' Bedyr said this with vague surprise, as though it were so common an item of knowledge as to be unworthy of discussion. 'She forsook Andurel for Estrevan when she was little more than a child – her talents manifested early.'

'King Darr did not mention it,' said Kedryn as they rounded a corner to enter a corridor leading to an upward flight of stairs lit by smoking flambeaux.

'He would not,' Bedyr responded. 'Why should he? Those of Estrevan forsake all family ties when they take their final oaths, and it was a matter of some dispute between Darr and Valaria. The Queen opposed the move, while Darr supported his daughter. Valaria ever hoped that Wynett would change her mind whilst she remained still an acolyte, but she was disappointed.'

Kedryn nodded, thinking that Wynett must be a woman of great spirit to forego the White Palace for the rigours of High Fort: he liked her the more for that.

'My Lords?' The telleman halted before an oaken door, interrupting Kedryn's musings. 'Lord Rycol awaits within.'

Bedyr thanked him and pushed the door open.

The chamber was shuttered against the darkness, candles burning in columns of carved crystal that magnified their radiance, lending some semblance of normality to the scene. A fire burned in the hearth, sending long shadows from the furniture that cluttered the room with a homely disorder, two great brindle hunting dogs stirring as they entered, returning to their places at a murmured word from Rycol.

The chatelain was changed, as Wynett had been. He seemed more gaunt to Kedryn's eyes, his face deeper lined, his movements slower, his voice husky as he said, 'My friends, welcome to this sad place.'

Beside him his wife smiled, her own plump features thinned, her hair all grey now. Kedryn saw that she wore a dirk at her waist.

'Rycol, Marga,' Bedyr said, 'I bring good news: the Kingdoms are raised.'

'Good news indeed,' Rycol murmured with a tired smile. 'But

please, come in. Sit. You are hungry?' He motioned to the chairs set about a circular table on which stood glasses and a flask of wine.

'I will see to the kitchens,' said the Lady Marga.

'Galen took us south,' Bedyr explained as the chatelain filled glasses. 'And with the aid of the Sister Grania, north again ahead of the main force.'

'Grania?' Rycol favoured Galen with a brief nod, more interested in news of the Sister. 'Where is she?'

'In the hospital.' Bedyr shed his cloak, settling at the table to cup his hands about the glass Rycol passed him. 'She used her talent to speed us from Andurel with the news that Darr follows with all the army. The task exhausted her and she remains under Wynett's care until she is full rested.'

'Can she lift this darkness?' Rycol asked. 'Whilst this prevails there's little any army can do.'

'She believes so,' said Bedyr, 'and meanwhile the Kingdoms arm to fight.'

Kedryn listened as his father explained what had transpired in Andurel, how Hattim Sethiyan had prevaricated and been forced to raise Ust-Galich when he lost the duel, how Jarl even now brought the Keshi horsemen north to the Lozins, and Tepshen Lahl marched from Caitin Hold.

'It will all take time,' said Rycol when Bedyr was done, 'and though I am ashamed to admit it, I cannot say how much longer we can withstand this sending. Listen.'

He gestured to the shuttered windows through which came the full thudding of catapult missiles, the sharper crash of breaking masonry.

'They keep this up unceasingly. Night and day it goes on, and all the while this accursed darkness grips us. Wynett is able to fortify us somewhat with her potions, but they run short.'

'So an innkeeper called Talkien Drass informed us,' Bedyr said. 'The darkness ends beyond the town, but there spirits are low.'

Rycol nodded. 'Drass has spoken for flight, but gave up that idea when I told him I'd brand him traitor. The other burghers are of somewhat stronger stuff – or more frightened of me than I knew.'

He laughed shortly, bitterness in the sound, and Bedyr studied his face with anxious eyes, seeing there the effects of the endless night.

'Have you word of Brannoc?' he asked.

'Nothing,' said Rycol. 'Your Commander of Auxiliaries is gone.'

'He will return when the time is right,' said Bedyr. 'I feel confident of that.'

'Perhaps,' grunted Rycol, doubt in his voice.

'Old friend, you are weary,' Bedyr said. 'This darkness leeches your spirit.'

'Mine and all those here,' Rycol agreed. 'It is no easy thing to maintain the spirit in the teeth of this fell glamour.

'Sister Grania will change that,' Kedryn offered enthusiastically. 'When she is recovered, she will lift the darkness and we shall see our enemy. Then we shall defeat him.'

'Well said,' Rycol allowed, 'but I fear that when we do, we may yet have scant cause for hope. The barbarians use catapults, they have brought a ram to the north gate – so what else might they have hidden behind that damnable pall? And how many do we face?' He turned to Galen, 'You command a river craft? Might you sail this blackness?'

'I might,' Galen answered. 'But to where? I had thought to remain here and lend what strength I can to your defence.'

'I thank you for that offer,' smiled Rycol, 'but you may be of more use as a messenger. I would ask you to cross the river to the Keshi side.'

'To Fengrif?' Bedyr frowned. 'Can you not contact him?'

'Not since this darkness fell.' Rycol shook his head. 'The signal towers cannot pierce the gloom, nor our boatmen make the crossing. Seven times have we tried, and each a failure. Navigation is impossible, it seems. Five boats turned back, and three drifted far south. Perhaps a larger vessel, though, might succeed.'

'I can attempt it,' promised Galen. 'The *Vashti* lays anchored below the fort now, on the west bank. Were I to cross the river and hug the east bank, mayhap I could find the Keshi fort, darkness or no.'

'You do not know whether Fengrif comes under attack,' said Bedyr, perceiving the larger problem.

'No.' Rycol shook his head. 'I do not know whether we share the forest folk between us, or if every warrior in the Beltrevan stands at my gates.'

'When Grania dispels the darkness you will know,' said Kedryn.

'I have great faith in the Sister's powers,' murmured Rycol, 'but this gramarye may be too much even for her, and if we learn too late that we stand alone against the tribes . . . well, it may be too late. I would glean all the information I can, as quickly as I can. You say the Sister spelled you north? Will the landbound armies arrive as swiftly? I may need reinforcements from the Keshi bank, but for all I know, Low Fort may have fallen.'

Kedryn stared at the chatelain, seeing the grim appraisal was all too real a possibility. 'If that were so,' he murmured softly, the prospect terrifying, 'then the barbarians might even now march through Kesh.'

'Aye,' Rycol nodded. 'Through Kesh to Andurel. Or cross the Idre lower down to march against our rear. In this darkness we know nothing!'

'Let me use what daylight I may find,' said Galen, 'and I will attempt the thing on the morrow.'

'Thank you,' said Rycol.

'Meanwhile,' said Bedyr, 'we must await Grania's wakening, and until then there is nothing we may do, so let us eat.'

'And eat well,' said Rycol with grim humour, 'for if she lifts the glamour there will be little time for such pleasures with the Horde seeking to join the feast!'

Chapter Thirteen

Kedryn woke to the same encroaching darkness that had accompanied his retirement, looking to the glass-encased candle set beside his bed to find the hour a little after what should have been dawn. For a moment he lay still, hearing the stones of the barbarians' catapults thudding down as they had fallen when at last he slept, then he climbed, shivering in the unnatural chill, from the warmth of the sleeping couch to light a torch, anxious for the comfort of its radiance. He could better understand now the waning morale of High Fort's defenders, for to wake each morning to this endless night was a thing that sapped courage, leeched resolve. It was as though the bastion stood isolated from the world, wrapped in darkness until the pounding of the ballistae should break down even those massive walls and the forest folk come through. He had spent only three nights in High Fort, but he felt the leaden weight of the Messenger's sending despite the preparation Wynett had administered, though the strange tingling sensation in his wounded shoulder had ceased under her care. Grania still slept, exhausted by her labours, and Galen Sadreth had reported angrily that his attempts to cross the Idre to Low Fort proved fruitless – each time he tried, he found himself unable to locate the eastern bank, and had now given up the venture in disgust, fearful that the *Vashti* might be lost.

He performed his ablutions and tugged on an undershirt and breeches of soft linen, topping those with leather and mail, deciding that he was not yet ready to don the heavy armour of full battle kit that many now favoured. He belted his sword and dagger to his waist. Then, carrying a torch and moving warily along the shadowy corridors, he found his way to the dining hall, where Bedyr already sat with Rycol and several tellemen, sipping a tisane laced with Wynett's remedy as they discussed what measures might be taken to raise the siege.

No useful suggestions were offered for it seemed there were no measures Rycol had not attempted. A sally from the north postern had been beaten back from the ram with the loss of thirty men, and the assault on the gate continued despite the rocks tossed down. The use of fire was still ruled out, save as a final, desperate measure, and the defenders could not tell whether the missiles they sent from their own ballistae did any damage. They knew only the darkness.

The situation lay at stalemate, waiting Grania's revival.

Kedryn took a place across from his father, murmuring his thanks to the hollow-eyed servant who filled a clay mug with tisane and set a steaming bowl of porridge before him. He spooned up the cereal without enthusiasm, then turned as a buzz of excited conversation from farther down the hall aroused his interest.

Through the shadows that braziers and flambeaux could never entirely dispel he saw Grania approaching, Wynett protective beside her. The elder Sister's face was thinner than he remembered, but colour had returned to her cheeks and the smile she sent in his direction was fierce with determination. He rose, aware that the others did the same, and made a place for both women.

'You are recovered?' he asked, smiling his pleasure.

'She is better,' Wynett answered him, a note of disapproval in her voice, 'but she is not fully recovered.'

Grania snorted dismissively, favouring all at the table with her smile. 'Wynett was ever careful of her charges. She would have me abed yet, even though there is clearly work to be done.'

'Work you cannot do effectively while you are still weak,' said Wynett.

'Work that cannot wait, child,' returned Grania. 'Do you not sense the malaise? Can you not feel the power of this sending growing stronger? It feeds on the very despair it creates. And your remedies are near finished, with no hope of replenishment. Besides, I shall have your help in what I intend to do.'

Wynett sighed helplessly, unable to counter that argument for it was so obviously true.

'So,' Grania continued, 'I have discharged myself from the excellent care of my Sister and shall attempt to counter the Messenger's glamour. Now let me eat, and bring me something a little stronger than tisane to drink.'

Servants hurried to comply and Kedryn watched as she consumed two bowls of porridge and a jug of mulled wine, then asked for bread and fruit which she ate with equal gusto.

'I feel better,' she announced when she was done, wiping daintily at her lips with a handkerchief produced from the folds of her gown. 'Now let us discuss the raising of this gramarye.'

She outlined those things she would need and Rycol sent men hurrying to fetch them to the north wall, where Grania intended to mount her counter offensive. She would have gone there immediately, but Wynett insisted she first take medicine and then fussed about the warmth of her cloak, which the older woman permitted with increasingly ill-concealed impatience.

Finally all was ready and Rycol, the most familiar with the gloom-enshrouded corridors and catwalks of the fort, led the way to the battlements.

A brazier stood unlit midway along the rampart, surrounded by soldiers whose fear of the missiles still flying out of the darkness was overcome by optimistic curiosity. Grania beamed at them and said, 'Stand to your posts, my friends – you'll have work to do ere long,' and they faded reluctantly back into the darkness.

Wynett produced a small satchel from beneath her cloak and passed Grania several bundles of herbs that the Sister sprinkled over the cold coals, murmuring indistinctly as she did so. When she was satisfied she requested a flint and struck sparks to the brazier's tinder. At the base of the metal basket dull fire glowed, rising slowly through the kindling until tiny tongues of flame licked upwards to consume the stuff she had placed on the top.

'Give me your hand, child,' she asked Wynett, 'and you, Kedryn.'

He was surprised by this request, tugging off his glove to take the tiny, warm hand she held towards him as Wynett took the other, the three of them standing facing the unknown across the wall. Instantly he experienced a sensation of drowsiness, such as precedes the descent into slumber, but instead of sleep he felt a tremendous calm that was both alert and confident. It was similar to the feeling that had gripped him when he spoke out against Hattim, but more, stronger, as though the joining of hands merged his being with those of the two Sisters so that they became simultaneously independent beings and a single entity empowered by their purpose, his will enlarged and guided. He saw the coals in the brazier glow brighter, white smoke rising, giving off a sweet pungency that made him think of summer meadows, of streams, the scent of Wynett's hair. He saw it rise and he thought of larks swooping across a clear blue sky, fish darting in crystal brooks. He saw, without at first realizing that he saw it, the darkness draw back from the brazier. He heard Grania's voice utter words he did not understand, growing louder as the gloom receded. He felt a surge of power flood through him, an utter certainty such as he had known when he entered the arena to face Hattim, but again much stronger, brooking no opposition. He was unaware of his father or Rycol standing close by until he heard Bedyr's gasp.

'By the Lady, it goes!'

And then he realized he could see the wall with perfect clarity, that the brazier sent its white smoke up into daylight that grew ever stronger, revealing a lengthening section of the wall, that above a column rose through the gloom, mingling at its uppermost extremity with an azure mid-morning sky.

He felt triumph then, and that feeling swelled and grew, and he was not sure whether it was because the darkness waned, or if the darkness fell back before the feeling. His spirits soared as he watched the occultation begin to swirl like wind-riven fog, tendrils of black coiling about the albescence that rose from the brazier only to be consumed by that purity, the darkness dissipating at an ever increasing rate. He heard the excited shouting of the defenders and became aware of sun on his face, warm and clean after the foulness of the Messenger's night. He looked up and saw the sky was clear, and when he brought his gaze down he saw the ramparts stretching out to either side, the flame of the torches lost beneath the brightness of the day. Only before the wall did the obfuscation still hold sway, and even as he watched that he saw it roll back as might mud washed by cleansing waves.

He heard Grania say, 'Praise the Lady, it is done,' and felt her fingers lose their hold on his, heard Wynett's urgent cry as the contact ended.

Momentary dizziness clouded his vision and he turned to see Wynett clutch at Grania's slumping form, lowering the elder Sister gently to the stone of the ramparts. Instantly he was on his knees, his arm a cushion for the greyed head, his heart pounding a drum beat against his ribs as he saw the dulling of those bird-bright eyes.

Wynett still clutched a hand, but now her fingers sought not the contact Grania had demanded but a pulse, and when she looked to Kedryn her face was gaunt with sadness.

'Quickly, bring her to the hospital! There may yet be time.'

He swept the tiny woman up, uncaring of Bedyr or Rycol as he hurried after Wynett, following her down stairways now bright and busy with the soldiers who flooded out to greet the welcome day, their smiles faltering as Wynett shouted for them to clear a way.

They reached the hospital and he deposited Grania gently on her bed, kneeling beside her as Wynett turned to her potions, seeking that strength of purpose he had so recently known to infuse life into the failing form, willing her to live.

And then he heard her voice, once more uncertain whether it resounded in his ears or in his mind, knowing only that she spoke to him.

'I am dying, Kedryn, but we have given the Messenger a taste of defeat. The rest is up to you. To you and Wynett. Remember there are two sisters, Kedryn.'

'No!' he said aloud. 'Do not die!'

'It does not matter,' said the voice that was not a voice. 'Has your kyo not taught you what a small thing death is? You have power in you that I have not seen before. Learn to use it, Kedryn. And remember always that the Lady is with you.'

He was about to speak again, but Wynett brushed him aside, setting a mug to Grania's lips as she raised the fallen head, spilling drops of some dark liquid into the Sister's mouth.

Grania swallowed and began to choke. Instantly Wynett lowered her head and pressed her lips to the older woman's, breathing into her mouth. Kedryn watched helplessly as she rose and pounded her cupped hands against Grania's chest, then again bent over the paling face. Grania lay still and after long moments Wynett sat upright, reaching out to smooth a strand of hair that had escaped the Paramount Sister's bun. She touched fingers to the eyes and lips, murmuring a prayer to the Lady, then turned to tell Kedryn what he already knew.

'She is dead.'

There were tears in her eyes and Kedryn reached unthinking towards her, seeking comfort for the loss he felt as much as he sought to give it. Wynett folded into his arms, her face pressed against his chest, ignoring the hard metal links of the mail shirt as she sobbed her grief and he realized that moisture ran down his own cheeks. He held her, stroking her hair, noticing incongruously that it was fresh-washed, its scent sweet in his nostrils. Behind her, on the bed, Grania lay still, as though asleep, a slight smile upon her lips.

'She spoke to me before she died,' he murmured. 'She told me it does not matter.'

'The Lady teaches us it does not,' Wynett answered, her voice muffled, 'but she does not forbid us mourning the loss of a loved one. She knew she would die. I warned her she was too weak to attempt the casting, but she argued High Fort would fall should she refrain.'

'She was right.' Kedryn knew this was so, though he did not understand how the certainty came to him. 'The Fort could not have withstood the glamour much longer, and if High Fort falls the Kingdoms go down with it.'

He felt Wynett's sobbing ease against his chest, then felt her stiffen, her face turning up to stare at him, surprise mingling with the grief in her eyes.

'You said she spoke to you? She was too weak to speak.'

'I do not think it was with her voice,' he answered, looking down at her. 'I seemed to hear it inside my head, before she died. She said there was power in me.'

Wynett's eyes grew large and he could not help thinking how lovely they were, which made him aware that his arms were still about her, and that despite the circumstances he liked that.

'Only the adepts can hear with the mind.' Her voice was awed. 'And no man has ever possessed the talent.'

Kedryn did not know how to respond. 'She said we had given the Messenger a taste of defeat,' he repeated, 'and that the rest was up to us. To you and me.'

'I do not understand,' Wynett murmured, blinking tears.

'Nor I,' said Kedryn, 'but that is what she said.

'A man with the gift.' Her voice was soft with musing and she seemed unaware that he still held her, or not to care. 'What are you, Kedryn Caitin?'

'I do not know,' he answered honestly.

'Nor I, though now I am certain you are more than Prince of Tamur.'

She looked long into his eyes, her own bemused, then seemed to become suddenly aware of his arms around her and rose to her feet so that he must release his gentle grip. She faced him, smiling uncertainly, and he reached to touch a tear from her cheek, her skin soft beneath his fingers.

At that she pushed him gently back and the distance imposed by her status as a Sister came between them again. 'The sending is lifted now,' she said, 'perhaps you had best attend the wall.'

Kedryn nodded, wanting to touch her again, to say something, but he could not find the words. Instead he smiled and turned from the chamber, leaving Wynett to prepare Grania for burial, not looking back as he strode swiftly through the ward, seeing hope in the eyes of the wounded now where before there had been only despair.

Outside, that hope was as palpable a thing as had been the darkness.

Where mean had previously fumbled through the gloom, their voices forlorn, they now ran, shouting in triumph for the sheer joy of knowing daylight again. Tellemen bellowed orders and cordors responded; the yards echoed with the clatter of weapons; a sense of purpose once more filled High Fort and Kedryn felt joy mingle with the sadness of Grania's death. That sacrifice had not been in vain, for once again High Fort was become a viable defence against the barbarian invasion and its men, released from the awful burden of the sending, were eager to prove their merit as warriors.

When Kedryn reached the north wall he saw they would have their chance. Bedyr awaited him with Rycol grim-faced at his side.

'She is dead,' he told them. 'The effort was too much for her.'

Then he looked to the north and gasped.

Three catapults faced the wall, between them three great towers, ramshackle constructions of rough-hewn timber hung with hides and shields, mounted on wheeled platforms, but for all their makeshift air, threatening enough should they come close to the fort, for each was high enough to meet the ramparts, and he could see that the topmost levels were hinged, so that bridges might come down to allow men access across the gap. Ahead of those constructions stood two low hut-like things, a massive log protruding from each, three wheels on either side. But more impressive – more threatening – than any of these was the sheer mass of forest folk. They filled the Beltrevan road in a human tide, a countless sea of swarthy, bearded faces, each one turned towards the wall, eyes hungry as wolves', swords and spears and axes raised in threat. The Horde extended across the trail to the banks of the Idre and to the scarp of the Lozins; it stretched back as far as he could see, covering the road, going on and on as though the forest itself reached out towards High Fort, as though the Beltrevan spewed out its people in a living stream. He had seen their campfires sprawling along the valley in the forest, but now, in the clear light of the hard-won day, that vast press of bodies was somehow more tangible, more deadly in its threat.

He could hear them, too, for they shrieked their rage, clashing blades on shields, the roaring of their anger drowning the sound of the river as would a thunderclap overpower the crying of a child, the dinning echoing from the mountainside with mind-numbing force.

They stood in unthinkable numbers and Kedryn felt cold dread knot ugly in his belly: how long could even High Fort stand against such a mass?

Then he saw movement in the ranks and the shouting died away to an ominous silence, men parting as a knot of heavily-armoured warriors pushed to the fore, themselves moving aside to reveal a group of five who stood surveying the fortress.

There was one there he knew instantly, for as his eyes fell upon the tall, fur-swathed figure, a stab of fierce pain shot through his shoulder and he knew that he looked upon the Messenger again.

He was taller than his companions, dressed all in furs from neck to feet, as though he hid his body beneath the guise of some animal, and where their skin was dark his was the colour of new-fallen snow, the mane of hair that draped his skull pale as milk. Across the distance that separated them Kedryn saw the curiously triangular face turn in his direction, deep-sunk eyes burning red. He stilled the instinctive terror that gaze aroused, clutching the hilt of his sword as he glared back, fury rising within him as he studied the creature who would bring down the Kingdoms, whose fell magicks had caused Grania's death, and in that moment he knew that he could not inhabit the same world as the creature, that he must destroy the Messenger or be himself destroyed.

To the mage's left he saw a warrior who stood out there because he was so simply accoutred. His head was bare, save for a bronze torque that went some way to holding his wild black mane in check, and he wore a leathern breastplate above homespun trews, a shortsword sheathed at his waist and a battleaxe in his right hand, a round buckler strapped to his left arm. The others were more regally bedecked. The man standing on the Messenger's right resplendent in burnished armour, breastplate, vambraces and greaves glittering in the sun. He carried a magnificent shield and at his waist hung a longsword sheathed in a bright-decorated scabbard. To his right, the remaining three wore motley armour, metal and leather mingled, one with bared legs, another with a basket helm concealing his features, a third clutching a great bearded axe.

Unthinking, prompted by the rage seething within him, Kedryn turned, seeking an archer. He snatched the man's bow, notching an arrow to the string he drew back until it touched his lips, sighting down the shaft at the fur-clad figure of the Messenger. As he loosed the shaft he heard Bedyr say, 'The range is too great,' not caring, willing the arrow to pierce the black heart, if heart was what the Messenger had.

It did not span the distance. Bedyr was correct and the arrow rattled off stone paces from the figure.

Kedryn ground his teeth in impotent fury as he saw the mage

glance carelessly at the wasted missile, then towards him, fleshless lips peeling back in soundless laughter.

He would have fired again had Bedyr not set a hand upon his shoulder saying, 'Not yet – he is too far away. Leave it to the catapults.'

He returned the bow and set his hands on the warming stone of the ramparts, his body trembling so that his father tightened his grip, frowning, seeking to calm him.

'Kedryn, you'll have battle enough when they reach the walls.'

Slowly, he felt the shuddering ease and cease, realizing that Bedyr thought battle madness gripped him. He shook his head, his voice harsh as he grunted, 'He will not come to the walls. That is not his way. His way is the dark path, yet I *must* kill him.'

'You or someone else, it does not matter,' said Bedyr. 'That we destroy him is the important thing.'

Kedryn turned then to face his father, his tone grave as he said, 'I do not think there is another who *can* kill him. I think it must be me.'

Bedyr stared at his son, aware of a change he could not define. 'What has happened to you?' he asked gently. 'You are . . . different.'

'Aye,' Kedryn nodded, 'I am different. I do not know what has changed, but I know that I am different. I heard Grania speak as she died.'

'Is that so unusual?' asked Bedyr. 'What did she say?'

'Not with her voice,' Kedryn responded, seeing that his father did not understand, 'I heard her in my mind. Wynett said that no man has had that talent. And she told me there is power in me.'

'Alaria's text,' Bedyr murmured. 'Oh, that we understood its meaning.'

Any further conversation was abruptly precluded by the rattle of the ballistae and the shouting that sped their missiles on their way. Rycol had ordered a volley and the catapult teams, delighted to find visible targets at last, responded with noisy enthusiasm. The great arms were wound down and stones loaded into the baskets, then on Rycol's shout, the latches knocked free to send the rocks hurtling through the clear air at the massed ranks of forest folk. Kedryn watched, aware of a fierce joy, as the stones crashed down amongst the foremost ranks of the tribesmen, seeing bodies fall, crushed, sorry only that the Messenger and the chieftains had withdrawn beyond range.'

'When Grania took my hand,' he said as the catapults prepared to fire again, 'I felt a strength – a power – that filled me. I cannot describe it, but it was unlike anything I have known. I felt peace, and ... purpose, I think. We joined, Wynett and Grania and I, of that I am sure. She knew it was in me.'

'Grania knew much,' nodded Bedyr. 'She . . .'

Again the rattle of the ballistae hid his words, and they turned to see the missiles land, the Horde falling back, save for the groups about the barbarian catapults, who now wound down their own throwing arms and began to return the fire.

It was impossible after that to speak, for the air became filled with flying stone, volley answering volley, boulders crashing against the walls to shatter blocks of stone loose from the ramparts, High Fort's catapults seeking to pinpoint the barbarian's siege engines, which were shifted constantly by crews careless of their safety, willingly reinforced from the innumerable ranks whenever men went down under the barrage.

The Messenger, too, had a part in that duel, for he could be seen moving amongst the ballistae, his hands moving in intricate patterns that sent blue fire sparkling from his fingertips to shroud the engines of the forest folk so that the defenders' stones fell short, or were deflected just far enough so they caused no damage.

'He uses magic,' Bedyr shouted above the din, 'but I do not think he is powerful enough to bring it directly against us. Perhaps he needs to stand closer.'

'Would that he did,' Kedryn answered fiercely. 'Within arrow range!'

'He is too canny,' Bedyr said. 'I do not believe he will chance his own life whilst there are others he may spend in Ashar's cause.'

It appeared he was right, for despite the glamours protecting the barbarian engines, men continued to fall, and by the north gate Rycol sent Istar's hundred out against the ram.

Kedryn would have joined them had the order not been given unbeknownst to him, but as it was he watched the combat from the vantage point of the wall.

The defenders continued to rain stone on the shelter, but that, like the catapults, seemed protected by both solid wood and less tangible magic, for no matter how heavy the blocks that crashed down, none succeeded in piercing the roof above the ram. The gate, however, was beginning to show the effects of the steady battering. Cracks showed on the inner face and Istar reported a loosening of the bolts retaining the lowermost hinges. With Rycol's blessing, the tellemen sallied from the postern to fall on the barbarians with eager swords. This time two score of Tamurin fell, but all the forest folk manning the ram were slaughtered, the archers on the wall repelling the tribesmen who attempted to relieve their fellows, giving Istar's force time to shove the ram back from the gates and set it to the torch. While the structure burned Istar and his warriors regained the fort safely, and for a while the gate was safe.

A great shout of triumph went up from the defenders as the ram was consumed, dark smoke coiling against the azure of the sky, while from the barbarian ranks there came a howl of fury. As Kedryn watched, a second ram trundled from amongst the ballistae and siege towers and Rycol shouted for the closest mangonel to lay fire on the structure. Three missiles landed close, then a fourth crashed against the roof, though without halting the ram's forward momentum. The barbarian catapults concentrated their fire on that ballista attacking the ram and it seemed to Kedryn that the Messenger lent some magic to the stones, for Rycol's engine was destroyed, its timbers shattering in a great explosion of shrapnel that left the crew dead and twenty men wounded while still the ram came on.

Archers sent shafts flying as the thing came within range, but their arrows were useless against the fortified roof and the ram reached the north gate, where it promptly took up the work begun by the first.

Again, Istar's hundred went out from the postern, but this time with worse fortune.

As the telleman led his sally the forest folk brought mobile barricades forward, their archers sending a rain of arrows towards both the north wall and the exposed defenders. Many of Istar's men went down and then tribesmen emerged from the cover of the ram, charging with berserk fury to drive the deplenished hundred back from the structure. Istar and his men fought bravely, but they were outnumbered and the barbarians forced them back from the ram in bloody retreat. Some twenty warriors succeeded in penetrating the fort, and even though they were instantly cut down, it was a small victory for the attackers, for sixty of Istar's men died and thirty more were wounded.

Then a second mangonel was wrecked as a section of the wall broke under the pounding of the enemy ballistae, toppling the catapult from the ramparts, and Rycol came hurrying along the wall to where Bedyr stood with Kedryn.

'Their accuracy is uncanny,' he frowned, 'and they appear protected. We cannot seem to hit them, whilst if they keep this up, our own engines will be destroyed one by one.' He ducked as he spoke, for the barbarians appeared intent on confirming his words, sending missiles crashing about another of the fort's ballista. 'We must destroy them.'

'How can we?' Bedyr retorted. 'As you say, they appear impregnable.'

'Balefire,' suggested the chatelain. 'If stones cannot harm them, mayhap fire will.'

Bedyr was dubious, but Rycol pushed his point, arguing that if his own mangonels were destroyed there would be nothing to prevent the approach of the siege towers, and should those massive structures reach the wall then nothing would prevent the forest folk from penetrating the fortress.

'It is dangerous,' Bedyr responded, 'Remember what Brannoc said.'

'What choice do we have?' grunted Rycol. 'If this continues, they will bring the walls down.'

Screaming from farther along the ramparts caught their attention, and when they looked to its source they saw a third catapult smashed, half its crew mangled by the falling stones.

'So be it,' Bedyr agreed, though Kedryn could hear the reluctance in his voice, 'use the balefire.'

Rycol nodded and sent a cordor running with word to the catapult crews. Kedryn felt a great sense of unease, feeling instinctively that this was an unwise move, but he could not put words to his trepidation and was loath to argue with the more experienced warriors.

The afternoon was lengthening towards dusk as the sacks were loaded, and when they were fired the fuses left long trails of sparks glittering against the darkening sky. Kedryn watched nervously, wishing that Grania were still alive, for he felt that her advice would have been of much use. He saw the sacks land, flame splashing across the Beltrevan road, gobbets of raw fire striking the barbarian engines. Men screamed, burning, running from the catapults with blazing hair and scorching flesh, but his heart sank as he saw that none of the ballistae were harmed. They appeared impervious to the flames and as he watched he saw the Messenger again, moving through the fires unharmed. The creature stood there, impossibly wrapped in licking tongues of incandescence, smiling.

'Again!' he heard Rycol bellow. 'Fire again!'

He shouted, 'No!' but his words were lost unheard as the eager crews slung fresh sacks into the baskets.

He began to run towards the nearest mangonel, screaming for the men sweating over the windlass to cease their labours, but even as he did so he saw the Messenger standing wreathed in fire, arms upraised towards the fort. Then he felt himself lifted up and hurled backwards, crashing hard against the angle of the wall as the balefire in the catapult exploded. Heat washed over him and his nostrils filled with the stink of scorching hair, of roasted flesh. He heard men screaming and all along the wall saw High Fort's catapults consumed in columns of flame, the sacks of balefire stacked nearby igniting, the flammable material splashing over soldiers who writhed and fell, those not instantly killed hideously burned. He saw a man hurl himself from the ramparts to the yard below, his body blazing, continuing to burn long after the corpse had struck the flags. More threw themselves outwards, lost in madness as flesh blackened and eyes melted. It seemed the whole wall was a curtain of flame, and he crouched, huddling against the heated stone as he waited for death.

It did not come and he sprang to his feet as he felt the heat lessen, peering about him, seeing a man whose tunic blazed rolling in a fruitless attempt to douse the flames. He moved towards the figure, but Bedyr's hands snatched him back, holding him as he struggled.

'You cannot help him,' his father groaned, his voice hoarse with anguish. 'The balefire cannot be extinguished.'

He watched as the soldier's movements slowed and ceased, the screaming that had filled his ears becoming a low moaning that finally ended, even though the flames continued to lick over the charred shape of the corpse.

Along the wall he saw the skeletal outlines of High Fort's ballistae, most reduced to smouldering piles of blackened timber, but a few still standing, no more than frameworks now, of no more use than charred kindling. The air was filled with the ghastly, sweetish smell of burned flesh, and where before the wall was thronged with men there now stood huddled groups of survivors, staring about them with wild, frightened eyes as they surveyed the wreckage of their defence.

'May the Lady be with us now,' he heard Bedyr murmur, releasing his grip. 'It will go harder now.'

Kedryn nodded without speaking. There was nothing he could say and his mind was filled with guilt that he had not spoken out earlier, argued against the use of the balefire when he felt that compulsion, that certainty that it was the wrong thing to do. He would never allow that to happen again, he promised himself. No matter whom he might argue with he would say what was in his heart, for he felt sure that something guided him, something that had awakened when Grania took his hand and joined his spirit with hers. He did not know what power was in him, but he felt sure now that the elder Sister's dying words were true – there was power.

He looked out across the fire-darkened rim of the wall to where the siege towers stood, his face grim.

'They will attack soon. How long can we hold them?'

'How many have we lost?' Bedyr turned, staring with stricken eyes along the wall. 'Three hundred? Four? Without catapults, perhaps five days. No longer, I think. Darr and the rest *must* come soon, else we are lost.'

There was anguish in his voice and Kedryn realized that he blamed himself for allowing the balefire to be used. Rycol, too, would doubtless share that guilt – if the chatelain still lived.

He did, for he came towards them, a pain in his eyes that stemmed not from the burns decorating his hands and face with ugly red blemishes, but from the loss of his men.

'What have I done?' he groaned. 'May the Lady forgive me, Bedyr, for I have killed my men.'

'No,' Kedryn said, impelled to speak, seeking to assuage the guilt that rang in the chatelain's voice. 'You did what you thought best. If there is guilt here, it belongs to me – I knew the balefire was wrong, but I kept silent.'

'You?' Rycol turned hollowed eyes from which the lashes and brows were missing on Kedryn. 'How could you know?'

'I felt it,' Kedryn said. 'I cannot explain it, but I *knew* it was wrong.'

Rycol made a dismissive gesture, wincing as seared flesh drew taut, but Bedyr said softly, 'Heed him, Rycol, for he is changed. When Grania used him there was something entered him. He speaks the truth – you advised as you thought best, and I agreed for I could see no other way. If there is guilt, then we share it.'

The chatelain stared long at Kedryn then, wonder in his eyes. Finally he said, 'Even so, we have lost better than three hundred men, and all our catapults. Whoever is to blame, those facts remain. As do the barbarians' engines. If they bring those up during the night . . .'

'We repel them,' said Kedryn, not caring that he spoke out of turn, that it was rightfully Bedyr's place to answer.

'Tonight, mayhap,' Rycol allowed, 'and again on the morrow. But for how long after that? Look!' He pointed into the growing twilight, northwards to where the fires were already dead about the catapults and siege towers, the mass of the Horde a deepening of the darkness that pooled along the canyon. 'With walls intact – and mangonels to keep that army at a distance – perhaps we might hold out. But now? Four days, five if we are very lucky.'

'Remember that Tamur marches,' Bedyr said, 'and Kesh. Ust-Galich follows Darr north.'

'How fast?' Rycol murmured, his voice weary.

'Sisters aid Darr's force,' Bedyr assured the chatelain. 'He might arrive on the morrow.'

'Or might not,' Rycol answered. 'And how strong is the King's army? Three thousand? Scarce enough to hold the Horde.'

'Enough to reinforce us,' Bedyr said firmly. 'Long enough that my Tamurin and Jarl's Keshi may reach us.'

'If any of us still live,' grunted Rycol. 'Do you hear that damnable ram pounding on the gates? They will not last five days! Tears of the Lady, Bedyr! They should not have had the chance to come that close. The darkness was our undoing.'

'And may,' Kedryn said speculatively, 'prove theirs.'

'How so?' Bedyr asked him. 'We can ill afford to chance another sally, even under the cover of night. Nor can we risk the use of fire against it.'

'The signal tower is in use again, is it not?' asked Kedryn, and when Rycol nodded, 'And does Low Fort come under attack?'

'No.' The chatelain shook his head. 'Fengrif reports no barbarians on the east bank. But that does not help us – these forts were designed to stand independent of one another and there are no boats to bring reinforcements across.'

'There is the *Vashti*,' said Kedryn. 'If Galen were to ferry Keshi over in the night, we might attack the ram from two sides.'

'The Lady bless you,' gasped Rycol, 'though I suspect she has already. That might work.'

'Aye,' Bedyr nodded, looking to his son with a respect in his eyes that gratified Kedryn, 'it might.'

They found Galen with the stretcher crews, grim-faced as he lifted bodies that crumbled in his hands, dusting him with ghastly flakes of burned flesh. They took him aside to explain the strategy.

'The *Vashti* will carry fifty men,' he responded instantly. 'Is that sufficient?'

'It must be,' Bedyr said, 'and we shall have surprise on our side. Fifty of Fengrif's Keshi attacking from the river wall and a hundred from the postern should be sufficient.'

'With a second hundred standing by to cover the rear it should be necessary,' added Rycol.

'Then send word,' beamed Galen, 'and I'll alert my men.'

The signal tower flashed the request to Low Fort, eliciting immediate agreement from Fengrif, and the plan was laid. Under cover of the night Galen would take the *Vashti* across the river, returning two hours before dawn, the two forces converging on the ram to slaughter the barbarians and haul the structure into the fort – it seemed unwise to attempt burning it after the debacle that had cost the defenders so dear.

Kedryn found it hard to contain his impatience as he waited for the sally. He had no appetite, for the stink of burning flesh still assaulted his nostrils, though he forced himself to eat and afterwards occupied himself with checking his equipment and honing his sword. Bedyr suggested he sleep, but he could not, his refusal to make the attempt bringing a tight smile to his father's lips.

'The waiting is always the hardest,' Bedyr advised. 'The hours drag before any battle, but you will become used to it.'

'Shall I?' Kedryn murmured, thinking of that fur-swathed figure he had seen amongst the flames.

'Eventually,' Bedyr replied, his eyes grave as he studied his son, 'this is merely the beginning. We may remove the threat of the ram, but there are still the catapults. And the Horde.'

'And the Messenger,' Kedryn murmured. 'What of him? If the King arrives in time and we drive the Horde back, what of the Messenger?'

'He must die!' Bedyr's voice was fierce. 'If he survives the siege we must go into the Beltrevan and destroy him. Ashar's minion cannot be allowed to live. For the sake of the Kingdoms he must die.'

'Aye,' Kedryn replied with utter conviction, 'but it will not be easy.'

'No,' agreed Bedyr, 'but we shall do it.'

'*I* shall do it.' Kedryn's voice was soft, almost musing, 'It must be me.'

'You said this earlier,' Bedyr frowned, disturbed by the strangeness he perceived. 'How are you so certain?'

'I do not know.' Kedryn shook his head, unable to explain the certainty he felt. 'I feel it, but I cannot say why or how. I think I have known it since first I saw him – and I suspect that he knows it, too. I felt it when I saw him amongst the catapults today.'

'I did not see him.' Bedyr's voice was wondering, his eyes curious. 'I saw the catapults struck by the balefire, but I did not see him.'

'He was there,' Kedryn shrugged. 'He walked unharmed amongst the flames and raised his hands towards us, and then the burning began.'

'He is a powerful mage.' Bedyr set a hand upon his son's shoulder. 'Tread carefully in your dealings with him, Kedryn.'

'I shall,' promised the young man.

'Perhaps it were better you did not accompany me this night.' Bedyr spoke cautiously, studying Kedryn's face. 'Mayhap you should remain behind the walls. If the Messenger knows of you, you may stand in danger.'

'No!' Kedryn answered fiercely. 'I will not hide from him. And I will be with you tonight.'

'So be it,' agreed Bedyr, seeing determination in the features so like his own, 'but guard your back well.'

Kedryn grinned then, setting down the whetstone and sliding his blade into the scabbard. 'I shall, father, fear not.'

Bedyr smiled at his resolution and glanced at the waning candle. 'The hour approaches – let us find the rest.'

Kedryn nodded, glad that the waiting approached its end. He felt a mixture of emotions, some that he could understand, more that he could not define. Nervousness was amongst them, for this would be his first real combat, sword to sword with men who genuinely sought to kill him, and he was concerned that he should acquit himself well. He was aware of the danger, and that brought a small taint of fear that he pushed away. He was unsure how he would feel when he brought his blade against flesh: he had thought it would be a proud, wild feeling, but that had been when he saw his first combat as a coming of age. Now he felt he *was* come of age, and saw less glory in the killing, for he began to perceive the forest folk less as the faceless enemy of his youth and more as pawns of the malign creature that had raised the Horde. Were he able to strike down the Messenger he knew he would not hesitate, for he felt in his bones that the mage was the quintessence of evil, a thing with no rightful place in his world, but he felt less eager to take human lives.

Equally, he knew that he would have to take lives, and that seemed somehow to taint him with the Messenger's evil, as though that malignity rubbed off, fouling everything it touched. He wondered if this sensation represented a new maturity, and worried that it might be a form of cowardice. It was necessary, he told himself; there was no choice in the matter, for if the ram were not cleared from the gate it would gain the barbarians an entry and the Kingdoms would fall.

But he could not help remembering Sister Grania's words, that the men of the Kingdoms should not hate the forest folk, and he wondered if that was the cause of his confusion – that some part of Grania's spirit had entered him when they joined to defeat the Messenger's sending.

It was as it had been when Bedyr spoke to him of Alaria's text: more questions were raised than he could find answers for, more doubts than certainties, leaving him wondering and confused, aware of a purpose, but not of the path he must travel to fulfil it.

And then he remembered another teacher, and employed the doctrines of Tepshen Lahl to clear his mind, focusing solely on the fight ahead.

He followed Bedyr out into the yard that fronted the north postern. The torches that would normally have burned there were doused and the night was dark and chill, though not now with the absolute blackness of the Messenger's sending. He could see the men waiting there, albeit faintly, and the few stars that pricked through the overlay of cloud filling the river canyon struck tiny answering points of light from helms and blades. He heard the shuffle of booted feet as the warriors shifted position, either to offset the chill or from the eagerness for action that he now shared. He was committed to the task in hand, all doubts, all questions, banished from his mind. He knew only that he must go out through the postern and do his duty as a soldier of Tamur – if men should die as a result, then so be it.

He stood patiently as Bedyr consulted with Rycol, who commanded the second hundred, then experienced a surge of relief as his father turned and murmured, 'Stand ready.'

The word was passed down through the ranks and he heard the faint chinking of mail as swords were drawn and shields adjusted. He had foregone the use of a buckler, preferring both hands free to wield his blade as Tepshen Lahl had taught him, and he had never favoured a helm, finding the weight cumbersome, the reduction of hearing and vision a nuisance. His head was bare, hair drawn back in a tail, his torso protected by the fine links of his mail shirt, his arms by vambraces, whilst the breeches he wore were sewn with larger links strong enough to prevent leg cuts, and his boots were high and of cured leather. Like all the men there he wore a surcoat emblazoned with the fist of Tamur, stark red against the encircling silver.

'Now,' he heard Bedyr say, and the bolts of the postern were drawn back, silent in their oiled fixings, and the gate opened.

He half expected barbarian arrows to rain down, but there was only silence. It seemed that the forest folk reverted to their traditional ways with the sending lifted, and waited for dawn to resume their attack for no outcry was raised as he followed Bedyr out down the passage that bored through the massive width of the wall.

Beyond, clear of the fort's confining bulk, the night grew fractionally brighter. On two sides the bulk of the Lozins and the bulk of the north wall rose sheer and black, but up the Beltrevan road he could make out the stark frames of the enemy catapults, skeletal against the glow of a myriad barbarian fires, and from the east he could hear the steady murmur of the Idre.

He moved silently along the wall, trying to pick out the shape of the hut-like construct that protected the ram, his ears tuned for any sound of alarm. His sword was in his hand, though he had no recollection of drawing the blade, and he lowered it to his side for fear that starlight might sparkle from the steel to alert some barbarian sentinel. Then, from the river bank, he heard the clarion of a battle horn and saw Bedyr's blade lift high, his father's voice loud in the night.

'For Tamur and the Kingdoms! Attack!'

From the darkness came an answering shout: 'For Kesh! For Kesh and the Kingdoms!'

Then he was running, unaware that he, took, screamed the battle shout, or that it was echoed by the warriors who paced him, intent only on reaching the ram and joining in combat. He heard a babble of sound ahead and then saw the ram for the first time. It was much larger than it had appeared from the vantage point of the wall, standing twice his height, the eaves of the slanted roof overlapping the solid timbers of the walls, the wheels enormous, larger than a stone dray's. The perception was brief, for tribesmen poured from the thing as ants from a disturbed nest, their own voices raised in war-shouts, the night abruptly filled with the babble of men intent on killing one another.

A shape loomed from the darkness, seeming more animal than man for the furs that draped the torso, but wielding a double-headed axe that swung towards Kedryn's head with lethal intent. He sidestepped the blow and brought his sword round in a two-handed stroke that cut deep into the warrior's side, eliciting a gasp of pain but not halting the barbarian. He ducked a backhanded cut and drove the point of his blade between the man's ribs, feeling the steel grate on bone, the cry on the tribesman's lips becoming a bubbling sound as a lung was pierced. Kedryn dragged the blade free and struck again as the man staggered, this time hacking down two-handed against the shoulder. The barbarian fell to his knees and in the instant before he toppled on to his face, Kedryn saw the whites of his eyes and the blood that spurted from his open mouth.

He turned, sensing as much as hearing the warrior who came at him from behind, lifting his sword to parry the blade that slashed viciously at his throat. He turned the attack, but the barbarian drove a leather buckler hard against his chest, sending him tottering backwards as the enemy blade was backhanded at his head. He felt the tip send cold air rushing over his face and thrust forwards, seeking to reach in over the buckler. The tribesman deflected the stab, dropping to hack at Kedryn's knees, but Kedryn jumped, raising his own blade as the sword passed below him and bringing it down in a tremendous blow that clove through the leather of the warrior's helm and deep into the skull beneath. The cranium split and the tribesman fell face down, the spillage of his brains slippery beneath Kedryn's boots as he spun to hack at a shape in a dented breastplate perceived from the corner of his eye. A scream of rage answered his blow and he felt a spear slam hard against the mail protecting his ribs. He reached out, fastening his left hand about the shaft and tugging it towards him, in tight against his side as he rammed his sword low into the attacker's belly, finding the soft flesh beneath the protective cover of the breastplate. He twisted the blade, leaving the barbarian on his knees, hands pressed to his stomach as the rage in his scream was replaced with agony.

Kedryn moved on, the screaming of the dying man lost beneath the clamour of battle, pressing steadily towards the hulking shape of the ram. He saw Bedyr cut down a man in a knee-length mail shirt and then retreat as three barbarians pressed in, a spear driving him back as two axes hacked at his head. Kedryn ran in and stabbed the nearest tribesman, his sword almost wrenched from his hand as the warrior turned, swinging his axe even as he died. He saw the second axeman swing a doublehanded blow at his ribs and let go his grip, throwing himself down to allow the heavy blade to pass above his head. He rolled, desperately seeking to avoid the blow he was sure would descend on him, then saw the woodlander drop the axe, lifting both hands to his throat as blood jetted from the cut Bedyr delivered. The spearman was already down, his furs soaked with the gore that came from his ravaged chest, and Bedyr stood above his son, sword raised defensively.

Kedryn scrambled to his feet, seeing his own blade jutting from the corpse of the warrior. He retrieved it, smiling his thanks to his father, who answered with a curt nod, eyes probing the darkness, turning as more warriors charged from the direction of the ram.

Father and son stood back to back then, surrounded by howling warriors, cutting and parrying, their blades working in unison as the woodlanders pressed in, hampered by their own ferocity, for they vied with one another to bring down the pair, jostling to thrust spears that threw the swinging axes off balance. Kedryn despatched one with a slash to the throat, then knocked aside a blade that would have taken Bedyr in the back, turning the thrust and driving his own blade along the length of the barbarian's arm to stab between shoulder and ribs. He cut another man across the face, sending him blind against a companion, and took the second man with a backhanded swing across the chest. Two more went down with opened bellies and then the remainder were suddenly gone beneath the press of Tamurin who came at them from behind, scything them down like summer grass.

'The ram!' Bedyr yelled. 'Make for the ram!'

And the Tamurin formed in a fighting wedge, Bedyr and Kedryn at the head, and charged the woodlanders who grouped before the structure.

It was butcher's work then, rather than swordplay. The forest folk stood shoulder to shoulder, intent on holding off the Tamurin force until reinforcements arrived; Bedyr's men were equally determined to despatch them and drag the ram clear before the main group could send more warriors to thwart the venture. The two forces clashed bloodily, war-shouts and the screaming of wounded men mingling in deafening cacophony as cries of alarm rang from the encampment to the north.

The woodlanders fought bravely, but the weight of the Tamurin wedge drove them steadily back against the ram. Kedryn cut and thrust and ducked, his blade darting out to stab into faces and bellies, hacking down at exposed arms, slashing across chests, unaware that some of the blood he felt warm on his face and hands was his own. He took a blow to the ribs that sent sharp pain lancing through his side, and gutted the warrior who delivered it, turning in reflex action to parry the axe that swung towards his shoulder, bringing his sword up to slash a gaping wound across the wielder's throat, down to sever the hand that drove a shortsword at his groin, forwards to stick the man.

So fierce was the blow that it emerged from the woodlander's back, the force of it jarring Kedryn's arm as his blade drove into something more solid than flesh. He grunted, tugging at his sword even as he wondered, with incongruous clarity, why the man writhing before him did not fall down and free the blade. Then he realized that he had reached the ram: his sword was lodged in the timber of its side. He raised a foot, planting his boot against the barbarian's belly and yanking back with both hands, tottering as the blade came loose, the dead weight of the tribesman counterbalancing him so that he remained upright. He freed the steel and hacked into the ribs of a barbarian to his right, seeing the man go down under the slashing sword of a Tamurin who whooped with joy despite the ragged slap of hanging skin that disfigured one side of his face. He cut to his left, severing the tendons of a woodlander's shield arm so that the buckler dropped, exposing the belly to the sword that thrust forwards, opening it.

Then, suddenly, there were no more barbarians, only Tamurin standing about the ram, mingling with swarthy Keshi in black armour, the raven horsehead picked out against the paler green of their surcoats.

'Sound the clarion!' he heard Bedyr shout. 'Give word to the fort!'

The Tamurin bugler lowered his sword and lifted his horn to his lips, blowing a sequence of notes that rang lustily from the silent walls of the mountains.

'Now set your shoulders to it!' Bedyr ordered, and the attackers clustered about the ram, driving their weight against the ponderous construction as the gates of High Fort were swung open and Rycol led a hundred out to snatch the forward ropes and begin to pull the ram in.

Kedryn sheathed his bloody sword and put a shoulder against the timber, straining as he heard the clamour of angry shouts from the north. He had no idea how long the battle had lasted. It seemed that he had fought for hours, yet when he thought about it, he felt that only minutes had passed since he rushed from the postern. He shoved, aware that the shouting was drawing closer, urgency lending him strength as he gritted his teeth, willing the massive bulk to move, fearful that the barbarians might yet reclaim it. Then he felt the timber give as the ram moved slowly forwards, and heard a ragged shout go up as it began to trundle ponderously through the open gates.

It passed between the gates and filled the yard beyond, awesome now that torches were lit, illuminating its bulk. He heard Bedyr shout, 'Bring it around,' and felt a change in direction as the men on the ropes turned, swinging the thing about. Glancing over his shoulder he saw the gates swing slowly closed, the crossbars dropped into position, sealing the fort again. Bedyr shouted once more and the ram was swung about, set hard against the gates, its massive weight now counteracting the damage it had done.

'A good night's work,' Bedyr said, coming towards him. 'The gates are secured and there are widows in the Beltrevan. You fought well.'

Only then did it come to Kedryn that he had killed. And felt nothing as he did it.

Chapter Fourteen

Kedryn's wounds were slight, even the pain of the spear-cracked rib abated swiftly with the ministrations of the Sisters, and he left the hospital wards without gaining opportunity to speak with Wynett, who was occupied with men worse hurt than he. He had wished to discuss his absence of feeling with her, for it seemed to him that he should have experienced some greater emotion at the taking of life once the exhilaration of the fight had faded, but he did not. He had killed as a soldier in battle and even as he rested after, he felt no remorse, nor any feeling other than the vague satisfaction of a task well done, and that, annoyingly, seemed to produce a sense of guilt that he considered out of proportion. He could not understand it, for it seemed to him that if he was to feel anything, it should be at the killing, not at the negation of emotion, and he felt that the Sister hospitaller would be able to enlighten him, for he was certain that these emotions stemmed from that joining with her and Grania.

As it was he had no chance to discuss his mood with anyone: Bedyr retired promptly, pragmatically intent on gaining what rest he might before the woodlanders pressed some fresh attack, and Galen took the *Vashti* over the river with the Keshi on board, ordered to remain on that side for fear the barbarians might mount a raid on so potentially valuable a craft, one that might later be used to bring fresh reinforcements from Fengrif. Kedryn was left alone with his confusion.

He slept a while, and then rose as he heard the barbarian catapults commence their pounding of High Fort, buckling on full battle armour against the danger of flying stone chips – half the men tended by Wynett and her Sisters were hurt by that shrapnel. Even his dislike of helmets had faded when he saw the facial damage done by fragments of dislodged stone.

The sky above High Fort was clear and blue, save for the crows that wheeled there in anticipation of carrion, the sun a golden disc, promising the advent of autumn, its light showing stark the damage done to the wall.

The geometric crenellations were lost now, the stone jagged as sharded teeth, long lengths of the upper walkway exposed where blocks had broken and tumbled loose, the men stationed on watch huddling behind the shelter of those areas still protected by upright sections. Where the sacks of balefire had exploded there were blackened areas, the stone slick from that awful burning, and where the mangonels had stood on their raised platforms there were only ashes and charred lengths of timber. The barbarians remained out of arrow range, seemingly intent on maintaining their bombardment until the wall was breached, for now their fire concentrated far less on the upper levels and much more on the lower reaches, especially about the gates and the postern, and they made no attempt to bring up their third ram, nor – yet – to storm the wall in frontal assault.

Craning over the ramparts, Kedryn saw great indentations in the wall, patches of lighter stone showing like open sores on the weathered surface, cracks radiating ominous webs from the impact points. He drew hurriedly back as a missile landed, crashing in a spray of splintered stone against the wall close to his vantage point, feeling the vibration under his hands.

'If they keep this up there'll be no fort for Darr to relieve. Only rubble.'

He turned at the bitter sound, seeing Rycol in burnished helm and breastplate, left hand clasped in frustration about the hilt of his sword, his narrow features hollowed by concern.

'What if they succeed?' he asked. 'In breaching the wall, I mean.'

'A few more days of this and they will.' Rycol turned angry eyes to the north. 'Then we fall back on the keep. This wall is our main line of defence, but not our last. They'll have a hard time coming through, for the yards and passageways are designed for defence and we'll slaughter hundreds there. But they have thousands upon thousands to throw against us and eventually we'll be forced to retreat to the keep. Once there it will be a matter of time.'

Kedryn turned enquiring eyes on the chatelain, not yet accustomed to this kind of fighting.

'The keep is our last resort,' Rycol enlarged. 'From there we have only two gambits left – we remain inside and hold as long as we can, hoping for relief; or we concede the battle and flee south.'

'Can Fengrif not reinforce us?' Kedryn wondered. 'The *Vashti* can ferry men across the river.'

'Fifty at a time,' Rycol grunted, 'and that but slowly. To ferry sufficient over the Idre would leave Low Fort unmanned. The Horde would need only to cross higher up the river to fall on the Keshi as they have come against us. Only if we were able to transport men swiftly from bank to bank would that be viable.'

'Why was such provision not made?' Kedryn asked, adding quickly as he saw Rycol's face darken. 'I mean no criticism, but surely such a measure makes sense?'

'Aye, now it does.' Rycol banged a fist against the wall in physical expression of the angry frustration Kedryn could hear in his voice. 'But when these forts were built there was no thought of such strategy – the forest folk did not use catapults, or rams more sophisticated than tree trunks. Nor did the Messenger lend his magicks to their cause. Our mangonels were enough to hold them at bay, and if they reached the walls they came with ladders, not those accursed towers.'

Kedryn followed his gaze to where the siege towers loomed menacing against the sky. Should they come close the fate of High Fort would surely be sealed, for fire could no longer be relied upon to destroy them and combined with the openings the catapults must surely make, the barbarians would then have several entry points.

As though sharing his thoughts, Rycol said, 'We might well hold the ramparts against the towers alone. Or the inner yards, should they breach the wall. But if they effect entry at both levels we shall have a hard time of it.'

'A raid against the catapults?' Kedryn suggested. 'Go out under cover of the night as we went against the ram?'

'Suicide,' Rycol answered, shaking his head. 'The ram lay against the gates whilst the catapults sit with the full might of the Horde about them. A raiding party would not even get close.'

'Might the *Vashti* take men up river?' Kedryn asked. 'Perhaps if Galen sailed with Keshi on board . . .'

'They'd hear her coming,' said Rycol. 'Or see her. She's too large a craft to go unnoticed, yet too small to carry sufficient men. Fifty warriors would stand little chance. And even if they succeeded, they'd not get back, and I doubt Fengrif wishes to sacrifice his men any more than I.'

'Then all depends on Darr and the armies of the Kingdoms.' Kedryn glanced up at the crows circling above, their dark pinions more threatening now.

'All,' Rycol confirmed grimly.

With that he left Kedryn, continuing along the wall to pause at each watch station and exchange a few words with the men waiting there, affecting a more cheerful demeanour than he had shown the young man. Kedryn studied the catapults a while longer, but without finding any strategy that might shift what now appeared a horrible imbalance, and then made his way to the dining hall, aware of the emptiness in his stomach.

He paused at the entrance, removing his helm as he studied the men seated at the long tables. Their faces showed a mixture of emotions, some weary, others laughing, all determined. Many called greetings as he strode towards the high table where Bedyr sat, speaking with the Lady Marga who smiled a wan greeting to Kedryn and excused herself as he sat down, nodding his thanks to the servant who placed bread and meat before him.

'You are grim,' Bedyr said. 'I thought to find you in better spirits after your first battle.'

Kedryn swallowed, his eyes troubled. 'I was on the wall. I spoke with Rycol.' He outlined the gist of their conversation, Bedyr's features growing sombre as he spoke.

'Rycol presents the most pessimistic view,' his father said when he was finished. 'He must, for he must allow for that as Chatelain of High Fort, and he cares for his men. Also, he cares for this fort and he sees it daily reduced a little closer to destruction. He is accustomed to thinking in terms of the Lozin Forts as isolated things, impregnable. I believe we shall hold out until Darr arrives. The three thousand he brings will allow us to last a while longer, until our Tamurin and Jarl's Keshi arrive. With our Tamurin on this bank we'll have men enough to stem the advance while the Keshi ferry over – using the boats that bring Darr and his men. And the Ust-Galich force should come soon after.'

'Will they be enough?' Kedryn asked.

Bedyr met his son's stare with an even gaze. 'They will have to be,' he said.

'Is that an answer?' Kedryn demanded.

'It is the only one I have,' Bedyr responded gently. 'The Kingdoms have never faced such an enemy. Not even Corwyn faced such a threat when Drul raised the Horde. I cannot offer you better. Were the Messenger not with them, I should be more sanguine, but his presence introduces the unknowable. Were Grania alive, she might be better able to answer you – I can only tell you what I know.

'Against the Horde alone I believe the combined might of the Kingdoms could prevail. If all goes as I hope and Darr reaches us in time, then I do believe we can hold. With Tamur, Kesh and Ust-Galich massed against the Horde I believe we can fight the forest folk to a standstill. They are not accustomed to long campaigning, nor much to working in unison, and that must tell against them. It might well be a long and bitter war, but we should win eventually.

'But the presence of the Messenger changes that. Already he has robbed us of our greatest weapon – as Rycol told you, without our catapults the barbarians are able to draw close, and at present they are in such numbers as would overwhelm us. If the Messenger brings some new sorcery against us, I cannot predict the outcome. Do you not see, Kedryn? I am a soldier, accustomed to thinking in soldier's terms – of men and weapons, numbers, defences, strategies. I cannot predict the unknown, and the Messenger *is* the unknown. I cannot answer you other than in the way I have.'

'But Grania might have done?' Kedryn pressed, mopping gravy with a hunk of fresh-baked bread.

'Grania was an adept of Estrevan,' nodded Bedyr, 'Andurel's Paramount Sister – yes, she could have answered you. Or stood against whatever sendings the Messenger might bring against us.'

'Are there then no others?' asked Kedryn. 'No other Sister in all the Kingdoms who might help?'

'Some, in smaller ways,' Bedyr murmured. 'Wynett gives us men who would be lost without her skills, and there are Sisters – as you know – who speed Darr's passage north, but none to equal Grania.'

'In Estrevan?' Kedryn finished the bread and wiped his mouth clean. 'The sacred city must have Grania's equal.'

'Certainly,' Bedyr agreed. 'There are many in Estrevan whose powers equal or surpass Grania's. But they are in Estrevan, not here.'

'Did the King not send mehdri with word of our plight?' Kedryn pushed his plate aside and sipped from the mug of tisane the servant poured him. 'And are the Sisters of Estrevan not in touch with those of Andurel?'

'Aye, Darr sent messengers,' Bedyr agreed, 'but even for the mehdri it is a long way to the sacred city, and any Sisters coming to our aid must travel overland, where such magicks as Grania used are of no use. As to your second question, I no longer know. There was never much magical communication between Estrevan and Andurel – I believe the bulk of the Gadrizels renders that difficult – and there was talk of the Messenger's presence imposing a clouding of mental communication.'

'It always comes back to the Messenger,' said Kedryn angrily.

'Aye,' nodded Bedyr, 'he is our greatest enemy.'

'And one we cannot seem to touch,' Kedryn muttered.

'No, all we can do is wait,' said Bedyr.

They waited through another long day and a longer night, spirits that had lifted with the capture of the ram falling again as the barrage of stones continued and the damage to the wall grew worse. Blocks weakened by the bombardment were beginning to shift, threatening to fall loose and open gaps that might well bring down whole sections. The north gates began to splinter, the bolts securing the hinges visibly weakening as the barbarian missiles struck with uncanny accuracy, loosening in their mountings as boulder after boulder pounded the timbers. It continued through the following day, the sheer remorselessness fraying nerves, frustrating men who longed for honest combat but could do nothing except wait, knowing that eventually the Horde must reach the wall, not knowing any longer whether they could hold the barbarians.

Kedryn shared that frustration, but at least the waiting gave him the chance to find Wynett and talk with her.

She was less busy now, for the wounded were tended and Rycol had reduced the numbers of men on the battlements, holding the bulk of his force in reserve for the main assault. Kedryn found her in the small garden he had first seen from his chamber in the hospital, seated on a bench with her face turned to the sun. The weariness that had marked her pretty features was gone with the banishment of the Messenger's sending and she wore a fresh gown of pale blue, her hair unbound so that it cascaded over her shoulders, reinforcing her resemblance to Ashrivelle.

Kedryn coughed discreetly as he approached, not sure if she drowsed and unwilling to disturb her, but she opened her eyes and smiled at him, beckoning him forwards.

'Sit beside me.' She patted the smooth wood of the bench and he smiled in return, adjusting his sword as he lowered himself, the bench small enough that their shoulders touched.

'Your rib is mended?' she asked.

He nodded, entranced by the golden spillage of her hair. It seemed the same colour as the sunlight, falling across her face as she turned towards him, a hand lifting to sweep the curtain from her face.

'I no longer feel it,' he said.

'Good.' Wynett continued to smile, eyes of cornflower blue studying him. 'But something troubles you.'

'Am I so easy to read? he asked, deciding that she was as lovely as her sister; perhaps lovelier, for there was a strength of character about her that he had not seen in Ashrivelle.

'I am Estrevan trained,' she reminded him. 'We are taught to read faces.'

He chuckled. 'And what do you read in mine?'

'I am not absolutely sure, but I see something. Tell me what it is.'

He looked into her eyes and found it suddenly easy to describe his confusion. 'When we took the ram I killed men. I am not sure how many – five or six, perhaps more. I felt nothing then, but I assume that is normal in battle. Yet afterwards I could not help remembering what Grania said – that we should not hate the forest folk, for they only do the Messenger's bidding – and then I felt that I should have experienced some emotion. Guilt, I suppose; or regret. Yet I felt nothing, and feeling nothing made me feel guilty. Is that normal?' He paused, not sure he was making sense.

'Have you spoken of this with your father?' Wynett asked.

Kedryn shook his head. 'No, it did not seem . . . proper. I am a soldier of Tamur. It is my duty to destroy her enemies, and my father praised me for the night's work.'

'Does it not make your duty easier?' she asked gently. 'To kill without feeling?'

Kedryn thought for a moment then said, 'I suppose it should, but it does not please me. I knew that I would kill in this war and when we first entered the Beltrevan I looked forward to it.' He laughed, mocking his own innocence. 'But I was a child then: I thought it would all be glorious. Now I see it is not and I realize that I do not particularly wish to kill anyone. Save for the Messenger.'

'The forest folk do his bidding,' Wynett murmured, 'and they have long desired to invade the Kingdoms.'

'True,' Kedryn agreed, 'and I know that I must kill them to prevent that, but I take no joy in it.'

'That is good,' she said softly, her expression serious.

'But I still feel nothing,' he said.

'Do you not?' she asked him. 'You did your duty as a soldier – you went to the defence of the Kingdoms and killed our enemies. You had no choice in that, so how can you feel guilty when what you did was your duty? Perhaps that is what you mean when you say you felt nothing. You had no choice in the matter, so could not feel any guilt for that. But you think on a larger scale than some common soldier, and you have been touched by Grania's wisdom; consequently you are torn between what you *must* do and what you would prefer.'

'Prefer?' he asked. 'I am not sure what I would prefer.'

'Are you not?' Wynett said. 'Look into your soul, Kedryn and tell me what you see.'

He stared at her, frowning, then slowly shook his head. 'I would prefer peace. I see now that killing is not very glorious and I think I should prefer we lived in peace with the Beltrevan. But we cannot.'

'No,' Wynett's tone was sad, 'we cannot. But that is not your fault, and if you were to be racked by guilt each time you are forced to do your duty, how well could you serve the Kingdoms? I think that what you did feel was remorse, but you could not understand it.'

He nodded, taking her hand unthinkingly, not noticing that she did not withdraw it. 'I think I see now. I could not regret what I had to do, but I did – *do* – regret the circumstances that make it necessary.'

'I think that is part of growing up,' she murmured, 'and that is not always an easy thing.'

'No,' he agreed, 'but you make it easier to understand.'

'I am pleased,' she told him.

He became aware then that he held her hand, but made no move to let it go because he found he enjoyed the touch. Her skin was smooth and warm and he felt very comfortable sitting there. The garden was quiet, the thudding of the barbarian missiles muffled by the weight of the intervening buildings, and it seemed they occupied a private world removed for a moment from the threat of war. He felt at peace, and wanted the moment to go on.

When Wynett at last made to remove her hand, he clutched it, reaching out to stroke her cheek, letting his fingers drift through the silk of her hair.

She said, 'Kedryn,' in a soft voice that was part admonishment and part plea, but did not draw back and he could not resist the impulse that sent his hand to the back of her neck, drawing her face towards his.

He felt their lips brush and began to tighten his grip, wanting very much to kiss her, and for a moment he felt her lips part, but then she trembled and turned her face aside so that he found his lips on her cheek. And then she rose, swiftly, blushing, her eyes troubled as she said, 'I am of Estrevan, Kedryn.'

There was something of regret in her tone and for a moment longer he held her hand, then let it go reluctantly as she drew back, fussing with her gown as she regained her composure.

'It would be a lie to tell you I am sorry,' he said, hearing the huskiness in his voice.

'Then do not,' she replied softly, and turned quickly away, hurrying from the garden.

Kedryn sat a while longer, wondering if any Sister had ever relinquished her vows.

He did not see Wynett as he left, but that night he was dreaming of her when the shouting woke him.

He came swiftly from his bed, reaching automatically for the linen undershirt he wore beneath his mail, tugging both garments hurriedly on, stamping into his breeches and boots and running from the chamber as he buckled his sword about his waist. The laces of his boots flapped loose and he paused to fasten them, listening to the cries that rang from the north wall, anticipating an assault.

Warriors poured from the barracks and halls, forming in their hundreds as tellemen and cordors shouted orders, weapons at the ready, squads running to their appointed stations in well-drilled chaos. Kedryn flattened himself back against a wall as a troop of bowmen pounded past, then raced up a stairway, ducking into an alcove to make way for a cordor and his twenty-five pikemen as they surged in the opposition direction. He reached the wall at the tail of a century of archers and stared out into the night, not sure that he could trust his eyes.

To the north, on the Beltrevan road, where the barbarian catapults and siege towers stood, he saw three great columns of flame rise into the darkness. Bright yellow light glared against the sky, sparks rising in dancing clouds like stars thrown at random against the heavens. Through the confused shouting of High Fort's defenders he heard the roaring of fire and the furious clamour of the barbarians.

'What is it?' he asked of a tellemen who stood with squinted eyes, trying like everyone else along the length of the wall to discern the source of the triple conflagration.

'I cannot see,' replied the officer. 'Some fresh sorcery?'

Kedryn felt not, though he could not say why, and left the tellemen peering into the flame-lit darkness to make his way farther along the battered ramparts.

He found Bedyr, bare-chested, with a cloak about his shoulders and sword in hand standing with Rycol, who wore full armour as though he slept in momentary readiness of attack, and repeated his question.

'It comes from the barbarian positions,' his father said. 'Look!'

One gouting column seemed to crumple in on itself, becoming a fireball that sent a great explosion of sparks blowing outwards as the height of the flames reduced, then a second leant sideways and slowly toppled, spreading a line of flame across the trail.

'Is this some new magic?' Rycol wondered aloud as the third column shed pieces of itself in a burning rain, smaller fires flaring all around.

'I think not,' Bedyr answered. 'Listen.'

The steady roaring of the fires had lessened now and the shouting of the barbarians was louder, drawing closer, no longer coming from around the bonfires but moving towards the fort.

'Stand to your posts!' Rycol bellowed. 'Ware night assault!'

Archers drew bowstrings taut as they peered into the darkness seeking targets. The shouting came closer still, angry. Kedryn grasped the stone of the ramparts, leaning out as he willed his eyes to pierce the night. He heard a bowman shout, 'There! I see them!' and heard the twang of a loosed string, the whistle of the departing arrow. Then an answering shout: 'Friends! In the name of the Kingdoms, hold your fire! We are friends!'

He recognized that voice and set a hand on Rycol's arm as he cried urgently, 'Hold fire! For the Lady's sake, tell them to hold!'

The chatelain stared at him, doubt in his eyes, then grunted and cupped his hands to his mouth as he yelled the countermanding order.

'Quickly!' Kedryn urged. 'Stand to the postern, we've friends coming in.'

'Friends?' The doubt in Rycol's eyes echoed in his voice. 'Friends from the Beltrevan?'

Kedryn pointed to the diminished fires, smiling. 'No sorcery, Rycol. Those are – *were* – the barbarian catapults!'

'What?' The chatelain stared at him in frank disbelief. 'Have they fired their own ballistae?'

'Not them,' laughed Kedryn, shaking his head, 'but the friends who approach.'

As if to confirm his point the shout from below rose up again, 'Friends! Stand to your gate, Lord Rycol, and open it for friends!'

'Who?' asked the bewildered chatelain.

'Brannoc!' Kedryn chuckled. 'My father's trust was justified.'

Bedyr had listened to this exchange in as much confusion as Rycol, but now he grinned and craned over the battlement to shout, 'Brannoc? Is that you?'

'Aye,' came the answer. 'Now will you open the gate and let us in? Or do you leave your auxiliaries to the hospitality of the forest folk?'

'Stand to the postern!' Rycol shouted, the order passed down from man to man.

'And hurry!' Brannoc added. 'We've half the Beltrevan on our tails.'

Kedryn turned, running to the stairway that led to the small gate, Bedyr on his heels, Rycol remaining on the wall, calling to his bowmen to cover the retreat. He heard the bowstrings twang while he was still descending the winding steps, the sound echoed by howls of pain and fury, then he was racing through the covered ways that devolved on the yard before the postern.

Brannoc stood there, hands on hips as he surveyed the warriors surrounding him and his party with drawn swords, his saturnine features mocking. He looked more barbarian than ever, his raven hair drawn into a series of plaits into which were woven feathers and shells, his torso hidden beneath a thick wolfskin jerkin and a homespun shirt, his breeches tucked into furred boots wrapped with leather thongs. The Keshi sabre hung at his side and a small buckler was fastened to his left arm. Kedryn noticed that the rings he had worn were missing from his fingers. His companions, some forty or so suspicious-looking fellows, wore similar garb, carrying a barbarous assortment of weapons that ranged from bearded axes to long, curved spears. They stared about them with wary eyes, as though anticipating a sudden attack, and ready to meet it ferociously.

The telleman commanding the surrounding soldiers, a warrior called Temleth, eyed them doubtfully, his blade at the ready.

'Bedyr Caitin!' Brannoc cried as he saw the two Tamurin enter the yard. 'And Kedryn! Will you tell these stalwarts that we are friends?'

Bedyr called to Temleth, assuring him that this was indeed the case and the telleman stood down his men, perplexed by these unlikely allies.

Kedryn crossed the yard to Brannoc and took the man's hand. 'You fired their catapults?'

'We did indeed,' Brannoc nodded cheerfully, 'and it was thirsty work. I've a few good men here who'd welcome the hospitality of the fort they just saved.'

Behind Kedryn, Bedyr chuckled and took Brannoc's hand in a firm grip. 'We owe you much, my friend. Come with me and I'll see you fed and wined, and you can tell us all about it.'

'Certainly,' Brannoc agreed, smiling mischievously.

They went to the dining hall, where Rycol joined them, calling for the kitchen folk to provide food and drink for the unexpected guests. The outlaw band settled cautiously at the tables, as though not yet certain of their welcome, or more accustomed to a different reception. Brannoc raised his hands and called aloud, 'Set down your weapons, friends. You've nothing to fear in High Fort – save the barbarians outside,' which brought a bellow of laughter as they grouped on the benches and set to eating and drinking with noisy enthusiasm.

Brannoc was more fastidious, shedding his buckler and jerkin and washing his hands before accepting the goblet of wine Bedyr offered him.

'You destroyed their catapults?' Rycol queried, a hint of doubt still in his voice.

'Aye,' nodded Brannoc. 'Did you not see them burning? I thought they made a pretty display.'

'Where did you come from?' Kedryn asked. 'How did you manage to get close?'

Brannoc winked, spearing a slab of roasted beef from the platter a sleepy-eyed servant set before him and carving off a chunk as he replied.

'After our last meeting I put High Fort's gold to good use,' he stared innocently at Rycol as he said this, not quite smiling, 'and sought out a few old friends who agreed that life in the Kingdoms would not be the same with woodlanders running roughshod over the land. Better the devil you know, they felt! They promised to rally on my call and when I heard of High Fort's plight, I sent for them. These,' he gestured at the rough-looking crew on the lower tables, 'are the first to answer, but more are coming. In the circumstances, I thought that better than waiting for the barbarians to come south as we first agreed.'

'We can use every man,' nodded Bedyr.

'I thought as much,' Brannoc grinned, 'when I saw that blackness hang over the forts. The Messenger? Who lifted it?'

Bedyr explained Sister Grania's part in that, and how the effort had killed her.

'A pity, a talent such as hers might well prove useful in the days to come,' Brannoc responded, 'but when I saw it lited I saw the catapults begin their work, and yours destroyed. It seemed then to be an opportune time to remove them.'

He broke off to swallow beef and sup his wine, clearly enjoying the telling. Kedryn watched, smiling, and even Rycol curbed his impatience in tribute to the night's work.

'So,' Brannoc continued at last, 'I gathered a few stalwarts about me and went to my old friend Fengrif. We were not sure whether the Messenger is able to read your signal codes, so we decided it would be the wiser course to say nothing. In any event, if we had failed there would be little to say, so we chose secrecy. There are no forest folk on the east side of the river and we were able to go out from Low Fort unobserved. We marched north and crossed the river higher up, then worked our way down the west bank until we reached the Horde.'

'You were in amongst them?' Kedryn asked wonderingly.

'I could see no other way to get close to the catapults,' Brannoc replied, shrugging with elaborate modesty as he said it. 'As you see, we bear a passing resemblance to forest folk, and it was night, so we simply moved through them until we came to the ballistae. Then we killed the guards and put them to the torch, and the rest you know.'

'You burned all three?' Rycol demanded.

'To the ground, as best I could tell with angry warriors on my heels,' nodded Brannoc, beaming. 'I would have tried for the towers, but I did not have sufficient men or time.'

'The catapults are more than we could have hoped for,' Rycol said, a slow smile spreading across his stern features. 'We are in your debt, Brannoc. I thank you.'

'Please,' murmured the former outlaw with a modesty that was almost believable, 'I did no more than I promised.'

'Nonetheless,' Rycol thrust out a hand that Brannoc took after carefully wiping his fingers, 'my judgement of you has been harsh, and I ask you to forgive that.'

'Of course,' agreed Brannoc expansively. 'Let bygones be forgotten, say I.'

Rycol smiled thinly. 'And now I had best stand down the men,' he said, rising to his feet. 'This news will put fresh heart in them. You'll find quarters for your men in the barracks.'

Brannoc nodded, watching the chatelain depart.

'He looks older. Has it been so hard?' His tone was abruptly serious, his dark eyes troubled.

Bedyr nodded. 'The darkness was the worst for that sank into the soul and Rycol suffered much of it alone. The lifting of it – as I told you – killed Grania, and it seemed after that we could do nothing save wait. The destruction of the ballistae hit him hard.'

'You reached Andurel?' Brannoc enquired.

'Aye,' Bedyr confirmed, 'and Darr must be on the Idre e'en now. The Kingdoms close on this place with all speed. Hopefully, we shall defeat the Horde here.'

'They'll bring the towers against the walls now,' warned Brannoc. 'Are they breached?'

'No, nor shall be thanks to you,' smiled Bedyr. 'The catapults have weakened them – and the north gates – but they stand.'

'It will be bloody fighting.' Brannoc reached out to draw the wine jar close and fill his goblet. 'My forty will make scant difference, but soon there'll be more. Three hundred, perhaps.'

'I did not know Tamur held so many outlaws,' Bedyr murmured.

'*Auxiliaries*,' Brannoc corrected, grinning again. 'And patriots to a man – in their own way.'

The roseate light of the early dawn reflected off Niloc Yarrum's breastplate as the hef-Ulan sat sullenly on a boulder overlooking the Beltrevan road. His ornate scabbard was set across his knees, his knuckles white where he gripped it, his swarthy features dark with rage. Behind him, their own faces hidden behind the nasals- and cheek-pieces of their helmets, stood his Gehrim, forming, with the bodyguards of the other Ulans, a semi-circle about the chieftains. Balandir sat to Niloc's left, tugging at his white-streaked beard, his great axe planted between his feet, Ymrath and Darien beyond him, as though seeking to distance themselves from the hef-Ulan's fury. Vran stood to his right, close-set eyes wary as they switched from Niloc to Taws, who stood with his back to the group, Borsus a few paces off, trying hard not to look at any of them. Before them, littering the roadway, lay the smouldering wreckage of the catapults, thin plumes of smoke still rising into the morning air.

'I do not understand,' snarled Niloc. 'How could this happen?'

The mage turned to face the hef-Ulan, his snow-pale features set in a hard, cold mask, the red pits of his sunken eyes bright with rage. 'I had thought to see them better guarded.'

'They were guarded well enough,' Niloc retorted harshly. 'No Kingdomer came close.'

'Then who,' Taws asked sarcastically, his tone bringing a flush to the Drott's face, 'slit the throats of your guards and set torch to the catapults?'

'Traitors!' Niloc barked. 'Ashar-cursed turncoats!'

'From whose clan?' Taws's head turned slowly, accusing eyes surveying each Ulan in turn.

'Not mine!' Vran said quickly, fingering the gold and silver torque about his throat. 'No Yath did this.'

'Nor Grymard,' said Darien, shaking his head.

Ymrath said, 'Why should any Vistral do such a thing?'

'My brother speaks sense,' said Balandir evenly, returning Taws's stare. 'Why should any tribesman do this? What profit would there be?'

'Reward,' grunted Niloc.

Balandir waved a dismissive hand, 'My Caroc would not dare and I do not believe your Drott would stoop so low. And what reward might they hope for save the embrace of the blood eagle?'

'They entered the fortress,' Niloc said in a voice low with suppressed fury, 'yet they did not come from there.'

'Therefore,' said Taws, 'they came from within the Horde. Send your Gehrim to question your people and bring me answers.'

Without awaiting a reply, he spun round and stalked away, Borsus falling into step behind as he strode towards his lodge.

'Master?' ventured the warrior as they approached the shebang.

Taws's head cocked to the side. Borsus swallowed hard, not sure he should speak, but knowing he had gone too far to remain silent.

'Well?' Taws thrust the flap covering the entrance aside and went into the stifling confines of the shebang. Borsus followed, sweat starting on his face and chest as the heat of the braziers struck him.

'When you sent me after the Kingdomers,' he began, 'I saw one with them who looked to be of the forest. Do you remember? It was he gave warning of my arrow.'

'I remember everything,' Taws said, lowering his angular frame on to a couch. 'What of him?'

'What if he had mingled with us?' Borsus suggested nervously. 'He might easily have passed for a woodlander, especially amongst so great a mass of the people. If he were in the pay of the Kingdoms, he might have found others – outlaws, freebooters – willing to undertake the venture. Mayhap they did it.'

'Mayhap,' said Taws softly, his tone ominous, 'in which case he will pay. Come here, Borsus.'

The warrior took a reluctant pace forwards, sensing the rage that seethed beneath the mage's outward calm. Taws beckoned, motioning for him to step closer, and when he did a hand snaked out to clench long fingers about his cheek and jaw, drawing his face down towards the Messenger's.

For an awful moment Borsus thought to see the crimson fire burn in the pits of the mage's eyes and felt his legs tremble beneath him, dreading the soul-stealing kiss of those fleshless lips. Instead, he felt a sudden dizziness, his head spinning as it had done so long ago when first Taws walked out from the fire-racked forest. Then his vision cleared and he felt the talon-like fingers release their grip, taking an involuntary step backwards as he sucked air into his lungs in a gusting sigh of relief.

'So.' Taws nodded, his voice soft. 'One more to seek out.'

'How, Master?' Borus asked.

'I know him now.' Taws's smile was an ugly thing. 'And you know him. When the time comes, I shall send you to him. To him and the other.'

'Me?' Borsus was alarmed.

'You,' Taws nodded, 'for you are the only one I can trust.'

'Master, you need but tell the hef-Ulan and when we take the fortress he will give you both their heads,' Borsus suggested.

'Yarrum becomes ambitious,' murmured the mage. 'What service he renders me is in return for the elevation I offer him; a matter of balances. You, Borsus, are more modest. What have you asked of me? A woman, no more than that. Such a little thing, yet you prize her do you not?'

Borsus nodded dumbly.

'Would you wear the hef-Ulan's torque?' asked Taws abruptly. 'I could make you leader of all the Beltrevan if you desired.'

'No!' Borsus shook his head fervently. 'I am a simple warrior, Master. Nothing more. I seek no more than to serve you.'

'And you shall,' promised the mage. 'Better even than Niloc Yarrum, for there is one who must die and I can trust only you to kill him.'

Borsus stood perplexed, wondering why a single man should be so important to the Messenger and why he so obviously wished to hide that importance from the hef-Ulan. Was it that Niloc might utilize that man as a counter-weight against Taws's dominance? Was that what Taws had meant when he spoke of balances?

'Do not trouble yourself with it.' The cold voice startled the warrior from his musings. 'Find the hef-Ulan and tell him to call off his Gehrim. Tell him I would speak with him by the towers. With him and all the Ulans.'

Borsus ducked his head and hurried from the sweaty lodge, thankful to be once again out in the clean air. There was a part of him that loathed that closeness to the Messenger enforced by Taws's selection of him as servitor, and another part that resented the fear he felt. There were rewards in compensation, certainly: he had Sulya, and the gifts bestowed by those seeking to curry favour with one so close to the mage had enriched his lodge, he enjoyed a position of undefined status; but hand-in-hand with all those things went the constant fear of his master's wrath. And the feeling that he was no longer his own man but a mere puppet jerked this way and that by unbreakable strings gnawed at him, even as he knew he would never dare rebel. Perhaps when the fortress fell things would change: perhaps then he would find independence again.

For now, however, he would do Taws's bidding dutifully and keep his thoughts very much to himself.

He found Niloc Yarrum lounging outside his opulent lodge, a horn of dark beer in his hand, his black eyes surveying the skulls hung from the trophy poles as though he sought answers in the bleached bones of his victims.

He slapped a fist to his chest in salute and said, 'Lord, the Messenger asks that you recall your Gehrim and meet him at the towers. You and the Ulans, Lord.'

Yarrum surveyed him for a while with surly eyes, then nodded and shouted to the handful of warriors who remained with him, telling them to find Dewan and take word to the chieftains. Borsus waited to be dismissed, but Niloc continued to fix him with that sullen glare.

'You are his man, warrior – what does he know?'

'Who fired the catapults, I think,' Borsus mumbled, unwilling to admit his part in this discovery, for he still recalled the threat-induced vow of silence Taws had set upon him.

'So,' Niloc grunted. 'A pity he could not use his powers to prevent it, eh?'

Borsus nodded, unwilling to speak.

'We nearly had them,' the hef-Ulan continued. 'Those walls could not have stood much longer, but now . . .' He drained the horn and tossed it carelessly to the grass. 'Is there a limit to your master's power, warrior?'

Borsus licked his lips, feeling himself caught between fire and flame. 'I have not seen it,' he responded cautiously.

'His darkness was lifted,' Niloc murmured, brow furrowing thoughtfully, 'and he would not use sorcery to bring down the walls. Or *could* not, which do you think?'

'I am only a warrior, hef-Ulan,' Borsus shrugged, 'I do not know.'

'And would not say if you did, eh?' demanded Niloc. 'No matter. When we take the fortress and conquer the Kingdoms we shall see where we all stand.'

With that enigmatic comment he rose to his feet and strode towards the siege towers, Borsus trailing behind, pondering the import of his words. Best, he decided, to forget them, for they smacked of dissatisfaction with the Messenger, and if some duel for mastery of the people was to foment, Borsus wanted no part of it.

They came to the towers and found Taws waiting for them, standing silent as he stared towards the battered walls. He said nothing, giving no sign that he was aware of their presence and Niloc Yarrum settled himself against a sun-warmed boulder, seemingly content to await the mage's pleasure. Only when the four Ulans were come did the Messenger turn and begin to speak.

'The catapults were burnt by mercenaries in the pay of the Kingdoms,' he told them. 'There is no point seeking amongst your people because they are safe now, behind those walls. What we must do is seek them there. They are weakened by my sending and the catapults and now we must breach the walls and take the fortress before fresh troops arrive.'

'Fresh troops?' demanded Niloc. 'From where? Winter will be on us before the Kingdoms can bring an army here.'

'The Sisterhood has powers,' Taws retorted. 'Not to match mine, but sufficient they may aid the fortress by speeding the arrival of the army. Before that happens, I want to cross that wall. I want that fortress in our hands!'

'Then we attack?' asked Niloc, a wolfish smile splitting his sullen features.

'We attack!' Taws confirmed. 'Send the towers forwards.'

'Praise Ashar!' shouted the hef-Ulan. 'Dewan, take word. Quickly!'

The leader of Niloc's Gehrim ran to obey as the other Ulans barked commands to their own men, sending the warriors of the Gehrim racing to alert the camp. Horns rang out, bringing the forest folk in their thousands to the trail, swords and spears clattering noisily against upraised shields as voices brayed war-shouts and the women screamed their encouragement. The chieftains remained on the side of the trail as teams of brawny tribesmen hurried to the ropes connected to the great tower platforms, whilst more massed behind, setting their shoulders to the bulk of the massive constructions. Bowmen huddled behind the mobile barricades, pushing them alongside the towers as the slow advance down the wide stone roadway began.

Borsus moved to join the warriors massing behind the towers, but Taws called him back, shaking his head.

'Not yet.' The mage beckoned him to his side. 'I have a task for you, but I must prepare you for it.'

'Master?' Borsus asked, not liking this unexpected development. He looked forward to honest battle and the honour to be won there after the long days of waiting, and the mood of the Horde as it surged remorselessly towards the fortress was a palpable thing, stirring his blood and calling out to him. He wanted to be there, ready at the ladders as the towers reached the walls, ready to take his share of skulls or die in glory, not hang back, tethered by the Messenger's will. He saw warriors he knew fall in behind the great constructions that would grant them access to the Kingdoms, the bar-Offas sending their axes whirling high in the dusty air, catching them as they fell with shouts of pride and battle-lust bursting from their lips, echoed by the men they led, the cries filling the river canyon with the wild, joyous sound of impending fight. He saw the dust raised by their feet swirl, dulling the sun, the crows that wheeled above them screaming their own cacophanous answer to the yelling of the Horde, and he trembled with the desire to join them.

'Wait.' Taws's voice was soft in his ear, insistent and promising. 'The glory they will find is as nothing to that which awaits you, Borsus.'

The warrior fingered the rim of his buckler, scarcely able to contain his impatience and yet unable to deny the command of the Messenger. He drew the strap taut about his left forearm, hefting the weight of the leather-covered disc; grasped his sword hilt, sliding the blade a little way from the scabbard and thrusting it back.

'There is time enough,' Taws murmured. 'Let them reach the walls. Let them open the way and then I shall unleash you. Then shall you do Ashar's work and earn a place for all eternity at his hearthside.'

Borsus tore his gaze from the vast throng of stamping, shouting warriors to look upon the face of the Messenger. It had an almost dream-like quality, as though Taws saw beyond the great column of marching men to what would be. Borsus wondered what it was the mage saw there, and what his part in that vision might be.

'What would you have me do?' he asked.

'Find your woman,' Taws said, 'and bring her to my lodge. Wait for me there, for this concerns both of you.'

'Sulya?' Borsus felt sudden confusion and more than a little apprehension. 'What do you want of her, Master?'

'Do as I bid you,' Taws ordered, rubescent eyes fastening on the warrior's. 'Now!'

A chill slithered down Borsus's spine, but he nodded dumbly and turned away as the mage gestured, teeth clenched in frustration as the column marched past him. He ignored the shouts that followed his passage away from the impending battle, promising himself a great skull-taking when at last Taws permitted him to enter the combat, but still wary, and more than a little confused by the mage's instructions. What could the Messenger want with Sulya? And what great destiny was he to fulfil? He could find no answers, and as he approached the lodge-covered slopes where the women stood watching he began to doubt he *could* find Sulya in that chaos.

The craggy foothills denied the customary groupings of lodges, the tribes pitching their dwellings in loose configurations rather than the formal circles, the undulations mixing Drott with Caroc, Vistral and Grymard and Yath mingling with them, finding footing where they might. Now, save for a few oldsters and the children left in their care, the lodges stood empty, the women clustering about the edges of the road, or on the surrounding hummocks, anywhere they might watch the advance and shriek encouragement to their men. It took Borsus a long time to find Sulya, perched on the out-thrust limb of a scraggy tree that grew partway up a knoll, her face red with shouting, eyes wild with excitement.

They grew bewildered as he stamped towards her, irritable from the loud questioning of the other women, and grasped a well-formed ankle, raising his voice above the screaming to bid her climb down.

She obeyed, eyeing him doubtfully, asking, 'Why are you here? Why do you not march?'

'Because I do the Messenger's bidding,' he snapped, deliberately loud enough that the others might hear. 'Come with me.'

'Where?' she demanded.

'To his lodge,' Borsus told her, taking her wrist and dragging her behind him. 'He would speak with us both.'

'With me?' Sulya's free hand rose to her mouth in alarm. 'Why with me?'

'I do not know,' he grunted in reply, 'I only obey.'

Her eyes clouded, but she fell into step beside him so that he let go her wrist, shouldering a way for them through the crowd, Sulya smoothing her robe and dragging fingers through her thick blonde hair as she prepared herself for the meeting.

Borsus came to the Messenger's lodge and halted at the entrance. There was no response to his shout, so he shrugged, telling Sulya to wait as he surveyed the warriors still marching noisily towards the fort. They covered the road like some dark, human sea, driving the siege towers before them. The towers were closing on the walls now and he could see the dark specks of falling arrows driving into the foremost ranks, the men hauling on the ropes falling as the Tamurin archers found easy targets. Answering volleys came from behind the barricades that now lined either side of the trail, and from the towers themselves. The road before the fortress was hard stone and the dust that clouded above the latter part of the advancing column faded there, so that he could see clearly how the hauliers went down until finally the survivors retreated behind the safety of the towers, adding their weight to the mass pushing the construction forwards.

It went slower then, but the towers continued to roll inexorably towards the walls and by the time the sun had climbed to its zenith and was shining directly into the chasm of the Idre they stood scant feet from the ramparts.

'You should be there,' Sulya muttered.

'Aye,' Borsus replied irritably, 'but would you have me gainsay the Messenger?'

Her answer was a gasp and Borsus tore his eyes from the towers, where warriors now clustered, preparing to mount the internal ladders and bridge the gap, to see Taws approaching.

'Come.' Without further ado the Messenger swung the entry flap aside and ducked into the lodge.

Borsus saw Sulya lick her lips and took her wrist again, hauling her behind him into the overheated confines of the place. She made a small, whimpering sound of protest as the heat struck her, her eyes darting about as though seeking escape.

'Sulya,' murmured Taws, his voice soft as falling snow, 'you are honoured above other women.'

She looked at the mage with doubt and fear in her blue eyes and he twisted his mouth in a serpentine smile, adding, 'Your man will live in the legends of the Drott. His name will be spoken throughout the Beltrevan and all the Kingdoms, and yours with him, for without you he cannot do what he must. Ashar's purpose depends on you, Sulya.'

'How so?' she asked, transfixed by his glowing crimson gaze.

'I will show you,' Taws promised, eyes turning to Borsus. 'Do you prize her?'

'Aye,' said Borsus.

'That is good,' said Taws. 'Give me your sword.'

In that instant Borsus felt a ghastly presentiment of what was to come. He opened his mouth to do what he had never before dared: to deny the Messenger; but Taws's eyes grew brighter, burning with hellish light and he felt his will become slack, refusal dying stillborn on his lips. His hand wrapped itself around the hilt of his sword and drew it from his plain leather scabbard, turning it that he might present it hilt foremost to the mage, aware of what he did but no more able to halt the action than he could halt the progress of a dream.

Taws took it and set a thumb to the edge, nodding in approval as Borsus watched, his limbs leaden, unmoveable.

'A good blade,' Taws said, his voice seeming to come from far away, 'a blade that will do good work. Ashar's work!'

He held the sword negligently, letting it hang loose by his side as he faced Sulya, reaching out his left hand to cup her chin, tilting her head back so that she stared up at him, transfixed.

'I gave you to this warrior,' Borsus heard him say, 'and now I take you back in Ashar's name.'

He let go her chin then, stepping back as he lifted the blade to his lips, first kissing it and then murmuring things difficult for any human tongue to form. Through burning eyes Borsus saw red light play about the steel. Saw the mage set the tip to Sulya's belly.

'I will make you invincible,' Taws said, his voice licking about the warrior's mind as might tongues of flame, whispering, half-heard yet indelible. 'There is one you must kill. You have seen him; you know him. You put my arrow in him and that will bring you to him. Nothing will stop you. Do you know him, Borsus?'

Borsus's answer came unbidden, torn by the Messenger's magic from deep inside him: 'Aye, Master, I know him.'

'Him first,' said Taws, 'and then the other, if you can. The one who fired my catapults. But the one with my mark on him is the one you seek first.'

'Aye, Master,' Borsus repeated.

'With this sword,' murmured Taws.

And drove the blade deep into Sulya's belly, twisting it so that she screamed and clutched at spilling entrails as he withdrew the bloodied steel, falling to her knees as her pain-racked eyes stared hopelessly at her slayer.

Taws stood above her, extending the blade to touch it to her lips, and then she moaned and fell on her side, her feet kicking feebly, slowing and stilling as death overtook her. And all Borsus could do was watch as hate filled him, a blind, seething hate that cried out for blood, demanding satisfaction, vengeance.

He could not move, nor speak. Could do no more than watch as Taws faced him again, the rubescent glare of his cratered eyes boring into the Drott's soul, filling him with an awful purpose that transcended the slaughter he witnessed, filling him with a hatred not of

Taws, but of the one whose image superimposed itself upon the mantis-features of the mage.

'His name is Kedryn,' said Taws. 'Go now and kill him for Ashar.'

'Aye!' snarled Borsus, taking the red-smeared sword. 'For Ashar!'

Chapter Fifteen

Kedryn donned full battle armour as the clarions sounded the alarm, buckling greaves and vambraces in place to complement the breast-plate embossed with the clenched fist of Tamur, that sat heavy on his chest, black against scarlet. He bound his hair back and set a helmet over the coif of his mail shirt, cursing softly as he tugged the chinstrap tight. His dislike of the confining metal was overcome, however, by the inevitable nature of the fighting that would take place along the wall once the siege towers rolled into position: the majority of the barbarians carried axes and those bludgeoning weapons were capable of striking through the most skilled defence, brute force overcoming finesse. He buckled his sword about his waist and drew gauntlets on to his hands, then found his way to the ramparts, where the defenders of High Fort waited, studying the enemy massed before them.

'Stay close,' Bedyr urged as his son joined him.

'Do you fear for me?' Kedryn asked, dry lips curving in a smile.

'I'd have your sword to guard my back,' responded his father. 'And mine yours.'

Kedryn nodded and turned his attention to the towers, the smile freezing on his mouth as he saw the warriors thronging the ground about the massive constructions. They held shields raised high against the rain of arrows sent by the archers along the wall, shafts sprouting like quivering stems from the bucklers, their voices lifted in challenge, animalistic in their fury. It seemed to him that he looked not upon individual men, but on some gestalt engine of destruction moulded by evil magic for no other purpose than the sack of the Kingdoms. Men fell, struck where shafts found a way through the shield wall, only to be replaced, their bodies trampled beneath the stamping feet, their cries lost in the ululation, their deaths ignored as the massed ranks of forest folk pressed inexorably forwards, the great wheels of the siege platforms turning ponderously, bringing the towers ever closer to the fort.

Closer and closer still, until finally they halted.

There was a pause then, an instant of silence, as though the Horde drew breath, and then a wild, ear-splitting shout went up from the myriad throats and the barbarians began to clamber avidly on to the platforms, climbing the ladders inside.

'May the Lady stand with us this day,' Bedyr murmured softly, the prayer echoed by Kedryn's 'Amen.'

Both Tamurin clutched their swords, waiting for the drawbridges to come down and disgorge the vanguard. Kedryn felt a calm descend upon him, an objectivity that erased fear, even hope. It seemed impossible that Darr should arrive in time to stem this flood – it seemed impossible that anything could stem so vast a torrent of blood-hungry humanity – and he felt that he would most likely die on the wall, but did not care. It no longer seemed to matter. Only duty mattered now, and that observation was made easy for him: he had only to fight.

He heard a bull horn trumpet sound and saw the drawbridges fall loose, rough-cut planks smashing against the battered edges of the ramparts, barbarians emerging even as the gaps were bridged. Cordors shouted and the first wave of invaders fell beneath a whistling storm of arrows. Were shoved carelessly aside to tumble down to the ground below, replaced by more. And more still as the second wave fell, replaced by a third until the bridges were crossed and barbarians set foot on the walls of High Fort.

Then it was bloody sword-work, Rycol's disciplined men against the wild fury of the Horde. Bedyr glanced, smiling grimly, at Kedryn and raised his blade high, roaring a battle cry. Kedryn answered with a shout and together they charged headlong into a cluster of forest folk carving a way on to the ramparts.

Kedryn sidestepped a downswinging axe and hacked his blade deep into a fur-covered shoulder, turning as another hatchet glanced off his armour to backhand his sword across a screaming face, reverse the swing to stab into yielding belly and kick the warrior back into his fellows. He saw Bedyr stagger as a mace thudded against his head and took the wielder through the ribs, pivoting to deflect a gisarme and carve a bloody line across the barbarian's throat. A bearded axe hooked his left arm, yanking him close to a tribesman who spat foul breath into his face as a buckler was slammed against his chest, sending him staggering back as the axe lifted to cleave his skull. He saw it drop from dead fingers as Bedyr's sword lifted the man's head from his shoulders and spun

338

to ram his blade deep into the chest of a warrior who came at his father from behind.

The forest folk drew back then, forming a defensive semi-circle about the drawbridge as fresh warriors mounted the internal ladders and came screaming over the planks. Again Bedyr and Kedryn charged, seeking to drive the invaders back over the wall, but able only to hold them briefly at the egress of the tower. Kedryn felt his head ring as an axe clanged loud against his helmet and moved instinctively inside the reach of the barbarian to drive the pommel of his sword against the tribesman's teeth, sending him back on to the point of Bedyr's blade. He shook his head, dizzy from the blow, and ducked beneath the howling arc of a longsword, striking two-handed to sever the wrist and send the blade with hand still attached to the hilt on to the blood-stained stone of the wall. He saw Bedyr down two men with a cut and riposte and fell a third who came in from the side with a savage slash to the stomach. Then he found himself facing a wall of shields that advanced remorselessly along the ramparts and heard his father shout, 'Back! Fall back!'

Unwillingly, he gave ground, knowing that the barbarians gained surer hold with each retreating step, seeing Rycol's men hurl themselves desperately against the shields, only to fall beneath stabbing spears and swinging axes. He snatched one pole beneath the head, drawing its owner close enough he was able to stab out an eye, then he was thrown back by the weight of a buckler that drove into him and fought defensively as axes and blades sought to bring him down.

For a spell there was stalemate, the defenders grouping in dogged bunches to halt the forward movement of the invaders, but all the time more barbarians clambered on to the ramparts, and as the afternoon drew on the forest folk secured their footing on the wall by sheer weight of numbers, establishing their hold on the ramparts until the Tamurin fought in groups surrounded by the tribesmen.

Kedryn's sword was blunting, losing its cutting edge from the endless hacking, when he heard the unwelcome sound of Rycol's trumpeter blowing the signal to retreat. The stones beneath his feet were slippery with spilled blood as he saw Bedyr gesture towards the steps leading down to the yards below and heard him shout for the men about him to begin the descent.

The Tamurin began to clamber down, Bedyr, Kedryn and a handful of soldiers covering their backs as a yammering howl of triumph went up from the forest folk. Along the wall scattered groups of defenders were cut off and butchered, their corpses hurled on to the men descending the stairs, Kedryn found himself shoulder to shoulder with Bedyr, their crimsoned swords darting and thrusting as the Horde took possession of the ramparts, pressing ever harder against the two armoured warriors who denied them their pursuit of the retreating defenders. Slowly, a step at a time, they began to descend, holding back the forest folk until they reached the lower level and were able retreat under cover of Tamurin arrows along a corridor.

A messenger from Rycol found them there, bringing word that the third barbarian ram was brought against the postern to threaten attack from the rear, and the chatelain's suggestion that they concede the wall to the Horde and concentrate their defence on the inner yards.

'We can hold them,' Kedryn argued. 'Make them pay for each step.'

'There are too many.' Bedyr shook his head, looking about him at the wounded. 'They overwhelm us by sheer weight of men. Had Darr come in time it might be different, but now ... No, we must fall back and seek to hold them from the southern gate.'

As though to emphasize his point, the barbarians mounted a charge along the corridor. Those at the forefront went down under a volley of arrows, but then the rest closed with the Tamurin and the swordplay began again. Screams of rage and agony filled the vaulted passage as the defenders retreated slowly, forced back as much by the insurmountable pressure of the warriors filling the corridor as by battle skill, for more barbarians entered by the minute as the siege towers disgorged the limitless numbers of the Horde on to the north wall. Behind the retreating defenders stood a thick oak door, and Bedyr shouted for men to stand ready to close the portal. Kedryn stood beside him as they worked furiously to clear sufficent space, the steel of his sword no longer visible under the slick coating of blood that decorated the blade from tip to guard. He hacked at a yelling face and thrust at a skin-clad chest, then saw a gap and shouted to Bedyr. His father turned the swing of a gisarme and disembowelled the user, leaping back even as he bellowed for the doors to be closed. Kedryn darted through, followed closely by Bedyr, and the heavy oak was slammed shut, held in place by Tamurin shoulders as the bolts were driven home and the pounding of axes shuddered the wood.

'Back,' Bedyr ordered. 'We group on the inner yards before they cut us off.'

The defenders ran, leaving the forest folk to batter a way through the door.

When they emerged into the yard Kedryn was surprised to see that the sun had fallen behind the rim of the mountains. The interior of High Fort was already in shadow and torches were lit, illuminating blood-streaked faces, tired, angry eyes. The yard was filled with men and as he paused to catch his breath he saw Rycol coming towards him. The chatelain's face was gaunt beneath the peak of his helmet, his armour dented, and his left arm thrust stiff under his sword belt.

'It is broken,' he said by way of explanation, 'like my fort.'

'We are not beaten yet,' Bedyr answered. 'There is still time for Darr to reach us, and the others.'

'Since this began we have lost hundreds,' Rycol said wearily. 'With those lost to the catapults, we have no more than six centuries. I have sent word to Orgal Leneth to begin the evacuation of the town – Galen is taking them across the river in the *Vashti* – and the women are seeking refuge in the hospital. The signal tower is cut off, and the north postern will fall before long. We have no choice but to retreat to the keep. Or abandon the fort.'

Kedryn stared at him, shocked by the hopelessness in his voice.

Bedyr said, 'We do not abandon High Fort. Not while we live.'

'It is an option,' Rycol shrugged, 'no more than that. I did not intend to take it.'

Bedyr glanced around. 'How many stand at the postern?'

'The remnants of Istar's and Temleth's hundreds,' said Rycol, 'and Brannoc's freebooters – they make a hundred now.'

Kedryn shivered, battle sweat cooling fast in night air chilled by the approach of autumn. It had all happened so fast, as though the Messenger had opened floodgates to sweep away the defenders before the awful tide of humanity he released.

'It is my fault,' he heard Rycol say. 'I should not have risked the use of balefire. Had we been able to use the catapults they would not have brought those accursed towers against the walls. We could have destroyed them before they reached us. But now . . .' He broke off, shaking his head wearily, his features haggard.

'We have discussed this,' Bedyr snapped, 'and it was no more your fault than mine. That responsibility does not rest on your shoulders alone.'

'I am chatelain,' Rycol said in a low voice. 'High Fort is my responsibility.'

'And the defence of Tamur mine,' said Bedyr. 'Now we must plan for that.'

'How?' asked Rycol helplessly. 'With High Fort fallen the Lozin gate is open.'

'High Fort is not fallen yet,' countered Bedyr, 'and even if they come through, they will find the army of Tamur approaching.'

He sheathed his sword and placed a hand on Rycol's good shoulder, looking the older man straight in the eyes. 'I'll have service of you yet, old friend. Organize the keep. Let them pay for each step they take towards it, and when they reach it we'll deny them access. If we can hold there until Darr comes, we have a chance. So long as we can prevent them taking the south gate we can deny them entry to the Kingdoms. Do that now, and I'll see to the postern.'

Rycol nodded, smiling wanly, and Bedyr turned to Kedryn. 'Will you ward my back again?'

'Aye,' Kedryn responded. 'Willingly.'

'Good. Then let us see what we can do.'

They moved at a brisk trot to the postern, where Brannoc and the two tellemen waited with their men, listening to the steady hammering of the ram. The wall surrounding the gate was already weakened by the pounding of the ballistae, as was the gate itself, and now cracks began to appear in the stonework, accompanying the splinters that sharded from the battered wood.

'They'll be in before we see the moon,' Brannoc announced cheerfully. 'Do reinforcements follow you?'

Bedyr shook his head. 'We hold them as long as possible. While Rycol organizes a retreat to the keep. No more than that.'

'I had thought I might die in High Fort,' Brannoc murmured, his dark eyes twinkling with wry amusement, 'but on the gallows, not in Tamur's service.'

'You need not die,' Bedyr said, 'You are free to go.'

'I think not,' Brannoc answered, smiling.

Bedyr nodded and produced a whetstone from his sabretache, setting a fresh edge on his blade. Kedryn found a seat and did the same, listening all the while to the sound of the ram and the howling of the barbarians already inside the fort. Brannoc unstoppered a waterbottle and passed it around, the contents tepid but still welcome to throats dry from shouting. Then Istar called a warning and the men waiting about the postern rose to their feet, grim-faced as they watched the gate.

Livid gaps showed in the wood now, great splinters flying loose where metal rivets tore out under the pressure of the battering, the crossbar itself buckling. Then, with a dramatic abruptness, the bar cracked clean across and broke in two as the head of the ram burst through. It withdrew and struck again, sending rivets clattering over the flags. Three more blows and the gate fell inwards, revealing the outline of the ram's shelter, from which came a yammering shout of triumph.

That sound blended into another, a feral baying that was blood-curdling in its animal ferocity.

'War hounds!' Brannoc screamed as low, leaping shapes poured through the gap.

Kedryn clenched his teeth as he saw the dogs, all glaring yellow eyes and slavering jaws, and braced himself to meet their attack.

The archers brought some down, but the animals were more agile than men, presenting harder targets as they raced towards the de-fenders, moving fast enough that the bowmen had time to loose only a single volley before the animals closed. Kedryn saw a massive brindled form come bounding towards him, lips peeled back from vicious fangs, hindquarters bunching as the hound gathered itself to spring at his throat. He brought his blade round and forwards in a two-handed grip, driving the steel between the jaws as the dog leapt, feeling his arms jarred by the force of its charge. He saw the point emerge bloody from the neck and staggered as the dog's dead weight fell against his chest, dragging his arms down. Instantly a second was on him, fangs closing on his wrist, the pressure numbing through the protective mail. He let go his sword and reached left-handed for his dirk, drawing the long blade and stabbing into the grey neck. A furious growling answered the blow and the hound shook its head, tugging him sideways so that he stumbled and went down on his knees, only the desperate will to live retaining his grip on the dirk. The dog began to back away, seeking to pull him down, ignoring the gore that dribbled from its wounded throat, and Kedryn felt his arm drawn out, amazed at the strength of the animal. He dragged the dirk free and stabbed again as he felt himself toppling forwards, knowing that if he fell he was unlikely to rise again. The dagger's point took the dog in its sensitive nose and it yelped, releasing its hold. Kedryn slashed viciously, cutting across the muzzle, driving the hound back. He got his feet under him and pushed upright, his free hand snaking to the hilt of his sword, snatching it free as the grey beast gathered for a fresh attack, swinging as it sprang so that its leap was turned aside by the blade that carved into its ribs.

He left it howling and turned about, seeing Brannoc despatch a great black beast with a savage sabre slash; Bedyr thrust a gauntleted

343

fist between gaping jaws and crush the skull with the pommel of his sword; Temleth go down with three animals worrying at him. He tried to reach the tellemen, but two hounds came at him together and he was forced to ignore Temleth's plight as he fought for his own life.

He clove a skull with his sword and then felt jaws fasten on his throat, grateful for the mail he wore, but still smashed down under the weight of the beast. He stabbed between the ribs, blindly, and battered at the great head with his pommel. His breath was cut off by the pressure and he felt a roaring in his skull, his vision clouding beneath a pall of red, the war hound's grip unrelenting despite the wounds he inflicted. Then the grip released and he sucked air into tortured lungs, feeling the dog's weight kicked from him and a hand clasp his wrist, hauling him upright. Brannoc stood there, sabre bloody and smiling through a mask of crimson, spinning and slashing as another hound launched itself, sending the animal yowling to the side, where Kedryn despatched it with an angry stab.

All around the yard men were engaged with hounds. Temleth lay silent beneath the corpses of three dogs and as Kedryn panted, his throat bruised by the pressure of the fangs, he saw Istar fall, and rise only to fall again. He saw one of Brannoc's outlaws skewer a hound and then go down as another fastened teeth in his calf, his throat ripped out by a third before he could use his blade again. He charged into the thick of the fighting, breaking a beast's back with a great downswinging slash and ramming his dirk into a shaggy throat even as the animal sprang at his face. He killed another, and another, and then the dogs were gone and he saw that he stood surrounded by canine bodies. Bedyr stood a little distance away, his face grim beneath his helmet as he drove his blade into the neck of a beast that crawled towards him, jaws still snapping despite its broken spine.

Then, howling as fiercely as their dogs, the barbarians poured into the yard.

Bedyr shouted, 'To me!' and the remaining defenders grouped about the Lord of Tamur.

Kedryn was shocked to see how many had been taken by the war hounds, and how many more carried ragged wounds, wrists broken and faces slashed by the fangs, hamstrings severed and fingers lost.

They were the first to fall to the tribesmen's charge, for they asked no quarter but threw themselves with desperate courage at the screaming forest folk whilst those better able to defend themselves thrust and cut and hacked at the baying, bearded faces that filled the yard. The moon appeared as they fought, full, seeming sad at the

344

carnage it lit with its wan, silvery light. Kedryn found himself positioned between Bedyr and Brannoc, their blades working in a natural unison as they defended themselves and the men to either side. Warriors fell before them, but for each one that fell there was another and another and then yet another to take his place, and gradually they were forced back across the yard, towards the covered passageway that led to the interior of the fort.

Again Bedyr gave the order to fall back, and the depleted hundred gave ground, withdrawing into the passageway.

They fought down its length, ceding it inch by bloody inch until it opened on to the larger courtyard beyond.

'Ten men!' Bedyr yelled over the bedlam of the fighting. 'Ten men to stand by me! The rest withdraw! Bowmen stand ready across the yard!'

Kedryn and Brannoc were two, the others five outlaws and three of Rycol's men, none wounded seriously. They grouped on the exit, allowing the rest time to retreat across the open ground with the wounded. They held the invaders there, desperation lending them a strength that stemmed the flow of the barbarian advance until a cordor bellowed that the archers were in position.

'To either side!' Bedyr called. 'Now!'

And they darted from the mouth of the passageway, hurling themselves against the walls of the courtyard as the bowmen loosed their shafts directly into the tunnel, not needing to aim, for the forest folk pressed forwards so densely that the arrows found targets presented thick enough the worst archer would find it difficult to miss. It was not archery but slaughter, the falling bodies in the front rank presenting a fleshy barrier over which the others clambered, only to fall as a fresh volley sang across the moonlit yard, adding to the obstacle so that more went down as the ten scurried around the walls to join their fellows.

Kedryn found himself separated from Bedyr, running at Brannoc's side with the outlaws close behind, moving along a colonnaded walk that ran around the perimeter of the yard. Behind, he could hear the angry shouts of the forest folk as they baulked at the entrance, held at bay by the archers, then from ahead he heard an ominous sound and slowed his pace.

'What is it?' Brannoc demanded, his breath ragged.

Kedryn raised a hand, not sure, for the coif of his mail shirt and the bulk of his helmet deadened sound, making it difficult for him to be certain of his suspicion.

He halted, tugging at the fastenings of the helm to lift the casque from his head and push the coif back, able then to hear more clearly.

'Blood of the Lady!' growled a burly outlaw. 'Why do we wait?'

'Hold your breath!' Brannoc snarled in response. 'What do you hear, Kedryn?'

'Listen,' he said, motioning for silence, 'I think they have reached the lower levels.'

'Then for the Lady's sake let us move on,' grumbled the outlaw.

Brannoc made an impatient gesture as Kedryn cocked his head to one side, trying to discern the source of his doubt. He was not sufficiently familiar with the configuration of High Fort to be sure exactly which passages queued into the yard, but he knew there were some that wound down from the north wall, and what he heard suggested that men were even now moving towards the courtyard from that direction.

'I think they are ahead of us,' he said softly, 'not here yet, but coming towards us.'

'How many?' asked Brannoc, hefting his sabre.

Kedryn shrugged, shaking his head. 'I cannot tell. We had best move on.'

'Thank the Lady!' grunted the surly outlaw. 'I'd as lief fight with more men at my back as with we four.'

Kedryn cradled his helmet under his arm as he proceeded along the walk, moving slower now for fear of running headlong into a barbarian ambush. Moonlight shone in patches through the colonnades so that they darted from light to shadow and back again, their footsteps muffled by the pillars that supported the arching roof. From behind, the shouting of the forest folk at the passageway grew louder and he guessed they were entering the yard, advancing behind shields against the bowmen. He wondered if Bedyr was safely across the court, and where Rycol had set the outer perimeter of his defence. The sounds he heard might be those of High Fort's soldiers, though his sense of direction told him that was forlorn optimism, for by now the Horde must be in full possession of the north wall and moving steadily inwards.

He slowed again as he saw the dark maw of a vaulted doorway, approaching it cautiously, then realized the sounds came from farther ahead, magnified by the structure of the wall, and picked up speed again.

In the moonlight he saw a second doorway, pale light shining on steps that climbed upwards, and knew the sounds came from there, motioning for his companions to halt again.

'There,' he said. 'They are coming down from the wall.'

Brannoc glanced at him doubtfully and said, 'I hear nothing.'

'They are there,' Kedryn responded with absolute certainty, surprised that the others seemed unable to discern what he could now hear clearly. It was as though his ears possessed a preternatural ability, the sounds of advancing men as distinct as Grania's voice had been, and he started, suddenly no longer sure whether he heard with ears or mind. It made no difference: they were there and he said, 'Come! Before they reach us.'

He led the way past the door at a trot, anxious to reach Bedyr and the others before he might find himself cut off. Then halted, spinning round, with sword upraised as he heard a man scream. He saw one of Brannoc's outlaws stagger towards him, face contorted with agony, and crash down to reveal the spear jutting from his back. Behind the fallen man barbarians poured from the doorway, blood black on sword and axe heads. They paused, staring about as if seeking their bearings, and Kedryn saw that unlike the rest they were heavily armoured, mail shirts hanging to their knees, helmets with cheekpieces and nasals concealing their features. Amongst them, a full head taller, stood a massive man in burnished armour that glinted in the silver light. A breastplate covered his burly chest and the vambraces that protected his arms seemed to bulge with the muscle beneath. Legs corded with sinew thrust from beneath a leather kilt set with bright metal studs, greaves buckled over high boots. He held a richly-wrought buckler of leather and metal in his left hand and in his right was a crimsoned longsword. A thick, black beard covered the lower part of his face, the upper part concealed by a helm that exposed only a hawkish nose and battle-maddened jet eyes that locked on Kedryn's with a feral intensity.

'Gehrim!' Kedryn heard Brannoc gasp. 'And Ulan's bodyguard. Or the hef-Ulan's!'

What force compelled him then, Kedryn could not define, only react to. He stepped forwards, letting his helmet fall to the flagstones as he answered the huge man's glare with a cold stare, his sword raised challengingly in both hands.

'For the sake of the Lady, Kedryn, run!' Brannoc said urgently. 'The Gehrim will butcher us!'

'Find my father,' Kedryn answered, bracing himself.

'Kedryn!' Brannoc repeated. 'We cannot fight them. Not Gehrim.'

'If he is the hef-Ulan I shall kill him' Kedryn answered, his voice icy calm.

He saw the Gehrim advance, eyes bright with blood-lust beneath their helms, then halt as the huge man bellowed something in the language of the forest, turning in surprise as he strode through them to stand facing Kedryn.

'I am Niloc Yarrum,' he shouted in gutteral Tamurin. 'I am hef-Ulan of the Horde!'

'I am Kedryn Caitin, Prince of Tamur,' Kedryn replied. 'And I bid you go from here. Or die!'

Yarrum threw back his head and laughed, the sound ringing loud from the surrounding stone. He said something to the Gehrim and they spread to either side, making no further move as the hef-Ulan stared again at Kedryn.

'You have courage, Kedryn Caitin. I shall give your skull a place of honour on my trophy pole.'

He angled his sword in Kedryn's direction as he spoke, and when he did so, Kedryn experienced a prickling sensation in his left shoulder, where the ensorcelled arrow had struck. He had not felt that since the Messenger's sending was lifted, and he realized that he felt the presence of magic. It seemed not to matter, for he was gripped with the same calm that had enveloped him when he spoke out against Hattim Sethiyan and knew that in some manner he did not understand he followed a pre-ordained course. He felt a power in him, a sense of purpose that precluded flight or fear, or any other thought save that he *must* fight this man.

'Lady, stand with me,' he murmured. Then, louder, 'Come and die, Niloc Yarrum.'

The hef-Ulan nodded. Then, with an ear-splitting shout, charged forwards, sword lifted high to cleave Kedryn's unprotected skull.

The blade moved with appalling speed, slashing down as Kedryn sidestepped, hacking his own sword at the barbarian's midriff, seeking to strike where the breastplate ended. He saw the buckler move as though propelled of its own volition to block his cut, and felt his wrists throb with the impact of the blow. He danced back as Yarrum's sword sang round, slashing at his throat, feeling the wind of its passage rustle past his face, and turned his blade, aiming for the underside of the forearm.

Again the buckler turned his cut, smashing his sword arm up, crashing against his chest so that he was driven back, struggling to maintain his balance as Yarrum turned with deadly speed to send a reverse stroke hacking at his side. The steel caught his breastplate, numbing his ribs, and he spun round, letting himself be driven along the wall, looking for space as the hef-Ulan's blade darted and wove before him.

He backed away, fighting on the defensive as Yarrum bellowed a war cry and charged afresh, teeth showing beneath his beard as he grinned his anticipation of victory. The grin faded as Kedryn countered the attack, fighting with a skill that seemed to come from that core of purpose deep inside him, knowing now that blade and buckler both were ensorcelled; but knowing, too, that a different kind of magic dwelt in him. He felt a strength, both physical and spiritual, his own blade moving with a rapidity that matched the serpentine darting of Yarrum's, blocking cuts, clashing loud off the shield, answering blow for blow. He moved past a colonnade, seeing the hef-Ulan's sword crash sparks from the stone, and landed a vicious swing to the armoured shoulder before the buckler could deflect the blow. Yarrum grunted, as much in surprise as pain, and lost a little of his momentum as he advanced again.

They were out in the yard now, and behind Kedryn the sounds of battle died as the barbarian invaders recognized the figure of Niloc Yarrum, ceasing their forward rush as their attention focused on the duel. Amongst the colonnades, the Gehrim watched, ignoring the retreating outlaws, only Brannoc lingering behind, helpless to assist, but still reluctant to desert Kedryn. The moon was risen to a point directly above the scene, filling the yard with ethereal light that gleamed on silvered armour, the fist emblazoned on Kedryn's breastplate as black as the drying blood that decorated both swords.

He ducked beneath a horizontal swing and would have taken Yarrum's legs from under him had the buckler not defeated the cut. He felt the blade land heavy on his shoulder and turned beneath it, stabbing over the shield that slammed against his chest to send Yarrum lurching back for fear of losing his eyes. He cut to the head and saw his blow turned, twisting barely in time to escape the thrust aimed at his groin, barely knowing that as he did, he rammed his pommel into the barbarian's mouth, splintering teeth. He felt the shield arm wrap about him and for long moments they stood face-to-face, wrestling, Yarrum's size telling in his favour until Kedryn hooked a foot about the hef-Ulan's ankle and threw his full weight against the massive chest, sending Yarrum staggering back, arms flailing as he fought to remain upright.

Kedryn pressed the attack then, not hearing the shout that went up from the Tamurin line as he rained blows at the helmeted head, each one blocked by the upraised shield that seemed an impenetrable defence.

He drove Yarrum back across the yard, pressing him towards the colonnades, seeking to cut through that magical barrier until cold stone stood at the hef-Ulan's back and he screamed a war shout and launched himself forwards with berserk fury. Now Kedryn was forced back, concentrating on deflecting the blows that slashed and hacked at his head and ribs, moving around the courtyard oblivious of the onlookers, who themselves stood wrapt in the combat; barbarians and Tamurin alike ignoring their enemies as they waited for the outcome of the struggle.

Kedryn knew that it must end. He felt no weariness, despite the long day's fighting, for the power he felt inside him seemed to fuel his strength and his arms raised his blade effortlessly, his wrists turned and twisted with no sense of exhaustion, and his legs were strong beneath him. Yet he could not trust the watching barbarians to remain mere onlookers. Yarrum's breath was coming harder now, and the savage grin that had decorated the hef-Ulan's mouth was become a grimace. Kedryn sensed that the magic he had felt lay in sword and buckler, not man, and therefore Yarrum would weaken in time, whilst he – of this he was confident – would remain limber, for his power stemmed not from fell sorcery but inner purpose. And if the barbarians saw that – saw their hef-Ulan weaken – they might well end their neutrality and bear him down beneath a massed charge.

He allowed Yarrum to continue forcing him back, circling the yard, letting the woodlander expend his strength, seeing how the ensorcelled blade appeared to act of its own will, just as the buckler governed Yarrum's arm. He defended himself, no longer seeking to attack until he saw they stood at a point close to the Tamurin line, on the south side of the court, and that Brannoc had moved along the colonnades to where he might easily reach friendly arms.

And then he knew it was time, and he acted as though the Lady herself stood beside him, directing his actions.

He allowed Yarrum to back him against a pillar. Let his arms droop as if exhaustion claimed him. Saw the deadly blade swing savagely at his head as Yarrum's mouth opened in a shout of triumph, and fell to his knees as the sword cut above him. He heard it ring on the stone of the colonnade, the force of the blow turning the hef-Ulan's body so that not even the magic shield could move fast enough to block his riposte as he lifted his sword and drove the point deep into the barbarian's thigh.

Yarrum screamed then, more in rage than pain, and Kedryn felt the buckler slam against him, pitching him sideways as he rolled with the blow, letting it take him, turning as he fell to avoid the downswing of the sword. He came to his feet and cut ferociously at Yarrum's head, and this time the buckler failed to counter his stroke. His sword hit heavy on the woodlander's helm, rocking the great head to the side. He reversed the cut, but now the shield came up to take it, though Yarrum's riposte failed to touch him because the man stumbled, blood gouting from the wound in his upper leg. It was bad enough to make him limp, his balance failing him, and Kedryn pressed his attack afresh, forcing Yarrum to stumble back, foregoing the use of his sword as he concentrated on holding the buckler upraised. Kedryn struck two-handed at the shield, great overhead swings that had Yarrum's arm lifted high. Then he brought the longsword down and round in a whistling arc that undercut the shield to land the edge against the side of Yarrum's knee. He felt the bones break and saw dark blood gout as Yarrum screamed shrilly, buckler dropping as he stumbled and then toppled sideways, his leg no longer able to bear his weight. As he fell, Kedryn smashed a blow to his helmet, and before he touched the flags, a second, beneath the lower rim of the helm.

Yarrum's mouth sprang open, livid lips opening across his neck. Blood spurted, matting in his beard, and Kedryn brought his sword back, raising the blade and driving it two-handed into the throat, feeling it jar his shoulders as the point struck the flags beneath the hef-Ulan's body. He stood above the dying man as Niloc Yarrum arched his back and choked on his own blood, blade falling from his fingers as his arms stretched wide and his eyes clouded into death.

Kedryn stood above him, calm, as silence filled the courtyard. Then he heard a great wailing cry go up from the watching forest folk, and behind him, Brannoc's voice, 'They say the hef-Ulan of the Horde is dead.'

'Do you speak their tongue?' he asked, and when Brannoc confirmed that he did, 'Translate my words.'

Brannoc moved out to stand beside Kedryn, facing the forest folk across the body of Niloc Yarrum, his voice raised in the language of the Beltrevan as he told them what the slayer of their hef-Ulan said.

'I bade Niloc Yarrum go from here or die, and I say the same to you. I have slain your hef-Ulan, and if you remain you will die beneath the swords of the Three Kingdoms. The magicks of Ashar's

Messenger could not save him and they will not save you, or give you victory – only defeat and death.

'Take the body of your hef-Ulan and carry him back to the Beltrevan. Return to your forests! The Kingdoms are not yours and never shall be! Now take his corpse and go.'

He backed away then, leaving Niloc Yarrum outstretched on the bloodied flags as the woodlanders watched in silence, stepping between the colonnades where Bedyr and the handful of survivors waited.

'Well done,' he heard his father murmur, a hand firm and approving on his shoulder. 'Well said.'

Slowly, eyes wary beneath their casques, the warriors of the Gehrim emerged from the shadows of the walk, stepping cautiously behind upraised bucklers across the yard. Bedyr motioned for the Tamurin archers to lower their bows and the recurved heads of the war arrows dropped. The Gehrim reached the corpse and lifted it reverently, setting it on a platform of shields, then slowly retreated back across the court to where the rest of the attackers stood. No word was spoken, but the barbarians faded into the passageway and were gone.

'Will they leave us now?' Kedryn wondered.

'Mayhap,' Bedyr said. 'At the least, you have dealt them a blow they will not easily forget.'

'They will take him from the fort,' said Brannoc, 'to give him funeral rites. What they do then will depend on the Messenger, I think.'

'Aye, the Messenger.' Kedryn's voice was bitter. 'What of him?'

'We can only wait,' said Bedyr. 'Wait and see. I think, though, that you have bought us time – hopefully sufficient that Darr may reach us. In the meanwhile, however, we had best find Rycol and prepare a defence.'

The remnant of the hundred moved back, aware of the sounds of battle fading as word of the hef-Ulan's death was shouted through the fort. They followed a stone-walled corridor and crossed a yard where bodies lay bloody in the aftermath of battle, seeing groups of forest folk retreating sullenly to the north wall. The burning roof of a timbered hall lit their way, and all about them stood signs of the carnage. Kedryn found a rag and wiped blood from his sword, not yet ready to sheath the blade but holding it loose at his side. The calm sense of power and purpose that had filled him was fading slowly, replaced by hope that Yarrum's death would mark the end of the siege. Perhaps, he thought, that was the meaning of Alaria's text: that

352

he was the one destined to defeat the Messenger's designs by defeating the hef-Ulan of the Horde. Yet the Messenger remained, an imponderable threat, and perhaps he would find some fresh means of arousing the forest folk. For now, however, enough was done and he could do no more. The siege, albeit perhaps only temporarily, was lifted, and perhaps – as Bedyr had said – that would afford time for Darr and the rest to reach High Fort. What he wanted now, he realized, was food and sleep. He yawned, rubbing at his eyes.

Then he gasped as fire seemed to lance his shoulder, and started round, sword lifting.

'What is it?' Bedyr cried, his own blade rising.

Kedryn peered about him. He could see nothing save the outline of the burning hall and the dancing shadows the flames cast on the wall before him.

'Magic,' he said, voice gruff, for his shoulder seemed to burn. 'Close by.'

'I see nothing.' Bedyr scanned the yard.

'It is here,' Kedryn said, 'I feel it.'

'The Messenger?' asked Brannoc.

'I do not know.' Kedryn shook his head, flexing his shoulder awkwardly. 'Perhaps. Or perhaps another ensorcelled blade. I feel something, but I cannot tell what it is. Let us move on.'

Bedyr nodded and they continued across the yard, hurrying towards the entrance that led through a wide, low-roofed passage giving way to the inner walls of the keep.

They were passing beneath the arched entrance when it happened, so fast that for an instant there was only confusion. Kedryn felt the pain in his shoulder become a throbbing agony and winced, his steps faltering for a moment. As he slowed a shape detached itself from the shadows, leaping from the mouth of the arch with an awful scream, blade glinting red in the light of the fire. It landed directly before Kedryn and for an eyeblink he saw a bearded face contorted in an expression of rage so hideous as to be indistinguishable from agony. He lifted his sword, seeking to parry the cut that slashed at his face, and saw bright sparks flash as steel met steel. Then pain exploded through his head and he saw no more.

He did not see Borsus raise his blade again as the one the Messenger's sorcery had imprinted on the warrior's mind fell on hands and knees before him for he was blind, and blind, did not see Brannoc's sabre interpose itself between the warrior's descending sword and his unprotected neck. He did not see Borsus snarl, turning

353

in confusion as he recognized the outlaw, caught between the two imperatives of the Messenger's dictat, though that instant of doubt saved his life.

Borsus raised his shield to ward the cut that Brannoc swung at his chest and slashed again at Kedryn. This time it was Bedyr's blade that turned the blow, the Lord of Tamur driving his longsword out to sweep the woodlander's thrust clear of Kedryn's back. Brannoc hefted his sabre in an overhand stroke at the buckler, blade imbedding deep in the wooden rim, and Borsus growled in mindless fury and twisted the shield, striving to tear the sabre from Brannoc's grasp. Bedyr brought his sword back and slashed it hard into the warrior's ribs, the angry force of the blow sending the Drott staggering clear of Kedryn with blood coursing over his leather tunic. A second blow took Borsus in the side, opening a cut that would have stopped any man not possessed of the berserk rage that gripped the warrior.

Borsus howled and wrenched Brannoc's sword from his hand, bringing the buckler round to block a third cut from Bedyr even as he drove his blade at Kedryn's spine. Brannoc kicked out then, his booted foot meeting the Drott's wrist and turning the blow so that the sword clattered on stone a handspan from Kedryn's head. Then Bedyr's blade came over in a tremendous double-handed swing that parted hand from wrist and Borsus screamed as blood fountained from the stump of his arm. It was a scream of frustrated rage, not pain, for he felt no pain, only the desire to kill, to avenge Sulya's death, to satisfy the demands of his master. He lifted his buckler, intent on crashing the edge against Kedryn's skull and splattering the Tamurin's brains over the flagstones, but as he did so, Brannoc sprang forwards, driving a dagger deep into the warrior's chest, piercing the heart, his full weight behind the blow, sending Borsus tottering backwards.

Bedyr finished it then, his longsword swinging in a flat arc, all his strength behind the cut, the edge finding Borsus's neck and severing it, the Drott's head falling from his shoulders to bounce obscenely over the flags. As it fell, the rage went out of the eyes and the snarling lips closed over the parted teeth, air sighing from the mouth in a sound like a name: 'Sulya.'

'Kedryn!'

Bedyr went down on his knees beside his son, sword falling as he set hands to Kedryn's shoulders, turning the younger man that he might look upon his face.

He groaned as he saw the livid bruise where Kedryn's blade had been driven back across his eyes, the flesh already swollen, blood oozing from around the orbs.

'Father?' Kedryn's voice was strangely calm and that wrenched at Bedyr's soul. 'I cannot see.'

'Sorcery,' Brannoc rasped. 'This is the Messenger's work.'

'Help me.'

Bedyr lifted Kedryn to his feet, Brannoc moving to his side, the two of them supporting Kedryn as he raised hands to his battered face and said again, 'I cannot see.'

'Wynett,' said Bedyr. 'Quickly! We must find Wynett.'

They moved slowly along the passageway, encircled now by a ring of protective steel, one of Brannoc's outlaws thinking to retrieve the fallen swords and glancing at Borsus's severed head as he did so. He wondered why the fallen head had so contented an expression.

At the end of the passage they were met by the outer ring of defenders, bowmen and halberdiers waiting behind a barricade, not yet sure of the barbarians' retreat. They opened ranks swiftly on Bedyr's shout and Kedryn was led through to the enclave of the keep and the wards of the hospital. Rycol stood there, conferring with tellemen, his broken arm strapped across his chest, his gaunt face aghast as he saw Kedryn.

'What has happened?' he asked, motioning his officers away.

'He killed the hef-Ulan of the Horde,' Bedyr responded, 'but then a berserker attacked from ambush.'

'There was magic in his blade,' Kedryn said. 'I felt it. I can sense magic when it comes close.'

'Where is Wynett?' Bedyr demanded, and Rycol held his questions in check as he called for an hospitaller to find the Paramount Sister.

She came swiftly, anguish in her eyes as she caught sight of Kedryn's wound, wiping blood from her hands as she studied him briefly.

'Come with me.' She turned about, leading the way through the wards to a secluded chamber. 'Is this his only wound?'

'It is,' Kedryn answered for himself, 'and it does not hurt.'

'Help me with his armour,' Wynett instructed, and they stripped the protective metal from his body, leaving him in breeches and undershirt as the Hospitaller laid him carefully on the bed that stood against the wall and ushered them from the small room, setting gentle hands against his temples.

He waited in darkness as she touched him, feeling her delicate fingers probe the bruising, rest upon his temples, confident that her skill would restore his sight, unafraid for he had faith in her talent and was sure that before long he would see again.

'Sorcery,' she murmured after a while. 'Tell me what happened.'

While he explained she mixed a poultice and smoothed it over his eyes, setting a bandage in place about his head. It was cool and he found it reassuring, though not so much as the hand he sought, and clasped as he spoke.

'The Messenger sent him,' she said when he was done, retrieving her hand that she might prepare a draught and bring it to his lips. 'You are important to him, Kedryn. I believe he knows you can destroy him.'

'How?' he asked. 'I cannot get close to him. And now I am blind.'

He heard the words, spoken with a flat calm, and that somehow brought home the horror of it, and he shuddered, reaching for her hand again. He found it, small and warm, and then he felt her lips brush his and wet droplets fall upon his cheek. He realized they were tears and that leeched hope from his soul.

'Wynett,' he said, his voice faltering. 'You can heal me?'

'I will find a way,' she said fiercely. 'I swear it.'

Fear gripped him then and he clutched her hand tightly, fighting the cry that threatened to burst from his lips.

'How soon?' he asked slowly.

'I do not know,' she answered, stroking his forehead. 'Your eyes are not cut, merely bruised. But whatever magic lay in the blade has stricken you, and I cannot cure that; not here, not now.'

'Where, then?' he asked dully. 'And when?'

'In Estrevan, perhaps,' she said. 'Or when Darr's Sisters come.'

'If they come; if the barbarians do not overwhelm us first,' he muttered bitterly.

'They will come,' she promised, 'and the forest folk will not overwhelm us now. You saved us that fate, Kedryn.'

'And paid the price,' he retorted.

'Aye,' she murmured sadly, 'but I *will* find a way. Now sleep.'

He felt her hand withdraw from his grasp and an arm encircle his shoulders, lifting him that he might sip from the cup she held to his lips. Then, when he had drunk the draught, he felt her hold him still, cradling his head against her breast as a languor filled him and he drifted into tranquil sleep.

Wynett undressed him then and went out to inform Bedyr of his plight. The Lord of Tamur heard the news with stricken face, and Brannoc cursed. But neither man could suggest any other course than to leave him lying until such time as help might be found, either from the Sisters who would arrive with the King or in Estrevan itself, and as there was nothing they could do, they busied themselves with preparations for the last-ditch defence of the fort.

There was no further fighting that night, nor the following day, though the barbarians still held the northern reaches of the fort, for the forest folk prepared Niloc Yarrum's funeral pyre, and on the next night the conflagration lit the canyon and the wailing of the mourning Horde rang loud off the Lozin walls.

The defenders anticipated attack when the sun rose, but none came, and soon after dawn King Darr's fleet arrived, the three thousand soldiers of Andurel greeted with a cheering that woke Kedryn.

He felt panic when he found himself sightless still, rising to stumble about the chamber, not knowing in his confusion whether the cries he heard meant salvation or the final battle. A Sister came to aid him, urging him back into bed and administering a soothing draught even as he cried out, demanding Wynett attend him, alternately wracked with anger at his predicament and fear that he should be blind forever.

'Darr has arrived,' she told him when she came from tending other wounded men. 'And the forest folk have made no further move to enter the fort. They wait on the north wall, but no more than that.'

He slept again then, while Darr's men manned the defences, the King coming to his chamber to study him with saddened eyes, accompanied by Bedyr.

'He saved us,' Bedyr said, his face lined with grief as he looked on his sleeping son. 'Had Kedryn not slain the hef-Ulan, they would have destroyed us all.'

'He has saved the Kingdoms, I think,' Darr said gravely. 'This hef-Ulan was chosen by the Messenger, and by defeating him, Kedryn has shown the forest folk the Messenger is not all-powerful. Now they must appoint a new hef-Ulan, or go back to the Beltrevan.'

'Will the Messenger allow that?' Bedyr wondered.

'Can he prevent it?' Darr said. 'The tribes of the forest prey on one another and only a powerful man can unite them. This Niloc Yarrum must have been such a one, but now he is dead, and the lesser chieftains will likely squabble amongst themselves until your army and the others come. Can even Ashar's minion resolve their differences?'

Darr's surmise was correct, for even as he spoke, the Ulans of the

357

Horde vied for supremacy, their fear of Taws lessened by the death of Niloc Yarrum.

'Attack!' Taws urged them, eyes smouldering as he studied the sullen faces about the council fire. 'They are weak and you will overrun them as I promised you.'

'Promised Yarrum when you raised him to lead us,' muttered Vran, not meeting the mage's stare. 'And who leads now?'

'I lead,' said Balandir.

'You?' Vran turned to the fox-bearded man. 'Why should the Yath follow a Caroc?'

'You followed a Drott,' snarled Balandir.

'Yarrum won the right in battle,' countered the Yath Ulan. 'He defeated my father and I swore to follow him. Not a late-come Caroc upstart.'

Balandir's hand swept forwards, spilling the contents of his drinking horn into Vran's face. The Yath snarled a curse and came to his feet with dagger in hand. Balandir's ivory-hilted knife flashed out in answer and the two chieftains crouched in readiness to kill.

'Cease!' Taws commanded, but neither man heeded his words until he moved his fingers in complex patterns and blue light flashed out to strike their blades, sending the knives spinning from their hands.

'I will not follow a Caroc,' snapped Vran, rubbing at fingers scorched by the Messenger's magic, anger making him brave.

'Nor I a Drott,' Balandir retorted.

'We are undone,' said Darien. 'When Drul raised the Horde, it broke on the Lozin forts, and he died. Now Niloc Yarrum is dead and the Horde is leaderless.'

Ymrath said nothing, but his eyes agreed with the Grymard.

'Select a hef-Ulan,' Taws said.

'The hef-Ulan is not *selected*,' Balandir muttered, 'he *wins* his place.'

'Then win it for yourself,' Taws urged.

'In battle?' Balandir shook his head, his tone contemptuous. 'I can defeat any of these dogs, but at what price?'

'The Kingdoms as prize!' Taws snarled, deep-sunk eyes sparking red.

'Messenger, you do not understand,' Balandir responded, his tone measured now, for he knew he trod dangerous ground. 'You know how Yarrum won his place – would you see my Caroc fight Vran's Yath? Ymrath's Vistrals? Darien's Grymards? And what of the Drott? Who leads them now? Half their ala-Ulans died storming the wall and the survivors already vie for the Ulan's torque. They mourn Yarrum – they will not accept me as hef-Ulan. Unless you use your magic to persuade them.'

'The Yath will not accept that!' Vran barked. 'The hef-Ulan leads by sword-right, not sorcery.'

'You forsake Ashar's purpose!' Taws snarled. 'The Kingdoms lay open to you and you quarrel like dogs!'

Ymrath spoke then, his voice low, his eyes clouded with doubt. 'Ashar has forsaken us, Taws. You gave us Niloc Yarrum to lead us south into the Kingdoms and Niloc Yarrum is slain. The Horde is leaderless and we cannot agree on another. I say we return to the Beltrevan while we still may.'

'Coward!' Taws spat, and his hands shaped air that became blue fire, lancing out to engulf the Vistral Ulan.

Ymrath jerked upright as the witchfire touched him, rank terror in his eyes. His mouth hung open and his pale hair stood on end in a corona about his head as his arms flung wide and a low, rasping groan burst from his gaping jaws. Blood came in thick droplets from his mouth and nose and ears, and then he pitched on to his back as the blue light and his breath faded together.

'Now the Vistral stand leaderless,' Balandir said softly, accusingly.

Taws stared at him and the Caroc Ulan lowered his eyes, but the mage saw that he had over-reached himself, for now the others looked at him with enmity joining the fear in their gaze and he knew that he could not risk killing them all, for then the Horde would become a mere rabble.

'Ashar curse you!' he rasped, and rose to his feet, striding from the circle to stand staring at the walls of High Fort, knowing that he was defeated.

He stood there long into the night, unmoving, knowing that behind those battered walls lay the one who had wrenched victory from him, the one ordained to defeat his master's purpose, for Borsus had not returned and he could sense that Kedryn still lived.

'I will find you,' he said softly, his voice chill as grave-frost. 'Wherever you go, I will hunt you and destroy you. I will take your soul and feed it to Ashar. Beware the Messenger, Kedryn Caitin.'

Darr's Sisters could do nothing for Kedryn's blindness, and so he took no part in the skirmishing that followed the arrival of Tepshen Lahl with the Tamurin army and Jarl's Keshi, who crossed the Idre with their horses and massed south of High Fort as they awaited the coming of the army of Ust-Galich before taking the fight to the enemy.

The Vistral had already begun to drift back into the forest with Ymrath's death, and the Drott Ulans vied for supremacy amongst themselves even as Vran and Balandir quarrelled over the hef-Ulan's torque. Taws's power was doubted with Niloc Yarrum's demise, and the mage was nowhere to be found when King Darr, flanked by Bedyr and Tepshen Lahl, Jarl and Hattim, rode out from High Fort. Demoralized, the forest folk were beaten back, driven steadily northwards into the woodlands that had spawned them. The battle raged for nine days, and when Balandir fell it collapsed into sporadic fighting until the last bloodied remnants of the Horde withdrew into the Beltrevan.

'It is over,' Wynett told Kedryn as trumpets heralded the triumphant return of the armies.

'And I am blind,' he answered.

They were seated on the bench in the little garden where he had kissed her once; long ago, it seemed. Then, he had acted without thinking and she had withdrawn, reminding him that she was a Sister of Estrevan. Now it was she who initiated the kiss, setting her hands upon his cheeks and drawing his face towards her as she planted her lips on his.

'We will go to Estrevan,' she said against his mouth, 'Together. And I will find a way to cure you.'

Kedryn wondered what the future held for him as he reached for her and clutched her tight against his chest.